THE SON OF
THREE FATHERS

BOOKS BY GASTON LEROUX

THE SON OF
THREE FATHERS

BY
GASTON LEROUX
Author of "The Octopus of Paris," etc.

TRANSLATED BY HANNAFORD BENNETT

WILDSIDE PRESS

Printed in the United States of America

CONTENTS

6 CONTENTS

THE SON OF THREE FATHERS

CHAPTER I

ON that morning a wave of excitement passed through the great Bella Nissa Stores at the corner of the Place du Palais, before even the doors were opened to the public. From top to bottom of the huge establishment the staff spread the news: During the night Hardigras had been up to his old pranks again.

The chief saleswoman in the linen department complained that two pairs of hemstitched and embroidered sheets were missing. In their place she found Hardigras's visiting card. That devil of a Hardigras! He preferred to sleep in cambric sheets!

The saleswomen in the silk department, who had not received a visit from him since, to the delight of some and the terror of others, he began his visits to the stores, turned away to smile. From the fact that so far the mysterious gentleman had spared their assortment of silk stockings, they concluded that he had little or no love of coquetry in his lady friends. Assuredly, if he was not overfond of love-making he had some taste for the things of the table; for, the new provision department, opened at the beginning of the season, no longer counted the number of tins of preserved food which had disappeared as if by magic.

The young ladies in the lace department plaintively complained that they were unable to find their samples. Moreover that same day the absence of two pairs of pajamas and a bundle of bath towels was noticed, and in the perfumery department several bottles of eau-de-Cologne and a sprayer were missing. Hardigras was becoming a man of fashion!

To prevent suspicion falling upon the wrong person, he invariably left his own elegant card—of course his cards came from the stationery department—on which he had written with his fountain pen in large capitals: *Hardigras*—a name of an alluring sound in this great city of the Midi, famous for its carnival.

And it was impossible to lay hands on him!

The first intimation of his presence showed that he did not disdain to take up his abode in the stores. It was discovered that he had assumed possession of a complete bedroom in the furniture department. Obviously he could not resist the temptation to sleep in the superb Louis XVI bed which lay "ready made" with its dainty sheets and lace embroidered pillow cases. The directors had been considerate enough to place on the bedside table an exquisite lighted night lamp whose electric bulb was softened by a pink shade adorned with multi-colored beads.

How could he do other than accept the unspoken invitation? The room seemed to be awaiting its occupant. It may be assumed that Hardigras, as he mingled in the daytime among the throng of customers, determined not to allow it to wait any longer. And with the coming of night, after the staff had wrapped the furniture in its gray lustring covers, the Bella Nissa's uninvited guest took possession of his room. . . .

With no fear of the night watchmen on their rounds, Hardigras, as he lay between the sheets under the gray lustring, must needs have dreamed pleasant dreams! . . . Then, rising early, with a good appetite, he had found his way to the provision department; and from the articles of food and condiments which had disappeared, it was easy to establish the nature of his early morning breakfast. . . .

Availing himself of the same opportunity, he provided himself with kitchen utensils—casseroles, spirit-stove, nothing was lacking. On another occasion he replenished his wardrobe. Disregarding evening dress, he helped himself to several suits which would have rejoiced those workmen who are ready to join the Sunday fêtes and dance with the girls, or feast at Cimiez on French pastry.

By choosing clothes of different sizes he may have wished it to be believed that he had accomplices, but more probably he sought in this way to disguise his own size—a proof that he was not devoid of a sense of humor. As for footwear he seemed to fancy a particular number from which it was deduced that this was his size and shape. He did not wear gloves. Notwithstanding these precise clues which seemed to suggest that this was no case of a swell mobsman, it was impossible to discover who he was. Needless to say this devil of a Hardigras had become famous along the seaboard these last six weeks. From St. Raphael to Mentone he was the main subject of gossip. The daily newspapers of the Côte d'Azur had related his earliest exploits with such a wealth of detail that in the end the interest of the great public was fully aroused.

It was at first thought that the whole thing was a new form of advertisement brought forward at a time when the old establishment had to fight against the competition of the Galeries Parisienne, but the rage displayed by M. Hyacinthe Supia, the managing director—against newspaper reporters whom he sent to the devil whenever they managed to get near him—and his threats against the elusive miscreant himself, soon proved to the public, at first incredulous, that the incidents must be taken seriously.

Then they were more amused than ever.

It is well to say also that M. Hyacinthe Supia was liked by no one. To begin with he never laughed, which is a mortal offense in a place that is a paradise on earth. And then he was niggardly, cheeseparing, discharging old assistants under the most frivolous pretexts, and engaging younger persons at starvation wages. The staff called him the "tyrant".

On the particular day when new thefts were discovered, the result of Hardigras's night-time exploits, the assistants were naturally laughing among themselves; but our story, which opens in farce, was to develop in so dramatic a fashion that they soon ceased their jesting.

The tall, gaunt figure of M. Hyacinthe Supia came in clad in a long frock coat as in a black flag, and as he strode through the stores terror reigned. His grayish-blue eyes gleamed with a malevolent light. Never had the "tyrant" seemed more formidable. After him marched, solemn and formal, M. Hippolyte Morelli, the staff controller, nicknamed "his majesty" because of the overwhelming dignity of his gait and his manner of countersigning with his initials "H. M." the most disastrous decisions on the future prospects of his subordinates.

The chief entered his office without uttering a word to a soul. Other important persons joined him and it was soon rumored that they were holding a directors' meeting.

Half an hour later the result of the deliberations became known. M. Hyacinthe Supia had decided to dismiss the day and night staff, whose duty it was to keep watch, and engage a fresh one. Then it was learned that the meeting had unanimously resolved to dismiss henceforth every employee in any department in which traces of Hardigras were found.

It was no longer a subject of jest. The staff was flung into consternation. Since M. Supia had adopted this extreme measure he must have some suspicion that the thief had accomplices in the stores. In any case Hardigras's doings were looked upon as less amusing now that they involved the dismissal of the staff.   •

In spite of the seriousness of the circumstances there was an outburst of laughter when on the stroke of noon it was observed that some mysterious hand had fastened to the light iron railing of the chief cashier's office a placard on which was written:

Any employee dismissed from Bella Nissa on account of Hardigras will be provided with a new situation within a week, and will have no cause to regret the "tyrant's" starvation wages. I pledge my word for it.

Hardigras.

How had this insolent placard been placed there? It was hung in such a way as to be out of reach. And thus it remained displayed before the eyes of the secretly delighted staff and the openly amused customers.

"Look out," exclaimed one suddenly. "Look at hatchet face." This was another nickname used by the smaller shopkeepers in the Rue Droite in speaking of the proprietor of Bella Nissa who, of course, had determined to ruin them by opening a provision department.

M. Supia in fact came along forcing his way through. A ladder had been brought up; but before the placard could be removed he had time to read it.

He grew yellower than quince jam, seized hold of the offending card, turned to the public and, with the look of a man who would like to choke the life out of them, he glared at those who were laughing. At last he decided to take no notice, and beckoned "his majesty" to come with him.

Both entered the elevator and mounted to the fifth floor, to his flat. He well-nigh collided with the frightened maid who opened the door; presently the two men shut themselves up in the private study. The conference lasting over an hour, did not pass off without a row. At last "his majesty" left and M. Supia remained alone. Lunch was long since overdone. Consternation prevailed from the kitchen to the dining-room. Then, someone ventured to knock at the door. And, as there was no answer, the door was shyly opened and the radiant figure of a young girl of seventeen brightened the gloomy interior.

"Good morning, godfather, how are you this morning?" said the chit without enthusiasm.

"Bad," he answered ungraciously.

"Aunt and cousin are waiting lunch for you."

"Let them lunch without me and leave me in peace. . . . Do you understand, Antoinette?"

"Yes, godfather."

She closed the door but came back again almost at once.

"Godfather," she said with a simplicity that seemed too natural to be unaffected, "is that awful Hardigras upsetting you again?"

"Damn it Antoinette! . . . Are you making game of me?"

And he strode towards her with so threatening a look that she slammed the door in his face.

He thought he had rid himself of her when the door opened. It was the chit again.

"I'll tell you, godfather, the notion that came into my head. . . ."

"Notion about what?" he growled all but subdued by so much persistence.

"About arresting Hardigras. . . ."

"Well, keep it to yourself," shouted Supia. "And, still more, don't let me see your face again or else. . . ."

"All right, godfather, I'm going. . . ."

She ran off finally without waiting to hear more. Neither wife nor daughter dared approach him during the day. About five o'clock Hippolyte Morelli came back to report that he had taken the necessary steps to obtain new night watchmen who would be ready that evening. But, M. Supia declared that he needed no one that night, that he refused to allow a single person in the stores after closing time, and that he was discharging even the firemen.

"His majesty," who was not gifted with overmuch understanding, withdrew at a loss. But it was easy to see that the "tyrant" meant to ascertain for himself what

was going on in his stores during the night. He had no
intention of sending for the police, whose intervention
is usually accompanied by a regrettable publicity. He
would himself arrest Hardigras, question him, and know
how to unravel the tangled threads which moved this
insolent puppet, in the pay of his enemies.

M. Hyacinthe Supia was no coward. At nine o'clock
that night he descended to the deserted stores with a
revolver in each pocket. It is easy to imagine the hooligan
tricks that he prepared in order to capture his visitor.
Obviously he knew as much about the ins and outs of
Bella Nissa stores as the ghost-like Hardigras.

From the basements in which the delivery department
was situated, to the fourth floor reserved for household
utensils and ironmongery, he groped his way, throwing
now and again the rays of a small dark lantern on obscure
recesses which appeared suspicious. More than once,
too, he came to a stop fancying he heard a gasp, a breath.

For a moment, as with infinite precaution he drew near
the famous Louis XVI room in which Hardigras but
recently had savored such sweet repose between the sheets,
he seemed to detect a peculiar snore which could come only
from a man devoid of all moral sense, and as invulnerable
to remorse as to evil dreams. M. Supia suddenly flew to
arms lifting in a flash the lustring covers. And yet the
snores continued singly, rhythmic, but a little farther
away. . . . He searched the entire furniture department.
. . . And the snores went on, becoming calmer, more fre-
quent, blissful! It was enough to drive a man mad. The
lustring fluttered like huge black wings under the "tyrant's" angry fists.

The hapless man passed through a night of hallucina-
tions. At three o'clock in the morning he was wandering
about distracted, clambering up to the fourth floor from
the ground floor and then, suddenly convinced that an
unaccountable noise was proceeding from the basement,
darting down again like an arrow!

He no longer took any precaution. He stumbled, fell, rose heavily, wild-eyed, in a flood of perspiration, yelling loudly his startled cry: "Who's there!" and as no reply came, shouting in a threatening voice: "Answer or I'll fire!"

He felt that it would be some relief to him to fire his revolver. Suddenly he fired at a strange shape that started up before him in the gleam of a sinister light. There was a terrible clash. M. Hyacinthe Supia had shattered the mirror of a wardrobe.

At the same moment a smell, peculiar to burning, assailed his nostrils. Breathing quickly he bent over the gallery dominating the main hall. In the dim light of the glass windows he descried a somewhat opaque puff of smoke ascending to the men's tailoring department.

"Fire!" he shouted.

But what was the use? Had he not himself that night dismissed the fireman? Hardigras knew it, and was seizing the opportunity to set fire to Bella Nissa. M. Hyacinthe Supia rolled rather than ran down to the threatened department. He made a grab at the fire extinguisher but his amazement was great when he discovered that the apparatus had already been at work and the incipient fire put out through the intervention—yes by the powers! —the intervention of Hardigras.

Under the weight of this last blow the "tyrant" admitted to himself his defeat—for the time. Hardigras that night had perhaps saved him from ruin, for the new insurance policies on his latest extension of premises were not yet in order.

He returned to his rooms in a lamentable state. He refused, however, to be pitied. And he declined, moreover, the attentions of his wife and daughter, giving Antoinette a box on the ear for repeating that if he would listen to her, Hardigras would be arrested within forty-eight hours.

CHAPTER II

As though by a sort of witchcraft the entire staff became
aware next morning of the tragi-comic incidents of the
night. The disorder in which they found their departments bore witness to the disastrous ardor with which the
"tyrant," in his pursuit of the Unseizable, had been inspired. The story of the snores, though M. Supia had
kept it to himself, achieved special success. To be sure
that devil of a Hardigras was up to all sorts of clever
tricks. Indeed, M. Supia owed him a great debt. But
for him Bella Nissa would have been reduced to ashes.

Hardigras began to be regarded as a great man.

The small shopkeepers of the neighborhood to whom
he sent dismissed members of Bella Nissa staff, with his
card, made arrangements to find employment for them.
They had no wish to hurt Hardigras's feelings. When
the fact was reported to M. Supia he swore that the old
town would soon have reason to regret their action; for
he would yet get the better of this puppet and those who
were acting in league with him.

Meanwhile "his majesty" Hippolyte Morelli introduced
the new night watchmen to him. They stood before him,
four fellows of herculean strength who feared neither
man nor devil, well-known in the harbor and town and the
railway goods station where they dealt more or less in
smuggled goods, juggling with bales and boxes and wine
casks. The first man known as Noré Tantifla, said:

"As for me if he shows the tip of his nose I'll drag him before you thrashed to a pulp, and begging for mercy."

"I'll give him a licking and hand him over to you looking like strawberry trifle," said Tony Bouta.

"I'll have a regular go at him just to give me a thirst. Get your brandy ready," said Cioa Aiguardente.

"And as for me, if he shows himself at all he'll be reduced to a dirty rag," declared Peppino Pistafun.

After they left, "his majesty" asked M. Supia what he thought of them. The proprietor answered somewhat dolefully that he had no doubt of their strength. But it was for Hardigras to show the tip of his nose, and up to that day they knew nothing of the shape of his particular nasal appendage.

"Leave it to me, and I will answer for the success of the plan," returned "his majesty."

An idea had occurred to him. They were nearing Carnival time and Bella Nissa had been displaying masks, fancy dresses, dominoes, and other appropriate disguises, with a variety and profusion that drew a jostling crowd ever eager for a sight of these fripperies, the preliminary signs of the coming fêtes. In fear of Hardigras these varied wonders, at night-time, had been carefully put away in boxes until the next morning.

A splendid standard, which was a worthy companion to that of Carnival itself and was to fly bravely in the main hall until Mid-Lent, attracted universal admiration. It displayed the colors to be worn at the masked ball and bore in letters of gold the inscription:

Mardi Gras is not yet dead.

On that particular night M. Morelli decided that neither masks nor fancy dresses nor banners should be put away, alleging as a pretext that the best part of a morning was wasted in bringing them out and re-arranging them. As a matter of fact "his majesty" felt that Hardigras would not be able to resist the temptation to treat himself to a few of these gewgaws for a fête of such importance, and would fain cut a figure in the most becoming finery without the need of unloosening his purse strings.

M. Morelli took all the necessary precautions; and the four stalwarts were stationed in such a way that any person creeping into the domain of temptation must needs fall into their hands. He himself took command of the field of operations. At nine o'clock that evening each man was at his post.

Before taking up his own position the staff controller once again interviewed M. Supia, and his language was so cheering and he seemed so certain of success that the "tyrant" allowed himself to entertain some hope. That night therefore was spent by him in peace and quietness. Nevertheless when eight o'clock came, surprised to be without news, he descended to the stores. He was at once painfully impressed by certain remarks from the staff who, instead of busying themselves with laying out the stock for sale, were laughing and pointing to a wretched little paper banner which had replaced their splendid oriflamme and on which was written:

Your flag will suit me. I have only to change the M into H.

Thanks!

M. Hyacinthe Supia seemed about to choke. It was as much as he could do to summon, in a hoarse voice, the staff controller. One of the heads of departments ran up and told him that he would have to give up the idea of seeing the staff controller that morning.

"I hope that you will be able to question him this afternoon," he added, "but in any case he will certainly be better to-morrow morning."

"What's happened to him? Is he ill?"

"Yes, Monsieur, very ill, but it won't be serious."

"In that case I wish to see him at once."

"I beg you not to insist. M. Hippolyte Morelli is not fit to be seen."

"What do you mean 'not fit to be seen'?"

"We cannot hide the truth from you any longer. This morning we found the staff controller rolling about on a bed of tango dominoes in a very sad state. The dominoes are spoilt. . . . As to M. Morelli, he was dead drunk!"

M. Supia could scarcely believe his own ears. Bewildered, refusing to grasp the truth, he had to be told several times the incredible piece of news.

M. Hippolyte Morelli owed his high position at Bella Nissa less to his intelligence than to his irreproachable character, his reputation for perfect sobriety. Yet M. Hippolyte Morelli had been found dead drunk!

"And he is not the only one," added the manager.

"Not the only one! Who else. . . ."

"All four night watchmen."

"Damn it, what happened?"

"We do not know exactly."

"But the whole thing is incomprehensible," cried M. Hyacinthe Supia, who for the first time in his life became purple, seemingly on the verge of apoplexy. "Still you—you have seen him. Have you any theory?"

"Well yes, Monsieur, but I don't know if I should. . . ."

"Speak out. You have my orders."

"Well, it's like this. . . . Hardigras has assumed so much importance. . . ."

"What sort of importance? Where? With whom? . . . In the minds of asses!"

"Exactly, that's what I was about to remark. But as we have to do with the staff controller. . . ."

"He's the biggest ass of the lot! . . . Go ahead. . . . I'm listening."

"I assume that before pitting his strength against Hardigras of whose powers he had so high an opinion, he determined to give himself and his four men a little courage."

"Your assumption is preposterous. The staff controller has a horror of drink, and his four men are so accustomed to it that I should say it would be practically impossible to make them drunk. Hardigras is capable of poisoning them. . . . If Morelli is not dead this afternoon I will go and see him. . . . And as for yourself unless you can get rid of that *thing* within five minutes, you may consider yourself dismissed."

He pointed to the obnoxious banner which in the confusion had not been taken away.

CHAPTER III

M. HYACINTHE SUPIA determined without delay to apply
to the police.

By what trickery and by whose complicity had Hardigras been able to put Hippolyte Morelli and his four
watchmen out of action before, so to speak, they could fire
a shot? He was at a loss to understand, and as his own
detectives confessed their helplessness, it became the duty
of the properly constituted authorities to unravel the
threads of the plot. He was paying his taxes without
defrauding the revenue. The State owed him assistance
and protection.

At the police station he was told that the Chief of
Police was on leave, but that M. Bezaudin, the District
Commissary, was temporarily acting as his deputy and
would be pleased to see him. M. Bezaudin was distinguished by his extreme urbanity, and the highly philosophical manner in which he regarded the difficult duties
of his office.

M. Bezaudin smiled when he beheld the proprietor of
Bella Nissa enter his room. He asked him to sit down,
and listened with close attention to a story with which
he was already familiar. When M. Supia had finished,
the official reproached him for so long delaying his visit
to him. Ought he not at once to have appealed to the
one force which was able to rid him of such a nuisance?

"You may return to your stores reassured," he said.
"We will question M. Hippolyte Morelli and his watchmen this very day and let you know the result."

20

At five o'clock M. Supia received a telephone message. It was from the Commissary asking to see him. He hastened to the police office.

"We now know what happened," explained the Commissary. "Last night, M. Morelli after stationing his men, himself remained without moving under a counter, until midnight. At that hour, weary of a position in which he suffered from cramp, he tried to make some movement. But behind him was a taut rope over which he stumbled and fell. At once a number of dark forms made a rush at him and deprived him of his power of self-defense.

"A bandage was tied over his eyes and he was forced to walk blindfolded upstairs and downstairs for some time. When at last his sight was restored he found himself in a spacious room hung with a cheap colored cotton fabric and decorated with framed engravings borrowed from the Bella Nissa picture gallery. A table laden with good things and bottles of champagne stood in the middle of the room, and a dozen joyous guests clad in dominoes, their faces covered with the mask which is worn at fêtes on confetti days, were feasting and making merry. . . .

"The gathering was presided over by a domino in crimson who lolled in a splendid Louis XIV gilt arm chair."

"I am sorry to say I recognize it," interjected M. Supia.

"This domino whom they all addressed as Hardigras wore a perforated mask of such loud colors and was so comically made up round the eyes that the very sight of him provoked laughter. It was the funniest face conceivable. Nevertheless, M. Hippolyte Morelli did not laugh, for almost at the same time, he caught sight of a hanged man behind this extraordinary droll form."

"A hanged man!" exclaimed M. Supia.

"No, the dummy of a hanged man."

"It's just as I thought. They were playing at carnival."

"We should like to think so. The effigy had a very long tongue lolling out of its mouth. Well, we should not have given another thought to this effigy had it not, according to M. Morelli, been dressed exactly like you, and had there not been an attempt to give it some resemblance to you."

"Eh? What? . . . What do you say. . . . It was made to look like me!"

"This point is all the more significant," went on M. Bezaudin, "as the hanged figure bore a card bearing the words: *Until we get the other*."

"That's what we've come to with Hardigras," cried M. Supia, clenching his fists.

"Yes, that's what you've come to. But you may rely on us. We shall not allow you to be hanged like that!"

"I should hope not. . . . What did M. Morelli do then?"

"As you may imagine he felt less inclined than ever to laugh, especially as Hardigras gave orders for the guests to be admitted. . . . And they brought in, bound hand and foot, Tony Bouta, Noré Tantifla, Cioa Aiguardente and Peppino Pistafun. They had, of course, been deprived of their revolvers, and were forced to obey Hardigras's orders, which were to ply their glasses with a will to your health—in other words to the health of the hanged man."

"And well they might, Monsieur, for the entire feast was at my expense. What amazes me is that my staff controller should have agreed to drink like the others."

"More than the others, for they compelled him to propose the most absurdly fantastic toasts. Lastly, everything was so managed that after some hours of this junketing, the unfortunate man fell down exhausted and remembers nothing more."

M. Bezaudin ceased speaking.

"Is that all you have to tell me?"

"No, M. Supia. As you may suppose, we have drawn from this incident such conclusions as are obvious. To begin with it seems in no way natural that men of the strength of your watchmen should have so easily allowed themselves to be the victims of a practical joke by Hardigras's gang. It is certainly the first time that force was needed to make them drink! Does it occur to you that in this there is food for thought?"

"There is nothing to think about," declared M. Supia. "They are all in league with one another. That ass Morelli could think of no better way of arresting Hardigras than to apply to men who would go through fire and water for him."

"I think they are capable of it," returned M. Bezaudin.

"You needn't tell me that, Monsieur. Come, we must arrest these fellows at once unless they are already under lock and key."

At these words, uttered in good faith, the Commissary smiled.

"If you knew us better, M. Supia, you would realize that the chief business of the police is to leave ruffians their freedom. What could we do with them in prison? We should get nothing out of them. Whereas, if we seem to suspect nothing, if we let them go their own way, we are free to keep an eye on their movements and catch them red handed."

"I see," said M. Supia. "You will arrest them after they've murdered me. Meantime they will continue to rob me!"

"No," declared M. Bezaudin positively. "Do you know, M. Souques? . . . Still you must have heard of him. . . . and M. Ordinal? . . . Don't you know M. Ordinal either? . . . Well, M. Supia, I shall have an opportunity of introducing them to you. They are two detective inspectors from the Criminal Investigation Department whom the Chief of Police has had sent down from Paris to arrest a couple of notorious hotel thieves working at the present time on the Côte d'Azur—not an easy errand because these ruffians do not hesitate to use their revolvers when they find themselves too closely shadowed. Before coming here they had a score of burglaries and three murders on their conscience. You will understand that compared with these rascals your Hardigras cuts a very insignificant figure. Souques and Ordinal will arrest him over and above the hotel thieves just to keep their hands in."

"It sounds too good to be true!"

"Whatever you do, leave matters alone. These two detectives will see that a proper watch is kept in the stores to-night. And it will be devilish odd if we don't hear some news to-morrow morning."

Next morning they did in fact hear some news. And the story was told as early as six o'clock in the morning in the Cours Saleya, round the tables and tents set up for the early market sales:

The two expert detectives, MM. Souques and Ordinal, had been attacked in the stores by two armed ruffians who suddenly appeared in their path and were about to make short work of them when two revolver shots fired, by no one knows whom, laid their aggressors at their feet, seriously wounded. The detectives at once rushed after their rescuer but were unable to come up with him. Nevertheless it was generally believed that this man was Hardigras, himself. As to the two men who were taken to St. Roch Hospital in a grievous condition, they made a complete confession. They were no less than the two hotel thieves whose operations during many weeks had terrified the guests in the chief hotels.

Some minutes later there was a scramble for the local daily papers in which a report appeared under huge headings:

Dramatic Scenes at Bella Nissa
Hardigras's latest move.

A rush was made to the stores in the old town. M. Hyacinthe Supia, who that morning was green in the face, witnessed the assault from the balcony on the first floor. A hateful name, repeated unceasingly, went

up to him: Hardigras! Hardigras! Was the crowd
about to call upon him to present Hardigras with a
medal for saving life? Suddenly every face became im-
passive with expectation, and then a loud outburst of
laughter from the delighted crowd filled the huge hall
and rang horribly in M. Supia's ears.

He felt certain that this was another infernal maneuver
by his enemy. He, too, looked up and beheld, hanging
from the uppermost balcony, a strip of calico on which
stood out in black letters in the local dialect:

Sow the wind and reap the whirlwind.

And this was followed by a sentence in French addressed
to hotel thieves and adventurers of every nation:

Let all persons who walk about my stores at night
take warning.

CHAPTER IV.

THE COMMISSARY'S IDEA

His stores! His stores! Bella Nissa has become Hardigras's stores!

As poor M. Supia was returning to his rooms more cast down than ever, he encountered on his way the charming Antoinette, who already knew what had happened.

"Well, godfather, do you think it proper for Hardigras to call Bella Nissa his stores?" she asked.

He swooped down on her, menacingly; but the chit spun on her heels and slipped away. She, too, now, was furious and rapped out at him from the door: "I shan't tell you now what my idea was."

In the course of the morning M. Supia was summoned to the police office. He found there M. Bezaudin and MM. Souques and Ordinal, the two detective inspectors.

Both detectives were lean and gaunt, dressed in somewhat dusty clothes too tight for them. They were singularly alike. Devoted to one thing only— their profession —they thought wholly of their work; in other words, they were suspicious, crafty, reticent, looking at the worst side of life. When big game was left to them they followed up the trail with a quiet intensity which knew no pause until they brought back their quarry, gasping, in the clutch of the handcuffs.

Possessed of courage, moreover, which had withstood every test, they bore the marks of many scars. What differentiated one from the other was that while M. Ordinal occasionally spoke, M. Souques was invariably silent. He believed in the written word; and he accepted no

26

orders which were not in writing. That was his system.
M. Souques had the greatest contempt for M. Ordinal,
and M. Ordinal loathed M. Souques. This ill-will arose
from the fact that each one robbed the other of some
honor that might have accrued to him, in the pursuit of
a man. Nevertheless their experience of the night before
brought them together in a common bond—their feeling
of rage against Hardigras.

Hardigras, perhaps, had saved their lives. They would
never forgive him for it. They bore him a grudge for
shooting down two criminals whom they regarded as their
property—the two hotel thieves. In short they were in a
state of mind so closely resembling that of M. Hyacinthe
Supia's, that all three were soon in complete accord.
M. Bezaudin, on the other hand, was more smiling than
ever. He found himself relieved of two dangerous visitors.
That was the main thing; and his first words left no doubt
of his gratitude to Hardigras on that account.

"Well," he began, when M. Supia was shown in, "your
Hardigras did us a very great service last night."

This far too airy greeting mightily displeased M. Supia.

"Did you a service, perhaps," growled M. Supia taking
a seat. "But as far as I am concerned I take note that
Hardigras is particularly anxious to be the only one to
rob me. This is a privilege that he does not choose to
share with anyone else."

He threw upon the table the strip of calico which bore
Hardigras's cynical explanation of his courageous act.

"All this is not very serious," returned M. Bezaudin,
shrugging his shoulders, "and cannot make you forget
how he prevented your stores from being burnt down and
saved the lives of these two gentlemen."

Here M. Ordinal looked up and abruptly interrupted
M. Bezaudin.

"Pardon, Monsieur," he said in a thin, harsh, somewhat
disagreeable voice, "this is not the first time our lives
have been in danger. But believe me, we have never

needed the services of a professional thief to get us out of a difficulty."

"I am quite sure of that," assented M. Bezaudin good humoredly. "All the same you cannot deny, either of you, that after what happened last night you owe Hardigras some gratitude."

"Gratitude for what?" asked M. Ordinal, even more harshly. "I suppose you mean because he has debarred us, owing to this incident, from the professional satisfaction of arresting two thieves upon whom we already had our hands."

"And who were on the point of shooting you."

"Or missing us. That is a daily risk in our business."

M. Souques made an approving motion of his head.

"A smart piece of work, in truth, on the part of your Hardigras!" went on M. Ordinal. "Those gentlemen will perhaps die in hospital without the opportunity of turning informers. Henceforward this is a matter between Hardigras and us. We shan't leave Nice until we have arrested him. That's our last word."

M. Ordinal turned to M. Souques who in silence fumbled in his pocket and drew forth a pair of handcuffs. He had no need for speech. His meaning was clear. Thereupon M. Bezaudin laughed openly at them.

"Well, gentlemen, do as you please, but allow me to say that up to now you have not been any cleverer than the others."

M. Hyacinthe Supia had listened to the two detectives with marked approval and now turned brusquely to the Commissary, in a tone devoid of all courtesy:

"But if you are not going to arrest Hardigras what are you going to do?"

"Nothing," returned M. Bezaudin. "I shall do nothing. I shall leave the matter to you. I had an idea of my own; but let's drop the subject."

"Excuse me," returned M. Supia. "The other day you said: 'Don't let's arrest his accomplices,' and to-day you say: 'Don't let's arrest Hardigras.' I am entitled to know what your idea is since you seem to consider that your main duty is to avoid arresting anyone."

"Arrest Hardigras! Arrest Hardigras! Hang it all, I am not the man to prevent you."

"What is your idea, Monsieur? These two gentlemen and myself are very keen on knowing," persisted M. Supia in increasingly hostile tones.

But MM. Ordinal and Souques seated side by side gazed blankly at the ceiling to show how far from the Commissary they were in thought.

Observing that his idea was of so little importance in their eyes, M. Bezaudin, who though he was a philosopher was no less a man—in other words was not without a certain pride—decided to tell them.

"Well, this is my idea—I think we are taking the wrong course with Hardigras."

"What do you mean?" asked M. Supia, becoming more and more suspicious.

"I mean that instead of hunting him down as you have done up to the present . . ."

"You would, perhaps, come to terms with him?"

"A man in my position, M. Supia, does not come to terms with a man like Hardigras."

"I am very glad to hear you say so."

"But that is a consideration a man like you would perhaps be wrong to reject in present circumstances."

"Oh, you don't say so! I am to make terms with the scoundrel."

"Come, I say, that is using very strong language. . . . Scoundrel! . . . He did not behave as a scoundrel last night, and I want no further proof of that than the daily increasing sympathy of the crowd for him."

"The sympathy of the crowd?" yelped M. Supia. "What crowd do you mean?"

"Oh, not a particularly brilliant crowd, I admit, but not a vicious crowd either I assure you. The crowd that

loves a good laugh and a practical joke and is pleased
to see the Commissary outwitted. I know it, and you too
know it, for it represents the more substantial part of
your customers at your stores. . . . Well, it is the complicity of this crowd that I look upon as formidable. . . .
And I believe that if one gave Hardigras to understand
that the jest has lasted long enough. . . ."

"You call it a jest!" gasped M. Supia.

In his indignation he turned for support to the two
detectives, but they continued to gaze imperturbably at
the ceiling on which Hardigras had not as yet written
anything!

"Let me develop my theory, if you don't mind,
M. Supia," went on the Commissary. "Afterwards—
well, you may do as you please. If you were to say to
Hardigras: 'We are quite willing to overlook everything,
and you can go and get yourself hanged elsewhere, but
on one condition: you must restore everything that you
have. . . .'"

"Stolen, Monsieur, stolen. I like to call a thing by its
right name."

"Yes, 'everything that you have stolen from Bella Nissa
stores.'"

"Then you wish to bargain with Hardigras?"

"There's no question of bargaining with him. The
point is to get rid of him as soon as possible on the best
terms. Let him know that you will not proceed to ex-
tremities against him if he will restore the things—as far
as he can now—and I am sure he won't hesitate."

"Through whom would you make this proposal, seeing
that you have been unable to discover the room in which
he lives and entertains his friends at my expense?"

"Look here, I am convinced that your night watchmen—
the four gentlemen whom Hardigras compelled to drink
your champagne and liquors—will be only too pleased to
render Hardigras this little service in return for a night
which they will not soon forget. Will you allow me to

say a word to them on the subject, in your presence?"

"What an awful disgrace," moaned M. Supia, as he dropped into a seat. "Still, have a try. . . . In one way or another, as you say, we must put an end to it."

The Commissary rang for his secretary, said a word to him, and almost at once the four night watchmen were shown in. Bouta, Aiguardente, Tantifla, and Pistafun seemed more prosperous and jovial than ever. They declared that they had never felt so well since taking what they called: Hardigras's medicine.

In the presence of the Commissary they assumed an air of consternation.

"If it depended on me alone," said M. Bezaudin in his loudest voice, "I should have offered you, some twenty-four hours ago, hospitality which would have been a great change from that which you enjoyed with your friend, Hardigras."

"Hardigras is no friend of ours," interrupted Tony Bouta. "Otherwise, governor, we should be ill with high living, but to speak the truth we've no fault to find with him."

"Come, come, don't talk such nonsense if you please," said the Commissary. "I know all there is to be known about you, and I should have taken you before the magistrates had I not given way to M. Supia, here present, who chooses to consider that you allowed yourself to be lured into drinking more liquor than was good for you, though you cannot have been ignorant where it came from."

"What about Hippolyte Morelli? Did he know where it came from? How about him?"

"We are not discussing M. Morelli. He is a man above suspicion."

"Yes, he will be whitewashed, but it will be the penal settlement for us, and why, I ask, seeing that we were forced to open our gizzards?"

"Hold your tongue, Tony Bouta, and listen to what

M. Supia says. Where I see in all this an aggravation of your offense, he contrives to find some excuse for you. Well, you must show your gratitude to him."

"Our gratitude," groaned Aiguardente. "What must we do to show our gratitude?"

"Gentlemen, I don't ask you to show us the rooms where Hardigras's stores his plunder. . . ."

"May I be paralyzed if I have the least idea!" said Tony Bouta with uplifted hand. "But if ever I hear a whisper of it I will tell you or may the devil take me."

"As for me," protested Tantifla, "may I die of consumption if I have any suspicion where Hardigras hangs out."

"May I never eat cod stew again," declared Aiguardente, "never touch another glass of brandy, never have any luck at bowls if I know anything of his family or home."

"Well, we don't want to be disagreeable, governor," added Pistafun, "but we don't know Hardigras from Adam. You must not take us for what we are not. We were carried before him tied up like sausages and my legs still have shooting pains in them. If we told you anything else it would be lies."

"I don't ask you to tell me because I know where the rooms are!" said M. Bezaudin in his grand manner. "This very morning Hardigras would be in the New Prison had not M. Hyacinthe Supia in his boundless generosity come and entreated me to spare a man who had saved his stores from fire and destruction and, at the risk of his life, preserved for the state two of its most useful servants."

As he spoke he turned to Ordinal and Souques, no longer contemplating the ceiling but gazing fixedly at the tips of their boots.

"Of course," went on the Commissary, "these gentlemen cannot any more than I can make terms with a man so greatly in the wrong as Hardigras—a man whose criminal whims have placed him beyond the pale of decent society:

But it is within the province of the one who alone has been wronged to listen to the voice of mercy. Therefore I say to you—you who are ignorant of Hardigras's whereabouts but may by chance meet him—it would be well perhaps to let him know that M. Hyacinthe Supia is ready to spare him, in short to withdraw the charge against him if he will restore forthwith the articles that have disappeared from Bella Nissa through his agency—a fact which he cannot deny since all his thefts have been avowed by his own signature. . . .

"Let him know, too, that when he has restored the things, it will be in his best interests to decamp before the police can lay their hands on him, for if I happen to come upon him I shall, as you say, send him and his accomplices to the penal settlement. Do you follow me, gentlemen?"

"I say steady, steady on Monsieur," said Pistafun. "You are making a great fuss about a thing that's no business of ours. But though we can't help you we may all the same express our opinioin."

"Go on, Pistafun."

"Well, our opinion is that this devil of a Hardigras will never return the furniture."

"Never," echoed the others, shaking their heads gloomily.

"And what makes you say that?"

"He is too fond of it. He takes too great care of it," returned Pistafun. "If you only knew how well the things are kept—not a speck of dust on 'em—it's a pleasure to see 'em! Particularly his wardrobes. He has them everywhere—in the dining-room, the drawing-room, the bedroom and even the kitchen. And the floors—linoleum such as has never been seen in a palace. What do you expect? He takes a pride in his home this man. . . . And then his casseroles from the biggest in which you could cook enough grub for a feast down to the tiniest one which looks as if made for a doll. No, no. It's no

good asking the impossible. If I, Pistafun, were by chance
to run up against him and knew it was Hardigras, for he
did not take off his mask before us—well, if I were to say
to him: 'Hardigras, humor the worthy M. Supia by giving
him back his furniture,' do you know what he would say?
'Pistafun, you go to the devil.' No, no, governor, ask
some one else, or rather do the job without talking about
it, seeing you know where his hiding-place is. You have
no need of us, hang it all."

The Commissary had grown red in the face, his strata-
gem had failed miserably. He folded his arms, turned to
M. Supia, and said in an indignant voice.

"You see what comes of your making offers to Hardigras! Well, M. Supia, we can't listen to you any longer."
—M. Supia had not uttered a word—"Nothing can now
stop me. It's war to the knife. Hardigras must go to
prison. That's my last word."

On leaving the police office, M. Supia was joined by the
two detectives.

"Now that the Commissary has given us a free hand
we shall lose no time," said M. Ordinal. "But you must
leave things to us. We have obtained from the Municipal
Library maps and documents bearing upon the old town,
the castle, and the underground outlets to the Paillon
valley. These will help us in our search of certain vaults
which undoubtedly adjoin your stores and which Hardigras is using as a retreat. Don't worry about anything.
We shall disappear. Should the thefts continue, don't
make a public fuss about them. On the contrary arrange
matters so that no one hears anything about them. Have
patience—that's all we ask. Leave everything to us."

M. Supia listened to this advice with a somewhat lugu-
brious expression. Nevertheless as these two men were
his last hope he had no wish to discourage them.

Three days sped by during which Hardigras showed
some moderation. M. Supia, sick of the whole thing,
grew accustomed to his petty larcenies. But on the fourth

day, M. Morelli, now entirely recovered from his terrible
adventure, came to him and reported that a magnificent
silver plated dinner service had vanished. Meantime nothing was heard of the two detectives, and there seemed no
reason why things should not continue indefinitely in this
way. Thus M. Supia once more paid a visit to the Commissary of Police.

He found him in a state of alarm. The authorities in
Paris had begun to express surprise at the long absence
and persistent silence of the two men. Explanations were
demanded from the chief at Nice, who was at a loss. The
Commissary was aware of the last conversation between
the detectives and M. Supia. But, like M. Supia, he considered that the matter was being drawn out beyond all
reasonable expectation. During the last two days his
men had been set to work, but had reported nothing that
was worthy of attention. In the bars and country inns
where the light wine and brandy of the country unloosed tongues, the Commissary's men variously disguised,
pricked up their ears and listened to no purpose to the
idle chatter of the company. In the table d'hôte restaurants where the bachelor employees of Bella Nissa took
their meals, not only was no allusion made to the disappearance of the two detectives, but Hardigras's name was
no longer mentioned. They were aware that many of
them were under suspicion of aiding and abetting the
jovial cracksman's disappearance and for some days they
had known how to hold their tongues. Finally, if Ordinal
and Souques had not left Nice or if they had not been
made away with, certain police officers, who knew them
intimately, would have discovered their trail however well
they may have disguised themselves. But not—there was
nothing. After all, Hardigras may have been capable of
doing a wicked as well as a good deed. After saving their
lives, knowing that he had made but two new enemies
pledged to send him to the penal settlement, he may have
rid himself of them without a scruple of remorse.

M. Supia returned home wrapped in thought; for he had derived no consolation from his visit to the Commissary. For some time now life in his family had been far from agreeable; and possibly there were reasons apart from Hardigras's practical jokes for this absence of cheerfulness.

It is well that we should now enter M. Supia's "home" and make acquaintance with the persons who adorned it. We have hitherto been so fully occupied with the mystery of Bella Nissa that we have necessarily neglected anything not directly relating to Hardigras, and we have caught but a passing glimpse of Mlle. Antoinette who, like others, had a plan for arresting him.

CHAPTER V

OF M. Supia, himself, we know very little. In appearance he did not belie his name; for, Supia in the local dialect means cuttle-fish. Lean, ungainly, enveloped in a long, loose, black frock coat without which he was never seen by his staff, of a bilious complexion, grayish-blue eyes, sharp nose and chin, sparse hair brushed with meticulous care over a hard forehead, this man between fifty and sixty years of age, whose appearance was now so little attractive, had had his day, some twenty years earlier, with the fair sex. He had won among others the wife of his employer, M. Delamarre, the founder of Bella Nissa, of which Supia was then the chief accountant.

Thélise Honorine Conception Delamarre had discovered so distinguished a bearing in this man, one of the firm's principal employees, that she had had neither the will nor the desire to resist him. It was happily at this juncture that M. Delamarre, after an attack of indigestion, and before he had become aware of his wife's change of affections, had had the good taste to depart this life. Certain rumors were current regarding his death as always happens when a fortunate coincidence provides the opportunity for an unforeseen triumph. Such gossip in no way perturbed the distinguished Supia. The marriage between him and Mme. Delamarre was an honorable, an irreproachable one.

But a week had scarcely elapsed before Mme. Supia discovered that her husband was hard, cantankerous, tyrannical, and sparing of his money—or rather of her money. We already know how he treated his staff; in other words,

from the highest to the humblest member of it as well as
by his own household he was looked upon as the "tyrant."
It may be that this sobriquet went too far, but we are
dealing with a neighborhood in which there is no worse
crime than to be unpopular.

One person who had small love for him was his goddaughter, the very pretty Antoinette. She was not loved
by any one in the house except the servants, who worshiped her, for it is a remarkable fact that servants
invariably bestow their liking on persons whom their
masters cannot endure.

Antoinette was the daughter of Mme. Supia's sister
who had married an honest, clever, hard-working and
hard-living man of Nice—characteristics which are by
no means negligible with which to achieve success in that
district. Antoine Agagnosc started life as a tailor's cut-
ter in a firm of repute and he possessed the business
instinct. Some years later he launched out on his own
account, and it was then that he married Mme. Delamarre's sister.

Bella Nissa was at that time one of the oldest linen-
draper's shops in the town supplying the average towns-
man, the market sellers, and the country round. As
Delamarre's brother-in-law, Agagnosc had little difficulty
in making him understand that much was to be gained by
developing the shop in such a way as to attract a better
class of customer, and he offered to enter into partnership
with him. The suggestion was accepted to their mutual
advantage. Bella Nissa before long consisted of a block
of shops and made great profits. Delamarre died, as we
have stated, and Mme. Delamarre married M. Supia.

The partnership was continued between Agagnosc and
Supia. That same year the two sisters presented their
husbands respectively with a daughter. The baptism was
a beautiful sight. Agagnosc stood before the baptismal
font of St. Paul's Church as godfather to Supia's daughter, while Supia became godfather to Agagonsc's daughter.

Mme. Agagnosc was of delicate health and died when Antoinette was two years old. And Agagnosc himself, who worshiped his wife, fell into a state of great melancholy, and it was not long before he followed her.

He left a considerable fortune in addition to his partnership in the stores. Antoinette was the sole heiress. He imagined that he could do no better than leave the management of this fortune to Hyacinthe Supia, whose strict probity, allied to his consuming avarice, he was able to appreciate. Moreover, Mme Agagnosc's sister would be a second mother to Antoinette. He died, therefore, with his mind at rest, glad to rejoin the wife who lay waiting for him under the turf in the little cemetery at the Castle, in the full light of the Nice sun.

The Supias had a country house at La Nova Fourca, in the Grasse valley. It was here that Antoinette was brought up among jasmine and roses, on milk from Mme. Bibi's goats. She rarely left La Nova Fourca; for she took no pleasure in town, which suited the purpose of all concerned.

Nevertheless, in spite of her tears, when she grew up they had to uproot her from this life of a wild flower. She was sent to a boarding school in Nice. She had left it about a year before to the great joy of the mistresses, whose lives she had rendered somewhat difficult, even though she was endowed with a delightful nature. She thought only of play, had a horror of lessons, and knew so well how to obtain forgiveness for her pranks that it was almost impossible to punish her.

Despite the by no means justifiable recommendations with which the examiners were assailed on her behalf she could not pass her examinations. Nevertheless, she had a considerable success in geography when she mentioned among the polar seas "the arthritic sea"; she was asked about L'Hotel des Invalides and made answer that it was a dancing hall. It was to no purpose that she explained how she had been told that in every hotel in Paris there was a dancing hall. The examiners hardly knew whether she was making game of them or not. She was then fifteen years old. After such brilliant schooling M. Supia provided her with a teacher who, first and foremost a governess, was never to leave her. M. Supia had his own reasons for that.

It was not without dread that he saw the time coming when he would have to render to his ward an account of her stewardship. Her marriage would be a serious matter for Bella Nissa, particularly at that time when the business needed all its financial ammunition to fight against Parisian competition.

M. Supia intended to choose a husband for her. But did she intend to allow M. Supia to choose her husband? We may surprise many of our readers by stating that she did not care one way or the other, as we shall soon see.

M. Supia went up to his flat at lunch time. A maid servant told him in a trembling voice that madame and mademoiselle had not yet returned.

"Is Mlle. Antoinette out with them?" he asked.

"No, sir, the ladies went out alone."

"Tell Mlle. Antoinette that I want to see her."

He went into the dining-room where the table was laid for four persons. He cast a dissatisfied look round and called the maid.

"Were you not told that the Prince was coming to lunch?"

"No sir."

"Well, he is coming. Lay the best service and let's have a table center and some flowers. Tell Mlle. Antoinette that I am waiting to see her in my study."

Two minutes later the study door was opened and the same young girl with whom we made acquaintance when M. Supia was in a scarcely less disagreeable mood, displayed her bright smile, clear blue eyes, plump cheeks, tiptilted nose, and intelligent forehead framed in a tumble of golden hair which would have eluded all the combs and ribbons in Bella Nissa.

"Good morning, godfather. How are you this morning?"

"Bad," returned M. Supia ungraciously. "Look here, what's the meaning of this dress you're wearing? Were you not told that the Prince was lunching with us to-day?"

"I was going to tell you Aunt 'phoned the Prince. . . ."

"What did he say?"

"It seems that he finds it impossible to come to-day."

"That's all right. He'll come all the same. Go and change your frock and tidy your hair. Understand?"

"But he 'phoned aunt . . ."

"Your aunt doesn't know what she's talking about."

"All right, godfather."

"I told her to take you and Caroline to the Promenade des Anglais. Why did you stay at home?"

"I hardly know. Aunt and cousin didn't want me, I expect. They can very well do without me, you know."

"It's your fault. You behave so badly."

"Oh, godfather! But I can equally well do without them; so don't worry."

"What have you been doing to-day?"

"I worked all the morning with Mlle. Lévadette who had the toothache. She always has something the matter with her, and it doesn't make her any the more pleasant. Can't you find me another governess?"

"You won't want a governess when you're married."

"Then marry me at once, godfather."

"To whom?" asked Supia roughly, darting a suspicious look at her.

"Any one you please."

"Very well. I'll think of it. I promised your father to insure your happiness, and I shall do so against your will if needs be."

"Well, godfather, I only ask one thing—insure my happiness as soon as you can. . . . Send me back to the country, to La Fourca. . . . I was so happy at La Fourca."

"With Mme. Bibi's goats?"

"Yes."

"Little simpleton. Do you think I undertook to be your guardian to allow you to become a goat-herd?"

"What do you intend to do with me, godfather?"

"I'll tell you soon."

"Oh, I know as well as you do what you intend to do with me—make me a Princess."

Supia taken aback, said nothing. That the chit who was so sharp should have guessed as much did not surprise him unduly, but he waited to hear more. . . . Antoinette was wont to speak of the Prince only to make game of him, and had already played all sorts of tricks on him. And, besides, the Prince confessed to forty-five years of age. True he was still a very handsome man, but after all a handsome man of forty-five is attractive to a young girl of seventeen, only on the stage.

Therefore M. Supia was waiting to hear more, and as she remained silent, he lost patience and broke out:

"Well, suppose it were true?"

"That's all right. I don't mind being a Princess."

"I knew I should please you."

"And him as well."

"Did he tell you so?"

"What do you think! He is too discreet for that."

"To tell you he loves you?"

"No, to tell me he loves my money."

M. Supia coughed.

"So you've thought it over."

"No, it's you who've thought it over! . . . You said to yourself: It will be a good thing to have a Prince connected with Bella Nissa. It will infuriate the Galeries Parisienne."

"It's impossible to hide anything from you, Antoinette."

"It's the Prince who will be staggered."

"Because I give him my goddaughter?"

"No, because I accept him. . . . For after all he is stone broke, your Prince, and with the life he leads will soon need a bath-chair."

"Antoinette! I am speaking seriously."

"So am I. But he will be still more staggered after . . ."

"After what?"

"After we are married when I cast him off."

"What! Have you taken leave of your senses?"

"I have never been so sensible in my life. On the one hand I shall do all that you wish, and on the other, by dropping him after marriage, I shall be meeting his wishes. I have no desire personally to interfere with this man. I will leave him to you since you can't do without him, and I shall go back to La Fourca and Mme. Bibi's goats. . . . Oh, godfather, take it or leave it."

"All right. All right. . . . After all, when you are married you may do what you like. That's a matter for your husband."

"I say, godfather, won't aunt and cousin be furious?"

"Not to mention that they certainly will be jealous of you. Only fancy—you'll be a Princess. Go and change your frock. Ah, my girl—by the way—what is that idea of yours which you wished to tell me—you know in connection with that infernal Hardigras?"

Antoinette burst out laughing.

"So you've come to that! Well, you know, you don't deserve to be told what my idea is. . . . And on consideration I won't tell you. . . . I'll go and change my frock."

"Antoinette."

"Don't keep me. My lord may come, and I wish to be seen to the best advantage. . . ."

"Antoinette."

"And besides you wouldn't do it."

"Never mind, tell me."

THE SON OF THREE FATHERS

"Well, it was an idea that flashed across me. It's very simple. I feel certain there is only one man capable of arresting Hardigras."

"Who is it?"

"The thing always happens at night time, doesn't it?"

"Who is it. . . . Tell me."

"Well, as it always happens at night time you must have a head watchman who is a strong man, and who will be glad of the opportunity of doing something to please me."

"But who is it?"

"Not forgetting that at the same time you will be doing a good deed."

"Come, out with it."

"Well, if I were in your place, I should send for Titin."

M. Supia gave a start and then banged the table with his fist.

"Titin!" he cried. "Titin le Bastardon. . . . Titin the Carnival scamp. . . . You dare. . . ."

"Why not? He would soon ferret out your Hardigras."

"Antoinette, I've already told you not to mention that fellow's name to me. Titin is a hot-headed youth who will never do any good."

"You make a mistake, godfather. He is as artful as a monkey and nothing will stand in his way. If I told him to get hold of Hardigras he would arrest him."

"Why Titin more than anyone else?"

"Because Titin has always done everything I asked him to do."

"That'll do. Let's drop the subject. I hope you haven't seen him since I told you not to."

"No, the poor boy has never tried to come near me since you sent him away."

"Well, let it rest at that."

"As you please. Let it rest at that, but don't complain, godfather, if Hardigras ends by clearing out your shop."

CHAPTER VI

PRINCE HIPPOTHADEE

THE maid came in to say that Prince Hippothadee had arrived. M. Supia at once went to him and himself showed him into the drawing-room. He lamented aloud the furniture being still in its covers, but the ladies had not yet returned from their morning walk. He begged the Prince to excuse them.

"I readily excuse them," returned the Prince none too well pleased. "Mme. Supia in fact telephoned me this morning that you wished to ask me to lunch, but begged me to find some pretext for postponing until later the pleasure of accepting your hospitality, because she had a great deal of shopping to do this morning. She said she was returning for a hasty lunch and leaving again at once for Monte Carlo, where she and her daughter had an engagement to join some friends in an excursion. . . .

"I told them that the postponement would suit me admirably because I had already accepted the Comtesse de Domingo d'Azila's invitation to put the finishing touches to the program for a charity performance in aid of orphans of fishermen lost at sea."

Prince Henri Vladimir Hippothadee, lord of Transylvania, was a man of distinguished presence. His tall, upright figure, his easy gait, his manner of kissing ladies' hands, and leading them to dance the tango, seemed to belong to the period of belated manhood; but his worn, lined, made-up face, his mustache and hair a little too dark, and the glassy look in his eyes, betrayed the years spent in the furious pursuit of pleasure and gambling saloons.

45

He wore a monocle, but the ornament did not impart to him that expression of absurd insolence with which would-be fine gentlemen seek to enforce themselves on the mob. He played gracefully with it, a fact that added to his accustomed affability, for Prince Hippothadee carefully dissimulated under a charming exterior the instincts of a spendthrift and a wastrel. He was one of the most appreciated figures in select circles. But he no longer possessed the wherewithal to support his position apart from the grudging and restive liberality of the Comtesse de Domingo d'Azila. It follows from all this that it was high time for the Prince, as the phrase goes, to settle down.

Had the thought occurred to him? It was quite possible. In any case M. Supia had thought of it for him. He had listened without surprise to the Prince's story couched in a tone of some acerbity.

"There's no doubt the ladies have avoided you for some time," said M. Supia, with a grimace intended for a smile.

"If my presence no longer pleases them," returned the Prince, "they must know that I never force myself upon any one, and if I am here, M. Supia, it is more to have an explanation with them than to accept the personal and pressing invitation which you were kind enough to send me this morning."

"I asked you to come here, my dear Prince, to set things straight. We have to do with a simple misunderstanding. When you did us the honor of accepting Mme. Supia's invitations and of returning them by kindly introducing us to circles which we were not in the habit of visiting, Mme. Supia seemed to notice—you will allow me, my dear Prince, to speak out in all sincerity, for I think too highly of you not to deal straightforwardly with you——"

"You have my attention my dear M. Supia."

"Well, Mme. Supia seemed to notice that our daughter Caroline attracted your attention."

"Indeed, is that so?"

"Yes. Mme. Supia said to me: 'Don't be surprised, Hyacinthe, if Prince Hippothadee comes here often, for Caroline is concerned in this."

"Obviously. You have a charming home life, M. Supia, and Mlle. Caroline is adorable."

"Let me continue. My wife after telling me this said to Caroline: 'Don't be surprised if we frequently meet the Prince when we are out. It is certain that he has remarked you.' "

"Mme. Supia was right," confessed the Prince with a bow. Mlle. Caroline could not pass unperceived."

"With the result that both of them imagined—Great Heavens, don't be upset Prince . . . it is so extraordinary, what I am going to say——"

"Go on, my dear M. Supia."

"They imagined that there was in the world—in the world of the linen draper's trade—a Mlle. Supia who might one day become a Princess."

"Upon my word you don't say so!"

"But, my dear Prince, you continue to smile. Does not all this astound you?"

"Why should it astound me, M. Supia? We have progressed considerably since the war. Where are the kings of to-day? Look around us. They are in commerce, industry, trade. The world is in their hands. . . . No, no, I am not astounded. On the contrary, a prince cannot but be flattered at the thought that he may become the son-in-law of one of these kings of to-day. I am speaking generally, of course. I am not sufficiently enamored of myself or my title to assume that I am going to become M. Supia's son-in-law."

"Prince, you are laughing at me."

"Not at all, I assure you."

"Are you speaking seriously?"

"Quite seriously."

"Well, Prince, quite seriously, you were right in making

that assumption, for I should not have given you my daughter."

The Prince, taken aback, dropped his monocle.

"Why would you not have given me your daughter?"

"Because you are not in love with her?"

"Who says that I am not in love with her?"

"Something tells me that you are in love with another."

"Let's have done with riddles, M. Supia. I should like to know to whom you refer."

"You are in love with my goddaughter, Mlle. Antoinette Agagnosc."

"I? I have never paid her any attention. . . ."

"There are ways of omitting to pay attention to girls or women, my dear Prince, which cannot deceive a man of experience like myself. It is not that I am an adept in affairs of the heart, but I have learnt how to fathom the most secret desires, the most private thoughts; or, if you prefer it, the most cleverly concealed thoughts."

"Where did you learn all this, M. Supia?"

"In my stores, that's all. I assure you that klepto-maniacs have a tough job of it in my stores, and it is enough for one of my customers to stare fixedly, at the lace counter for instance, for me to be convinced that she is coveting the pair of silk stockings immediately behind her. Therefore, when I saw you making yourself so agreeable to my daughter, I suspected that you were thinking only of my goddaughter, Antoinette, whom you were not looking at."

"Tut! Tut!" said the Prince, reflecting that marriage with Antoinette would be no less brilliant than marriage with Caroline. "Tut! Tut! I hardly know if I am —— Ah, allow me to say frankly, my dear M. Supia, that you greatly embarrass me."

"But why?"

"Well. . . . Try to understand my hesitation. . . . If I were to confess, in fact, that I am not indifferent to Mlle. Antoinette, possibly you would answer me that I am

much to be pitied seeing that your fixed intention was to
refuse me her hand were I by chance to think of asking
you for it."

"Well, this time you are wrong. Ask me for Mlle.
Antoinette's hand, and I am quite willing to grant it."

"You are wonderful, M. Supia. To grant me at the
first endeavor the dearest of my wishes! . . . But tell
me—we are here to discuss the matter—suppose Mlle.
Antoinette who is always making fun of me. . . ."

"Why Prince, what an indifferent psychologist you are.
She is always making fun of you because she is in love
with you. Did you not guess as much?"

"Upon my word, no. Are you quite sure?"

"Absolutely sure."

"Has she told you so?"

"Not ten minutes ago."

"Are the ladies aware of it?" asked the Prince with a
certain misgiving, for despite his self-possession, he was
greatly excited by the stroke of good fortune so unexpect-
edly fallen from the skies.

"I spoke to my wife about it several days ago. Knowing
beforehand how it would end, and wishing to cut short the
lamentations of my daughter, foolishly mistaken as to
your feelings towards her, I took it upon myself to tell
them that your views were centered on Mlle. Antoinette
and you had not concealed from me that your dearest wish
was to make her your Princess as soon as may be."

"Now I understand," exclaimed the Prince.

"That's because you are so clever! Have you ever
doubted it?"

"I doubt it to-day. . . . Hang it all, I feel a child
compared with a man like you. You have such a way of
hustling things."

"That's business methods, my dear Prince. Talking
of business, confess that you are not making a bad
bargain."

"Oh, I know nothing of business."

"Still the dowry has some attraction for you."

"Good Heavens! . . ."

"Tut! Tut! As Antoinette says, you are cleared out. . . ."

"Ah, Mlle. Antoinette said that, did she?"

"You live by makeshifts."

"What?"

"But that belongs to the past, and the past is no affair of mine."

"My dear M. Supia," said the Prince in his most charming and languid voice, suggestive of the near East, "money has always been a second consideration with me where love is concerned. I have told you that I love Mlle. Antoinette."

"Tut! Tut! Business is business. Two million francs in the hands of her trustees . . . and her share which is very large in Bella Nissa! . . . That's clear. And the present is nothing compared with what the future will be."

"How do you mean, M. Supia?"

"Yes! You will put the two million francs in Bella Nissa and you will double your income."

"Allow me. . . . Allow me."

"What! Are you by chance hesitating?"

"I don't say that, but a moment ago you were good enough to hint at certain rumors about me. Allow me to say in turn that there are regrettable rumors in the town about Bella Nissa. The profits are said to have greatly decreased within the last two years."

"That's true, but there is nothing regrettable in that. We have had enormous expenses but they are already practically paid off. Moreover, with Antoinette's two million francs—your two millions my dear Prince—the business will receive a new impetus."

"I daresay. . . . I daresay."

"If you don't like the affair, say so."

"But I don't say so. Only when Prince Hippothadee

marries, you understand, there will be considerable expenses. . . . Moreover, I have debts. . . ."

"I suspected as much."

"If I marry I must repay that admirable woman, the Comtesse Domingo d'Azila, who during the last five years has advanced me the wherewithal to live on, or else there would be a frightful 'scandal."

"There will be no scandal seeing that nothing will be changed in your relations with this lady. You will continue to visit her as often as you please. Antoinette declares that she will be as fond of you when you are away from her as when you are with her. She will retire to the country and leave you in town. The Comtesse Domingo d'Azila will be all the better pleased, for you will cost her less."

The Prince rose from his seat, flushing to the temples.

"What do you take me for?"

"I'm not taking you. I'm buying you."

"Not at a high price, at all events."

"Do you think so? I am guaranteeing you one hundred and fifty thousand francs a year."

"I would remind you, Monsieur, to whom you are speaking. If I marry I must have a million."

"My duty as trustee does not allow that. One hundred and fifty thousand francs a year or nothing."

"And I shall be paid monthly. You will be charitable, M. Supia. . . . All this might pass, if as a wedding present. . . ."

"Not another word or I shall begin to believe that you are not in love with my goddaughter, and then I shall be compelled to ask myself what a prince of high descent like you, ruined like you, can have visited my humble abode for, unless it were in search of a dowry. What can have been the attraction here? Shall I have long to seek Hippothadee?"

The last sentence was rapped out in so doleful a tone and the hand which lay on the hapless Prince's shoulder

gripped him with so much unsuspected force, that the
Prince dropped into his chair, worsted in the fight by this
grotesque and formidable being.

"Oh, I am too devoted to Mlle. Antoinette to continue
any longer a discussion which exhausts me. But you are
very hard in business, M. Supia."

The other chuckled and held out his hand.

"Your hand upon it. I am guaranteeing your future,
prodigal son. Rely on father Supia, on the 'tyrant' as I
am called here. You will, of course, often meet 'tyrants'
like me to bring you on a charger, an income of one hundred and fifty thousand francs, and a handsome girl like
Antoinette! . . . Are you really to be pitied?"

The Prince took the hand held out to him if not with
effusion at least with as much good faith as he was
capable of. It was then that they became accomplices. It
was a critical and stirring moment. M. Supia did not let
go his hold. He had the look of a man who had taken per-
manent possession of a friend from whom he was entitled
to expect the utmost. Possibly he was about to give him
the accolade as is the custom in French middle-class households, but the maid came in to tell him that "the ladies had
just returned" and "were waiting for him in the dining-
room."

"They still frown upon you," said Supia, smiling.
"Come and make your peace with them, my dear Hippothadee."

The ladies were in fact in the dining-room. They
affected the greatest surprise to see the Prince though
the maid had told them that he was in the drawing-room
with M. Supia.

Mme. Supia was still a very handsome woman though
somewhat corpulent. Her plump neck was bedecked with
a magnificent pearl necklace, her podgy wrists shook with
heavy gold bracelets, and other substantial jewels lay
scattered over her bust carefully clad in silk and velvet.

Thélise's vigorous appearance stood out more fully

when contrasted with the hatchet profile of her bilious-
looking husband. Any other woman would have died of
despair on the morrow of her honeymoon on discovering
how greatly she had been deceived in him and on calcu-
lating the years of wretchedness that lay before her. But
Thélise was a true daughter of this enchanting country
where grief finds no place.

Biding her time, she said to herself that she was still
young, and a third experience might be more fortunate
than those which had gone before. It was this hope which
buoyed her up in her disappointment. The years sped
by. Was there a third experience? Was there more than
one before Prince Hippothadee crossed her path?

At all events it would be a mistake to assume that she
had not thought of having at last captured the bird of
paradise for which she was seeking. But her ill-fortune
continued, and she had barely tasted the consoling joy of
her new adventure when Supia told her that her prince
charming had asked for Antoinette's hand. It was to
succeed with Antoinette that he had paid his court to her!

For two days Thélise was like a person distraught.
Caroline had no suspicion that there was any reason for
her mother's dejection other than disappointment on her
account. For, Caroline had made no secret to anyone,
still less to the Prince, of her hope to become a princess.
Thélise made the most of this candor to give full rein to
her resentment against the Prince.

Moreover, mother and daughter's soreness was increased
tenfold by the thought that the princely favor was accorded to the youthful Antoinette, incapable of behaving
in society with propriety. Princess of Transylvania!
Was it not enough to make them die of laughter? Meantime they wept at the thought of it.

It was to no purpose that M. Supia condescended to
explain, in order to pacify his daughter, that in making
Antoinette a present of the Prince, he was making a gift
to himself which would not fail to be of advantage to

Caroline later on when he was dead. She declined to entertain the thought of so simple a plan. M. Supia had an easier task with Thélise. To put the break on her outbursts, it had sufficed for him to look her steadily in the face and say:

"If you persist in refusing to understand me I shall begin to believe that love which was blind is deaf as well. . . . When I speak of love, my dear Thélise, I mean, of course, the love of a mother for her daughter."

This second sentence, which punctuated so felicitously the first, did not quite restore her confidence, and she remained, for some moments, under the crushing weight of the first.

We have said enough to enable the reader to picture the lunch which brought together so charming a family around its head to celebrate a coming event—an event, seeming to possess its humorous side, but which bore within it the seeds of the cruellest tragedy. It was the starting point of terrible and mysterious dramas which for long convulsed an entire neighborhood hitherto devoted to the lighter side of life.

But since we are only at the beginning of the masquerade which is, as yet, still behind the scenes, we may be amused by M. Supia's ill-humor. In spite of his artificial spirits, he failed to get a word out of Caroline or to induce Thélise to eat anything. It was the first time in her life that she had lost her appetite.

She might well have done so. For the rest, she confided herself strictly to her duties as the mistress of the house. Antoinette, clad more or less becomingly in her best with a new ribbon in her hair, entered under the tutelage of Mlle. Lévadette, still suffering from toothache, Thélise, then, after a look from the "tyrant," pointed to a chair next the Prince, and then uttered these words in a somewhat harsh voice:

"I believe we are now all here. We can sit at table." And they all "sat at table."

Mme. Supia then subsided. To her husband, who pressed her to take part in the feast, she said:

"I have already 'done myself the pleasure' of telling you that I have no appetite to-day."

M. Supia, without stopping to serve his daughter, on the point, he felt, of bursting into tears, passed the dish to Mlle. Lévadette. But, Mlle. Lévadette, what with her toothache and the literal distress into which she was plunged whenever Mme. Supia indulged before the Prince, in any one of those expressions which showed that, in spite of her admission to upper middle-class society, she was still a daughter of the people, was in no mood to respond to M. Supia's culinary advances.

The Prince for his part scarcely touched anything. He vainly sought to catch the eye of Thélise and Caroline. But to all appearances he did not exist for either of them. Antoinette had not yet addressed a word to him; and he dreaded nothing so much as being spoken to by her. She herself was immensely amused. But she kept her thoughts to herself, and the gloomy and tedious lunch pursued its course.

Suddenly the clarion-like voice of the terrible child came from the depths of the plate over which she was leaning:

"It must be very funny to be called Madame Hippothadee."

The old servant was the only one to burst out laughing at this absurdily fantastic remark, and she was straightway turned out of the room by M. Supia, who apologized for his goddaughter's unbecoming playfulness and for the maid's notorious stupidity. After which he seized the opportunity to settle the matter so that it should no longer be in question.

"Antoinette, you are a silly little thing," he said.

"Yes, godfather."

"And you don't deserve the great honor in store for you."

"What honor, godfather?"

"Prince Hippothadee has surprised and flattered my pride by asking for your hand."

"You are making game of me. That's tommy rot."

"Hold your tongue, wretched girl, or be good enough to use different language. When one is to become a Princess. . . ."

"Oh, there's plenty of time to talk about that. I don't know even if he cares for me. . . ."

"Prince, I beg you to excuse her. She acquired these manners in the country, and we haven't had time to rid her of them."

"Oh, I find Mlle. Antoinette delightful," said the Prince, toying with the cord of his monocle, and craftily assuming his most agreeable air. "Under her freedom of speech I perceive an impulsive and clever nature capable of great development. We shall make a society lady of her. Mlle. Antoinette has only to set her mind to it to throw into the shade the best of them, I am sure."

At these words Thélise's eyes filled with tears and Caroline, growing as white as the table cloth, bit her lip till the blood came. The Prince congratulated himself on having thus roused from their icy and scornful attitude the two ladies whom he still regarded as his property. Then languidly bending over Antoinette, he went on:

"You said something just now which immensely disturbed me. You must know"—here he cast a sly look at Thélise and Caroline—"that real love is shy. But however great my reserve may have been I hoped that you had in some degree guessed what my feelings were towards you."

"Well, Monsieur le Prince, how could I have guessed them?" Antoinette made answer with her terrible candor. "Up to now you have only kissed my aunt and cousin!"

The effect was instantaneous, and indubitably more complete than the Prince had expected. Thélise let fall, and shattered to pieces, a carafe from which she was pouring

out some water. As to Caroline, she took the opportunity
of giving way to her first attack of hysterics. The tumult
disturbed M. Supia himself, who with the Prince, rushed
to her assistance. Mlle. Lévadette, tormented by a raging
tooth, left the room on the plea of going for the smelling
salts. Antoinette alone retained her self-possession, explaining in a calm voice that there was no reason to make
so much fuss because the Prince had kissed her aunt and
cousin on their birthdays. No one had ever wished her
many happy returns of the day which was the reason,
perhaps, why the Prince hadn't kissed her. . . .

M. Supia could have killed her; the Prince paid no
further attention to her. Thélise took her daughter in her
arms. M. Supia went to her assistance, but she pushed
him aside without ceremony.

"Leave us if you don't mind," she said. "You have
made enough hullabaloo for one day."

Contrary to expectation, Thélise accepted only the help
of the Prince, who had managed to whisper in her ear:
"I am not the wretch you imagine." And the three of
them shut themselves in.

When the door was opened again their eyes were red
but they were friends once more. Beaten in business,
Hippothadee had exercised all his powers in the domain of
love. He had no difficulty in satisfying Thélise that he
had been constrained to yield to M. Supia's suspicions
and avarice; that marriage in such circumstances was ruin
to him personally, but that he had not hesitated to accept
the "tyrant's" terms for the sake of peace and quietness.
Lastly, while Thélise continued her attentions to her
daughter, who had not yet come to herself, he gave her to
understand that it would have been unsafe to continue to
take advantage of Caroline's credulity, and the best solution of their numerous difficulties was to be found in his
marriage with Antoinette.

Having thus persuaded Thélise, he was not yet at the
end of his tether. When Caroline opened her eyes and

was able to understand him, he swore that he had never loved any one but her, but that since he was penniless M. Supia had rejected him as a son-in-law, which, moreover, was what was to be expected from the old miser. It was a wonder that he had thought of giving him Antoinette, a questionable plan from which his good faith revolted. But, he had agreed to it, nevertheless, because it would enable him to enter the family and see daily the one of whom he had never ceased to think. . . . In other respects it behooved them to have patience. With a nature like Antoinette's, and her peculiar tendencies, she would soon put herself in the wrong. And divorce had not been invented for nothing.

Thereupon, they all kissed affectionately, and having thus sealed their reconciliation sought out M. Supia to tell him the good news. But they failed to find him, for meantime that gentleman had received a shock. A notification had come from M. Bezaudin, the Commissary of Police, informing him that they had at last received news of Souques and Ordinal. The two detectives had been discovered in Naples in a very grievous state. They had been found in an old coasting vessel, in which Hardigras, with the help of a friend, had obtained a free passage for them. Details were lacking.

Souques and Ordinal still raging from their experience had telegraphed that they would shortly be back in Nice, and that they relied on nothing being done in their absence, for they would take everything upon themselves. But M. Supia had had enough of the police and he took advantage of being alone with Antoinette to put aside his self-conceit and ask her if she was still of the same opinion that only one man in the world was capable of arresting Hardigras.

"I still believe so, godfather," she returned. "You have only to call on Titin le Bastardon from me and say: 'Toinetta wants you to arrest Hardigras'. and he will bring him to you bound hand and foot."

CHAPTER VII

TITIN LE BASTARDON

It would have been beneath M. Supia's dignity to go in search of Titin le Bastardon, himself. Descending to his private office he had a brief interview with Hippolyte Morelli, who at once set out for the Place d'Arson.

This popular square afforded a pleasant sight with its bowlers, their "coats off" revealing under their open shirts their tanned muscles, broad shoulders, bull necks and brawny chests. They delivered the bowl with a spirit and a natural gayety that came to a head whenever one of them made a shot that swept the field.

Was it possible to be in ill-humor in the Place d'Arson? One would scarcely think so. And, moreover, what reason could there be for such a thing? None of the young fellows there could have had any excuse to pull a long face. They had never been condemned, like so many others, to work eight hours a day. Their desires, which were to eat and drink well, to amuse themselves within reasonable limits, and to take no heed of the morrow, demanded no great effort from them, and thus they were able to reserve their energies for bowls and public affairs—we mean politics—which should, at certain times, occupy the attention of every self-respecting man ready to do his duty as a citizen. For, he may find his reward in sundry good things such as banquets, junketings, fêtes and other festivities to which ladies are invited. . . .

The unfortunate M. Morelli's duty was to disturb these men at play.

"Look out!" exclaimed one of the players on catching sight of "his majesty".

Pistafun cocked up his nose and greeted Bella Nissa's staff controller with a wave of his hand.

"Well, Mr. Hippolyte," he rapped out without seeming to attach any importance to "his majesty's" unaccountable presence in a place reserved for popular sports. "How are you?"

"Gentlemen," said M. Morelli, doing his best to show a brave face amidst the general curiosity. "I was passing this way when I remembered that M. Supia had said to me: 'If by chance you see Titin le Bastardon, tell him that I should be glad to have a word with him. He is a good fellow and I have always wished him well.' "

He paused, but no one answered him. They seemed to ignore his presence. He went up to Pistafun, who had just delivered his shot and was now assuming an air of indifference.

"Come, Pistafun, can you tell me where Titin is?"

"Titin le Bastardon?"

"Yes."

"He hasn't played a game here for over a month," said one of the players. "Hang it all, he can't be in Nice or we should have seen him."

"The last time I saw him," said Pistafun, "was at Le Peillon where he was managing a wedding fête, distributing bouquets to the bridesmaids, handing round appetizers, arranging the ball and the firework display. That's some time ago."

"I saw him," said Tantifla, "at La Colle where he was organizing high mass, standing drinks before the concert and arranging various sports. That was long ago."

"I saw him last summer in St. Jeannet," declared Aiguardente, "in connection with the feast of St. John the Baptist, and then in Biot for the feast of St. Julian, and then in St. Vallier de Thiev for the feast of St. Constant. Oh, I was forgetting St. Julian in Roquebilliére. Titin is an honest man who would not miss a saint's day, as you may suppose, but would celebrate the event according to

custom and with the necessary ceremony which he knows
better than any one. That's why there's never a saint's
day without Titin. You've only to look at the calendar,
M. Morelli, and you'll find Titin."

"It's possible Titin will be in La Fourca to-night,"
suggested Tony Bouta. "To-morrow they're having a
goat show. He is to arrange the distribution of cockades
and rehearse the brass band."

M. Morelli thought the men were probably right. He
would see Mme. Bibi in La Fourca; she would know where
to find Titin le Bastardon. But it was too late to take
the train to Grasse and he postponed his departure until
next day. He did not leave the Place d'Arson without
thanking Pistafun, Bouta, Tantifla, and Aiguardente. But
he refused their invitation to have a drink with them at
the hut.

Next day at three o'clock, M. Morelli reached La
Fourca Nova.

La Fourca was an old town of no great size whose
golden pyramid of time-honored houses nestling one
against the other, stood on an eminence and was dominated
by a medieval tower from the top of which the surrounding
country, from far-off Grasse to the blue sea, could be
discerned. The tower in days gone by was surmounted
by a gibbet intended to remind the inhabitants of the plain
that the Lords of the Moat and Castle had power of life
and death over them; whence came the name of Fourca—
the fork, the gibbet—a name at long last adopted in all
the region watered by the Loup.

The river Loup which rose some miles distant from the
wildest and most precipitous gorges that the mind could
conceive, flowed to the coast through a country now as
verdant as Normandy and now as bedecked with flowers
as a garden in the Arabian Nights. These two tragic
names apart, it was a smiling and enchanting land.

La Fourca Nova which stretched to the foot of the old
town of Fourca was a holiday resort. The Delamarres

possessed a commodious square-built house with crimson-colored walls, tiled roofs and windows decorated in fresco in the Italian manner. Large grounds, a kitchen garden, an orchard, a poultry yard—these things were once the scene of great activity. But they were now more or less neglected, imparting to the villa an aspect of luxuriance and rusticity which failed, however, to attract M. Supia, whose leanings were towards the chateau style of domain.

Nevertheless, as the land increased in value year by year, he had retained the house and outbuildings. Better still, he had bought under different names, the adjacent fields. And it was in this way that, by making a bargain which completely had mystified Mme. Bibi—a disguised robbery—he had secured a small farm which the husband of this honest peasant woman had taken twenty years to acquire.

Since then Mme. Bibi had lived in a hut in which during the war, she had found shelter with her two goats. On his return from the trenches Titin le Bastardon, her adopted son, who had not a penny to bless himself with, but whose fertile mind was full of resource, secured for her a small grocer's shop in the street which led, from the old, to the new town.

Titin le Bastardon never went past the closed iron gates of the Delamarre's villa, La Patentaine, without a sigh. It was here that little Toinetta, in other words Mlle. Agagnosc, was brought up, and where he and she had played many games together. . . .

M. Delamarre had called his villa La Patentaine, which signifies in the local dialect, La Prelentaine—the gadabout —because it was here that he decided, once his fortune was made, he would live and die merrily on the fat of the land. Alas, he did not enjoy La Patentaine for long, and though he died merrily he died too early in his opinion, and in Toinetta's opinion, too—as we know.

M. Morelli strode past La Patentaine without a sigh, and began to climb the back lanes which mounted the hill

to the open space where, from time out of mind, the fêtes
were held. He turned down by the old church with its
Romanesque base reinforced by a Renaissance column,
inside as rich as a cathedral with relics and ornaments
dating as far back as the eleventh century, when every
Philistine purchased his place in Paradise with wealth that
he imagined he would no longer require in this world.

Then the labyrinth of lanes became steeper, and M.
Morelli passed under archways whose purpose was less
to connect one house with another than to hold them in
place. At last he emerged into the sunbathed glories of a
fête which had lasted for four hours and in which Titin
le Bastardon seemed the principal figure. Standing between the Mayor—a real old peasant of the outskirts, still
robust and drinking hard in spite of his seventy years—
and Mme. Bibi who was seventy-five and seemed at least
to resemble her goats in her sharp face, bright eyes, and
heavy quarters, Titin was in the act of delivering one of
those speeches of which he possessed the secret enabling
him always to hold his audience, whatever he said. He
was the mouthpiece, the organizer, the main-spring, to
use a common expression, of the general gayety.

His highly-colored style, harsh and flattering by turns,
lashed and cajoled his hearers according to the whim of
the moment. They invariably shouted "Hear! Hear!"
because he knew how to have the laugh on his side. The
authorities were often spoken of in uncomplimentary
terms. But not one dared take offense; for this youth,
without house or home, possessed an immense influence in
political matters.

Every girl fell in love with him. He was not so broad
shouldered as his friends, Tantifla, Bouta, Aiguardente,
and Pistafun. Of medium height and well-proportioned,
with admirably developed muscles, he had indulged in
every form of athletics in the army, and had endured
terrible hardships during the war on the Somme, Verdun,
and Champagne, receiving the compliments of his officers,

who all but condemned him to be shot for breaches of discipline. . . .

As a youth he fought all and sundry. Not one of the young fellows present who would not have admitted that he had received a good drubbing from him when he was first breeched, and even in his first games of bowls; for the rest they were all proud of the fact.

It could not be said that Titin was good looking, but he had fine eyes—two splendid dark orbs which gleamed under his long lashes. His mouth was a little wide, and the curl of his lips showed his dazzling teeth; all else vanished in the brightness of his smile. It was enough to have seen him once to say: "Here's a man glad to be alive." When his friends spoke to him of marriage he burst out laughing:

"Family life means perpetual quarrels. . . . No more comfort and enjoyment; and it's all up with honest pleasures which are—eat well, drink well, and don't worry."

"Well the race would die out."

"Not a bit. Nature which is responsible for everything did not invent marriage, particularly in our bright little country where men allow their wives to do what they please. . . ."

CHAPTER VIII

So Titin was making a speech. What we he talking about?

About everything and everyone. Everything that came into his head likely to please the good people who open-mouthed listened to him. Titin's speech, at the end of a feast, was interspersed with an incredible number of wishes and vows for the prosperity of each one and the community at large. Nor would it have been a success had they not risen to clink glasses, lift elbows, and let the brandy flow as was proper after a banquet.

He had the gift of exciting good-natured laughter at the expense of the guests whom he dealt with in turn and held up under the most humorous aspects. He wound up with a few bold moral and philosophical reflections couched in the form of aphorisms of which he seemed to possess a rich supply, ready at hand. And his sayings usually displayed a wisdom and an experience of a man far beyond his years: "It is not enough to be an honest man, you must above all appear to be one." "A favor is always thrown away." "Many relations much trouble." "Too great cost too little pleasure." And he invariably concluded by remarking: "It's no good worrying" because "when one door closes another opens."

M. Morelli prudently waited until Titin had finished his speech amid a great hubbub and thunders of applause. He had waited quite an hour. And when, at length, he went up to him, young women already were surrounding

him; for, the sound of the fiddles could be heard, and he
was about to open the ball.

Mme. Bibi already had turned up her skirt showing her
two drumsticks in their new white stockings. He led the
old lady to the dance as though she were a young lass.
She was proud of the encouraging cheers and clapping of
hands that greeted her on the way. But, she was still
prouder of her Titin on whom she beamed enraptured,
showing her last tooth. . . .

When Titin led Mme. Bibi back to her seat after kissing
her on each lean cheek, "his majesty" was able to approach him.

"M. Supia would like to see you as soon as possible,"
he said, taking him by the arm. "It would be as well to
come at once." Then putting his mouth to his ear: "I
come from Mlle. Antoinette."

At the mention of Supia, Titin seemed ready to send
M. Morelli about his business; but, on hearing Antoinette's
name, he made an affirmative sign that he would follow
him at once. The company had no inkling of what was
happening, and the fiddles were waiting. When they saw
Titin put on his coat and make for the archway, leading
to the old town, where M. Morelli was waiting for him,
there was general amazement and consternation. He left
without offering any explanation; not even a good-bye
to the poor peasant mayor, nor a friendly wave of the
hand to Mme. Bibi.

"All that for Supia!"

"Oh, of course, he'll come back," said Anais, the elder
daughter of d'Esteve, the baker in the Rue Montante.

"Not at all," returned Nathalie. "He won't come back.
He wouldn't put himself out for Supia, that's a certainty.
It's for Toinetta."

"Well, what about it?" interrupted Giaousé Babazouk.
"He puts himself out to please himself. He has no need
to explain what he does to anyone. It's no business of
ours. It's not for us to interfere in his policy, I suppose."

Nothing more could be said. After the mention of Titin's "policy" no one was clever or daring enough to breathe another word. They started the dance again. But it was not the same thing. . . .

M. Morelli at once took Titin to M. Supia. He told him nothing. But Titin was so pleased at the thought of seeing Antoinette again that he did not even ask himself what she wanted him for. When he was confronted with M. Supia instead of Antoinette he began to pucker his brows. The two men had small love for each other. On his discharge from the army Titin had called to see Antoinette. He had been received, but Mlle. Lévadette was present at the interview, and showed clearly how unbecoming she regarded the young man's persistence in wishing to see again a "young lady" with whom he may have scoured the country when he was a boy, but about whom it was his duty no longer to think.

This first rebuff had not discouraged Titin. On the contrary, whenever he got back from La Fourca his first business was to hasten to Bella Nissa with some of Mme. Bibi's cheese and flowers as offerings to his young friend. On each occasion M. Supia cut short the interview. One fine day he wrote Titin a letter in which he asked him to put a stop to his visit to his goddaughter, and to act in future as though he did not know her. He had consented to open his door "to a soldier who had returned from the war after honorable service," but that Mlle. Agagnosc could have nothing to do with a youth who was "the scandal of the town."

M. Supia considered it strange that Titin should always have money in his pocket, though he had no regular occupation.

He had no occupation! He had a dozen, according to the season, the day, the hour. Now it was some difficult work of negotiation, now a helping hand to a friend, now his sardine fishing—in short a number of occupations which called for considerable skill and understanding.

And then came politics. And then, a wonderful venture which provided him with the wherewithal to live on a lavish scale without doing a stroke of work. . . .

M. Supia seemed that day as courteous as his temperament permitted it. He tried even to smile at Titin, who failed to notice it; for, he was not looking at him.

"My dear Titin, I asked to see you . . ." began M. Supia.

"There's no 'my dear Titin' in it," interrupted the other. "I was given a message from Mlle. Antoinette. I am waiting to see Mlle. Antoinette."

"I am very sorry she's out," said M. Supia, assuming a paternal tone, "but you will certainly have an opportunity of seeing her to-morrow morning. She will, I know, be anxious to thank you for the services you are going to do us. But please take a seat, my dear Titin."

"I am not your dear Titin. Please call me Monsieur Titin. Apart from this, you have my attention. . . ."

Titin sat down with an increasing frown on his face, thrust his hands into his pockets, and tried as far as possible to avoid looking at M. Supia, whose expression repelled him as it became more friendly.

"M. Titin, I owe you an apology," began M. Supia. "I was mistaken about you. I shall never forgive myself for failing to perceive your merit. I know how important you have become in our town, and the services you have rendered to the common weal by your influence on the most interesting class of our population, and by your tact, intelligence, initiative. . . ."

"That'll do, M. Supia. Cut the blarney. You want me. What's it for?"

"Well, it's like this, M. Titin. For more than a month we at Bella Nissa, have been the victims of shameless robberies. . . ."

"Ah, so that's it. It's this Hardigras business."

"You've got it, M. Titin. You are aware, like everybody else, I am sorry to say, of our misfortunes. You

know what happened to our night-watchmen, to our
worthy M. Morelli, to the detective inspectors. . . . This
confounded fellow has always managed to slip through our
fingers. To come to the point, I was in despair of ever
laying hands on him when my goddaughter, Antoinette,
said to me: 'Why, there's one person who could arrest
Hardigras right away. I mean Titin, who has always
done what I asked him to do.' That's the whole story
my dear Titin. I have given you Antoinette's message.
What do you think of it!"

"You may thank your stars, M. Supia, that the request
came from Mlle. Antoinette. Had it come from you
there would have been nothing doing, as sure as my name's
Titin, and I will tell you why. When Hardigras began
his tricks do you know whom you at once suspected? Do
you remember, M. Supia? . . . Well, you said to yourself: 'There's only one scamp round here capable of leading me such a dance like this Hardigras. That's Titin le
Bastardon.' And you had me watched. I was followed
night and day by your detectives. It was no end of fun
for me, believe me. I held my tongue and took the
thing with a laugh because that is my nature. Now that
you have recognized your mistake . . ."

"I do recognize it."

"You come to me and say: 'Only a fellow like you can
arrest Hardigras!' You will admit that I have every
right to tell you to go to Jericho! . . ."

"M. Titin don't fire up. I am not the only man who,
at first believed what you say. I don't want to mention
names. . . ."

"Let's get on with it. I don't care a hang what people
may or may not say. When one has an easy conscience. . . ."

"I had a watch kept on you and I offer you my apologies. But I gave up interesting myself in your doings
long ago. . . ."

"Yes, when you were certain I hadn't left La Fourca."

"I've had no idea of your whereabouts for the last three weeks, and our worthy M. Morelli went to the Place d'Arson on the off chance of finding you there."

"Did you tell Mlle. Antoinette of your first suspicions?"

"I am not such a fool, M. Titin."

"You made a mistake for you would have got rid of them at once. I know Mlle. Antoinette. It would have been useless to tell her that I was a burglar, a thief, a shop plunderer, a regular ruffian, a hangman. . . ."

"A hangman?" echoed M. Supia, staring at Titin with a look of dismay in no way assumed.

"Well, was it not said that this burglar had erected a scaffold in the stores?"

"That's true, I'm sorry to say," returned M. Supia. "He had a dummy hanging from it which it seems was intended for me."

"But if we are to believe Pistafun, Tantifla and company, it bore a placard on which was written: 'Until we get the other.' "

"Don't you think it's monstrous?"

"Monstrous—there's no other word for it. That's exactly what I was saying yesterday to my friend Babazouk: I may dislike M. Supia, but I should never think of erecting a scafford with the avowed object of hanging him on it."

"You don't like me, M. Titin?"

"No, M. Supia, I don't like you. But to please Mlle. Antoinette I will arrest your Hardigras."

"When?"

"To-night."

"Are you certain of arresting him to-night?"

"As certain as you are standing there."

"You are a wonderful man, M. Titin."

"Pah, we are what we are," returned Titin modestly.

He left M. Supia promising to return at nine o'clock. He asked only one thing—that M. Supia should himself take him into the stores in such a way that no one should

suspect his presence. Afterwards he would take everything upon himself. . . .

"And may I really hope. . . ?" stammered M. Supia,
amazed at so much assurance.

"Antoinette will be satisfied. You may tell her so, and
sleep soundly on it."

On leaving Bella Nissa, Titin made straight for the
Quay des Ponchettes, where he took the opportunity of
greeting some dozen of his fishermen friends. With bent
head he retraced his steps to the Rue de l'Hotel de Ville,
whence he could see, beyond a block of houses, the fifth
floor of Bella Nissa, and at a corner of the building a
window which however showed no light.

"If she were there a light would be burning. Supia
was speaking the truth," he said to himself. He returned
to the old town, still wrapped in thought. Obviously
he was considering how best to capture Hardigras. Thus
he reached a popular restaurant famous for its fish
dinners.

Sometimes the well-to-do local tradesmen came to this
quarter of narrow lanes—blackened walls, tall, decrepit
houses, whose perpendicular was broken by centuries of
humidity—for the pleasure of visiting the common room
of the old restaurant with its homely tables, and enjoying
the native dishes with which they had been wont to regale
themselves in their younger days.

That evening, as it happened, the worthy Papajeudi,
Mme. Papajeudi and their three daughters were dining
at a table at the back. The Papajeudis had started business in a small way like many others, and by dint of econ-
omy, cheerfulness, and hard work had made good in the
business of foodstuffs, butter, cheese, and so forth. They
now owned one of the most valuable businesses in the Place
du Marché, supplying hotels and restaurants; but this did
not prevent them from continuing their retail trade and
attending daily to the chance customer. As soon as the
market was opened, Mme. Papajeudi was to be seen in

the cash desk, while her husband, apron turned up at the waist, a wooden pallet in his hand, cut up pats of golden butter and weighed out other commodities, to the satisfaction of his customers. On the other hand, the three girls were never seen. They were at boarding-school learning to play the piano and to sing. For, it was intended one day they should grace drawing-rooms with their presence —a fitting reward for their parent's persistent toil.

Titin always had been spoiled by the Papajeudis from the time when, still a lad, he came straight to Nice because his Toinetta had been taken away from him. He wandered about the market, picking up his food here and there, running an errand, now receiving a tip, now a rebuff. Yet, he was delighted with the life because, from time to time he could catch a glimpse of his young friend, who waved her hand to him behind her maid's or governess's back. Too, he was certain, in hard times, always of receiving the gift of a little stockfish, a handful of olives, or other titbit from the Papajeudis. Papajeudi found him great fun, this youngster who made him laugh till the tears came. And, sometimes he drove Mme. Papajeudi frantic when she saw him juggling with her new-laid eggs.

"Why, it's Titin," exclaimed M. Papajeudi when he saw him. "Have you heard the news?"

"No. What is the news?"

"Well, Toinetta is to be married."

"Oh," said Titin, making no attempt to conceal his surprise and perhaps his agitation. He turned somewhat pale, but sitting down unfolded his napkin and added in a normal voice: "Well, no, I had not heard the news."

"Do you mean to say Toinetta has not told you?"

"I haven't seen her for a long time," returned Titin simply, ordering a small bottle of Chianti from Caramagna, the proprietor, who had hastened up from the kitchen on hearing of his coming.

"Bah! though Toinetta may have said nothing to Titin

she probably has whispered a word or two to Hardigras," interposed Caramagna with a wink.

"You are all a lot of asses," said Titin with a shrug. "What do I know about Hardigras?"

Caramagna burst out laughing. But he stopped short at the hard look in Titin's face.

"Go and drown yourself. You are too silly," he rapped out.

Caramagna discreetly returned to his kitchen; for, he knew that it was unsafe to provoke Titin when he had that look in his eyes.

A silence ensued. Then Titin asked:

"Anyway, is she making a good match?"

"What! Making a good match," cried Mme. Papajeudi. "Why, of course she is. She's marrying a Prince."

"What Prince?" asked Titin, having seemingly recovered his self-possession.

"No more or less than Prince Hippothadee, who may perhaps one day be King of Transylvania, you can never tell. At least the dear gentleman himself has spread a rumor to that effect."

"Is he handsome . . . young?" asked Titin with the same composure.

"I consider him very smart," cooed Mme. Papajeudi.

"Oh, you women!" exclaimed her husband, pouring the last of the Chianti into a glass. "With you women it's enough to be a Prince—nothing else matters. Toinetta's Prince is over fifty. He is made up like an old cocotte, his fortune consists of debts, he lives at the expense of a bewigged Comtesse. What does it matter? Toinetta wants to be a Princess and she'll be a Princess."

"When?" asked Titin, rejecting with an involuntary gesture the plate of smoking hot tripe that Caramagna, as an act of propitiation, had just brought him with a smile.

"Why, I believe it's to be within the next three weeks," returned M. Papajeudi. "I met the 'tyrant' this morning

in the Rue de l'Hotel de Ville. He was coming from the
Town Hall, and on his way to St. Reparate Church to
make the necessary arrangements. He seemed as pleased
as if he were going to be married himself. . . . Why,
Titin, what am I thinking of! I can see that I've hurt
you."

"Oh, no."

"You *are* hurting him," said Mme. Papajeudi, a good
soul moved to pity by Titin's distress.

"I am hurt, it's true," confessed Titin. "I've always
been very fond of Toinetta. At La Fourca when we were
kids we used to play together. She liked me, too. When
she grew up she didn't put on any side when she saw me.
In spite of old Supia we managed to say a word to each
other here and there in remembrances of old times. What
more could I do? I have only one wish—to see her happy.
She was not happy with the Supias, and I said to myself:
'If only she makes a good marriage!' Now you tell me
she's going to be married to a good-for-nothing. Well,
I am very sorry, that's all."

Titin's voice trembled slightly. His agitation spread
to the Papajeudis and even to other customers near
enough to overhear him. Caramagna wiped away a fur-
tive tear. A silence fell. At last Caramagna, dusting the
table with his apron, thought it well to show that he par-
took of Titin's grief:

"My dear old Titin, I am very sorry for you, believe
me."

Titin struck the table such a resounding blow with his
fist that he might have made the crockery fly heavenwards had not Caramagna darted forward in time to save
his possessions.

"Silly ass," rapped out Titin, now as red as before he
was pale. "It's not for me you should be sorry, but for
Toinetta."

Realizing that his intervention, however well-meant,
was not to his customer's liking, Caramagna made off to

his kitchen abandoning the idea for that day of putting
himself in the good graces of this hasty-tempered youth.

"You, M. Papajeudi, who spoke to M. Supia," went on
Titin, after an effort to recover his composure. "You
who saw him so pleased with himself—did it not occur
to you that he might be working some scheme of his own
in this matter? He is not very often to be seen rejoicing
at other people's happiness. Besides, from what you tell
me I imagine that he may have forced poor Toinetta's
hand—if I may say so."

"Believe me," interrupted Mme. Papajeudi, whose
opinion had not been asked, "Toinetta is not such a young
girl as all that, and Supia is not the man, hard and tyrannical as he may be, to force her to do anything she
doesn't want to do."

"I understand that," returned Titin, in a doleful tone.
"But this marriage is so utterly unforeseen that we are
entitled to ask certain questions about it. . . ."

Just then two men from Bella Nissa's staff came in.
One held an evening paper in his hand.

"The news is official," they said to two friends waiting
for them. "Mlle. Agagnosc is engaged to be married."

Each tried to snatch the paper. One of them read out
aloud:

"We have the pleasure to announce the engagement of
Prince Hippothadee of Transylvania, one of the best
known residents in Nice, to Mlle. Antoinette Agagnosc, the
charming niece and ward of Mme. Supia and M. Supia
the proprietor of Bella Nissa. The many friends of this
old and highly respected family will rejoice at a union
which does no less honor to the royal representative of a
friendly nation than to the merchant princes of the Côte
d'Azur."

"That's Supia all over!" exclaimed one of the employees.

Titin was silent. He cast a stealthy glance into the
adjoining room, a continuation of the room in which he
and the Papajeudis were seated. Two newcomers had just

made their appearance. They wore such a gloomy expression that it was no pleasure to watch them. To judge from their clothes and their flaxen hair they were foreigners. The Teutonic features of these two persons— they had taken a seat in silence at a side table, whence they had a view of both rooms—was emphasized by their huge horn-rimmed spectacles.

One of the Bella Nissa's staff was not to be deceived.

"I recognize them," he said, loud enough for Titin to hear. "They are the two detectives who had a narrow escape at our place."

"We thought they had gone back to Paris," said the other.

"I heard they had disappeared," said another customer in an undertone. "I know a search was being made for them everywhere. The police here were absolutely run off their legs. And, of course, they put it down to Hardigras. Yet it was he who saved their lives."

They all looked at Titin. He rose from the table, paid his bill, and rammed his hat upon his head with his fist. He seemed in a very bad temper.

"Are you off?" asked Papajeudi, surprised.

"Yes, I'm clearing out. I've had enough of all this talk about Hardigras. Damn it, to prevent any further question about him, for I'm sick and tired of hearing of him, I'm going to arrest him myself. I'll hand him over to Souques and Ordinal before long—if he's the man they're looking for."

Thereupon he strode, as stiff as a post, through the room, pressing against the detective's table as he passed and went out in a dead silence.

"Bah, he's not worrying about Hardigras. I'll stake my life on that," said M. Papajeudi.

"He was very fond of Toinetta. He loved her as though she were his sister. He is very upset about this marriage."

Souques and Ordinal silently, gloomily, and without enjoyment ate their stockfish. Caramagna, who took them for what they were not, gazed at them with concentrated rage. At last he said:

"These gentlemen do not like my fare. Do they want some 'kartofeln'? I can send out for some 'sauerkraut.'"

They made no reply, paid their bill, and stalked into the street. They turned their steps slowly towards Bella Nissa. They had no intention of entering it. M. Supia had plainly expressed his attitude towards them. He had no wish to hear any more from them, and had even prohibited them, in somewhat discourteous terms, from concerning themselves with his affairs. The assistance which, up till then, they had rendered him had not been sufficiently effective to enable them to persist. They had no other object in prowling round Bella Nissa than to keep a watch on Titin.

Stopping in the shadow of a wall at the corner of the Place du Palais, they soon discovered the man whom they were seeking. He was gazing intently, his hands in his pockets, at a window in darkness and closed, on the top floor of Bella Nissa. He repeated the operation three or four times, walking from one pavement to the other and escaping in this way the light.

At last he seemed to make up his mind and took a stroll in other directions. And so by out of the way flights of steps he came back once more to the Boulevard Mac-Mahon. After wavering for a second, he continued his way under the arches skirting the casino, and emerged into the Place Masséna. His attention was attracted by the crowd thronging round the entrance to the casino, adorned with hangings and bedecked with flowers as though for some great gala performance.

A theatrical performance in aid of charity was in fact being given at the casino. Motor cars were beginning to flow like a torrent, stopping under the arches, where the police were regulating the traffic. Showily dressed couples and those brilliant figures in society on whom fortune had smiled, enabling them to help a good cause without unduly boring themselves, were set down there. It was a glorious night for the time of the year, one of those marvelous winter nights of which Nice seems to possess the secret and which so greatly astonish the visitors.

In their open fur cloaks, the women, bedecked with jewels, roused the admiration of a double line of sight-seers. . . . Suddenly Titin gave a start. He recognized, alighting from a car, between her aunt and cousin, Antoinette, attired in a dress of exquisite taste and rich simplicity. A light cloak trimmed with silver leaves lay in unstudied grace over her shoulders. Titin was fascinated.

As this young queen stepped from the car she touched lightly the outstretched hand of a man of distinguished presence, with a monocle in his eye, and a courtly manner of bowing to the ladies.

To be sure he was not in the first flush of youth; but Titin found the sight of him sufficiently resplendent to be intolerable.

Everything, everyone, was a torture to him. Antoinette was the greatest torture of all! How he suffered to see her pass so remote from him, the admired of all, with the bright smile that he knew so well. But alas, it was no longer for him! That smile was perhaps the one thing that had not changed in her. Her aunt and cousin followed as though they were her servants. What was the meaning of it? Titin fled like a person distraught.

Where did he pass the next three hours? How many streets did he cover? Only Souques and Ordinal could have told. Oh, he led them a pretty dance! They found themselves at midnight once more outside Bella Nissa, still at his heels.

By that time they no longer had a doubt of anything. They merely wondered by what unsuspected means he would enter the dark building and betray Hardigras's secret to them.

They held their breath. Thus their surprise was great

when they saw him calmly knock at a small door, though some time elapsed before it was opened. The two detectives calculated that they had no time to lose and shot forward before the door was closed again. But they came up against not Titin, but a figure which they certainly did not expect to see there. And, straightway the door was slammed in their faces. To have been kept on the run for three hours and in the end to see M. Supia open his door to Titin le Bastardon!

However much, in their profession, they were prepared for surprises the shock was so great that the ever silent M. Souques exclaimed:

"That explains everything."

In order to seem equal to himself and any occasion, M. Souques had adopted the manner of saying, "That explains everything," when an incident seemed particularly hard to solve. Utterly stupefied they returned home to bed. . . .

It was two o'clock in the morning. A light was burning in Toinetta's room. She had just returned from the casino where Prince Hippothadee had entertained her and her aunt and her cousin at supper.

Truth to tell it was an evening that stood for a great deal in her life. And it was not surprising that instead of going to rest at once, she opened her window and lingered awhile, leaning on the balustrade, reflecting on the delight of those recent hours during which she had realized that she was destined to achieve every triumph in society.

Her success had been complete. The fashionable world of Nice, in friendly relations with the Supia family, had not failed to offer their congratulations. Moreover, the Prince introduced his friends to her, and they made no secret of their admiration for her youth and beauty.

But it did not seem as if the memory of her success completely occupied her thoughts, for her gaze wandered to the right and left and above and even beyond the roofs rising one above the other, over the great stores. Now her eyes remained persistently fixed heavenwards. Was she offering up thanks for her coming happiness? Or, was she amusing herself by counting the stars?

On following her gaze we should discover, perhaps, that it was centered less on individual stars than on a certain dark form which appeared on a level with a rain-pipe, and with the greatest caution, now clinging to a window in the roof, and now to a skylight, not omitting the protecting shadow of the chimneys, was creeping towards the roof that sheltered the future Princess.

It was not, indeed, without a certain anxiety that Mlle. Agagnosc followed, with her eyes, the movements of this daring figure, and when it seemed as if he might lose his balance, it was not for herself that she shuddered, but rather for the madman, risking his neck for a purpose which the reader will have divined. Let us not expect her to call for help. On the contrary it was with as little sound as possible that she went back to her room, switched off the light, and returned quickly to the window.

O Romeo, Juliet's balcony stands before you! But when the two young lovers of Verona met at night in an agony of suspense lest they should be discovered they knew that they loved and they risked their all for a kiss. . . . But poor Titin. He was staking his life to learn from Antoinette's own lips whether she had become engaged with a glad heart to a man whom he hated to the death. . . .

Did Toinetta know that he loved her? Did she know his secret before he knew it himself? Had she suspected what was in his heart before the thought of it began to make him suffer? No, of course not. The gulf that lay between Titin le Bastardon and Mlle. Agagnosc was too deep; so deep, indeed, that neither of them had ever thought of bridging it. It was this which made them both so frankly pleased when they met, unconscious of any danger. And now that he knew it, he was terrified. But

he came just the same. He knew that he had nothing to
say to her. But he wanted to see her. . . .

So that night in Nice, as beautiful as an Italian night,
Titin tremblingly crept to the light balustrade on which
Antoinette was leaning. She was greatly touched by his
wonderful dexterity.

"Big silly," she said, kissing him as in the old days.
"I felt sure you would come. I didn't know how. But
you were in the building, thanks to me. The 'tyrant'
told you all about it, of course. Yes, it was I who had the
idea of sending for you to arrest this practical joker,
Hardigras, who infuriates my uncle. Personally I don't
care one way or the other about Hardigras. But I wanted
to see you. It's so long since we met. And I waited up
for you. I wondered whether you would come from above
or below, or from north, south, or west. I had a laugh
beforehand, but I didn't laugh when I saw the risk you
were running through me. I was terrified just now when
you stumbled near the chimney. . . . If you had fallen
to the pavement I should have followed you. . . . You
mustn't do these rash things again. . . . But to-night
let's make the most of it. . . . Tell me about La Fourca.
How is Mme. Bibi?"

"Toinette . . . dear Toinetta. . . . Is it true what
you said just now?"

"What did I say?"

"You said you would have followed me to the pavement."

"I promise you I would, Titin. It would have been
my fault if you had been killed. I should never have got
over it. Do you think I'm not fond of you?"

A silence fell and then Titin making an effort to speak
in a natural tone said:

"You're going to be married?"

"Oh, you've already heard the news. I was going to
tell you. . . ."

"No need to. It was in the paper to-night."

"It looks as if it had upset you."

"Not a bit of it, Toinetta. You will have to marry one day."

"Yes, yes. You've got something to say to me about it. Well, out with it. . . . I'm listening."

But Titin remained silent. She began to lose patience.

"Can't you speak? . . . You silly old Titin."

Then he asked her seriously:

"Do you . . . do you like him?"

"I neither like nor dislike him. I scarcely know him."

"What about him?"

"Him?"

"Is he in love with you?"

"What about you?"

"Me?"

"Yes, you ask me one question and I ask you another. Are you in love with me?"

"We are not discussing me," stammered Titin. "You know that I have liked you since you were a baby."

"Is that all?"

"Well, of course . . ." muttered Titin.

"It isn't much," she said, laughing nervously.

"I couldn't very well like you before then," returned Titin fatuously.

"We like each other, as much as we did when we were kids, don't you think?"

"Well, yes. You know that as well as I do, and even better."

She laughed again, but with a laugh that was not without bitterness and, perhaps, not far removed from tears.

Then she became silent and Titin said nothing. In truth he was more perturbed than he cared to show. He forebore to look at her. He felt that were he to turn his eyes to her it would be all over with him. He would take her in his arms and fiercely clasp her to him. He, too, leant on the balustrade, his hands before his face, his heart on fire, striving to recover his calmness, and restrain his

emotion. . . . Nor did she look at him. At last she
spoke:

"You asked me if my fiancé loved me. Of course he
does. He's devoted to me. He does everything I tell
him. I shall be happy with him. I shall be a Princess.
He possesses every charm."

"He is no longer young."

"He is still very handsome. Very smart. All the ladies
are infatuated with him."

"I know that," said Titin. "But speaking of ladies he
has, it seems, a very curious reputation."

"It's his enemies who say that. There are plenty of
jealous, spiteful, envious people about. He has ruined
himself for the ladies."

"It's their turn to support him. They at least owe him
that."

"Why do you say so? Because of the Comtesse d'Azila?
She's an old family friend and has lent him money. But
he will repay her."

"With your money."

"What then? I can do what I like with my money.
He will make me a Princess. I can make him rich. That
sort of thing forms the basis of a good marriage."

Titin made no answer. Tears stood in his eyes. Suddenly she noticed them. It was her turn to be perturbed.
She tried to lift his head.

"What's the matter, Titin? What are you crying for?
. . . Tell me."

"Because I should like to see you happy," he returned,
in more cheerful tones, as if he were ashamed, "and because I can't believe that you'll be happy with that man."

"Then with what man do you think I could be happy?"

"How do I know."

He left her abruptly. With the agility and readiness
of a monkey he sprang upon the baluster rail, laid hold
of the wooden shutters, and climbed to the roof. Antoinette was furious to see him slip away from her. She

begged him to stay a few minutes longer. But he made
answer that it was high time for him to think about
Hardigras. She laughed once more, the laugh that is the
premonitory sign of tears.

"Well, go then. Go to your Hardigras and leave me
to my Prince. If I am miserable it will serve you right.
After all, as well be miserable with the Prince as with
anyone else."

But Titin was already some distance away. Antoinette
angrily closed her window.

Meantime M. Supia, who had not gone to bed, was
waiting in his office for the event which Titin had promised him. As we have seen, Titin reached Bella Nissa late,
after his wanderings about the town, but he satisfied
M. Supia that his time had been taken up with the working
out of his plan, which could not fail to bring the best
results. M. Supia refused to leave him until he had
escorted him from top to bottom of the stores, stopping
more particularly at those places which Hardigras had
plundered.

On arriving at the furniture department, M. Supia,
a dark lantern in his hand, showed Titin the famous
Louis XVI bed, in which the impudent Hardigras had
calmly spent the night. Since that incident no bedclothes
had been placed on it, and the room had been specially
committed to the care of the fireman succeeding the
nightwatchman, in whom M. Supia had lost confidence.

"My best room," groaned M. Supia. "A style complete
in itself and worthy of a museum. However, I have just
made it over to Prince Hippothadee of Transylvania,
who is to marry my niece. I recommend you to keep a
special eye on it."

"Leave it to me, M. Supia. You may sleep soundly on
it. I have a plan of my own."

On reaching the fourth floor, M. Supia showed Titin,
before returning to his flat, a small repast which he had
placed for him under the counter in the hardware depart-

ment. It consisted of half a chicken, a bottle of wine, and a small flask of brandy.

"You will have something to sustain you if you feel hungry, or to keep you warm if you need it," he said. "Are you armed?"

"Armed to the teeth now," returned Titin, with a loud laugh.

"Hush?" said M. Supia, who failed to see the joke. "Be careful, and if you keep your promise . . ."

"Can you doubt it, M. Supia?"

"Unfortunately I do doubt it. I have had so many promises."

"Have no fear. You shall have your Hardigras to-morrow morning at latest. Good-bye everybody. . . ."

"What! Are you going off like this without seeing my niece?"

"I've seen her. I saw her not long ago as she was going into the Casino with her future husband. How can you expect poor Titin to have anything to do now with a princess? . . . Look here, I will make her a present of Hardigras. That will be my wedding present to her."

"I always knew you were a good chap. I have confidence in you. You see this electric button. If you want me during the night, press it. I have taken my precautions, and help will be forthcoming. Good-bye for the present, Titin. I'll leave you my dark lantern. . . ."

"Whew!" gasped Titin as soon as M. Supia had gone. "I thought he would never leave me. How he bored me with his Hardigras!"

As a matter of fact, Titin had been thinking of something else. When he climbed over the roofs it was not in search of Hardigras. And when he got back to the stores after the scene on Juliet's balcony he was not the same Titin—the Titin who, as we have seen, was in a state of depression and tired of everything. He had recovered his delight in life, his sprightliness, his wonderful spirits, and his incredible contempt for all those things which lead

men to lie awake, hustle, trim their sails, work, fight—
in a word, the thought of the morrow. The splendid
present alone existed for him as it lay before his eyes.
What would he do with his wonderful discovery? He
could not say. But at that moment and in that place he
cried out: "She loves me!" And unable to restrain himself
he proclaimed the fact aloud to the pots and pans.

They were in love with each other! They had discovered it on that charmed balcony between the hard
words that came to their lips because they feared to utter
the real truth, though it would have relieved their hearts,
too long kept in ignorance.

Suddenly he ceased shouting. How careless of him!
"Why, if Hardigras heard me," he thought, "he would be
capable of going and telling old Supia. Hang it all, how
happy I am!"

And by the light of the "tyrant's" lantern he soon disposed of the half chicken. The bread and cheese followed
to the last crumb. Not a drain remained in the bottle
of wine. But he set aside the brandy for the work that
was still before him.

Satisfied with his meal, in merry mood, he told himself
that he was ready for the fray. Then, carefully, he began
his investigations. He moved noiselessly, contrived to
visit every floor without using the staircase, and was lost
to sight for a good quarter of an hour in the basements.
When he returned, scarcely needing the lantern, he passed
like a shadow amid the great wooden figures peopling these
dark and deserted rooms like ghosts, when a moonbeam
fell upon them.

He again mounted to the fourth floor, and, impelled
by the desire to make acquaintance with the brandy, he
crept to his refuge among the hardware. Then he descended again to the third floor and devoted his attention,
in accordance with his promise, to the Louis XVI room.
No sheets or blankets lay on the bed, but it bore a comfortable mattress. It occurred to him that Hardigras

could not have slept badly on it, and the best way of taking charge of the bed, to which M. Supia attached so much importance, was to lie on it himself. Like Hardigras, he drew the huge cover over him and waited the course of events.

It was a piece of cunning by which he obviously hoped to take the nocturnal visitor by surprise. And, it seemed to delight him. He laughed in anticipation over it. But his laughter did not last long, for son of Carnival as he might be, and even of three fathers, no one could lie down on a comfortable bed after the strain of such a day, with a flask of brandy inside, and not feel a pleasant lethargy steal over him—a lethargy calculated to sap the moral and physical resistance of the strongest being.

Titin soon fell into a heavy sleep. Like Hardigras, on a certain night, he snored. But, as far as we remember, Hardigras's snores were those of malice aforethought to keep poor M. Supia on the run. Whereas, Titin's snores were as real and as steadily rhythmic as ever were heard.

Titin was still snoring at seven o'clock in the morning, the hour at which M. Supia, unable to sleep a wink, resolved to descend to his stores for news of Hardigras. Alas! Titin was unable to give him any news for he was still snoring, and the worst of it was that he lay snoring on the floor on which the bed in the famous Louis XVI room once stood.

Now the bed and the furniture had disappeared. Nothing remained in the room but Titin snoring on the floor. At the sight before him, M. Supia uttered great cries betraying his utter despair. At the same time he shook Titin as though he were mad.

But Titin continued to snore. Five men tried to rouse him, but he did not open his eyes, and seemed in no way inconvenienced in his extraordinary slumber by the rough usage to which he was exposed, so that it was thought better to remove him to a garret adjoining M. Supia's flat.

They threw him upon the bed. He was no longer snoring, but he did not wake. He merely smiled. Though his beaming face was turned to M. Supia, he was not, in all probability, smiling at M. Supia; he was smiling to himself. He was smiling above all at the miracle which had fallen upon him from above—he was smiling at his Toinetta!

Enraged by this smile, which seemed to set him at defiance, M. Supia flung himself once more upon him. Then Titin began to snore again. . . . At eleven o'clock he still slept. . . . At two o'clock in the afternoon he still slept. . . .

On the suggestion of Antoinette, who at first was amused by the incident, and then grew alarmed and was with difficulty kept in the flat, they sent for a doctor, who after carefully examining him declared that someone must have administered a powerful narcotic.

"Where did he have his last meal?" asked the doctor.

"Well, doctor, I prepared his supper myself," returned M. Supia.

"I should like to see the remains."

The plates, glasses and bottles were brought to him. He noticed that a little brandy remained in the flask. A few minutes later the plates and glasses and brandy were examined in a laboratory in the Avenue de la Victoire. The analysis was conclusive. Titin had been sent to sleep by a drug which some mysterious hand had poured into the brandy.

Some mysterious hand! Ah, M. Supia knew only too well that mysterious hand. . . . Hardigras! Hardigras again!

Just then Titin woke up and expressed the same opinion.

"That confounded Hardigras has had me," he confessed unmoved. "But I'll come back this evening, M. Supia, and . . ."

"Clear out," yelled the "tyrant." "Clear out and don't let me see your face again."

"You are extremely rude, M. Supia," said Titin, putting on his trousers. "I should never have thought you would make so much fuss over a mere Louis XVI room. And I have been nearly poisoned on your account! Give my respects to Mlle. Antoinette, and say how much I regret my failure in this damned Hardigras business."

But M. Supia already had departed to the refuge of his own room. Once more he began to think things over, and this time he recognized his powerlessness. "Bezaudin was right," he said to himself. "I shall have to bargain with Hardigras and make the best possible terms with him."

M. Supia was to know that very day at what cost he could bargain, perhaps, with Hardigras. Having retired to bed early after the exertions of the night and the severe excitement of the day, he learnt what to expect, before nine o'clock. On slipping his handkerchief under the pillow his hand encountered a letter, which he certainly did not expect to find in that place. The envelope bore the address in capital letters:

"TO M. HYACINTHE SUPIA. URGENT AND STRICTLY PERSONAL."

With a trembling hand he tore it open and read:

"The marriage between M. Hyacinthe Supia's ward and the 'good-for-nothing' Prince Hippothadee of Transylvania is prohibited."

It was signed: *"Hardigras."*

CHAPTER IX

IN WHICH IT IS SHOWN THAT TITIN LE BASTARDON HAS GENIUS

THE following evening at seven o'clock, Titan had recovered completely from his enforced sleep. Wider awake than ever, he was walking along the Avenue de la Victoire, with his henchman, Babazouk, when suddenly turning round he perceived two gentlemen. From the cut of their clothes it was impossible to regard them as regular frequenters of first-class hotels.

Nevertheless we should do MM. Souques and Ordinal the justice to say that their make-up was so unlike that of two days before when they were in Caramagna's restaurant that Titin himself wondered if he were not mistaken in assuming that they were the two famous detectives. But Babazouk said:

"You can walk up to them, Titin, it's they right enough. They'll never leave us."

Titin went up to them and saluting them in military fashion said:

"MM. Souques and Ordinal, I believe? . . . Yes, it's certainly you. Three days ago you were dressed like Germans and to-day you look like Englishmen. I have no objection to that—it's all in your day's work, and as we are on the eve of Carnival it's as well for you to get your hand in. . . .

"But I am beginning to be fed up with you. You don't leave me by a foot's breadth, and in face of such misplaced persistence, I should be entitled to complain to the Commissary of Police. I only ask you, since you are so bent

on keeping our company, to take your walks abroad
with us. Let me introduce you to my friend, Giaousé
Babazouk, who was telling me a good story just now about
this Hardigras, who has been playing such nasty tricks
on us. . . .

"As to Hardigras, don't you think, gentleman, it would
be wiser for us to join forces rather than scatter them to
no purpose? We should end by having the 'rogue,'
though you would have to put your backs into it, and give
up once for all the notion—so fatal to poor M. Supia,
who had to retract and apologize to me for it—that
Hardigras and Titin le Bastardon are one and the same
person. . . .

"Gentlemen, here we are at Négrin Passage. There
are some very decent bars round here. Allow me to offer
you, since you are Englishmen to-day, a cocktail such as
you have certainly never tasted in England."

MM. Souques and Ordinal listened with perfect composure to Titin's little speech, and when he finished M.
Ordinal said:

"Hardigras invited M. Morelli to have a drink."

"Hang it all, how suspicious you are."

"Look here, Titin, that's quite natural after what
happened to these gentlemen," broke in Babazouk.

"What do you mean?" asked M. Ordinal, casting a
black look at Babazouk.

"Well, after your experiences in Naples," said Titin.

"Tut, tut," said M. Ordinal, looking uneasily round
him.

They walked down the passage. Titin led the way into
a bar. They found themselves in a bodega, where drinks
of varied character were being consumed round elegantly
polished wine vats circled with white metal hoops. Behind
the counter Fred, with a masterly skill that never flagged,
was shaking up glasses in the preparation of his concoc-
tions. On entering, Titin gave him a friendly nod and
asked:

"Has my accountant arrived?"

"Not yet, M. Titin," returned Fred, "but he won't be
long. . . . He was waiting for you yesterday, but it was
rumored that you were ill."

"I am never ill. I was poisoned."

"Poisoned!" exclaimed Fred. "Who poisoned you?"

"Hardigras!"

He did not seem to notice the outburst of laughter
which filled the saloon, but strode with his three companions to a small room at the back of the bar. MM.
Souques and Ordinal exchanged glances and had no need
to give utterance to their thoughts, which were the same:
"This time we've got him."

After drinks were served M. Ordinal opened the fray.

"You were speaking just now of what happened to us
in Naples. Did anything happen to us?"

"We know every detail of the affair," returned Titin.

"You know it as well as Hardigras himself," said M.
Ordinal casually.

"Oh, it wouldn't surprise me you know if Hardigras
told the story," returned Titin.

"I should be curious to hear it," said M. Ordinal,
winking stealthily at M. Souques, "just to be able to tell
you if by chance he has introduced any fanciful details."

"Well, gentlemen, you shall judge for yourselves how
much we know about it."

Titin related every particular of the occurrence alike
so extraordinarily successful and yet so simple in its
methods. . . .

One evening the two detectives were informed that
Hardigras, realizing that he was being hunted down, had
taken refuge on board a coasting vessel due to sail that
night. While waiting for the vessel to put to sea, he
descended to the hold for greater safety, and hid himself
behind goods bound for Naples. Since they were bent on
trapping him, it was a favorable opportunity; no time was

to be lost.   At that very moment the crew were on shore
and the vessel was in charge of an apprentice.

Acting boldly on their own impulse, MM. Souques and
Ordinal hastened to the harbor.   To board the vessel and
seize the apprentice in charge did not take long.   The
hapless young man protested to no purpose against the
outrage inflicted on him.   They silenced him, revolver in
hand, and forced him to show them the hold.   They made
him lead the way down the companion ladder which descended to the lowest part of the vessel; and they began
their search.

Suddenly as they were entering a dark corner in which
the cases consigned to Naples were stored, a blow from
a stick coming from above struck down the lantern in
M. Souque's hand.   At the same time they were hustled,
belabored, and thrown to the ground, for they dared not
use their revolvers lest they should shoot each other.

When they recovered themselves they noticed that they
were imprisoned in a sort of cell, in which their captors
had taken the precaution on humanitarian grounds to
place something to eat, which, however, they forebore to
touch, for they were in no humor for food.   They were,
in fact, a prey to sea-sickness, and when they arrived at
their destination were more dead than alive.

The captain and crew of the vessel did not fail to lavish
the most assiduous attention on them while waiting instructions from the authorities, to whom they reported
the occurrence as soon as they made their discovery.
From the explanations that followed it seemed certain
that the detectives had once more fallen to the wiles of
the accursed Hardigras, assisted by the apprentice, who,
the Captain learnt, was no longer on board ship and could
not be traced.   To show his good faith and regret that
MM. Souques and Ordinal should have been compelled to
make so unpleasant a trip, he offered to take them back
to Nice on his vessel free of charge, but they declined
his generous offer.

When he had finished his story, Titin ordered another round of drinks and proposed the health of the two detectives, wishing them a speedy revenge.

"Neither M. Souques nor myself," said M. Ordinal slowly and almost solemnly, "interrupted your story because we readily admit that it is as near the truth as possible. But we have taken the necessary measures, believe me, to prevent the details of this unfortunate affair, which reflects no credit on us, from being known to anyone but ourselves. . . . As a matter of fact, how did you learn all this, M. Titin? Would it be indiscreet to ask you?"

"Why, we heard about it like everybody else."

"What do you mean?—'like everybody else'!"

"He's getting at us," muttered M. Souques on thorns, feverishly rattling in his pocket the handcuffs intended for Hardigras.

"Well, like everybody else—through the newspapers."

"Newspapers!" exclaimed M. Ordinal, turning pale. "Is there anything in the newspapers about it?"

"They are full of it," returned Titin ingenuously.

"Here you are," said Babazouk, taking two Paris newspapers from his pocket.

He unfolded the papers. The detectives seized them and were amazed at the headlines, which left no doubt of their misfortune:

"EXTRAORDINARY EXPERIENCES OF TWO WELL-KNOWN DETECTIVES OF THE CRIMINAL INVESTIGATION DEPARTMENT. LAMENTABLE STORY."

For the moment they could not bear to read more. They looked at each other in despair.

"Our turn will come," muttered M. Ordinal, in a harsh and threatening voice.

"Yes," added M. Souques, and relapsed once more into silence. But Titin pursued the subject:

"Your position is nothing to laugh at. I am speaking seriously now. . . . Hardigras saved your lives in spite of you and sent you to Naples against your will. He deserves his punishment. You won't always miss him. I, too, failed to get him. Well, gentlemen, let's see if between us we can't do the job. But don't look under my jacket for him. You won't find him there. 'Pon my soul, it's maddening to see my friends look at me and laugh when they speak of Hardigras. I have always acted like an honest man. I have never done harm to a single soul. How can anyone take me for a burglar? I have always worked in the light of day. Everybody knows what my business is. I began with nothing and to-day I occupy a position which I won't allow to be jeopardized by a silly story. By my life, no! It's not by playing practical jokes on M. Supia that I have managed to start a business which shows sufficient profits to enable me to entertain my pals and friends from one end of the year to the other. Is that not so, Giaousé?"

"There's nobody in the world like Titin. That's all I've got to say," returned Babazouk.

"What business do you mean?" asked M. Ordinal, under the impression from his special inquiries that Titin was without resources.

"What business! You ask me what business! Why, have you been merely basking in the sun all the time you've been here and never heard of 'Bastardon's Kiosks'?"

"Tut, tut," said M. Ordinal, thinking that Titin was jesting, "Have you any kiosks?"

"You are the only man, M. Ordinal, to be unaware that I employ two hundred persons, not including my auditors and chief accountant."

"Where are your kiosks?" he asked, more and more disposed to believe it some hoax.

"Why, they're in the streets. They're all over the town and in the early hours of the morning they're besieged."

"It's extraordinary. I have no idea what that may be like. What do you sell in your kiosks?"

"Well, the best things in the world, unless of course you consider them the worst—newspapers," returned Titin chaffingly, waving in their faces the two papers containing the story of their discomfiture.

"Where are your offices?"

"Here."

"Here?"

"You may take my word for it. Here on this wine-vat. Perhaps you would have preferred an American desk?"

"He's getting at us," growled M. Souques once more. "We've had enough of this."

"Yes, M. Titin, we've had enough of this," repeated M. Ordinal, rising to his feet. "But never fear, I have a vague idea that we shall meet again."

"Always at your service, gentlemen. You will find me in my office on every first Saturday of the month. I am obliged to turn up here to check my monthly accounts. As we say in these parts: Method means money, lack of method, bankruptcy."

Just then Fred crossed the room and said:

"Your chief accountant has come."

"Show him in, Fred. I shall be delighted to introduce him to these gentlemen. He is the most honest man I know. You can't often meet such men in your business?"

"No," agreed Souques.

"Come in, my dear Gamba Secca. We are very glad to see you again, particularly if you've got any good news for us."

"Couldn't be better," said Gamba, adding, "I say, Fred —a glass of wine!"

"Gamba Secca" signifies in the local dialect a game leg and also any person whom nature, sometimes a harsh mother, has inflicted this infirmity. The man who came in had one "stump" shorter than the other, in fact. This caused him to limp; but his limp did not apparently trouble him overmuch. He was alert and he slipped gayly into the room. He did not give the impression of wealth, and his clothes were somewhat dusty. But, apart from this, he did not appear to lack either food or drink.

"M. Gamba Secca, my chief accountant and staff controller," introduced Titin. "He is not so ornamental as 'his majesty,' Hippolyte Morelli, but for keeping accounts he has no equal. Have you brought the books, Mr. Chief Accountant?"

"They never leave me," declared Gamba Secca, taking from his pocket a dirty notebook, about the size of the palm of his hand, and the veriest remnant of a pencil.

"What about Mr. Auditor?" asked Giaousé. "Figures are all very well. But money is money."

"At the present moment, Mr. Auditor must be at the Café de Provence, at Peron, waiting for the day's takings," said Titin.

"No, he told me to wait for him here as he would soon be ready with the cash."

"Here he is," said Babazouk.

"Cheerio Le Budeu," said Titin. "Come here, I want to introduce you to MM. Souques and Ordinal, two of the glories of Paris anxious to make acquaintance with your talents. . . ."

Mr. Auditor saluted Titin with dignity. His clothes scarcely differed in character from the chief accountant's. But, instead of "bringing the books" like Gamba Secca, he swung before him two fat, well-filled canvas bags which gave forth a metallic sound when he threw them without ceremony upon the wine-vat.

"Still going strong, Titin?" inquired Le Budeu. "So your illness was nothing much then. I said to myself: Hang it all, he's not the fellow to die young."

"Are you satisfied with business?" asked Titin.

"Well, we did twenty-five per cent. better last month than the month before. Aren't you delighted?"

"Yes, yes, I am delighted, my dear fellow, immensely delighted."

"Bring me a glass of wine also, Fred. . . . And now for our accounts."

He drew from his waistband and unfolded a handkerchief containing a decent sized wad of bank notes. Then he emptied the money from the two bags upon the "desk" in a double jingling stream. Titin, now as serious as a Prime Minister, proceeded to count the notes and while Giaousé placed the money in little piles, the chief accountant checked and put down rows of figures.

Titin turned round for a moment to gaze at MM. Souques and Ordinal, who wore an increasingly bewildered, suspicious look. .

"If you will lend us a hand we shall get through it quicker," he said. "As a reward I will explain my little scheme."

The two detectives were longing to know where the money came from. But they could not make up their minds to play the part of "supers" in Titan's business. He bore them no malice and explained it all the same. He told them that at the hour when shops were still closed, and newsagents had not yet begun to make a show, when the shutters of even tobacconists were still up, a large number of shop assistants, laborers, mechanics, seamstresses and milliners—in short all early workers on their way to offices, factories, works, or shops—felt a longing to know, before starting their day's work, something of the latest news, and even of the serial story. When Titin himself used to arrive at the market at dawn, he suffered from his lack of mental pabulum, and it was on thinking about it that the idea occurred to him to start Bastardon's Kiosks.

The business needed no greater outlay than the sum involved in the purchase of a rather large number of bags. Here, he found certain persons willing to supply him on credit. "I will give you in place of money 'founders' shares," and thus he had established his business on a limited liability basis.

The bags were hung up more or less everywhere from the Place Massena, the heart of the town, to the most distant suburbs. This was the work of Le Budeu, the staff controller, who soon added to his first office that of auditor. He was Gamba Secca's brother-in-law. Le Budeu was seen sometimes ; but his staff never.

And even to-day it is a surprise to some people to observe, in the early morning hours, bags filled with newspapers, still redolent of the printing press, hanging to a nail in the wall, or to shutters still closed, or to the bars of shop awnings not yet down—bags which no one seemed to guard as they were emptied of their newspapers by passers-by who dropped their coppers into them. . . .

A bag of coppers was a temptation. And also we are no longer in the days of Rollon! Was Titin then guilty of imprudence? That would be to show little knowledge of him. His staff was not to be seen, but it was in existence. And it was numerous for it was made up of men employed by the electric tramways—as many of them as he needed—without expense to himself.

The kiosks were planted along the lines, at turnings, stopping places and so forth. While engaged in their own work, drivers and conductors and others kept an eye on the bags and the customers. They would have done anything for Titin, who in return entertained them to a great banquet every year in May.

The banquet cost him nothing—too great cost, too little pleasure. For, he made some important person, eager for popularity, pay regally for the feast, promising him, when the next election came, the "votes" of his entire staff. Here, moreover, was the beginning of Titin's influence in the election of deputies and senators. . . .

Thus was demonstrated once for all Titin's genius. A new idea enabled him to fill his own pockets by getting others to work for him, and to uplift the world in the doing of it.

The world of politics, of course.

CHAPTER X

IT is not surprising that MM. Souques and Ordinal left the Passage Negrin before Titin, Giaousé, Gamba Secca, and Le Budeu.

The accounts were made up. All was in order. After dealing with serious business Titin and his friends could well afford a little diversion. Never had he been in such a lively mood—at least so merry in a fashion unlike himself. He laughed without reason and without offering any explanation of his sudden outbursts of gayety. Giaousé, who knew him well, cast a surprised look at him now and then.

"Titin, you are hiding something from us," he said.

"Yes," returned Titin.

"You seem different somehow."

And he began to sing an old song:

> *We are Moors,*
> *We know it.*
> *We look like Africans,*
> *And if we wash*
> *Perhaps you'll like us more!*

The three others joined in the song which never failed to awaken the good citizens of Nice at the hour when revelers return with their lady friends from the May fêtes or other celebrations of which there is no lack at any season.

"That's not all, we've rather cut into returns," he said. "We shall want some money for Carnival."

100

They left the bodega after unloading their money into
Fred's drawer. Fred walked with Titin almost to the
doorstep, thus showing his respect for a reputable tradesman whose custom is an honor to his establishment.

Titin le Bastardon was not to be seen again before the
coming of Carnival to his beautiful town of Nice—a
memorable coming which saw Carnival, Titin and, finally,
Hardigras himself.

.   .   .   .   .   .

On that day unwonted excitement reigns on the streets,
crowded as if by magic, multitudes flocking in from the
outlying districts, all prepared to make merry. At
fabulous cost foreign visitors snatch up positions still
vacant in windows, in balconies, in stands. Here and
there a few solitary masks dance in the streets—masks too
impatient to wait for the start of the procession, aspiring
only to gain the vote of the jury whose work it is to
present the awards.

From midday onward the aspect of the streets and
squares through which the procession is to pass entirely
changes. Each person takes up his position in the battle
and prepares his munitions—confetti, flowers, serpen-
tines. Over a distance of nearly two miles, thousands
of banners and flags of all nations flutter in the breeze
above a double row of engarlanded masts. Shops transformed into stands, their windows richly bedecked with
flags, swarm with spectators.

The battle begins. Confetti is thrown in handfuls;
entire bags are emptied over heads; multicolored ser-
pentines fly in spirals through the air; the throng on
the pavements with hands uplifted, charged with mis-
siles, are ready for the fray. Hawkers of ammunition
stand at intervals but have no need to look for customers.
Their wares are quickly seized.   Here and there a few
strangers watch, with bewildered air, a spectacle so novel
to them.

In the middle of the road all join in. It is a unique throng knowing how to be merry without annoyance, how to make good cheer without sinking into drunkenness. Thus the carnival amazes the visitor. No guys! Behold the children of the sun intoxicated with the glory of the day!

And now comes the march past.

We will not describe the effigy, nor the form in which His Majesty, King Carnival, appears to his faithful subjects. Nor will we dwell on the swaggering originality displayed in the construction of the local cars. It is not the first part of the procession but the last in which we are interested. For even though King Carnival is received with the accustomed enthusiasm, a tremendous tumult greets the last car—a car which is not included in the program and springs from no one knows where. Let us follow the crowd as it marches up the Avenue de la Victoire, the better to understand the incident which unloosed so great a tempest of gayety.

The actors in the procession turn round, the "big wigs" come to a stop in spite of their personal success, and every group pauses in its riotous dancing. . . . And suddenly, little by little, a shout makes it way: Hardigras! It is Hardigras who brings up the rear!

And then another name arises in every throat: Titin! Titin le Bastardon! . . . And nothing can be heard but the two names: Titin! Hardigras! . . . At last the rumor spreads: Titin has arrested Hardigras! He is bringing him bound hand and foot to the police!

As the rear of the procession draws near, the delight of the crowd knows no bounds. A thousand shouts greet the coming of Titin, who helped by Pistafun, Bouta, Aiguardente, and Tantifla, pulls along the car on which a pasteboard Hardigras lays stretched, bound down with fetters on a wooden framework.

The giant effigy shows its distress by its wide open mouth whence a scarlet pennant hangs like a tongue,

bearing the words: "To prison with Hardigras!" Ahead
of the triumphant Titin two masked figures made up to
resemble MM. Souques and Ordinal, walk backwards waving a huge pair of handcuffs that jingle like the sound
of bells. Now and again the detectives bow in token of
their admiration and gratitude to Bastardon. When the
procession stops they shake hands with him, while Hardigras gives forth a tremendous bellow, manifesting his
sorrow and shame.

"Poor Hardigras! Good old Titin!"

At the Place Massena, opposite the grandstand, Titin's
triumph is complete. Young girls greet him with an ova-
tion, throw their bouquets at him, empty their bags of
confetti over him, kiss their hands to him. . . . Suddenly a great shout goes up from the crowd: "To Bella
Nissa! To Bella Nissa!"

The car is now dragged towards the Place du Palais.
The crowd rushes after it. From the balcony of the fifth
floor Prince Hippothadee and the Supias look down upon
the people who accompany the sacrifice of the wretched
Hardigras with song and dance.

Toinetta is the first to grasp the meaning of it.

"I say, godfather," she cried, clapping her hands, "it's
Titin bringing you Hardigras."

The "tyrant" turned pale. The joke struck home.
Below him a thousand voices shouted his name: "Supia!
Supia! 'Tyrant'! Titin is making you a present of
Hardigras!"

Such seemed to have been his intention, for after making a tour of the sqaure, the car drew up outside Bella
Nissa. But it was not to Supia that Titin was making
the offering of Hardigras—it was to Toinetta herself.
Raising his carnival hat he laid his prisoner at her feet
with the grace of a toreador dedicating the bull to the
queen of the fête, who is so often the queen of his heart.
The gesture was so splendid, so happily inspired that a
shout went up: "For Toinetta! For Toinetta!"

Antoinette bowed and gracefully waved her handkerchief in acknowledgment. And then, as if by inadvertence, let the precious piece of cambric fall. It fluttered at first like a bird on the wing and then, swept by a favorable wind, floated towards Titin who, leaping forward, caught it before it touched ground.

The incident had not escaped the notice of the crowd.
. . . They all knew of the friendship that existed between the two youngsters. . . . Alas! our greatest triumphs often prove to be the most fleeting. At the moment when Titin saluted Toinetta and in his turn waved his trophy, the cheering gave way to an outburst of laughter—some unforeseen incident had occurred behind him.

He looked round and saw a spectacle that might well have made him shudder or it might have overwhelmed him with shame. But a Titin, on a Carnival day, laughs at everything, and he began to laugh louder than the others as he threw his arms up in the air with a gesture that bore witness if not to his concern at least to his amazement. The huge skull of the pasteboard Hardigras was lifted, and a Hardigras in flesh and blood sprang out waving the banner that not long before had adorned Bella Nissa and now bore the words: "Hardigras is not dead!"

Just then a voice came from the fifth floor: "My banner!" It was M. Hyacinthe Supia in a state of feverish excitement pointing to his property and the man who had secured it.

"Seize him! Seize him! That's Hardigras!"

He seemed indeed to be the man as he appeared to M. Hippolyte Morelli on the memorable night which had reduced him to so grievous a condition. . . . A long red gown hung from his shoulders like the toga of a grand justiciar, and the perforated mask concealing his face bore the expression, at once smiling and good humored, that persons of good cheer and good health wear when they pretend to fly into a passion. A gilt pasteboard crown covered his abundant hair, and he held in his hand

a banner—a banner which in itself was sufficient evidence.
For, it was M. Supia's banner!

"Come on, lads. Let's get him!" cried Titin as he shot
forward.

His friends started after him—the sham Souques and
Ordinal as well as the real detectives. Disguised in carnival dress they had followed the car from the moment
of its appearance, ready at the right moment to intervene.
When the man with the banner appeared they elbowed
their way through the crowd. They would have to arrest
him. He had the banner. It would be for him to explain
how it came into his possession.

Titin in a few bounds reached the giant effigy, climbed
to its mouth and clung there; and then by a final effort
pulled himself up to the huge skull serving as a platform
for Hardigras who, heedless of the general uproar around
him, continued to wave his banner. Titin at once caught
hold of his feet. But, just then the skull opened and
Hardigras slipped into it with the same agility with which
he had emerged from it.

"I'll follow you to hell," shouted Titin. And before the
skull was reclosed he, too, vanished from sight.

Inspired by such a splendid example, his men also
plunged into the cavity. At last Souques and Ordinal in
their turn found themselves on the brink of the abyss still
open and seemingly waiting for them. They exchanged
glances, understood each other, and remained standing on
the giant's nose in a somewhat grotesque attitude. The
skull seemed to wait for a few minutes, and then slowly
closed.

Now the confetti fell upon the two detectives, with a
hundred disagreeable allusions to their prudence, pardon-
able after all in men who had already experienced Hardigras's methods in their Naples adventure.

They were so nonplussed and dissatisfied with themselves that at first they paid no attention to the movement
which set going the mechanism on which they were stand-

ing.   When they realized that the car was starting, they discovered that Pistafun and his three companions had harnessed themselves to the ropes ; and the whole equipage seemed to be guided by Hardigras, who emerging from the lower part, took up his place on the shafts, still holding his banner.

The car went on its way again.   The crowd followed. But Hardigras seemed to be made of India-rubber, he bounded so lightly between one and the other, returning to his place on the head of the giant while his adversaries could do no more than shake their fists at him.

It is easy to imagine the glee of the crowd as they followed the successive phases of the chase, uttering quizzical encouragement to one and the other, while their cheers were reserved for Hardigras.   At one time it seemed as if MM. Souques and Ordinal had got him.   But, at the crucial moment the head of the giant effigy was on a level with a window on the first floor of Bella Nissa looking directly into the deserted offices.   Hardigras slipped through this window and vanished.   MM. Souques and Ordinal did not hesitate to follow him this time.

The car pulled up and a silence succeeded the tumult of a moment before.   Every eye was fixed on Bella Nissa. On the balcony from which the Supias watched the scene there was a great stir and confusion to which Toinetta alone remained indifferent.

Hardigras appeared again on the roof, towering above the whole town, seeming to bless it with his banner outstretched to the four cardinal points in turn.   There was so much dignity, so much audacity, so much amusing mockery in his bearing that the cries of "Bravo Hardigras !" that went up were a flattering tribute from the mob.   They seemed to see in him the magic being in whom the very spirit of Carnival was personified.

But he had no time to rest on his laurels.   The roofs were being rushed.   From every side came firemen, led by MM. Souques and Ordinal, showing on this occasion a

courage all the more uncommon as they were almost
entirely ignorant of the manner in which firemen and
slaters scrambled over roofs.

M. Supia once more began his frantic gesticulation,
revealing Hardigras's many ruses to escape his pursuers
by shouting out: "There, behind the chimney! Look
out! The skylight! The dormer! The rain-pipe! This
way! Have you got him?"

For a moment Hardigras vanished from view, and
suddenly Supia uttered a terrible cry. Hardigras had
alighted upon his shoulders! Prince Hippothadee, who
was not lacking in courage, made a movement to dart forward. But Hardigras delivered a well-aimed blow from
the handle of his banner, which kept him at a distance,
and, giving another leap, he disappeared through the
upper part of the window and closed it behind him.

The crowd gave way to shouts of delight.

The "tyrant," whom his wife and daughter vainly
strove to hold back, followed Hippothadee, who had
smashed in the French window. He reached the door
between the private apartments and the store rooms, and
here he met Souques and Ordinal with the entire body of
firemen engaged in the pursuit. But, Hardigras had
climbed down the iron pillars supporting the main building, and he had succeeded in reaching the basements. . . .
The basements were searched from end to end without
result. . . . Not the least trace. . . . Nothing!

It was Titin, appearing near his car from no one knows
where, who conveyed the news to the crowd, and they loudly
cheered him as he set himself once more to pull along the
car containing the effigy. They almost wept with joy.

That evening in Caramagna's restaurant, the customers
round Titin continued to laugh over the events of the
day. But he said nothing. Gamba Secca and Le Budeu
had as much as they could do to settle the score for their
diversion. For it made a considerable hole in the cash
resources of Bastardon's Kiosks.

CHAPTER XI

FROM that day onward many people were convinced that Titin le Bastardon and Hardigras were one and the same person. But it still remained to be proved. As to Titin, himself, when any person rashly allowed himself to express such an opinion, he treated it with contempt, declaring flatly that he would have been the veriest of fools to waste his time in hanging the "tyrant" in effigy as suggested by M. Hippolyte Morelli. He would have hanged him in good earnest, and have been recognized as a public benefactor!

"I believe you," said the excitable Nathalie with a laugh, "for there are certain things that cannot be forgiven and should be punished with hanging."

"What are they?" asked Titin.

"Marrying Toinetta to Prince Hippothadee for instance."

He angrily left her standing there and went back to paint Mme. Bibi's shop, which displayed his talent as a fresco painter. For, Titin carried on that business besides the others—he was an "artist". He had acquired the taste from his friend Giaousé, who was not unskillful with the brush, and he covered the walls and ceilings of La Fourca Nova with paintings of birds, flowers, fruit. Titin found the time, no longer graced with Toinetta's presence, hang heavily on him, and he started to daub Mme. Bibi's modest shop in La Fourca.

The counter itself was decorated. And, even the drawers were an agreeable sight with their designs of

108

flowers, fruit, greenery. The composition of the whole
was so violent and primitive in its brightness that persons
holiday-making in the place were amused, thinking that
one must needs be mad like Titin to dispense so much
color over a poor little shop where it would have been
better to sell the paint.

There was, in particular, on the wall at the back, a
painting of a village rising like a pyramid whose con-
fused and ill-balanced mass was treated with a vividness
of light and shade which would have made the Spanish
school of painting blush—and it claimed to be a picture
of old Fourca.

A member of the "Artist's Club" in Nice, who was
passing through, wished to see this particular "Picture
Gallery" where art rubbed shoulders wth groceries and
sweets. Afterwards, he surprised everybody by declaring
that Titin was a born artist.

In truth only Mme. Bibi—whose opinion was of no
great weight in view of her worship of the artist—and
the ordinary people of La Fourca went into ecstasy over
this luminous riot of color with the childish candor of
persons knowing nothing of nature but that which nature
has taught them. They appreciated, best of all, Titin's
signboards. These shone from afar like stars. And, too,
he always managed to suggest the business for which they
were intended, by little designs which made people choke
with laughter, and by nice big capital letters with twists
and flourishes like vermicelli—called in the district
"angels' wings."

Titin executed these masterpieces when he was feeling
bored to death, and they afforded sufficient proof of the
wonderful work he might do one day when he consented
to take a pleasure in his painting. But, for some time
now he had lost his gayety, and it was not Nathalie's
dubious jests that were likely to restore his good humor.
Accordingly, he painted with desperation, scoring Mme.
Bibi's walls with his impetuous brush.

The good woman had set out that morning, no one knew where. She hardly ever left her shop. She put on her best clothes and sarted off at an early hour without waking Titin. But it was not of Mme. Bibi's absence that Titin's thoughts were filled! As he painted he apostrophized himself, aloud, in bitter terms:

"Silly Titin! Ass! Fool! What a duffer! Does she know, poor dear, that I love her? Did I tell her so when I saw her on the balcony? . . . And you, Titin, were waiting to hear from her! . . . Hear what? Read the newspapers. Go to the Town Hall. You will be able to see the announcements. . . . And why shouldn't she marry a Prince I'd like to know? Are you as good as the Prince? You hadn't the pluck to say: 'Toinetta, I love you.' At your age, too! Therefore she thinks you don't care for her. The Prince did not wait for you before telling her, you know."

When he reached this point in his lamentation the door bell rang and Mme. Bibi came into the shop. Her eyes were red.

"Titin," she said, "you must go into mourning. You must be brave, my dear; your mother is dead."

And she sat down, worn out in part by her journey and in part, it seemed, by grief. She was still vigorous, the old dame, in spite of her age, slightly bent and withered, but her eyes were bright and her voice young. She had had her share of troubles in the course of her long life. But Titin had been her consolation.

After a pause Titin said:

"You've been crying, Mme. Bibi. But perhaps it's as well that she's dead."

Titin himself knew no other mother than Mme. Bibi. He had heard vaguely that his real mother had lost her reason and was in St. Pons Asylum. He had asked to see her but Mme. Bibi had always answered:

"Better not. They tell me it wouldn't do her any good. And besides, she wouldn't recognize you."

Nor would he have recognized her. All the same he was cast down. But that was on Mme. Bibi's account.

"You had better have a cup of coffee," he said.

"No, thank you, I must talk to you about your mother. When you were young you sometimes used to ask me: Why do people call me son of Carnival or son of three fathers? I answered: For no reason, Titin, and I added: When they say such things give them a good dressing down. And you did what I told you, and they got so many dressings down that they left off calling you these names. Therefore you refrained from asking me anything more. But to-day I must tell you more. I had a message to say your mother was at death's door. I went to her. . . . Think of it—a little of her reason had come back to her before she died. . . . She recognized me. . . . I was sorry I didn't take you with me, for she asked after you, Titin. Yes, she asked after the son of Carnival. You know she lost her reason before you were born. . . . Poor Tina! . . . She was a good, honest girl and you can respect her as you should respect your mother. Certainly she loved dancing after a fête like many another girl. But there's nothing to be said against that. . . . There were three of them after her one Carnival. . . . They all had had too much drink. . . ."

Mme. Bibi paused and a tear fell down her cheeks. A silence ensued and then Titin said in a voice that she had never heard before:

"I suspected something of the sort. But why do you tell me about it if you can't give me the names of the three villains."

"I'm telling you about it, my dear, because poor Tina before she died gave me the name of one of the masks. It was the only one she recognized. But you may be able to get the names of the other two out of this man."

"What's his name?" asked Titin.

"Menica Gianelli."

"Menica Gianelli," repeated Titin, thoughtfully.   "I fancy I've heard that name before."

"'The Gianellis are big ironmongers in the Rue Gioffredo. Well, it was the proprietor's son who, with two others, enticed your mother away.   The Gianellis are rich.   I thought you might get something out of him."

"Yes, you are quite right, and when I have got this something out of him there won't be much blood in his veins.   Have you anything else to tell me?"

"Yes, Titin.   Poor Tina is to be buried to-morrow."

"Well, you go to the funeral.   I will go and pray on her grave when I can tell her something about my three fathers."

He rose to his feet, kissed Mme. Bibi, and straightway left La Fourca Nova.   He wore such a grim expression that Giaousé and Nathalie dared not speak to him.   He reached Nice that evening, walked to the Rue Gioffredo, and stopped outside the ironmonger's shop.   He gazed at the signboard which bore the words: Durando and Gianelli.   He did not know Menica but he remembered often seeing the elder Gianelli, a somewhat miserly, not over sociable, little man.

"I wish to see M. Gianelli," he said to a clerk who was hastening into the office with some account books under his arm.

"It's very late," the clerk returned.   "We are on the point of closing.   Could you not come to-morrow?"

"No, I am in a great hurry.   Tell him it's Titin le Bastardon."

Two minutes later the clerk returned.

"The partners can't see you.   Cannot you tell me what you want?"

"No.   I must speak to M. Gianelli."

"I must tell you, M. Titin, that the partners are wondering if it is anything serious.   On the other hand, they don't want to put you to any inconvenience.   But they are very busy just now."

"Is M. Menica with them?"

"M. Menica," repeated the clerk, lifting his eyes heavenwards.

"Ask them if I can see M. Menica. Tell them it's a matter of great importance."

Another short absence of the clerk and then:

"This way, sir."

Titin removed his hat and took a seat. MM. Durando and Gianelli stood before him.

"You asked to see M. Menica," said M. Gianelli in a harsh voice. "We don't know what's become of him."

"Do you mean to say you don't know where your son is?"

"Menica is not my son. He is only my nephew. It's many years since I heard anything of him. Is that all you desire to know?"

"That's all. I wish you good evening, gentlemen."

He strode towards the door and then turning round:

"M. Durando, I should like to have a word with you."

M. Durando accompanied him into the shop.

"The old man is angry with Menica," said Titin. "There's nothing to be got out of him, and it's a pity; for I have some good news for Menica. I have found a very valuable article which he lost some years before he left Nice. An article worth its weight in gold. Something which has increased in value as it has grown older. I can't tell you anything more about it, but if you could give me some information that would enable me to restore it to M. Menica. . . ."

"Look here, M. Titin, I should be only too pleased to be of service to you. You did make me laugh that first Sunday in Carnival! I was in the Place du Palais, and I am not anxious to be treated one day as you treated poor M. Supia. Well, when Menica left us he went to Marseilles and opened a grand bazaar in the Allées de Meilhan. Perhaps you could get some information there."

"Thank you, M. Durando."

Next morning Titin arrived at Marseilles and at eleven
o'clock was outside the grand bazaar in the Allées de
Meilhan. He could not be mistaken. "Menica's pipes"
were sold there. The business seemed a very prosperous
one.

"By my mascot," said Titin to himself, "my father does
not belong to the riff-raff. We shall be able to talk."

We have mentioned that when Titin left La Fourca
Nova he was no longer thinking of Toinetta. But the
night before he had dreamed of her again, and now when
he thought of vengeance it was in connection with his love
for her. These two sentiments, instead of being in opposition in his mind, on the contrary, were combined; and
he dared not allow his mind to dwell on them. The night
before nothing would have satisfied him but bloodshed,
even if it had meant the sacrifice of his own skin. But
now it was different. The vision of a Titin enjoying life,
rich, in possession of an acknowledged position as a citizen—of a Titin who could honorably aspire to Mlle.
Agagnosc's hand—began to take shape. . . . Suddenly
the thought of his mother being at the very moment laid
in some grave near St. Pons, flung him back into a feeling
of horror of himself.

No, no, he had not come there for that. Titin le
Bastardon was certainly not going to represent himself
as a beggar. He had come for something quite different.
And, if he were to lose Toinetta and perhaps die for it on
the scaffold—he must allow for every possibility—he
would leave this vale of tears at least, with head held
high, and without dishonor, as befits a Bastardon!

It was fortunate for Menica that he failed to offer
himself at that moment to Bastardon's revengeful blows.
For by the time Titin entered the bazaar he had worked
himself up to such a pitch of excitement over his filial
duties that he might have sent this first father whose
identity was certain to another world, leaving himself
plenty of time to think of the other two. . . .

Titin learnt that Menica had not made a success of his pipe business but had sold it and had settled in Montpellier as a wholesale wine merchant. And now he journeyed to Montpellier, where he learned that M. Menica had failed as a wine merchant and been reduced to buying a retail dram-shop in Cette. He went on to Cette and discovered that M. Menica, having set himself to consume in detail the wine intended for his customers, sundry unpleasant experiences had followed, forcing him to leave the place. Thereupon, he returned to Marseilles and set up on the quay as a vendor of mussels and other shell-fish to be eaten on the spot.

Titin returned by train to Marseilles. On his way he said to himself: "That's all right. You have only got what you deserved. Instead of considering how to avenge your mother, you were hoping your father was a rich man, able to give you a big wedding present. And here you are the son of a mussel man! . . . You may well run after the girls now. If Toinetta heard of it she would die of laughing. It will be better to let her know nothing about it I assure you."

He inquired of an oyster man on the quay where Menica was in the habit of fixing up his stall.

"Menica! Oh, poor fellow, he's no longer in the business. That's not his fault. He's had trouble in the Courts over an American millionaire who tasted his stuff and, with his wife and daughter, was poisoned. It seems the mussels were picked up at Pierres Plates. Since then he has lived from hand to mouth, worse luck! Hullo, here he is. Menica! . . . I say, Menica! . . ."

A poverty stricken creature in rags was passing and it was a marvel that this miserable specimen of humanity had sufficient strength to carry the sack of peanuts under the weight of which he was bowed down. He stopped when he heard the oyster man call out to him. Clearly he was staggering under his load. Titin took it from him and threw it over his own shoulders. For the rest of that morning he did the work of a porter. He uttered no word and the other left it to him, stupefied. . . .

When he had shot the last sack of peanuts on to a van Titin said:

"Come along."

"Who are you?" asked the old man without excitement. For nothing could now surprise him.

"Son of Carnival," said Titin.

"Oh," was the answer, and he seemed to be trying to search the depths of his memory.

"I am Titin—Titin le Bastardon."

"Le Bastardon?"

"Yes, Menica. Just test your memory. . . . Poor Tina. . . . I am your son, Menica."

Menica gazed at him for some time.

"It may be so," he returned at last; and then after a moment's reflection: "But there are three of us, you know."

"Do you know the other two?"

"I should have to think," said Menica, shaking his head. . . . It's so long ago—that story. . . . But hang it all I am thirsty."

"Come along."

Titin gave him food and drink and clothes, and took a small room for him in the old quarter near the Town Hall. In short, he behaved like a good son. He was rewarded to some extent by awakening the poor fellow's vague memories. For Menica recalled to mind a long drinking bout with a milkman whose Christian name only he knew. This man Noré (Honoré) was a great wag in his way. He had made his acquaintance at Olmiez, at a fête, the year before the Carnival, when the grievous incident had occurred. And he had continued to see him on Sundays in the country inns where players of bowls were wont to congregate and where clerks took their lady friends. . . .

Noré had no equal in those days for setting the company off and making the girls dance while he played the mandolin. As to the third man, it was Noré who had brought him along. Menica did not know him nor had he seen him since.

Titin returned to Nice dissatisfied with everything and himself. The feeling for revenge no longer moved him. Having set out to kill his three fathers he had emptied his pockets in coming to the assistance of the first. Perhaps he would discover the gay milkman in the workhouse and have to rescue him from destitution. If the third one were of the same type as the other two, Titin might well ask himself whether his many occupations would be sufficient to provide suitably for so numerous an ancestry!

While roaming about the country beyond Cimiez, Titin met an old innkeeper who remembered perfectly well a man called Noré, an adept at inducing the girls to dance to the music of his mandolin.

"He married a good-looking St. Maurice girl and was not seen again. I heard he had taken a milk shop near Petit Piol."

At Petit Piol Titin learnt that Noré and his wife had left the district and had settled in Nice in the Rue Massena near the Passage Négrin. The dairy was still in existence. But, it had developed into an important and high-class shop, greatly frequented during the season. The proprietor soon made his fortune. And after a few years sold the business on very favorable terms.

Titin was still ignorant of Noré's surname, a fact which did not render his task any the easier. However, he discovered from an old English woman who had been a customer for years, that the former proprietor had acquired a provision warehouse, called the "Silver Rabbit", in the Rue d'Angleterre.

The size of this shop made some impression on Titin. He asked to see the proprietor. A respectable looking

individual in a white apron, carving behind the counter
an appetizing cold fowl, was pointed out to him.

"Are you M. Noré?" inquired Titin.

"Noré? Never heard of him," returned the carver as
he calmly removed a wing. Then after a pause: "Oh, you
mean my predecessor. Well, you are behind the times,
my friend. That was nearly eighteen years ago. Why,
but you belong to Nice."

"Yes, my name is Titin."

"Titin?"

"Titin le Bastardon."

Two assistants were standing near and one said:

"Yes, governor, that's Titin—Titin le Bastardon."

"Oh then, that explains everything," said the governor,
making up his mind to see a joke. "You're being funny."

"I assure you that I was never more serious."

"I'm not Supia, you know. No need to pull my leg.
You are Titin le Bastardon and you come here and ask
me about a man who sold me his business eighteen years
ago!"

The assistants burst out laughing.

"Why, governor, no one knows him better than he does."

"Well, of course. Good-bye, M. Titin, and if it was
Papajeudi who sent you tell him from me that he might
have found a better joke."

Titin had already departed. He strode, like a person
distraught, in the direction of the old town. . . .

Papajeudi! It was true that Papajeudi was called
Noré—Honoré Papajeudi. He was the one-time milkman.
Well, he had gone far since those days! He was undoubtedly one of the richest tradesmen in the town. It was said
that he could give each of his daughters a dowry of three
hundred thousand francs without inconvenience. And he
would have to put himself to a little more inconvenience.
He would have to reckon with his son also.

When Titin entered Papajeudi's shop he was surprised
at Mme. Papajeudi's absence from the cash desk. But her

eldest daughter was in her place and he noticed that her
eyes were red with weeping.

"Can I see M. Papajeudi?" he inquired.

"No, M. Titin, father is very ill," she returned in a
low voice.

"You don't mean it, Mlle.?" said Titin, sincerely sorry,
for Papajeudi had always been "good" to him even in the
days of his poverty.

"It is the truth, unfortunately."

Just then the two other Mlles. Papajeudi came up.
They, too, were weeping.

"But what's the matter with him?" asked Titin. "Only
a few days ago he took the chair at a trade banquet."

"Exactly," said the young cashier. "The pastry gave
him indigestion. He took some medicine and he felt cold
shivers. Then he drank some old Belet to warm himself
and afterwards some brandy which made his head swim
without bringing any relief. So much so that to-day he
sent for his solicitor and asked my sisters to fetch the
priest from St. Francis de Paul."

"He takes a very gloomy view," said Titin, greatly
disturbed.

"Yes, he is very gloomy about it," she wailed. "He
does nothing but pity himself, poor thing."

"Tell him that I called and was very sorry when I
heard of his illness."

"We certainly will do so, M. Titin. Did you wish to
see father on anything urgent?"

"Oh no, Mlle., I only wanted to pass the time of day—
that's all."

He was making for the door when Mme. Papajeudi
appeared, bathed in tears.

"Is he worse, mother?" cried the three young ladies.

"Oh, my dears, he is delirious. He doesn't know what
he's saying. He is constantly calling for Titin—Titin
and the priest."

"But M. Titin is here."

Mme. Papajeudi turned and saw him.

"Oh my poor boy," she sobbed. "Our dear Papajeudi is very ill. You must go up and talk to him. Besides, he does nothing but ask for you."

"I will go up," said Titin.

When the son of Carnival entered the room the invalid, who was in a high fever, seemed to wish to get out of bed to meet him.

"There you are at last! Oh Titin, my good Titin, I didn't want to die, you know, without telling you . . . without telling you that I am very fond of you. . . ."

"But you are not going to die, M. Papajeudi. I am very fond of you, too. . . . You have always treated me. . . ."

"Calm him," whispered Mme. Papajeudi.

M. Papajeudi looked at his wife.

"You must leave us," he said.

"I will go now, dear." And she whispered as she passed behind Titin: "My goodness, I have often told him, 'whatever you do Papajeudi, don't eat that pastry,' but he always will puff himself out with it. . . . Oh you men!"

When she had left the room Titin drew nearer the bed.

"Bolt the door and come here. Give me your hand."

Papajeudi's hand was burning hot.

"I'm in a very bad way, my boy. . . . Yes, yes I tell you, I'm in a very bad way. . . . It's the good God punishing me. . . . Sit down here Titin. I've got to talk to you. . . . Listen, I sent for my solicitor this morning."

"It's safer, M. Papajeudi and, when all is said, that won't kill you. . . ."

"I am going to die. I know what I'm saying. So everything is settled as far as the solicitor is concerned, but there's still the priest and you, Titin."

"Me?" asked Titin ingenuously.

"Yes, and I am glad to see you before the priest comes.

Provided you will forgive me, of course. . . . He, too, will have to forgive me."

"What are you talking about? What have I to forgive you for, M. Papajeudi?"

Papajeudi gave way to tears again and clasped Titin's hand.

"My poor Titin . . . my poor Titin . . . I am a wretch . . . a wicked man. I deserve. . . . Oh, if one only knew when one is young! But it was not altogether my fault. We took too much champagne that evening. I have suffered from remorse all my life, Titin."

M. Papajeudi began to "blub" loudly and then hugged Titin, who could not restrain his own emotion.

"There were three of us. We didn't know what we were doing. I did as the others did. . . ."

"Yes," said Titin coldly. "And my poor mother went mad. She has just died."

"I know. . . . I know. . . . And I, too, am going to die. . . . Ah, if one only knew! There, I would give ten years of my life to wipe out the past. You may believe me, Titin."

"I believe you all the more, M. Papajeudi," declared Titin in increasingly cold and distant tones, "as ten years of your life is not worth much now seeing, as you say, you are going to die."

"That's true. But I wanted to tell you how bitterly I regret it. . . . Listen, Titin. Put yourself in my place. I was a married man. I was in business. I could not give myself up and say: I did it. You can imagine even now the scandal—prison. And my poor wife—she would have gone mad, too. There would have been two mad women instead of one. What good would that have done? All the more as it was me and yet it was not me. The others lured me on. Besides, the others held their tongues. And then what could they have said seeing the evil was done? . . . But when I knew that you had come into the world I said to myself: 'That's not the end of it. I must look after the youngster. . . .'

"Then I went to La Fourca and saw you with Mme. Bibi. You were as nice a little fellow as could be, and you caught hold of my nose in great glee. Oh, you won my heart right away! Then I made inquiries. 'He will want for nothing," said Mme. Bibi. 'With me and the goats nobody need pity this child. . . .'

"And then you grew up there. . . . I kept an eye on you. I was proud of you. I should have liked to tell everyone: Le Bastardon is my son. But I could not, of course, on account of Mme. Papajeudi and my daughters. Afterwards you settled down in Nice."

"Settled down?"

"Yes. You came to live in Nice. You had no money, you know."

"I know that," said Titin.

"You had a few miserable rags on your back and you did not always eat your fill. Well, you had but to come here. Have I ever refused you anything?"

"Never."

"Admit that I've always been very good to you here."

"That's true, M. Papajeudi. Had you been my acknowledged father I ask myself, what more could you have done for me."

"Yes, and what about Mme. Papajeudi? More than once she gave you my old clothes; and she never suspected anything. You must not forget that Titin."

"I am not forgetting it."

"Titin, I am going to die. . . . You must forgive me."

"Even if you don't die I forgive you, M. Papajeudi, because I'm of no account."

"How do you mean—you are of no account? I am more anxious to have your good opinion than the priest's, you understand."

"Oh, it's not a matter for the priest. It concerns some-

one who may perhaps stand in your way up above—poor
Tina."

"Alas, I have often thought of her of late I assure you,
and I said to myself, if I do something for you here below
poor Tina up above will be pleased."

"Oh, you have already done a great deal for me."

"No, no. That's why I sent for my solicitor. I said
to him: 'I am going to die and must make amends for a
youthful folly. I have a son; no one knows it, not even
he, himself, and I want to leave him something to set him
up in life, without Mme. Papajeudi knowing anything even
after I am gone. This son was born after I was married
and I don't want my wife and daughters to hate my
memory. What must I do? Do you know what he
answered?"

"That these matters can always be arranged," returned
Titin.

He answered that nothing could be done, that Mme.
Papajeudi and I were married under the law by which all
our property is held in common, and that a legacy of that
nature could not be concealed. He told me that I should
be acting to the prejudice of my daughters—a material
prejudice and above all a moral prejudice. And this, too,
at the very time when they were going to be married.
That, my dear Titin, was what the solicitor told me. . . .

"Then what could I do? I had no wish to see Mme.
Papajeudi and the girls suffer for a wretch like me. For
I am a wretch, Titin."

"Yes, yes, M. Papajeudi, you are an old wretch," said
Titin, rising. Papajeudi wildly held out his arms to him.

"What are you going to do? It's all the solicitor's
fault."

"Go to blazes with your solicitor."

"What are you going to do?"

"Nothing. I am disgusted with you."

"Titin. . . . Titin. You're not going to leave me without forgiving me. I'm dying, Titin."

"Well die," said Titin.

Papajeudi started up and then fell back upon the bed, remaining motionless. Titin darted forward, called to him, took him in his arms, but held only a limp, heavy form, clammy with an icy perspiration.

"God, I have killed him," he cried. . . . "I forgive you, M. Papajeudi, I forgive you."

Papajeudi opened his eyes again, sighed and asked for something to drink.

"Oh, that's better," he muttered, "I'm burning like a soul in hell. You may be satisfied Titin. I'm going there right enough."

"You must live for your wife and daughters' sake. You have nothing more to fear from me. I forgive you— on one condition. You must help me to find the man who made you drink so much champagne that night. Menica told me you knew his name."

"Menica! So you've seen Menica. What's happened to him? They told me things had gone wrong with him."

"Yes. He has been down on his luck," said Titin.

"He had money too early. It's a bad thing to have money too young. Think over what I am saying, Titin. Work—there's nothing like it. . . . When one waits for dead men's shoes. . . ."

"That'll do, M. Papajeudi. It's my turn to speak now. This other man—was he a rich man?"

"Yes, very rich, but he is not rich now. It's not worth while to trouble about him, Titin."

"I should like to know his name all the same."

"I can't tell you. It would cause too much unpleasantness—unpleasantness in which I should necessarily be involved. . . . And seeing you have forgiven me. . . ."

"His name."

"I can't tell you. He is a man who would shrink from nothing."

"His name."

"I have forgotten it, Titin. You know, I wasn't per-

sonally acquainted with him. It was quite by chance, so
he said, that he wanted to enjoy himself with the crowd.
One Carnival day we met on the grandstand, and his name
was mentioned, but I have forgotten it. He left Nice
many years ago. When he came back he had greatly
changed. I didn't recognize him."

"His name."

Papajeudi shook his head. Titan strode towards the
door.

"Don't leave me like this."

"I am going to call Mme. Papajeudi."

"Titin, my dear Titin. . . ."

"You will have to tell me his name before her. Seeing
that he is to blame and seeing he led you on, he must pay
for the others. Mme. Papajeudi will understand that,
because someone, you know, has got to pay in this
business."

"But I tell you he hasn't a sou. . . ."

"That's not the question. I know what I am about,"
returned Titin, opening the door.

"Don't say anything, Titin. You shall know his name.
But you must swear not to give me away."

"Of course. Come, I'm waiting."

"Well, it was an aristocrat, a foreign nobleman, a
prince."

"Is he in Nice at present?"

"I should think so."

"Do I know him?"

"Yes, you must have seen him."

Titin, who had sat down again, sprang from his chair.

"It's that Transylvania Prince," he rapped out at the
terrified Papajeudi.

"Yes, Titin, that's the man."

"Hippothadee?"

"Oh, calm yourself. Calm yourself. Don't shout. Oh,
I wish I were dead."

"The man who is to marry Toinetta," cried Titin,

striking the bedside table such a terrible blow with his
fist that it rocked and collapsed with a deafening crash of
broken china and glass.   At the sound of the tremendous
clatter Mme. Papajeudi and her daughters came running
into the room while Papajeudi, on his sick bed, fainted
again.

"What's the matter?   Good heavens, what's the matter?" cried Mme. Papajeudi.

"Nothing, madame, we did it while having a good
laugh," said Titin, rushing downstairs, cursing and
swearing like one possessed and fingering a knife in his
pocket that would indubitably make a few extra button-
holes in the new clothes presented by the Comtesse d'Azila
to Prince Hippothadee, on his engagement.

On chance, and possibly impelled by his unerring
instinct, which manifested itself at moments of extreme
excitement, Titin rushed straight to the magnificent new
flat which the Prince with the help of M. Supia's cash
had taken in the Promenade des Anglais.

Arriving in the entrance lobby, he came up against
carpet layers, decorators, and other workmen who stood
aside scared by the grim look on the face of him whom
they scarcely recognized as Titin. . . . He tried to open
a door.   A flunkey appeared.   The man uttered a few
words but was flung violently to the landing to join,
almost at once, the workmen now fleeing from the scene.
Titin felt convinced that the Prince was in.   In fact he
was in and greatly surprised at the commotion in his
entrance lobby.   When he saw Titin he grasped that
something was about to happen on which he had not
reckoned, and that he was face to face, perhaps, with one
of the most serious moments of his life.

But the Prince had seen a great deal in his day.   He
had escaped so many past dangers that he did not lose his
presence of mind.   On the contrary, seeing before him a
demented enemy, he summoned up all his self-control.

"I am sorry to have come into your flat without being
announced," said Titin, "but the matter is so urgent that

I thought I might dispense with the usual formalities. Monsieur, I am Titin le Bastardon, and I have come to tell you that I intend to kill you."

While the Prince's composure was impressive, Titin's was not less so. But Hippothadee could not control a start, though he quickly recovered himself again, adjusted his monocle, and eyeing Titin from head to foot, asked:

"Fight me . . . or kill me?"

"Kill you. I know that you are not lacking in courage and are an expert with the sword and pistol and saber. No, I do not intend to risk giving you an advantage of which you might avail yourself at my expense. I am going to kill you and have done with it, because one does not fight a duel with a man like you."

"You are afraid?"

"Titin le Bastardon is not afraid of anyone. Only I don't intend to be taken in and allow a low hound like you to run me through so that you may be able to continue calmly your little games."

The Prince had stealthily drawn nearer the button of an electric bell. Moreover, he had maneuvered in such fashion that a desk stood between him and Titin.

"I did not expect such a long speech from an assassin," he said in his quietest tone.

"It means that I wanted you to know before you die why I am taking your life."

Titin was in deadly earnest. He fixed a bloodshot eye on this detestable man who, after victimizing his mother, wanted to make Toinetta his wife. He opened his knife. The Prince thrust his hand towards the wall and with unexpected strength shot the desk at Titin's legs. But Titin, as nimble as a monkey, leapt over it and fell upon him before he could touch the bell. He threw him to the ground, put his knee upon him, and clutching him by the throat pressed hard. He lifted his knife.

"For Tina," he shouted in his ear. "Think of the Carnival in eighteen hundred and eighty. . . ."

But he had scarcely uttered these words when the

Prince managed for a moment to thrust aside the fierce pressure of the fingers that were choking him and gasped:

"Some mistake . . . mistake. Tina—never heard of her. Was not in Nice that year."

Before striking the decisive blow Titin thought it well to give the Prince further information.

"Tina was my mother."

"I don't care a rap about your mother. I never heard of her."

"I am your son."

"Why, you are mad—quite mad. I can tell you that at once. You are confusing me with someone else. . . . Let me get up. You have been misinformed. . . . You must be mixing me up with my brother."

"Are you or are you not Prince Hippothadee?" shouted Titin.

"All our family are called Hippothadee. . . . Let me explain, and you'll see that we shall end by understanding each other. . . . Hang it all, how violent you are! It's no easy matter to talk to a man like you, you know. In our family, we are all called Hippothadee, after a famous ancestor who, it seems, rendered great service to the country at the time of the first Turkish invasion. Since then all Princes of Transylvania have been called Hippothadee. And so I am called Vladimir Hippothadee and my elder brother is called Marie Hippothadee. In the West every one calls us Hippothadee. But at home I am Prince Vladi and my brother is Prince Marie. Well, it was Prince Marie who came to Nice at the time you mention and behaved so badly towards your mother. As for myself, I had nothing to do with the matter. I did not come to Nice for the first time until some fifteen years later."

"I beg your pardon, Monsieur Hippothadee. . . . Vladimir. . . . You may get up," said Titin, closing his knife. "But we haven't finished our talk for all that. I was on the point of killing you but it only depends on you for us to become good friends. . . .

"Besides I have made inquiries about you. The result is most unfavorable. . . . Let me continue, if you will. You are entirely on the rocks after ruining several of your mistresses. You are living at the moment at the expense of the Comtesse d'Azila—that's your business. All the same you are not a very pretty gentleman. Well, in spite of these miserable affairs of the past, I might have some respect for you if you give up a plan which covers a last act of depravity, in which you have certainly allowed yourself to be drawn by the criminal schemes of a man I despise even more than I despise you. I mean M. Supia. Understand me, my reason for speaking to you on this matter is because I am interested. I have known Mlle. Agagnosc since she was a baby, and she has done me the honor to continue her friendship. She lost her parents when she was very young, and is not happy with the Supias. She is so far from being happy that to get away from them she has agreed to marry you. You or anyone else, it's all the same to her. She does not know you. But I do know you."

"You mistook me just now for my brother."

"Let me continue. I know what a poor gentleman you are. Well, I who all but consider myself Mlle. Agagnosc's foster-brother, say to you: this marriage shall not take place, and I ask you if you wish to remain good friends with me—I mean by that if you don't want me to interfere in your affairs—I ask you to give up Mlle. Agagnosc on your own initiative."

"Well, M. Titin, suppose I tell you that the charm which I find in Mlle. Agagnosc has made a new man of me? Suppose I tell you that I feel quite capable of making her happy—that I am in love with her? Don't you see in these circumstances, the difficulty? . . ."

"No," interrupted Titin savagely. "No, that won't do."

"And suppose I tell you that Mlle. Agagnosc loves me?"

Titin gave a start; but he managed to calm himself and said in a hoarse voice:

"I should not believe you."

"You would make a mistake, for I assure you we are
the most devoted of engaged couples. Now, monsieur, I've
had enough of this. You came here to kill me. Kill me or
let me go and dress. Mlle. Agagnose and the worthy Mme.
Supia and her charming daughter are expecting me. I
have to take them to a reception. . . ."

Titin rose to his feet. He had regained his composure.

"This marriage shall not take place. I have an account
to settle with the Transylvanians. I shall tell the world
what sort of man a Hippothadee is, and put such a blot
on your escutcheon and"—he added with a smile expres-
sive of all the sarcasm that only an aristocrat could put
into a smile—"and *mine* that M. Supia himself will shrink
from the scandal of giving you his ward."

"That's a fine idea," cried the Prince. "Tell the story
of my brother's rascality. I cannot offer you too much
encouragement. Prince Marie will only get his deserts.
I shall myself be even with him! M. Supia, so far from
refusing to give me his ward, will understand why I had
to leave my country. Prince Marie has stripped me of
everything. He is the worst of tyrants. He terrorizes
the king himself. Avenge Transylvania! Avenge me,
M. Titin! Oh, you scarcely realized the truth of what
you said a moment ago—that we might still be good
friends. I am your man. I won't keep you to-day because, as I told you, the ladies are waiting for me. But
you know where to find me. And whenever you require a
little information for your purposes . . ."

"Enough of this patter," shouted Titin, wishing he had
strangled the Prince before hearing the nature of his rela-
tionship with his third father. "This is my last word—if
you marry Mlle. Agagnosc . . ."

"If I marry Mlle. Agagnosc as everything leads me to
hope, I will invite you to the wedding."

"I shall be there," said Titin.

CHAPTER XII

HARDIGRAS AT THE WEDDING

TITIN LE BASTARDON's confusion was unmistakable. His expedition in search of his three fathers had failed to yield the result that he had a right to expect either because he had intended to avenge his mother or because he had counted upon some fortunate change in his circumstances which would assist him in his relations with Mlle. Agagnosc. . . .

After his interview with Hippothadee he thought it well to obtain more definite particulars about him. The evidence that he was thus able to gather was quite enough to set Toinetta in revolt against marriage with the Prince. Titin had done his utmost to approach her. Unluckily for him, the "tyrant" on the one hand, and the Prince on the other, had anticipated his intention of seeing her privately, and they had taken their precautions accordingly. Toinetta was never left to herself. When she went out, it was for a drive and she invariably had a suitable companion with her.

The night still remained open to him. Nor could he have forgotten that it was possible to climb over Bella Nissa's roofs to Toinetta's balcony. Unfortunately since Carnival day the roofs were so closely guarded day and night that Hardigras himself had given up the attempt to mount them.

It was all the more regrettable inasmuch as Titin could imagine Antoinette lingering more than once at her window in the expectation of seeing him again. As she certainly had not been informed of the precautions that

131

were being taken, she must have concluded from Titin's failure to appear that he had made up his mind to say no more to her. . . . Thus the days sped by and the date of the wedding drew near.

While making his inquiries about Prince Vladimir Hippothadee, Titin had gathered some valuable information concerning Prince Marie. He learnt that no better nor more honorable man was to be met in the kingdom; that after sowing his wild oats he had wisely settled down and was regarded at Court as a model of all the virtues. He had displayed unbounded patience and generosity towards his brother. Moreover, he had continued to supply the exile, whose property was confiscated, with an allowance sufficient for any self-respecting man.

"Unless Prince Marie is a hypocrite," said Titin to himself, "he will not fail to take the opportunity of repairing as far as may be his youthful sin—sin did I say, I mean crime." And he wrote:

"To His Highness Prince Marie Hippothadee of Transylvania, Mostaregevo.

Your Highness,
I have been told, that you possess too high a character to have forgotten a certain Carnival night in Nice—a night which you spent as a very young man in a terrible drinking bout in company with MM. Menica Gianelli and Noré Papajeudi, and which must have left in your mind some feeling of remorse.
I need not remind you of poor Tina and the calamity that befell her as the result of that evening. I learn that you left Nice the following week, and it may be that you are unaware that poor Tina lost her reason after giving birth to a son whom everybody here calls the Son of Carnival. Tina has just died. She was my mother and you are one of my three fathers. The first is almost penniless and is on my hands. The second has entreated me not to destroy his home by creating a scandal from which innocent persons would suffer. As a last resource I appeal to you, who can do a great deal for me. . . .
If you consent to what I am about to ask, you will never hear of me again.
Your brother, sire, who is a despicable creature, has succeeded in worming himself into the society of an honorable family, and is engaged to marry Mlle. Antoinette Agagnosc whom I love, though

she is not aware of the fact, for a man like myself, poor and without a name, must not speak of love to a rich young girl whom he cannot marry. But I would willingly lay down my life to prevent this marriage. Mlle. Agagnosc cannot be happy with so infamous a person as Vladimir Hippothadee. Intervene, sire, to the extent of your power. Do not allow this rascally deed to be done, and you will have no further duty towards me."

He signed his letter Titin le Bastardon, Son of Carnival, care of Mme. Bibi, La Fourca, Nova, Alpes Maritimes, France. Then after posting it he took the train to La Fourca.

When Mme. Bibi caught sight of him she ran to the roadside with her goats as though she had been waiting for him since he left her. She kissed him with tears of joy and then gazing at him with the bright, piercing eyes of an old woman, asked:

"Are you satisfied, Titin?"

"No, I am not satisfied. What's more, if you wish to please me you will take me to my mother's grave."

They set out together. The mound was bedecked with flowers, and in the center Mme. Bibi had placed a cross which bore simply one word: Tina.

Titin opened the knife with which he had intended to kill his three fathers and carved under Tina's name: Mother of Titin le Bastardon.

Then he closed his knife, put it back in his pocket and knelt down:

"Mother," he said, "while you were going on your last journey I was making a useless one. Could I allow my first father, Menica, poor fellow, whom divine justice has reduced to beggary, to starve to death? And this big, wretched Noré who has always suffered from remorse and been so good to me, could I inflict shame and despair to his board at the moment when his daughters are about to be married, bringing down in sorrow to the grave poor Mme. Papajeudi, who believes in him as she believes in her religion? Could I do these things? No, you would not have wished it—you who have suffered so much for others.

So much for my first and second fathers! As to the third, nothing would have prevented me from sending him to the devil as was his due—but he was not my father! Mother, speak to me, for I am listening."

When he rose to his feet he said to Mme. Bibi:

"She has spoken to me. She said to me: 'Why are you dissatisfied, Titin? I am satisfied. You are a good son.'"

Still Titin did not recover his natural high spirits until some days later, and then he seemed to reach the height of that transcendent philosophy whence he was able to control, by making fun of everything, his successive moods of restlessness. He laughed and chaffed and joked with his old friends of La Fourca. Never had there been such keen contests at bowls. Pistafun, Aiguardente, Bouta, Tantifla, Giaousé were delighted to perceive that he was his old self again.

As to Nathalie, she exerted all her ingenuity in dress to appear more comely in his eyes. She had a scene with Giaousé because she was now wearing silk stockings every day. But nothing in the way of adornment was too good where Titin was concerned.

Nevertheless this flame of gayety which glowed within Titin seemed all the more extraordinary to some of them; for they knew how deeply mortified he was at Toinetta's coming marriage. The event was to take place the following Monday. . . .

Nathalie told Titin one day that he had been extremely patient with her, rejecting but weakly—possibly because his thoughts were elsewhere—her advances which she made no attempt to dissemble.

"Are you going to the wedding, Titin?"

"Of course I shall go as I've been invited," he returned smiling.

"Good gracious me! You've been invited to Toinetta's wedding! Who invited you? Not Supia, that's very certain."

"Oh, no, not Supia as you say," said Titin, bursting out laughing. "It was the Prince who asked me."

"The Prince—that low hound—invited you?"

"Don't speak ill of a man who is going to marry our dear Toinetta."

"Well, I can hardly believe my ears, upon my word. And so you intend to go?"

"Of course I shall go, and you ought to go, too. And Giaousé and all our friends even though they haven't been asked. Why, if there's no room for them in the procession, there'll be plenty of room outside. It seems it's going to be a gorgeous affair. I shall be curious to see it, you know."

"I can't get over it," said Nathalie, "but all the same I'm very glad you're accepting the inevitable."

"Oh, what I said about it was on Toinetta's account. Once being assured of her willingness to marry him, I'm not the one to stand in the way."

"Oh, Titin, I must give you a kiss."

"If you like, but you'll end by making our dear Giaousé jealous. . . . Giaousé, come here a moment. Your wife wants to kiss me."

"What a fool she is," said Giaousé.

She gave him a black look.

"Are you jealous, Giaousé?" she asked.

"No need to be jealous of women!" said Babazouk, in a tone of contempt.

"Then I needn't worry," said Nathalie, giving Titin a resounding kiss on the cheek.

"You don't know what I was saying," Titin explained to Giaousé. "I was telling her we all ought to go to Toinetta's wedding."

"That's not a bad idea," agreed Babazouk, "especially as it's rumored there'll be rather queer doings. Hardigras, I hear, has warned Supia that he won't allow him to marry Toinetta to Hippothadee."

"That devil of a Hardigras!" said Titin, laughing.

136 THE SON OF THREE FATHERS

"But what can it matter to him whether Toinetta marries the Prince or anyone else?"

"I didn't ask him!" grinned Giaousé. . . . "It's just to annoy Supia, I suppose."

"Who told you so?"

"Pistafun. Hullo, here he is! I say, Pistafun."

Pistafun came up rolling a cigarette. He seemed to be chuckling over some thought which he kept to himself.

"How are you, Titin?" he said, "I am very glad to see you. They're dull without you in the Place d'Arson, you know."

"I say, Pistafun, is it true what Giaousé tells us that Hardigras has made up his mind to prevent Toinetta's marriage with the Prince?"

Pistafun darted a glance at Giaousé and then at Titin and seated himself opposite Nathalie.

"It is true," he said. "He won't have it. He has written to the 'tyrant'—several times in fact. Bezaudin the Commissary of Police has the letters now, and believe me, they've taken their precautions."

"How did you get to hear all this?" asked Titin.

"From Tantifla, who heard it from Le Budeu while playing cards at Caramagna's after dinner. He got it from Gamba Secca who heard it from the milliner in the Rue Lépaute. She had it from Mme. Supia's cook, to whom she sells hats, and the cook got it direct from Mlle. Agagnosc. So you see, Titin, we couldn't have better authority! Why, everyone in the town knows it! It's the one subject of gossip. And you can imagine how amused they are about it already. There'll be a great crush outside the Town Hall and St. Réparte Church to a certainty."

"And what does Mlle. Antoinette say about it all?" asked Titin.

"It seems she's like a little madcap. She says that for ever so long she's been wanting to make Hardigras's acquaintance. When she was trying on her bride's dress

she made them laugh: 'Make me look beautiful,' she said
to the dressmakers. 'I hear Hardigras has invited himself
to my wedding. I want to dazzle him. . . .'"

"We'll all go to the wedding," said Titin.

M. Supia was anxious for the mayor himself to marry
his ward, and had been obliged to postpone the date of the
civil ceremony to the day fixed for the religious service;
consequently the marriage before the mayor and in church
were both to take place on the Monday.

As early as nine o'clock in the morning the neighbor-
hood of the Town Hall was overrun by an eager multitude.
The event of the day was not so much the marriage as the
intervention of Hardigras, foretold by all and sundry.
Crowds had flocked in from the surrounding country.
The throng reached as far as the railings of MacMahon
Square, whence the eye could take in the whole of the
Rue de l'Hotel de Ville.

Units of both the local and state police were placed on
duty to insure the safety of the wedding party. Moreover,
the Supias' residence in the Place de Palais was not more
than a hundred yards from the Town Hall—a distance
which the bride and bridegroom and their friends were
to traverse in motor cars. It was whispered that a number
of plain clothes policemen were dispersed over the adjoining streets. Moreover, MM. Souques and Ordinal, each
in a car with his own men, would precede and follow the
procession.

All kinds of rumors were rife. Some gossips alleged
that Hardigras would know how to play a last trick on
Supia in his own particular fashion, in spite of every
precaution. Others again diffidently and prudently suggested that Hardigras was going too far in interfering in
a family matter which, after all, was no business of his.
But opinions were divided.

It was well known that Toinetta was in the Supias'
hands and was not a free agent: was in fact their prisoner,
their victim, marrying only to get away from them. She

was unaware, poor thing, that she was escaping one evil to fall into a worse one, for no fate on earth could be more hateful than that which was to unite her to an individual with Prince Hippothadee's past. . . . Since she had suffered so much she should have displayed a little more courage. There was no lack of worth-while young men in the district; and she would have been happy with any one of them, dear little Toinetta, as everyone wished her to be. Such was the opinion of the worthy people of Nice. And it was obviously the opinion also of the hot-headed Titin le Bastardon, that one of them in particular would be sure to provide her with happiness.

At Camousse's restaurant in the Rue de l'Hotel de Ville, from which the entire proceedings could be witnessed, the customers winked whenever Titin's name was mentioned: "No, he is not here," said one. "He has other things to do." What was he doing? What scheme had he prepared? No one knew. But, it was bound to be something out of the ordinary.

The advent through the yard of Gamba Secca and Le Budeu, followed by Giaousé Babazouk, was greeted with cheers, the significance of which was not to be mistaken. But, a greater demonstration burst forth when the formidable quartette, Pistafun, Aiguardente, Tony Bouta, and Tantifla came in. The company shouted; stamped their feet. The newcomers appeared in no way conscious of what was happening. . . . They were there as sight-seers like everybody else.

"Where's Titin?" was asked.

"Titin! We haven't seen him for several days," was the reply with a look of surprise that excited general merriment. "We should be very glad to have news of him. Isn't he here?"

The laughter broke forth louder than ever. No, no, he wasn't there!

"He was invited to the wedding," said Giaousé. "He'll be with the wedding party."

There was a veritable explosion.

"Who invited him?"

"The Prince. It seems they're great pals."

They held their sides. Indeed, if the day continued like this they would die of laughter.

The guests driving direct to the Town Hall began to arrive in motor cars or carriages. Some were pointed out by name and discussed. A few good-natured jests were indulged in, more particularly in criticizing the ladies' dresses, for they had attired themselves in all their finery and were blazing with jewels. Indeed, the gentle folks of Nice cut a very respectable figure. Young girls in white frocks listened smilingly to young men in evening dress. As the guests alighted outside the Town Hall gates, their cars and carriages were parked in the Rue St. Francis de Paul.

The police service was admirably arranged. Prince Hippothadee's friends in the foreign colony appeared in uniform, accompanied by ladies clad in the latest fashion. The Comtesse d'Azila, more flaxen and berouged than ever, was observed inquiring after the health of sundry respectable dowagers. She seemed more at ease than anyone on this day which would see the last of her best hopes. They could not help admiring her courage. Her friends displayed some pride in her: "She is, indeed, a great lady," they said.

The entire party had but one thought—Hardigras!

Something like stupefaction arose at Camousse's when the company saw Titin le Bastardon stalking up the middle of the road alone wearing a flower in his buttonhole, a new black hat a little on one side, a dark blue suit with a low cut waistcoat, an embroiderd shirt, white tie, and patent leather boots, his hands carelessly stuck in his pockets.

"Hullo! There he is! . . . It's Titin. . . . How well he looks!"

"Babazouk was telling the truth. It's a fact he's going to the wedding."

Now they crowded the door and windows. They all wanted to see Titin. Hands were outstretched to him.

"Oh, Titin—there's plenty of time, my boy."

"The bride hasn't come yet."

"Come and have a drink."

"Come in, hang it all, and let's have a look at you. The Prince will be jealous."

"We didn't expect to see you."

"We were waiting for Hardigras and here's Titin."

"Have you any news of Hardigras?"

"You call him, Giaousé. He'll come in to a certainty."

On hearing Giaousé's name Titin looked round, smiled at everybody, consulted his watch, a fine silver watch with a chain that hung from his breast pocket beside a white embroidered handkerchief—a final touch of smartness—and made up his mind to enter.

A closed car filled with unknown persons whose countenaces were not that of wedding guests pulled up immediately behind him, and M. Ordinal alighted. He had abandoned any attempt at disguise. He entered the restaurant after Titin heedless of the difficulties of elbowing himself through and the agony which he suffered when his corns were trampled on.

Titin as usual shook hands with Giaousé, whom he loved as a brother, though Giaousé was far from possessing his talkative disposition and philosophical way of looking at things. Giaousé was by nature somewhat reserved, never displaying any great jubilation, and remaining silent in his troubles. Without demur, he always did as Titin directed. It was in the early days when he received a good drubbing from Titin. After that he had accepted Titin's ascendency as inevitable, and whenever he expressed an opinion he never forgot to add: "Don't you think so, Titin?" When Titin thought otherwise, Giaousé thought otherwise, too. . . .

Nathalie and Giaousé obviously were none too happy together. It is possible that Titin was the cause of their conjugal differences. But who was to blame? At first Nathalie had often shown jealousy of the friendship existing between the two young men. She despised her husband for passively accepting the subordinate place. He rebuked her sharply: "You must try to be as fond of Titin as I am," he said. And she did try. Possibly she became a little fonder of him than Giaousé had bargained for. Women can never observe the happy medium! . . .

"Isn't Nathalie here?" asked Titin.

"No," returned Giaousé. "She's been in the dumps since the other day. Perhaps you know what's the matter with her?"

"One must be very clever to know what's the matter with a woman," said Titin.

Meantime they ordered a drink for him and congratulated him on his appearance. He looked very handsome in his new clothes which threw into relief his clean-cut, robust figure. It was as though a bronze statue of the best Florentine period, a Benvenuto Cellini, had been dressed by a first-class tailor from Bella Nissa; that is to say, by a good craftsman who knows what is suitable for a son of the azure coast. His lady friends took advantage of Nathalie's absence to straighten his tie for him. But their little attentions veiled a crafty desire to know what was to be known.

"Toinetta will be very pleased to see you. Oh, if I were only in her place," said one.

"What if she were to introduce you to the Mayor and say: 'This is the man I want to marry,' " asked another.

"I hear she is going to see Hardigras."

"Well, she'll see Titin. What more can she want?"

"She will have a surprise, perhaps."

"We certainly have had a surprise."

Titin allowed them to talk. He noticed behind him M. Ordinal, who suddenly found himself hemmed in by

Pistafun and his three friends, unable to escape from the stronghold. Titin helped him to get clear and M. Ordinal expressed his thanks.

"Where's M. Souques?" asked Titin. "Isn't he with you? Is the dear man ill or dead?"

"Don't speak of him," returned M. Ordinal. "He is impossible. I've broken off all relations with him. We work on our own now."

"I see that," said Titin, smiling.

"And so to-day he's going to stick to the Town Hall and I'm going to stick to you on account of this Hardigras business, you understand."

M. Ordinal laughed.

"I should think I did understand! You seem much more cheerful now, M. Ordinal. If we've got to be together in future I shall be all the better pleased you know."

"It was that awful M. Souques who made me feel miserable. What a comfort it is to both of us to be rid of him, M. Titin."

"You can see for yourself how delighted I am."

"To say nothing of Souques being as stubborn as a mule. He is still in the same mind about Hardigras."

"Ah, yes. He is really a bigger fool than I thought. And what's your opinion?"

"Oh, I remember the little chat we had in Fred's bar, in the Passage Négrin. Don't you remember it?"

"Very faintly."

"What! Don't you remember suggesting our joining forces to arrest Hardigras?"

"Oh, yes, of course," returned Titin.

"Well, I'm agreeable to make this treaty of alliance, and to remain together until we've got the better of this rogue who now lays claim to prevent Mlle. Agagnosc's marriage."

"Yes, yes. In fact I've heard something about it. But do you suppose there's anything serious in the story?"

"I hope for Hardigras's sake there's nothing in it," returned M. Ordinal, "for between ourselves, if he makes a move he's done to a turn this time."

"Oh, he's done!" said Titin, so comically that those round him, taking good care not to lose a word of the conversation, burst out laughing.

"He's done to a turn," repeated M. Ordinal with greater emphasis, casting a keen look round.

"In what sauce?"

"The sauce of hard labor."

A silence ensued. Every eye was fixed on Titin. He took M. Ordinal's arm.

"Meanwhile, let's go to the wedding. Make way, gentlemen. Don't you see that M. Ordinal is now my best friend? I won't leave him either!"

Just then a low rumble came from the street and cries went up:

"Here she comes! Here she comes!"

It was, in fact, the bride, in a magnificent car bedecked with orange blossoms, the windows open, with M. Supia seated beside her, clad in dress clothes, looking like an undertaker's man. A car followed containing plain clothes policemen with M. Souques next to the chauffeur. Then came other cars bringing the bridesmaids, the best man, and the family.

"You saw his hatchet face," exclaimed Anais, who had climbed on Tantifla's shoulder. "Anyone would think he was going to a funeral."

They all noticed how thin Antoinette looked.

"Poor girl," exclaimed Ciaosa, "if she is waiting for Hardigras to save her from this business. She has every reason to pull a long face. He's in no hurry."

When Antoinette alighted from the car there was complete silence. M. Supia quickly led her across the courtyard, and then to the room in which the civil ceremony was to take place. The room soon filled up. Prince Hippothadee at once came to her. Looking round, he caught sight of Titin standing on a bench. He whispered to Toinetta who, turning her head, gave Titin a slight nod and then began to talk to Hippothadee in the friendliest manner. Her laugh even could be heard—a rather nervous laugh.

The Prince appeared to be in high glee. He assumed an air, and indeed his admirably cut frock coat showed off to advantage his tall stature and the outlines of a figure still supple for a man soon to pass his half century. When he was not talking to Antoinette he gazed on either side, smiling at some of the guests, and bowing to others. The attendants scarcely knew which way to turn. The secretaries had placed the papers on the Mayor's desk. They were waiting only for the mayor.

A clerk came up and whispered to the chief secretary. The secretary, in turn, told the family that they would have to wait another quarter of an hour as the Mayor—whom the Deputy Mayor, some minutes before had gone to fetch—had been obliged to attend an important meeting of stockholders. It was a meeting at which matters of great interest to the town were to be decided. He had telephoned an apology. The Prince was greatly distressed by the delay.

Soon, however, good humor was restored. . . . But the Mayor still failed to put in an appearance. Then as the passage in the center between the benches remained free, guarded at one end by M. Souques and at the other by M. Ordinal clinging to Titin, the guests began to move about and hold a reception.

The Prince shook hands with several guests, passing from group to group, and so came near Titin.

"How are you, M. Titin? I'm glad you didn't forget my invitation. Mlle. Agagnosc and I are much obliged to you."

"It's a very fine show," returned Titin. "I took good care not to miss it. Please offer Mlle. Agagnosc my congratulations."

"But go and talk to her yourself," said the Prince with cool audacity, looking at Titin with an air at once so quizzical and superior that he bitterly regretted allowing him to escape when he had had him under his knee.

"Offer Mlle. Agagnose my congratulations! I shall see her like everyone else in the vestry," returned Titin in his most innocent manner.

"That is no reason why you should not go to her now. She will be delighted."

Titin needed no pressing and he followed the Prince, saying to M. Ordinal:

"Whatever you do, don't leave me!"

Mlle. Agagnosc greeted Titin in a manner of unembarrassed cordiality.

"Ah, there you are, Titin! So you decided to come?"

"The Prince had the kindness to invite me," returned Titin as he shook hands.

"He was quite right. I can't tell you how pleased I am. And yet, you see Titin, what a joke it is. I should never have dared to ask you."

"Why not, Toinetta?"

"Pah, I can't tell you," she said with a slight grimace. "You are such a rum fellow. One tries to please you but doesn't always succeed. Anyway, are you glad you came?"

"I am glad to see you looking happy, Toinetta. . . . But I—I don't know if I ought to go on calling you Toinetta."

"Don't you worry. The Prince is very broadminded. And though I am to be a princess I needn't forget my old playmate. You ask me if I am happy. Very happy, And I want everyone else to be happy, too."

"I'm sorry for disturbing you. I will leave you to your happiness. Good-bye."

"Good-bye. . . . Oh, one moment, I hear everywhere that you are on excellent terms with Hardigras. Now there's a man who is having a game at everyone's expense,

you know! Why does he want to prevent my marriage?
For all that, I wouldn't mind making his acquaintance.
Tell him from me that he is a wicked old humbug."

"If only to deliver your message I'll manage to see him
one day," said Titin, and he strode back quietly, noncha-
lantly, to his place.

The company were still waiting for the Mayor and were
beginning to think that he was "overdoing" it. Moreover,
the public in the streets and neighboring cafés were of the
same opinion. What was the reason for such an excep-
tionally protracted ceremony? At what hour in these circumstances would the party reach St. Réparate Church?

At Camousse's café the Mayor was blamed for giving
way to his talent for speechmaking. Suddenly the rumor
spread, no one knew how, that the Mayor had not yet
arrived and that the wedding party was growing anxious,
particularly as on investigation, they failed to discover
whence had come the telephone message supposed to
explain his absence.

They exchanged glances, and a few minutes later as
the commotion outside grew more and more disturbing,
began to smile. They grasped the meaning of it. And
there was an outburst of laughter. So this was Hardigras's unexpected trick! He had captured the mayor.
Well, it was not such a bad move after all.

"It's a bit risky what he has done," said Gamba Secca.
"And besides, what's the good of it? It can't prevent the
marriage. It will be easy to find a deputy."

Le Budeu, who had been making inquiries, took it upon
himself to answer. The First Deputy had disappeared at
the same time as the Mayor. As to the other two they
had been hastily sent for. . . .

An increasing tumult came from the crowd standing by
the railings in MacMahon Square and from the Rue St.
Francis de Paul. . . . It was at this moment that Titin
reached Camousse's bar, still holding M. Ordinal's arm.

"You quite understand, I refuse to leave you. I am not

anxious to be mixed up in an affair of this sort. Between ourselves, our Hardigras is going a little too far."

Nevertheless the crowd laughed as he made his way through. When he entered Camousse's café, he was besieged with questions:

"What does the bride say? What does Toinetta say?"

"Well, she says she isn't married, and she cried."

"That's not true, Titin. I hear she is treating the whole thing as a joke," said one.

"Ask M. Ordinal," returned Titin.

But M. Ordinal had vanished.

Just then there was a startling new arrival. It was the bride's chauffeur and his satellite, the footman, tired of waiting, without a drink, for a bride who failed to come.

"No one knows how long it's going to last," he said. "It seems that the second deputy left for Paris last night and the third is in Cannes. They are now telephoning to Cannes."

The delight became a delirium. The two men were invited to have a drink. Moreover, they seemed no strangers to the place and on entering had shaken hands with Titin. But who would not shake hands with Titin?

Some minutes later an extraordinary commotion occurred in the street. The lines of policemen had great difficulty in holding their ground against the pressure of the crowd eager for a closer view of the guests as they came out, for they were leaving the Town Hall. The civil ceremony had in fact been postponed until the afternoon, and the religious ceremony until the next morning.

Each person in the crowd wished to see the faces of the Supias, and of Hippothadee, and in particular of how Toinetta was taking it. She was not long in coming and looked more cheerful on leaving than on arriving. In short, the failure of the ceremony had kindled a roguish light in her eyes which, during the last few hours, had not been there. The chauffeur grasped the wheel and made ready to drive off. The footman, as stiff as a poker,

opened the car door. Antoinette stepped in. Was it due
to some act of carelessness on the man's part. The door
was immediately closed.

M. Supia, taken aback, tried to utter a protest. But
he was too late. At that very moment the crowd broke
through the barrier of policeman on all sides. A number
of merry hot-heads, such as are invariably present at ex-
ceptional public functions, on the lookout for an opportunity to amuse themselves by creating a little confusion
in the best arrangements, broke the ranks with irresistible
force and gathered round the cars.

Tantifla, Bouta, Aiguardente, and Pistafun were con-
spicuous among the others for the energy with which they
hustled those who opposed them. Meantime the chauffeur drove through the tumult. Then, when he raised his
head, they noticed that he wore under his cap a mask
which was not unfamiliar in Nice. And a shout went up:
"Hardigras! Hardigras!"

Yes, it was Hardigras carrying off the bride! The
crowd opened out before him as if at the word of command, and when he swept through, closed up forming a
barrier which MM. Souques and Ordinal's police cars—
the latter without M. Ordinal—were unable to break
through. They would have had to run down the crowd.
When the square was at last cleared the bride's car and
Hardigras were far away. . . . The car was found during
the afternoon in a picturesque but somewhat secluded part
of the country, called Dark Valley. The bride, of course,
was not in it.

It was then that the Mayor and his deputy returned to
the town after an excellent lunch at a country inn on the
banks of the Loup, where they had been driven against
their will in a hired car ordered the night before. At that
period the Mayor of Nice had no official car.

Any spirit of resistance that they might have felt,
cooled on seeing the fighting attitude of two skillfully disguised men who crowded into the car behind him. More-

over, their protests ceased altogether when they were assured that it was merely a question of doing justice to a splendid blue salmon. The inn which had been unoccupied for some time seemed to have opened specially for them to close its doors again on the morrow.

M. Ordinal, too, was released from the room in Camousse's restaurant in which Pistafun had locked him. . . . But he was furious. That was because he had not the same reason for consolation as the Mayor and his deputy.

But no trace of the bride could be discovered. So daring an act of abduction, so cynical an outrage on the liberty of the chief magistrates of the town, was bound to set in motion the entire apparatus of the law. A beginning was made by putting Pistafun under lock and key. Then Titin, who had quietly returned to La Fourca, was requested by the District Commissary of Police to appear before him next day.

One of the most terrible tragedies in judicial annals was about to unfold itself.

CHAPTER XIII

IN WHICH THE BRIDE IS FOUND

WHEN Titin received the request to present himself at the chief police station there was no lack of counselors to endeavor to persuade him of the risk involved in such a step. But he refused to listen to them. Even Mme. Bibi's entreaties fell on deaf ears.

Gamba Secca, however, ventured to say:

"Take care! They have already arrested Pistafun. If Giaousé Babazouk were here, he would know how to persuade you."

Then a voice which was that of Nathalie said not without bitterness:

"Yes, but Giaousé is not here. Titin lent him to Hardigras to look after Toinetta. A nice man for the job, upon my word! So go to the police station Titin, and whatever happens you've only brought it on yourself."

"I shall go all the easier in my mind for if anything happens to me, I am pretty sure Giaousé will manage to get me out of it."

"Of course and we shall all be with him."

Nathalie clung to his arm.

"Stay, and go and join Hardigras," she said in an undertone.

He gently released himself for he knew how devoted she was to him and how much it pained her to speak in this way to him.

"Men are all crazy," she added.

At last he was able to get away. It was with a smile on his face that he appeared at the police station and, with the summons in his hand, asked to see the Chief Commissary of Police. Orders had been given. He was at once shown in, not to the Chief Commissary, but to M. Bezaudin. For all his philosophy, M. Bezaudin was beginning to harbor towards Titin the somewhat harsh feelings that Inspectors Souques and Ordinal had long entertained.

When some hours after the trouble had occurred the bride's guardian and her promised husband in a towering rage called at the police office—which Inspectors Souques and Ordinal had just left after being treated like regular blockheads—the Commissary made no attempt to soften their indignation. He shared it.

"This Titin ought to have been put in prison long ago," exclaimed the Prince. "He had already threatened to kill me if I married Mlle. Agagnosc."

"You ought to have told me so," said the Commissary.

"Ought I to tell you also that Titin and Hardigras are one and the same person."

"No!" said M. Bezaudin.

"You knew it and yet you failed to arrest him," shouted Supia.

"Well, M. Supia, you requested Titin to arrest Hardigras, and I was waiting. In reality, I wasn't sure of anything."

"What are you going to do now?"

"Why, I am going to ask Titin to tell Hardigras to give us back the bride."

"I've had enough of it," roared Supia. "You must arrest him and put him in prison."

"Very well, I am quite willing," agreed M. Bezaudin. "I've no fancy for him any more than you, you know. Ah, I'd like to tell him to go to the devil. He is causing me no end of worry. Everything I said just now to Souques and Ordinal who promised to be answerable for him and still were silly enough to let him go, is nothing compared with what I have personally had to put up with.

The District Commissary does not often fly into a rage. But this time I thought he was going to throw me out of the window pending my dismissal. Let's arrest this confounded Titin, then. . . . And we'll say no more about it."

"Yes, yes, and the sooner the better," agreed Supia, furiously.

"The ruffian is utterly unscrupulous," said Hippothadee.

"We know it," burst out the Commissary, "and Mlle. Agagnosc must take her chance."

"What do you mean?" asked Supia, nonplussed.

"I mean that since he has such a hostage as Mlle. Agagnosc in his hands, a fellow like Titin will know how to make the most of it. But as you want him to be arrested, let's arrest him. It shall be done to-night or to-morrow. He has no need to lie low. It is sufficient for him to have got Mlle. Agagnosc safely hidden away. But let's show him we're not the sort of men to shrink from these considerations. To prison with Titin come what may to Mlle. Agagnosc in the hands of Titin's friends, who won't hesitate to avenge him!"

"It's monstrous. Do you think he is capable of such a crime?" gasped Supia.

"I think he is capable of any crime," yelped Hippothadee. "I have never seen anyone more headstrong than that young fellow."

"But he is in love with Toinetta."

"Oh, you know nothing of love, M. Supia," roared Hippothadee. "Titin is the kind who would rather see Mlle. Agagnosc dead than the wife of another."

"That's how men in your country look at things perhaps," rapped out Supia, disconcerted.

"Yes, sir, and they call such men heroes."

"A nice thing! What an age to live in! Here's a man who has robbed me and carried off your promised wife. Do you call him a hero!"

"Gentlemen, I am sorry to interrupt this little argument," broke in M. Bezaudin, "but I should like to know what you have decided. . . ."

"You are always asking us what we want done," said M. Supia, irritably. "But it's for you, once for all, to act upon your own responsibility."

"Very well, I will sign a warrant for his arrest."

"No, don't do that," protested Hippothadee. "Above all else we want to save Mlle. Agagnosc—to part her from Titin. Well, first of all, get her away from him."

"It's not so easy as you may imagine," said M. Bezaudin, "but after all, it's one thing that we must try first. For that reason I must not arrest Titin. . . ."

It was as a result of this conversation that Titin was "invited" to call at the police station. He found the Commissary seated at his desk. M. Bezaudin was on the point of lighting a cigarette. He seemed to remember that Titin also smoked, and offered him his cigarette case. Titin helped himself, thanking him with a nod, and producing his pocket lighter in his turn, handed it to the Commissary.

"Why are you smiling, Titin?" he asked.

"What about you?"

"Allow me, but it's for me to question you."

"That's true, and I will answer you right away. I was smiling because I know what you're going to ask me."

"I'm glad of that," said the Commissary, laughing, "for if that is so, we shall not be long in coming to an understanding. Well, what was I going to ask you?"

Just then the telephone bell rang, and M. Bezaudin with a word of apology took up the receiver.

"Hullo! Hullo! . . . What? . . . What do you say? . . . Pistafun! . . . Oh, you don't say so. . . . No! It's out of the question. . . . Why, they are mad. . . . Run them all in. . . . All of them. . . . No. . . . Don't put them with Pistafun!"

The Commissary hung up the receiver.

"Your friends are making themselves very disagreeable as was to be expected," he said.

"What friends?"

"Tantifla, Aiguardente, and Tony Bouta. . . . They want us to give up Pistafun. It seems they're kicking up a devil of a dust about it."

"They are decent fellows and won't desert their pal in his hour of need," said Titin.

"They asked for Pistafun to be set at liberty or to be imprisoned with him. I didn't want to go against the wishes of these worthy fellows, and so the four of them are in jail! It is the best thing for all of us."

"Not for me," said Titin.

"Why not?"

"I will tell you presently."

"Meantime as you are so well informed, tell me why I sent for you."

"To ask me to restore Mlle. Agagnosc."

"Well, you do play the game. So you admit carrying off the bride?"

"I admit nothing of the sort. M. Ordinal will tell you that he did not leave me during the whole of the incident. Everyone could see us together at Camousse's restaurant at the very moment when Hardigras drove off with Mlle, Agagnosc."

"Allow me. At that time M. Ordinal saw nothing at all because your friend Pistafun had locked him up in some room."

"That does not agree with Pistafun's version of the matter. . . . I'm not surprised that M. Ordinal was hustled and found some difficulty in getting away seeing there was such a great crowd at Camousse's. Pistafun is very indignant at the treatment he received after assisting, once in a way, the police. I know him. He will never do it again! As to his friends, how could they be other than incensed by such injustice? And you nab them! Really, I'm surprised you haven't arrested me before now. You

are only asking for trouble to-day. And that's not like
you, let me tell you."

"You are making me out either better or worse than I
am, my dear Titin. Pending an agreement between us I
sent for you so that we might understand each other.
Do you know where Mlle. Agagnosc is?"

"How should I know? I'm not Hardigras."

"But Hardigras may tell you. . . ."

"Possibly."

"Do you know him?"

"No, but I have a friend who knows him. It seems
he is not a bad sort. I may as well say at once that I've
made arrangements to meet him. I have a great regard
for Mlle. Agagnosc, and don't want anything to happen to
her. On that matter we are in agreement."

"Look here, Titin, if you have a great regard for Mlle.
Agagnosc you will arrange for her to be taken home to her
guardian this evening. Her reputation depends upon it.
Her honor depends upon it. Have you thought of
that?"

"I have thought of it and also of this: No worse calamity can happen to a girl than to become the wife of Prince
Hippothadee. Are we still agreed?"

M. Bezaudin greatly perplexed, was silent. Titin rose
from his chair.

"What are you going to do?" asked the Commissary
quickly.

"I'm off. I can do nothing more here, now that we are
no longer agreed. I'm off, unless you're going to have me
arrested."

"You know quite well that I'm not going to have you
arrested; otherwise who will get into touch with
Hardigras?"

Titin bent over him.

"You know yourself that the Prince is a scoundrel and
Supia not much better, and this marriage an infamy."

"Why did she accept him?"

"She won't accept him again," cried Titin, his eyes all aglow with delight.

"Ah, you know that!" exclaimed M. Bezaudin, laughing loudly. "So you have already seen Hardigras!"

"Well, yes, I have seen him. There!" Titin could not help blurting out. He bit his lip until the blood came, and flushed. His joy as a lover had carried him off his feet and he had given himself away like a child. M. Bezaudin having scored did not dwell on his victory. He held the whip hand for the moment and kept it.

"If she won't accept him again what have you to fear on her account?"

"Everything," returned Titin. "Granting that she returns to her relatives and says she doesn't wish to marry Hippothadee, she will be none the less under the thumb of these people for some years. She is but a child. She will end by giving way."

"Then it means that she is not in love with you," said M. Bezaudin, ruthlessly.

Titin grew pale. He made no answer either because he had nothing to say or lacked the strength to utter a word.

"Titin, my friend, you are on a very slippery path. . . . But there is some hope for you. You are a better chap than you make yourself out to be. The people round here have spoilt you because they have been too fond of you. Take care! You will allow yourself to be involved in matters which will turn everybody's hand against you. When a man claims to be his own master, his own judge, when he puts himself above the law, a time comes when he stumbles and falls. And then he is trampled under foot. . . . Titin, my friend, listen to me as a Commissary of Police. It is none too soon. You have played the fool long enough as it is. I will even go so far as to say that you no longer have the right to do so because you are in love and perhaps also because you are loved. Send back Mlle. Agagnosc to her relatives at once if you are an honest man."

"Mlle. Agagnosc shall be with them this evening," said Titin in a voice broken with emotion.

"Thank you Titin. I know you better than all the others, believe me. One of these days, perhaps, we shall become good friends. By jove, don't take on like that."

"Hang it all, I'm not!" protested Titin, wiping his eyes with the back of his hand. "This confounded Bezaudin— I beg your pardon sir—can do what he likes with me!"

Just then the telephone bell rang again. With a gesture of impatience M. Bezaudin snatched up the receiver.

"What? . . . Again? . . . Did you not put them in prison as they asked. . . . Yes. . . . Well, what then? They're smashing up everything. . . . They want their Pistafun. Well, put them all together. . . . Give them a pack of cards and tell them to stop worrying us."

M. Bezaudin hung up the receiver.

"Your friends are very troublesome," he said.

"More than you think, sir, for they are only just beginning. If I were in your place I should get rid of them at once. It would be safer. You can't imagine what these fellows are capable of doing when they get together and are supposed to be playing a quiet game of cards."

"Still you wouldn't wish me to release Pistafun?"

"They want to be all together, and I would rather see them together outside than inside. . . . And then I will tell you my mind—one good turn deserves another. I know Hardigras. He won't agree to give up Mlle. Agagnosc unless you release his Pistafun, Aiguardente, Tantifla, and Tony Bouta."

"Are they, too, friends of Hardigras?" asked M. Bezaudin, smiling.

"Rather! Hardigras can't do without them. He can't play bowls without Pistafun."

"I perceive more and more that Hardigras's friends are your friends," said M. Bezaudin, signing an order for the release of the four friends.

"What conclusion do you draw from that?"

"That I shall be 'slanged' by Ordinal, and you'll end by getting me put on the retired list," said M. Bezaudin, showing Titin the order for release.

"There will always be a room for you at Mme. Bibi's—if that's any consolation."

When Titin had left, M. Bezaudin dropped into his seat with a feeling of unspeakable satisfaction.

"Whew! I had him."

Just then a messenger informed him that Prince Hippothadee and M. Supia were waiting to see him. When they learned that Mlle. Agagnosc would be home again that evening they were loud in their congratulations. The Commissary declared that it needed very few words from him to bring about this result.

"Titin is not such a bad fellow as you think."

"Perhaps you're right," said Supia. "And as to that, I should like to have a word with you in private. Will you allow me, my dear Hippothadee?"

"Why, of course, my dear Supia. I'll go and tell the good news to Mme. Supia, who is worrying herself."

"My dear Commissary," began M. Supia, when they were alone. "I shall end by thinking like you that we were greatly mistaken in Titin. But tell me, did it occur to you, when you were together, to suggest to him that old idea of yours which, perhaps, is not such a bad one after all?"

"What idea are you referring to?"

"What! Have you forgotten it? It was a question of promising Titin to pass the sponge over the past if he would restore the more important articles, particularly the furniture, which it amused him to take away from Bella Nissa."

"But it was Hardigras who took the things."

"Good lord, wasn't it Hardigras who carried off my ward, and isn't it Titin who is sending her back to me?"

"I agree. Hardigras does so exactly what Titin wishes that I might, of course, have said a word in passing and

settled the Bella Nissa affair; but I had already arranged
with him about Mlle. Agagnosc. Sufficient unto the day is
the evil thereof."

"Fix this up for me and you won't regret it," urged M.
Supia.

"If this matter can be fixed up, I will see to it for you
apart from any question of gratitude."

"It can be fixed up. It will be easier than arrang- '
ing Mlle. Agagnosc's return which you managed so
well."

"I don't agree with you. I was able to persuade Titin
in that matter because it concerned the honor of his old
playmate. But in your affair I fear I should meet with
many difficulties. I don't know what you've done to him,
but that youth hates you."

"Do you think it will last?

"Hang it, you must ask Hardigras that question."

"Look here, M. Bezaudin, I will tell you how you can
arrange this business."

"I'm listening," said M. Bezaudin, who had rarely seen
M. Supia in such agitation, and asked himself: "What am
I going to hear now? What piece of blackguardism is the
old pirate going to drag out this time?"

At last Supia made up his mind to speak:

"I know why Titin has a grudge against me. When he
was in the army, I made a deal over Mme. Bibi's land.
Oh, it was a small matter. But then she was very keen on
her little place, the confounded old woman. On the other
hand, it interfered with my plans. You understand, it
obstructed my view. At last I got hold of her land. She
didn't gain anything certainly, and she didn't lose either.
It was hardly worth anything. On returning to the district Titin let himself go in very strong language. Now
that we know for certain that Hardigras and Titin are
one and the same person, the whole thing comes back to
my mind. Mark me, Titin would never have robbed me,
probably, if I had not. . . ."

"If you had not robbed him," said the Commissary completing the sentence.

"You are very severe, Bezaudin. You were not so severe upon Hardigras. Anyway, you now see what happened. The whole thing has been done by way of retaliation."

"Reprisals."

"Do you say that—you who represent the law?"

"No, I certainly don't say it. But Titin says it—granting of course that Titin is Hardigras."

"Let's make an end of it. Please tell Titin that if he restores what he has taken, and promises to stop these Hardigras games, I will give back Mme. Bibi's land. It will be child's play for you to carry through this little affair. Can I rely on you?"

"I will repeat our conversation to him, and hope we may be satisfied with the result."

At six o'clock that evening the Supia family and Prince Hippothadee were together in the Managing Director's office at Bella Nissa. The two men were impatiently waiting for Antoinette's return. Mme. Supia and Caroline displayed much more composure. Caroline in particular was in no hurry to see the future Princess of Transylvania. And, indeed, in her heart of hearts she was still hoping that Titin would keep his Toinetta for good and all.

At last the bell rang. Almost at once the maid came in and announced:

"Mlle. Agagnosq."

They all rose to their feet and hastened to meet her. But they were amazed to see standing before them a lovely child clad in the old-time costume of the country which is still to be encountered occasionally in remote parts of the mountain districts.

"Well, don't you recognize me? Did you expect me to come back in my bride's dress?"

"What have you done with it?" demanded Mme. Supia.

"I gave it to Hardigras."

"Hardigras dressed her to the best of his power," added Titin, showing himself. "His wardrobe is not a very extensive one, you know."

"As peasant or princess she is equally beautiful," cried Hippothadee, feasting his eyes on her.

"Come in," said Supia drawing her into the office.

"May I come in, also?" asked Titin. "I have a word to say to you from Hardigras."

Now that Antoinette was home again M. Supia no longer had the same feeling of forbearance and conciliation that possessed him in the Commissary's office. In fact, he greatly regretted his avowal. He forgot that Titin, of his own accord, had surrendered his hostage. He remebered only the dastardly abduction which had almost reduced to naught his most cherished schemes.

"Monsieur Titin," he returned in his harshest voice and most disagreeable air, "you will understand that after what has happened we will not detain you. In fact it is rather strange that you should dare to inflict your presence on us."

"You are quite out of place," Hippothadee thought it well to add.

"My dear Hippothadee, leave it to me to tell him what he ought to know since he has had the courage to come here. . . . If M. Titin you had any friendship for my ward, and were in any sense an honest man, you would never have thought of embarking on such a disgraceful proceeding. You have made amends as far as you can by restoring Mlle. Agagnosc to us, but it is none the less a fact that you have prejudiced her future and but for Prince Hippothadee's magnanimity she might look a long time for a husband."

"Don't you worry godfather. I don't want to be married," broke in Antoinette.

The Prince made a gesture of surprise which was almost despair, while M. Supia turned to her angrily:

"Hold your tongue you little wretch. You are crazy and deserve what has happened to you."

"Very likely, but I don't want to be married," returned Antoinette calmly.

"And I tell you that you will be married," burst out M. Supia. "I have had enough of your fancies. I won't incur the responsibility of keeping you home any longer."

"You should have left me where I was."

"She no longer loves me!" groaned Hippothadee, placing his hand upon his heart.

"Well, I never," she said laughing. "Anyone would think it was a sin to hurt his feelings. What do you say, Titin?"

Amid the excitement Titin maintained complete composure.

"For my part," he said seating himself upon the side of an armchair, without being invited, "I see no reason to fire up, and it's for Hardigras to look after himself. I should never have come here to listen to such absurd arguments had I not agreed to deliver a little message to M. Supia from the said Hardigras."

Supia shot a terrible glance at him. Unable to restrain himself he pointed to the door:

"Clear out Bastardon. As to Hardigras, I don't want to know what his message is. But you can tell him this from me if ever you come across him: I shall show him no mercy, and I'll have him before a jury who will know how to put an end, once for all, to his abominable tricks. Do you hear, Titin?"

"I'm not deaf," returned Titin, rising and striding quietly to the door. "I won't forget to tell him what you say. We shall meet again, M. Supia. Heaven bless you!"

"Titin, kiss me before you go," called Antoinette, "and give my kind regards to Hardigras."

Supia made a threatening gesture as though he would like to strangle him. Just then Titin turned round:

"I really don't know what you have up against me,"

he said, twisting his hat between his fingers. "You wanted
your niece back and I have brought her back, and now
you act like a madman. Hardigras will be amazed when
I tell him. As for myself I shall not interfere again.
Hardigras must do his own work. He will write to you—
that's all. That will suit me all the better as the message
I had for you was no joke."

"This affair concerns me as much as M. Supia," interposed Hippothadee, who was seething at the tone of
contempt underlying Titin's apparent meekness, "and I
shall be obliged if you will tell us now what sort of message
your so-called Hardigras entrusted you with."

"It has to do with Mlle. Agagnosc, and I don't know if I
ought to. . . ."

"You must. Though M. Supia is Mlle. Agagnosc's
guardian, I am her fiancé."

"Well, here you are: he asked me to tell M. Supia to be
very good to Mlle. Agagnosc, so that her stay with the
family may be, if not agreeable, at least endurable. He
says she must not be thwarted in anything and above all
must not be driven by despair into marrying Prince Hippothadee. Should this marriage take place, he says, and
I am quoting his exact words, he will hold M. Supia and
his family responsible. A crime of this sort will not fail
to recoil on him and the whole of his family."

"Well, and what about me?" asked the worthy
Hippothadee.

"As far as you are concerned he said nothing. It seems
that you do not count. . . . Good-bye everybody."

Titin strode slowly from the room without troubling
about the storm that broke out behind him.

CHAPTER XIV

LIFE grew lively once more at La Fourca and the country round. Titin was ready always to contribute to the general happiness. Nathalie herself was treated kindly. But, she had no illusions. She knew now how matters stood. She said to herself: "Since he is easy in his mind about Toinetta and convinced that she won't marry Hippothadee, he has recovered his spirits again and enjoys life. It is because of his love for Toinetta that he allows us to flatter him. That's Titin all over—now like a lion and now like a lamb. He already fancies himself married to her."

"Oh, he won't have the patience to wait three years for her," said another admirer.

One thing that set Nathalie beside herself was the foolish persistence with which Giaousé rallied her for her fondness for Titin. Had he wished to throw her at Titin's head he could not have adopted better means.

Titin's confidence in himself now seemed to know no bounds. In the last resort he pronounced judgment in the quarrels arising between his friends. Nor would he allow any discussion to take place on his verdicts, dictated by his natural sense of justice. As a result, the sharpest disputes were amicably settled, and the settlement celebrated over a flask of wine.

Titin was in the state of mind when the most extraordinary tasks seem child's play. Hitherto he had merely painted sign-bords and landscapes, of an ingenuously cubist character, upon the walls of Mme. Bibi's shop.

164

But now he set about a huge work which was already the admiration of his subjects; for, in truth, no other word can convey an approximate idea of the ties which bound the neighborhood, in thrall, of its own free will, to his every fancy. He undertook to paint in fresco the marriage room in La Fourca Town Hall. The subject was a huge fête. In a beflowered setting young men and maidens danced with triumphant grace, not without reserve, in its artistic simplicity. On the wall facing the visitor was depicted a feast presided over by the peasant mayor of La Fourca whom Titin had portrayed with bold strokes, not devoid of cruel satire.

On a shield behind the desk where the register was placed during the ceremony, the words "Bastardon's wedding" could be read in curious capital letters adorned with flourishes. And on a large square was the dimly recognizable figure of Titin. On another outline was a sketch of the bride clad in her long white veil, though as yet no face could be distinguished. But they knew what was meant and gave expression to their opinions.

"I can see her from here," said Pistafun, "with her golden hair, her eyes like sea pinks, her rosy cheeks and little tip-tilted nose as she smiles 'good morning.' Is that not so, Titin I am not so very far out."

"Why yes, that's pretty well as I see her, too. But to make certain, I won't finish the bride until she comes herself and poses in her white dress."

"She will come right enough. You must have patience. Meanwhile finish the background. You've plenty of work to do. The picture is not finished."

"But what if she doesn't come?" said Nathalie. "It will never be finished."

"Yes it will," returned Titin as he began to mark out other figures in chalk.

"How he loves her!" said Nathalie.

Giaousé remained silent. But he laughed harshly when he looked at his wife.

The painting was an event in the district, and no progress could be made without the good cheer and diversion with which Titin contrived to reward his models. He asked them to attire themselves in the old costumes of La Fourca, which their grand parents had preserved in their wardrobes. The men came clad in short jackets and breeches in homespun with blue stripes. The youths wore linen shirts and shoes with leather straps. The women wore a swelling bodice to which a pad nearly six inches long was sewed and to which the petticoat was fastened. A gold cross held by a ribbon of black velvet was worn round the neck. The hair was gathered in fringes or fillets whose lower part, raised on the head and fixed with hairpins, ended in little tassels hanging down behind. Over the coif—in old people black, but in the more youthful red or yellow—was a little white wrap trimmed with an insertion of lace, the long ends of which were passed under the chin and tied over the head.

But so that this picture of an attractive and delightful past should possess some actuality, Titin would not allow them to pose in the traditional groups taught in schools, but made them amuse themselves in earnest in dancing and feasting. He engaged musicians and had the tables loaded with good things so as to gladden the eye as well as the taste; in short, to rejoice mind and body alike.

But these things cost money and the day soon came when Gamba Secca told him that the resources of "Bastardon's Kiosks" were exhausted. Then Titin grew depressed again and disbanded his models. It was while somewhat dejectedly painting the blue sea on the sky-line that he heard a musical voice of an unfamiliar tone asking if the artist at work was not the great and famous Titin le Bastardon.

Titin turned round and beheld a man very smartly dressed who bowed almost to the ground and drew himself up only to assure him of his unbounded devotion, his tried fidelity, his immense admiration.

"But you are making a mistake," said Titin frowning. He was in no humor to allow a stranger to laugh at him.

"No, no, I am not making any mistake. By the Blesséd Virgin and all the saints and by all I hold most dear, I am the humblest of your servants, M. Titin. It was you, was it not, who wrote that letter to Prince Marie Hippothadee of Transylvania?"

"Yes. What about it?" said Titin on his guard.

"What about it! His Highness was greatly affected by your letter. I read it. It was grand."

"No, it was neither grand for him nor for me."

"It was full of the finest sentiments. . . . It was easy to see the sort of man you are—a great and noble soul. There's no mistake, M. Titin."

"Well, get on with it. What are you driving at?"

"His Highness wrote to his Consul at Nice to obtain a few particulars, you understand."

"Why, of course."

"They were wonderful—those particulars. The Consul told the Prince the story of Hardigras with which the town is ringing."

"Hardigras! I don't know him," rapped out Titin, more than ever suspicious; and he said to himself: "You, my friend, have been sent here by Souques and Ordinal—"

"You don't know Hardigras!" cried the stranger and he burst out laughing.

"I think this joke has been carried far enough," said Titin.

"But there's no joke. Don't let's talk about Hardigras if it annoys you. Let's talk about yourself. I am sent to you by one of the greatest Princes in the world—Prince Marie Hippothadee, shortly to be crowned King of Transylvania, whose throne you may inherit one day, for the Prince, your father, to whom you wrote and who wishes you well, ordered me, his most unworthy servant, to tell you that he will not have a moment's happiness until he has recognized you, my lord, as the heir to his name and possessions—which are immense."

Titin let him talk, not a little astonished and not knowing what to think. Was it true that this astonishing stranger was an envoy from the Prince, his father, whose intervention in Antoinette's marriage, on the off chance, he had sought to obtain? After all it was quite possible. No matter. He hardly expected it. He had forgotten all about his letter to the Prince until suddenly this man came and declared the Prince's intention to interest himself in him of whose existence a few weeks before he was ignorant.

The stranger gave his name as Odon Odonovitch, Comte Valdar, Lord of Metzoras Trikala, and other places, and handed him a letter sealed with the arms of Transylvania. It was addressed:

To Monsieur Titin le Bastardon,
　　La Fourca Nova,
　　　　Alpes Maritimes,
　　　　　　France.

He opened it and read:

"My dear son,
　I learn of your existence with a joy which I scarcely expected from Providence. I was in despair lest the family without a male heir should become extinct. It is my will that the real line of the proud Hippothadees should be restored in you. My intention is to recognize you as my legitimate heir, that is to say when the political crisis, through which we are passing, is settled, and when I have become complete master of this realm—a result which cannot be long delayed.
　In the meantime I am sending you my faithful servant, Comte Valdar. He will give you this letter as well as a sum of money enabling you to maintain from this day forward the rank in society which is yours by right. He will supply also all your needs and establish you as befits a Prince destined to succeed me; moreover he will keep me informed of your wishes. Command him as I should command him myself, for he will refuse you nothing; he owes his life to me.
　As to your marriage, since you love this young girl it behoves you to marry her. But you must allow me first to confer upon her the titles essential to the rank that she will assume at Court. All this shall be done in due course. My wretched brother, the disgrace of

our house, will have but to stand aside and, if need be, to disappear. I will see to that. Have patience for a few months, my dear son, and your happiness will be equal to my own.

MARIE HIPPOTHADEE."

When Titin finished reading the letter which completed his amazement, he raised his eyes to Comte Valdar. The Comte smiled broadly and gave him a wallet.

"This is but a small part of the amount that I am to present to you, my lord; the rest has been expended in preparing an establishment for you. But you may spend as much as you like. I have written to His Highness that the expenses have exceeded my calculations, and I expect to receive a much larger remittance at the beginning of next month."

Titin, who in spite of his extravagant appearance, was a matter of fact man, opened the wallet and, without further ado, counted the bank notes. It contained twenty-five thousand francs. The matter was assuming a different aspect.

He asked the Comte to take a chair which the Comte did, declaring that it was a great honor to be allowed to sit for the first time in the presence of his king's son.

"I am overjoyed, as you may see, at the turn of events," said Titin. "I have always had a longing for wealth so as to be able to share it with persons very near to me, and if I ever dreamed of being a king's son, it was in the hope of enjoying life with my friends, telling them not to worry but to rely on me in their difficulties; therefore to-day is a red-letter day since it enables me to fulfill a wish that I have regarded as impossible. We will celebrate it here and now."

"You were born to be a king," cried Odon.

"Meantime, until I become one, do me the favor, monsieur, of calling me, like everybody else, Titin le Bastardon. From what you tell me and I have read, I wish to remember only this remarkable and obvious fact: I am still Titin le Bastardon, and thanks to you, have at my disposal a very decent sum of money that we will at once proceed to spend. Afterwards, time will show."

"Oh, M. Titin, if His Highness could only hear you he would say: 'He is his father's own son.' He too, the dear Prince, spends everything that comes into his possession."

"How is it that he has anything left?" asked Titin.

"But he never has anything left. Fortunately he is practically master of the realm which means that he receives a great deal. . . . That is one of the signs by which we recognize a true prince. You are a true prince, M. Titin."

"No, monsieur le Comte."

"Oh, M. Titin, call me Odon Odonovitch, I beg of you."

"My subjects won't ruin themselves for me. It's I who will be ruined by them."

"Hardigras will never allow you to want for anything," said Odon Odonovitch, with a satirical grin.

Titin frowned.

"Oh, don't be upset, M. Titin. Anything I say about him is meant in jest. But I know all about your lovely story, believe me."

"I notice that you, too, made inquiries before coming to see me."

"I had to, M. Titin. It was His Highness's express wish."

"Have you been in this country long?"

"I arrived in Nice a fortnight ago, and everything I have learnt, everything I have written to His Highness, has filled me with unspeakable pleasure. You are the chief subject of conversation round here. Everyone admires and fears you—which is the highest achievement in real politics. You are a great politician and a great artist. People have said to me: 'Go and see his paintings on the Town Hall walls. No one has ever done anything finer since the ancients!'"

"And now you have seen my work what do you think of it, Odon Odonovitch?"

"It's splendid."

Having said this the Comte rose and lifted his arms before Titin's paintings as though speechless with admiration. Titin with a curt gesture caught hold of his arms.

"Comte, I ask you seriously as a friend, do you like all this?"

"As a friend?" echoed the Comte embarrassed by the searching look in Titin's eyes.

"Yes, as a friend. Admit that it all seems hideous to you."

"Hideous? How can you say such a thing?"

"Come tell me. I insist. Tell the truth to the King's son."

"Oh, what a wonderful man you are! Well, yes, M. Titin, I think it is awful," he returned, adding at once scared by his own sincerity: "But I am no judge in these matters."

"Nonsense," said Titin. "I prefer the truth to empty words. If you wish to be my friend you must always tell me the truth."

"Of course, of course, truth is the one thing that princes never hear."

"It's very strange but sometimes you speak with a Slavonic and sometimes with a Spanish accent."

"That's because my father was a Slav and my mother a Spaniard—a beautiful Spaniard. My father met her in Las Palmas. They fell in love and were married. I inherited my mother's splendid dark eyes and my father's fortune which was splendid also."

"Are you a rich man, Comte?"

"I used to be but now I am penniless."

"Through mixing in politics?"

"Yes, through mixing in politics, which entails a big expense—too big an expense. You've got to live up to a certain rank, of course. Well, I overdid it. . . . I never know what money I'm spending—it's awful. There are times when I don't know what to do not to pay my valet."

"You mean you don't know what to do to pay him."

"No, no, I mean to pay him. When I have money, I never pay him and he never asks for any because he robs me. But now I am poor he doesn't leave me a moment's peace, and I don't know what to do not to pay him. I made no mistake."

"Have you any money at the moment?"

"Not a penny."

"Well, you may depend upon me to pay your valet. Where are you going now?"

"I have a car outside which will take us to Nice. I want to show you your new home."

They left the Town Hall. A crowd had gathered in the square round the car, greatly perplexed by the rich stranger's unexpected visit—at all events he seemed to be rich. He had a distinguished bearing, and Titin was so well pleased with himself and wore so lordly an air that the good people of La Fourca gasped with astonishment. They followed the car through the narrow, tortuous lanes and ran behind it as it traversed the whole of La Fourca Nova.

As they drove past La Patentaine, Titin lifted his hat with a sweeping gesture to Mme. Cioasa—M. Supia's poor sister who was the concierge. Mme. Cioasa turned yellow. It was her manner, as an old maid, of blushing. Then Titin bowed to right and left, like the Head of a State paying an official visit to a country town.

CHAPTER XV

THE journey was effected almost in silence. Odon
Odonovitch seemed absorbed in thought. Titin worked
out a plan of his own. When they reached Nice and the
car was turning towards the Place Massena, Titin asked
the Comte to drive to his Consul. Odonovitch at once
gave the order.

"I understand," he said.

"You must forgive me Comte, but you took your precautions and I am taking mine."

"That's quite natural," agreed Comte.

On arrival the Consul received the Comte and Titin with
the greatest deference. Titin showed him the envelope
containing Prince Marie Hippothadee's letter, and the
Consul identified the Transylvanian arms and seal.

Titin turning to the Comte, asked:

"Have you any objection to my showing him the letter?"

"None at all," returned the Comte.

"This letter is in Prince Marie's handwriting and it
bears his signature," said the Consul with a bow after
reading the letter.

Titin apologized to the Consul, thanked him, and was
shown out with all the honors due to a king's son. They
once more stepped into the car; and Titin gave himself
up to pleasant thoughts over the amazing occurrence
which would revolutionize his life. Doubtless for reasons
of policy, as explained by Prince Marie, he would have to
keep secret for a while the splendor of his birth. But, the

letter and Odonovitch's wallet of bank notes were some amends for the wretched past. They permitted him to indulge in every hope. Moreover, Odon Odonovitch's personality attracted him. Had it been in that worthy gentleman's power the truth would have blazed forth before the hour dictated by fate and Prince Marie Hippothadee's prudence. His entirely disinterested conduct was remarkable. A poor man, in a strange land, he had faithfully conveyed to Titin a considerable sum of money and at the same time all the advantages that money bestows. Titin had reached this point in his reflections when the car—a luxurious hired car—pulled up outside a house in the Promenade des Anglais, which was not unknown to him.

"This is the place," said Odonovitch.

To Titin's great amazement the Comte led the way to the floor recently occupied by Prince Vladimir Hippothadee for his marriage with Mlle. Antoinette Agagnosc.

"A bargain M. Titin!" exclaimed Odonovitch. "A splendid bargain. I bought the lease and furniture for a mere song."

"I know the flat, but I don't recognize the furniture."

"By all the saints, the furniture was not good enough for you," cried the Comte. "I sold it, and sold it at a good price. An excellent piece of business."

"And you bought this furniture, which is certainly very fine, with the money from the sale?"

"No. This furniture was delivered last night by the best house in Paris which has a branch in the Avenue de Verdun here. But it's not yet paid for. I expect to pay for it at the beginning of next month. We still have a good many expenses to meet, of course."

"What expenses?"

"Well, many little things are wanted here in the flat. I have ordered the linen. The sheets haven't come yet. Meanwhile I have retained a suite of rooms for you, next to mine, at the Palace Hotel where I am staying and where they'll bring you everything necessary to enable you to hold your own in the world."

"Do you know the name of the man who sold you the lease and furniture?" asked Titin with a satirical grin.

"I don't remember his name.. All I can tell you, your Highness—I beg you to allow me to give you this title in private—is that I made his acquaintance in the club, and during the evening he lost, as the saying goes, the very shirt off his back. We soon concluded the business. He said when I gave him the money: 'Lightly come, lightly go', and added: 'I bought this furniture from a gentleman who was in need of money as the result of a little game of chemin de fer'. Thereupon he left me, and went off to take the bank, and in ten minutes had lost every penny I paid him. Then I said to myself: 'This furniture will bring us bad luck. I must get rid of it at once.' "

"But you, my dear Odonovitch, you never gamble?"

"Never! Well, that's saying a great deal. A man in my position owes it to himself to play now and then to keep up his character as a gentleman."

"Yes? Well, gamble as little as you can for we have a saying here: 'When a man gambles the devil enjoys himself.' "

"By your respected father every word you say is wisdom itself!" exclaimed the Comte. "But let's hurry I beg, for your tailor must have been waiting at the hotel for over an hour."

"Before leaving the flat I want to tell you, my dear Comte, the name of the man who first furnished it. I mean the man who sold it to the gambler whom you saw losing his money at the tables. He is known to both of us. It was Prince Vladimir Hippothadee himself. He was then hoping to bring Mlle. Agagnosc here as his Princess."

"By the Virgin of Mostarajevo that's funny! . . . Mlle. Agagnosc will come here all the same. She will be Princess but another Prince will bring her here. I see in this sign that the Lord above is with us. But by my sainted mother, the furniture was a disgrace."

"It was Supia who chose it and Supia who paid for it," said Titin. "Obviously Hippothadee lost at the gaming table the money received by selling the furniture without Supia's permission. The thing is funnier than you imagine. As for myself, I am more pleased than I can tell you, for it proves beyond doubt that Vladimir has given up, at least for the present, the idea of marrying Mlle. Agagnosc."

"I see. He's afraid of that terrible Hardigras," said Odonovitch with a wink. Titin did not move a muscle.

That day and following days were spent in giving orders of all kinds; their rooms were besieged by tailors, bootmakers, hosiers, jewelers. Odon Odonovitch thought nothing too good for his dear Prince.

As to Titin, he had Prince Marie's letter in his pocket and, since it was the Prince's wish, he let things take their course. Moreover, his mind was occupied with the legitimate consideration that when it became known that he was no longer a nobody, Supia would withdraw his opposition to his marriage with Antoinette. The thought that she might soon be his wife made him bless the day that he wrote to the Prince, after giving up the idea of troubling Papajeudi and Gianelli.

From La Fourca to Nice and to the inner spurs of the Esterel, Titin's good fortune was the chief subject of conversation. Times had changed. The story of his sudden wealth, though they knew nothing of the real facts, seemed no more fantastic than others, equally extravagant, which daily fill the newspapers. There was a rumor, as rumors go, that underlying it all was a story about his father. But they knew nothing with any certainty, and it behoved them just to rejoice with him since he was in luck's way.

His transformation into a man of fashion came about in the most natural manner and with surprising rapidity.

It did not take him long to acquire manners and bearing in keeping with his new circumstances. He had been known as a light-hearted street boy living from hand to mouth, content to satisfy the needs of the moment, taking no thought of the morrow—a true son of Gianelli. He had been known, too, as a respectable trader making a success of his ingenious scheme for "Bastardon's Kiosks"—a true son of Papajeudi. And now it was his turn to reveal himself as a true son of the great Hippothadee.

And he did reveal himself! His ambition, soon outrun, had been at first to equal in smartness the gentlemen with monocles whom he used to see offering a hand to Toinetta as she alighted from the car at the casino.

If she could only see him now! But he looked in vain for her in the society circles where, fortunately, Hippothadee was no longer acting as her escort. She was not to be seen. Supia had set a closer watch round her than ever. She had even to change her room. A repetition of the balcony scene was no longer possible. . . .

But in spite of every precaution Supia could not prevent them from writing to each other. Titin would not have been Titin had he not, before sending her back to her relatives, contrived some means of corresponding with her which set at naught every vigilance. Toinetta complained in her letters of the enforced seclusion of which she was the victim. But she greatly enjoyed receiving Titin's letters and read them under the "tyrant's" nose without his suspicions being aroused. No more was said about the marriage. Hippothadee continued to visit the Supias, but he came as a friend of the family and ceased to make love to her. He allowed himself to be petted by the ladies, waiting the course of events. Toinetta wrote:

"Supia and Hippothadee imagine that I shall soon be tired of it all the first to revert to their schemes which they have by no means abandoned. They don't know me, especially since I have acquired a stock of patience by listening to my Titin. The Prince may say what he pleases, but whatever wedding present he may bring me will not be half so beautiful as the words that Titin has said to Toinetta. My Titin I love you. Nothing else matters. Have patience."

A few days after receiving her letter, Titin wrote telling her of the amazing change for the better in his prospects since the arrival of Odonovitch in Nice, and added not without pride that in marrying him she would be a princess and, perhaps, a queen one day!

"These things do happen," she wrote back, "but I love the old Titin and it is Titin I shall marry."

Meantime though Antoinette was no longer to be met in society, Titin was seen everywhere with Odonovitch. He was introduced to the more prominent members of the foreign colony. He proved to be a good shot at the pigeon shooting in Monte Carlo. He had insisted on being entered at the club as Titin le Bastardon, the name which he intended to bear until he had the right to use another.

"Why doesn't he sign himself Hardigras?" said one man with disdain. "Gentlemen, we are Hardigras's fellow members now."

But the fact that he might one day be a prince, owing to Odonovitch's unguarded speech, was soon an open secret. For, he was constantly blurting out "your Highness," and Titin had ceased to raise objection either because he was tired of calling him to order or because the title pleased him. But Titin found society life dull, and was only really happy when he managed to take Odonovitch off to La Fourca—which happened two or three times a week. . . .

It is not surprising that the contents of the wallet from Transylvania grew visibly smaller. None of the tradesmen was paid, of course, and bills were run up in all the hotels on the sea-coast. But then would they not all be settled at the beginning of the month when the money came from Transylvania? Moreover, Odonovitch gave it as his opinion that it would be well to leave some of them unpaid if only to show that they were not ordinary, middle-class folk without credit.

"That will allow us to have some money to play with, which is absolutely necessary for a gentleman in your position," he said.

"I never play. I have already told you so," protested Titin.

"That makes people chatter. I don't say you need play the fool, but just have a little flutter on the tables to show that you don't worry about money."

"We have a saying: 'Don't begin to gamble if you wish to keep out of danger' " said Titin.

"May I say I thought you took a broader view of things? You will certainly surprise your father. . . . Anyway, we'll talk of this matter when the money comes."

But the money did not come! Titin and Odonovitch lived sumptuously on credit, carefully guarding the few bank notes that remained to them. And the early days of the month sped by, and the tradesmen began to grow impatient. . . . Some of them became so pressing that he kicked them out. Then he was intensely humiliated. Disagreeable rumors were current, spread doubtless by Vladimir Hippothadee who had not been seen in his usual haunts for some weeks. Odonovitch himself grew anxious.

"I can't understand his Highness's silence. May I ask how much money you have left?"

"Fifteen hundred francs."

"Lend them to me and we shall pull through."

"What do you propose to do?"

"I have discovered an infallible martingale at trente et quarante. I begin with a stake of twenty francs."

"And you leave off with fifteen hundred thousand francs?"

"Possibly. But I must first have the fifteen hundred francs."

Titin put the notes back and returned the wallet to his pocket.

"You would only lose the money," he said.

Odonovitch hurried away so as not to betray what he thought of such niggardliness, unworthy of a Hippothadee. Next morning on leaving the hotel Titin entered a tobacconists to buy some cigarettes. As he had no change he took out his wallet and saw to his amazement that it was empty. He felt certain that Odonovitch had borrowed his last fifteen hundred francs to test the martingale. He went back to the hotel and ordered lunch in his room.

As he was sipping his coffee the telephone bell rang. It was Odonovitch who offered his apologies and confessed to borrowing the money, declaring that he would be back by four o'clock. The first sitting at trente et quarente had given undoubted proof of the excellence of his system. "It means the end of our little troubles while we are waiting for a remittance," he said, and again expressed his sorrow for having taken such a great liberty in his devotion to his master.

"My dear Odonovitch," Titin made answer with a lordly air, "another time I will leave the wallet with you so as to save you the trouble of taking the contents without my permission."

The Comte did not return until six o'clock. He was a little pale. He closed the door and fell at Titin's feet. He had lost everything.

"Don't let's speak of it," said Titin. "Gamblers always lose."

Odonovitch tried to enter into an explanation. Titin asked him not to worry himself.

"Don't you think, Comte, you're making a lot of fuss over those miserable fifteen hundred francs?"

But the Comte was in despair and Titin had much ado to console him:

"I assure you that it doesn't matter," he said.

"But I am much more guilty than you think."

At these words Titin pricked up his ears:

"What do you mean?"

"I mean that I am a wretch. I have abused your confidence and deserve to be punished. I have a bitter confession to make. But I want to tell you everything and afterwards you may do as you please with me. I do not deserve your pity, I assure you."

Titin remained silent. He lit a cigarette and waited. Under an appearance of complete indifference he strove to control the anxiety that oppressed him. What was he about to learn? He deemed the Comte capable of good and bad alike. He expected the worst.

"I came to France from our great Hippothadee with two hundred thousand francs."

Titin repressed a slight start.

"If I remember rightly, Comte," he said in a voice strained with suppressed rage, "twenty-five thousand francs were in the wallet you gave me."

"Yes, twenty-five thousand francs."

"And you ought to have handed over two hundred thousand?"

"No. . . . I ought to have handed over fifty thousand."

"What about the other hundred and fifty thousand?"

"They were to be spent for the country."

"What do you mean—'spent for the country'?"

"For propaganda purposes. You know what political necessities are. I had to back up the cause—the cause of the great Hippothadee. . . . In short, pay for publicity. Do you see?"

"Yes, I see. What then?"

"Well, I gambled with the hundred and fifty thousand and lost them."

"That was an irreparable crime," said Titin.

"No not irreparable," protested the Comte. "What has been lost on the tables can be won on the tables. I can therefore make good. I have tried to. . . ."

"Yes, I see that to-day."

"Oh, I have tried before to-day! . . . . I had fifty thousand francs belonging to you left."

"What then?"

"Well, I lost them too. . . . A run of bad luck. . . ."

"But you gave me twenty-five thousand francs."

"Oh, that's another matter. . . . You must know that I had an old jewel in my possession—an old family jewel. I sold it for thirty-five thousand francs. The jeweler robbed me as though he were a highwayman. But of course I couldn't allow you to be without money, and besides I had to take the flat for you. I had my mission— my sacred mission to fulfill. It was with this money that I bought the lease and furniture of the flat."

"But you told me you bought the furniture from a man at the club. Did you return to the club?"

"Yes. I still had the idea of winning back the money intended for propaganda purposes, nor did I forget my instructions to find a flat for you and give you fifty thousand francs. What could I do with thirty-five thousand francs I ask you? So I began to play, and I had good luck. I won a hundred and seventy-five thousand francs."

"That was a pretty good win!"

"Yes, I had the best of luck that evening. Seated next to me was a gentleman who had lost everything: 'Do you want to buy a furnished flat?' he asked. I said to myself: 'He's been sent to me by the saints.' I took him away from the tables, bundled him into a car, and we drove to the flat. I examined the furniture.

" 'It's not worth more than forty thousand francs,' I said.

" 'That's a bargain,' he returned.

"We signed an agreement and I paid him his forty thousand francs. He lost them right away as I told you. I had no end of luck that evening. Taking into account the thirty-five thousand francs received for the jewel and my winnings of one hundred and seventy-five thousand francs

I had one hundred and seventy thousand francs left after paying him. Well, I lost the lot."

"The lot!" exclaimed Titin.

"The lot," returned the Comte calmly.

"That's what you call good luck!" said Titin beginning to see the humorous side of the story.

"Great good luck. Had that gentleman not been sitting next to me, I shouldn't have bought the flat from him, and I should have lost the money received for the family jewel, whereas though I hadn't got the jewel I had the flat. Only you see I hadn't a sou left to give you so what do you think I did the next day?"

"You sold the furniture," said Titin.

"Ah, that's very clever of you. What you say is wisdom itself. I did sell it for twenty-five thousand francs."

"But it cost you forty thousand."

"Yes, but it wasn't worth more than twenty-five thousand for it was awful stuff. . . . Once again I did a good stroke of business, particularly as we mustn't forget the lease of the flat. . . . Moreover, I replaced that awful stuff with some splendid furniture, as you have seen."

"But you omitted to pay for it."

"One never pays cash down for furniture of that value. I suggested a little arrangement, but the dealer was not satisfied to take my word. So I signed bills."

"But suppose you can't pay the bills," said Titin, once more taking alarm.

"You must understand that one never pays a bill when it's presented for the first time, nor the second; that smacks too much of the small tradesman. You must get that into your head."

"But suppose they seize the furniture?"

"Let them seize it. We will get still better stuff."

"What about the twenty-five thousand francs that you received for the furniture? Did you gamble with them, too?"

"No. That confounded furniture had brought enough

bad luck to my predecessors. And then I was only too pleased to hand them over to you as representing the first smile of the new fortune that I came here to tell you about. I was a wretch to borrow those fifteen hundred francs from you. Nothing good could come from playing on the tables with them. In fact, I only got what I deserved. . . . And it's too kind of you to forgive me."

"Tell me, Comte, when you telephoned at midday what had become of the fifteen hundred francs?"

"They had become a thousand louis exactly."

"By jove," exclaimed Titin. "Why, a thousand louis is. . . ."

"Twenty thousand francs."

"That was splendid."

"No, it was not splendid. I played badly. There was a run of twenty-one on the black. I ought to have won at least a hundred thousand francs. But I was afraid of losing again. I was playing like an inexperienced youth; so during lunch at Monte Carlo I thought to myself: 'If there is a run of only ten this afternoon I shall have my revenge.' "

"But it didn't come off," said Titin.

"No. All the afternoon and part of the evening, I defended myself like a lion. But I came upon nothing but intermittances. I didn't win enough to pay the taxi which brought me back from Monte Carlo and those beggars at the hotel refused to pay the driver. It's a shame. I shall complain to my consul."

"So the taxi is still waiting?" said Titin.

"It's very good of you to trouble about these details. Let the driver go to the devil. Do you think I'm worrying about him?"

Just then there was a knock at the door and a servant entered.

"The driver refuses to go away," he told the Comte.

"Tell him I shall want him to-morrow morning at ten o'clock punctually," returned the Comte with complete indifference. "And whatever you do, don't pay him, and then I shall be certain he'll be here."

"Very good sir," said the man, and left the room.

"Thats one thing settled, you see. Everything in this life comes out all right."

"But what are you going to do to-morrow morning?"

"To-morrow is also a day, and I shall sleep over it. I have a taxi for to-morrow which is something."

Titin went to bed early. He had nothing else to do. Before he fell asleep he reflected that whatever happened, as a result of this adventure, he had learnt a great deal in that school of experience in which the Comte was a past master.

Next morning he remained late in bed and was not surprised that the Comte failed to pay him his usual morning visit. He assumed that the Comte, ashamed of his confession of the night before, would not dare to show his face again until he had received the long-expected remittance from Prince Marie Hippothadee. At eleven o'clock, after trying in vain to telephone to him, he went to the Comte's room. He learnt that he had left about ten o'clock, but nothing was known of his movements. . . .

He walked along the Avenue de Verdun stopping now and then to gaze in the shop windows. As he was about to pass the jeweler's shop at which he had bought his pearl shirt studs, he turned abruptly aside for he remembered that this man had not been paid and had shown some impatience. But he had gone only a few steps when he saw the jeweler bowing low before him.

"Are you looking for the Comte?" he cried with his most ingratiating smile. "He has just left the shop. Oh, he was only here long enough to pay my little bill. Really, M. Titin, there was no hurry. . . ."

Titin went back to the hotel. There could be no doubt about it! The Comte must have received the letter from Transylvana, and was settling the accounts before doing anything else. A good mark to the Comte for that!

Titin uttered a sigh of relief. He had lived the life of a Prince for far too short a time not to feel embarrassed by these worries with unpaid tradesmen, money lost, re-won, and lost again at the tables, and all the makeshifts which confounded the wildest imagination and from which the tables alone benefited.

Titin assumed that the Comte would appear at lunch time. Nevertheless, he thought it surprising that his strange mentor, well knowing how anxiously he was awaiting news from Mostarajevo, had not sent him word before of the receipt of the precious missive.

"He wishes to plant a surprise on me," he thought.

At two o'clock he could restrain himself no longer. He had lunched alone. Suddenly he said:

"I bet he has gone back to the trente et quarante table with the rest of the money."

He jumped into a taxi, and was driven to Monte Carlo. Here, however, no one had seen the Comte. He went back to the hotel, and met a member of the Club who told him that the Comte was in the Club at Cannes playing for high stakes. He hurried to Cannes. Here he found the Comte penniless, but he came up to him with a smile.

"Cleaned out I suppose," said Titin, boiling with rage.

"Well, yes. But I made a good beginning. . . ."

"Shut up!" growled Titin fiercely. "You don't know the sort of man I am. I'm going to show you. . . ."

"You are my Prince—my King's son. My life belongs to him."

"Very likely," said Titin, beside himself and pushing him before him with a violent gesture, "but my money doesn't belong to you."

"What money?"

"You know what I mean."

"The money from Transylvania! But it hasn't come yet. Oh, as to that money you can be easy in your mind —it is sacred. I should have brought it to you at once.

You do not yet know Odon Odonovitch, Comte de Valdar, Lord of Vistritza, Metzoras, Trikala. . . ."

"But in that case what money have you been playing with?" interrupted Titin, taken aback.

"I will explain. You gave me an idea yesterday about that furniture which hasn't been paid for. You said: 'If you don't pay for it they'll seize it.' I thought we ought not to wait until they seized it, so I sold it."

"But, wretched man, it doesn't belong to you."

"Allow me. It does belong to me. I paid for it—with bills, but I paid for it. Every business man will tell you: 'He who has credit owes nothing'—owes nothing while his credit lasts of course. Therefore I owe nothing. And you may rely on Odon Odonovitch to make his credit last, as I ventured to explain to you yesterday. . . . Therefore, I sold this furniture to another trader who, of course, robbed me. He gave me a mere trifle—sixty thousand francs for furniture which cost me one hundred and twenty thousand francs—not a penny less."

"In paper," said Titin.

"That paper bears the signature of Odon Odonvitch, Comte de Valdar, Lord of Vistritza. . . ."

"Yes, yes, Metzoras and other places. . . . Go on."

"And that signature is worth a great deal of money."

"So I perceive and so others will perceive," said Titin recovering his good humor on reflecting that the money due from Transylvania was untouched.

"I was saying that this thief bought the furniture from me for sixty thousand francs. But I made one stipulation—you will see how careful I am in business matters—namely, if within a fortnight I pay him seventy-five thousand francs, I am to remain the owner of the furniture."

"Ah yes, seventy-five thousand francs. But you lose fifteen thousand francs on the transaction."

"You don't follow me. It's the trader who will lose forty-five thousand francs, since the furniture is worth one hundred and twenty thousand."

"Yes, yes. Oh, that's very clever. A very fine transaction! Congratulations!"

"Isn't that so? Particularly as my buyer can't, during the next fortnight, touch the furniture which belongs
to me but which also remains the security of the first seller.
That may involve us in some little unpleasantness. Before the fortnight is up we shall have received the money,
and then we shall be masters of the situation."

"Yes, the masters who pay."

"We shall pay it if it suits us, for, as I have already
said, we can always let the furniture go, and buy other
and still finer furniture."

"Listen to me, Comte," said Titin. "If you don't mind,
I will attend to my own business in future."

"As you please. You are at liberty to put money into
tradesmen's pockets and ruin yourself."

"Still you made a good move this morning when you
began by paying the jeweler."

"Ah, you know that! I'm not surprised. That man
is a great gossip. I reckoned on that. I thought to
myself: 'Here's a chatterer who will say everywhere: The
Prince pays up.' So I paid him."

"But all the tradesmen will want to be paid now."

"You don't know tradesmen! If I were to take money
to them now they'd refuse it. When you can pay these
infernal tradesmen they will never accept it. It's only
when you can't pay them that they clamor for their
money."

"Do you know, Comte, you would make a wonderful
Chancellor of the Exchequer. . . . You have a real understanding of credit! But meanwhile we are once more
without a sou. What are we going to do to-night?"

"To-night we shall dine in Monte Carlo. It's some
time since you've been seen there. That has a bad effect.
I have invited a few Club friends, including the great
Tchertschanowska, the dancer, to dinner at the Hotel de
Paris. It's going to be a little gala, and will be talked

about. And we need it! When I think of those miserable flunkeys at the Palace Hotel refusing to pay the taxi— the taxi of Comte de Valdar, Lord of . . ."

"That'll do. What rot you talk! We haven't a sou."

"I am sorry. . . ."

"And so you ought to be."

"I am sorry because you no longer have faith in your servant."

The conversation was continued in the taxi which brought them back to Nice.

"Is this the taxi you engaged yesterday?"

"Yes."

"Have you paid for it?"

"No."

"Then how do you propose to pay for it when you get there? I warn you that I wont have any scandal when I'm about," said Titin frowning.

"I haven't paid for it because we are keeping it."

"Keeping it?"

"Certainly—so as to get to Monte Carlo. . . . Besides, we've arrived. Please go up to your room and dress. I shall be with you in half an hour."

Titin sprang from the taxi, and without waiting to see what would happen, hurried into the hotel and made for the elevator. Half an hour later the Comte, as good as his word, came in and spread before his astonished eyes nine thousand five hundred and twenty-five francs, fifty centimes."

"Where did you get that money from?" asked Titin, taken aback.

"Odon Odonovitch always keeps something up his sleeve. To-day the 'something' was the jeweler whom I paid this morning. I called on him just now. He almost forced into my pocket a case containing a very fine scarf pin—a diamond almost the size of a nut. I took it, without losing a moment, to the National pawnshop, and they lent me on it this money which I have brought to you."

"Odon Odonovitch you are a genius—a dangerous genius, but a genius," said Titin as he swept up the banknotes. "This money shall not go to the tables I promise you. It will enable us to live until we hear from Transylvania."

"That's what I thought. The money will be safer in your pocket than mine," returned Odonovitch with a loud laugh.

His good humor infected Titin who went off to dress. That evening they created a sensation in the great dining-room of the Hotel de Paris by a regal dinner presided over by Tchertschanowska clad in a robe of incomparable audacity. A number of well-known persons came to renew acquaintance with Titin and the Comte, and Tchertschanowska was more than gracious to her host. It was an elegant party and cost Titin a considerable sum. . . . Next day he made up his mind to live economically in spite of the Comte who assured him that after the magnificence of the night before he could give himself free rein, at least for the next fortnight, without putting down a sou. But Titin was not yet quite up to the mark.

The next week passed without further incident. But the life of a prince, in such circumstances, had no attraction for him, accustomed as he was to take the lead, and more than once he looked back with regret to the time when he was satisfied to be the chief figure in La Fourca. Had he not been restrained by his native honesty, inherited certainly from his second father, the worthy Papajeudi, who would have died rather than dishonor his signature, he would gladly have said good-bye to the luxury of hotel life now become hateful to him since he was no longer in a position to take advantage of it. And since he had to show himself so far sensible as to wait for money intended above all to satisfy his creditors, he became miserable, pale, restless. . . . The thought of Toinetta alone

buoyed him up. It was for her that he suffered; for her
that he had become a prince; for her that he still endured
the sight of Odon Odonovitch who, for his part, wore his
gloomiest air, stopped short, as he had been in his illusive
expedients.

At last the letter arrived from Transylvania. It contained a check for a considerable amount. But, as ill-luck
would have it, the money was dissipated while Titin, in an
increasing state of depression, had gone for a walk in the
country.

The letter was of course addressed to the Comte, who
had taken great care to leave Prince Marie Hippothadee
in ignorance of what had befallen the money "for propaganda purposes." All the same the Prince must have suspected something, or if he suspected nothing, thought it
wise to take certain precautions. Thus he threatened
Odonovitch with the worst penalties if he omitted to carry
out his instructions to the letter. These threats doubtless
alarmed him for he decided without further ado to win
back with the new money all that he had previously lost.

The result of his operations was soon apparent. When
Titin got back to the hotel at five o'clock that afternoon,
a taxi had arrived from Monte Carlo. The driver handed
him a letter:

"I do not deserve your pity, but if you wish to see your
servant come quickly in the taxi which is bringing you
this message. I shall be dead within an hour. I received
the letter from Transylvania, and I have again spent the
money intended for 'propaganda purposes.' "

Titin jumped into the taxi.

"If he is not dead, I will kill him," he thought.

Forty minutes later the taxi pulled up outside the
Casino. Titin observed the Comte seated with a book
before him at the open front of the Café de Paris. The
Comte rose to his feet with dignity:

"Don't touch me. I was wrong in saying that my life
belongs to you. My life does not belong to me or to you.

It belongs to Prince Marie Hippothadee. I have no wish to steal it from him. To die would be too easy. Here is the Prince's letter in which he threatens me with the direst penalties if I fail to carry out his instructions to the letter. . . . I'm going to him. To-morrow I shall take the boat to Genoa and go on to Venice. Before the end of the week I shall be in Mostarajevo."

Titin read the Prince's letter:

"I've had enough of your damned kidding," he shouted in a hoarse voice. "Come on."

He drew him to a secluded corner of the terraced gardens overlooking the sea. He had a mad longing to throw him into the harbor and told him so.

"Wait a bit, I beg you," cried the Comte. "Wait—a splendid idea has just occurred to me."

"I don't want to hear it," said Titin, "I'm sick of your splendid ideas."

"No, no, all hope is not lost," said the Comte as if speaking to himself. "And I was despairing of Providence. May the Virgin of Mostarajevo be with us and we shall be saved! Why didn't I think of it before? I ought to be ashamed of myself. . . . Tell me—it's important—have you ever played at the tables?"

"Never, and what I know of your experience as a gambler will never induce me to play."

"You make a mistake. Don't play more than once, but at least play this once. The beginner always wins. What do you risk? . . . Only to win a lot of money, because you can't lose since you have never lost !"

"How do you expect me to play without money?"

"You say you haven't any money when you have your sleeve links, shirt studs, tie pin. . . . What are they if they're not money?"

Titin took out his pearl pin, studs, and links.

"Here you are. I'll wait for you."

He was at the bottom of an abyss. He could escape from it only by a miracle. He would tempt fortune. For once, Odonovitch was right. What could Titin do, now that he was to be Titin once more, with those absurd jewels?

The Comte walked away without a word. Titin thought he might not return, but he was mistaken. Indeed, his faith in Titin's luck as a beginner outweighed every other consideration, and it suppressed his own passion for gambling. Titin made no effort to follow him. What will be will be, he thought.

In less than fifteen minutes the Comte returned with eight thousand francs. He surrendered the whole amount, and Titin went into the casino. The Comte remained on the terrace in expectation. . . . Half an hour later Titin came out. He had lost the entire sum. He seemed relieved.

"Now it's all over. You will take the boat to-morrow, and don't let me ever see you again," he said; and with a start: "Of course you've got your return ticket?"

"No," answered the Comte helplessly, unable to understand why Titin had lost. "But be easy in your mind I will get one."

"Have you got your passage money?"

The Comte shrugged his shoulders. This incredible stroke of fate had made him lose all sense of respect.

"But how will you manage to take the boat?"

"I shall get my viaticum," returned the Comte, at last recovering from a fit of despondency unworthy of his birth and position.

"What do you mean by viaticum?"

"It's the amount allowed by the management to persons who have lost their all, to enable them to return home. May I suggest another idea to you?"

"You want to gamble with the viaticum?"

"Oh no, that's impossible. Once I have received the viaticum it's good-bye to the casino. You are not allowed to enter it again. But what I want to propose is—you take your viaticum and come with me."

"No—you must return alone. . . . That would be quite outside the Prince's instructions, and I have business here. Go and get your viaticum."

When the Comte had obtained it, he of course suggested a gamble with the money.

"But I thought you weren't allowed to gamble with it?"

"No, I am not allowed to, but I can give it to you and you can build up our fortunes again."

"Hand it over," said Titin.

He put the money into his pocket, and did not return it to the Comte until next morning on the boat. There was a touching farewell. But Titin was not at ease until the boat was but a wisp of smoke on the horizon. Soon it was lost to sight altogether, and after that Titin disappeared too.

CHAPTER XVI

WHEN it was established that Comte Valdar and Titin
had disappeared without troubling about their very considerable debts, a great outcry arose along the coast from
Antibes Point to Cape Martin. Hotel and restaurant-
keepers, tailors, hosiers, bootmakers, and other tradesmen began once more to lift up their voices. But the
loudest note was struck by the victimized jewelers who
strewed the battlefield, over which Odon Odonovitch had
swept without a scruple of remorse or pity.

The little that we have related of his exploits was but
a minor incident in the great strategic operation that he
carried through successfully with the help of his faithful
Lombards—such is the name in Transylvania of the
admirable institution commonly called the National pawnshop—to enable him to maintain his rank.

Soon furniture dealers entered the fray as well as
buyers and sellers of old rubbish, pictures, engravings and
pottery, who had competed one with another to decorate
the rooms and walls of a flat in which no one had lived,
and to which a new occupant, on paper, appeared to have
succeeded daily, only to enable Odonovitch and Titin,
through the credit they were able to obtain because they
were its tenants, to scour all the hotels. . . .

Finally, as the one security which they left behind them
—the one definite souvenir of their passage—was furniture which each one, with duly authenticated legal documents, claimed to be the preferential owner, there followed

195

a veritable mobilization of the litigious tribe: barristers, solicitors, prosecutors, bailiffs, and every other legal quill-driver; and these were practically the only people to reap any advantage from the intricate situation except M. Hyacinthe Supia, who as will be seen presently, was not the man to leave his share to anyone.

The stir that rose over the matter reflected no credit on Titin. Many of his friends were sorry for him, but no one grieved more than Mlle. Agagnosc. She wept in secret when she learnt of his escapades. She was aware of the banquets at which a famous dancer and some doubt-ful characters were present. Before others, Antoinette would indignantly repel the calumny, and often silenced Hippothadee. But he never grew weary of returning to the charge.

After the incident of the abortive marriage and Antoi-nette's home-coming and revolt, the "tyrant" said to Hippothadee:

"Have patience. The marraige is only postponed. Un-less you are a regular ass, you will know how to disgust her with Titin."

Hippothadee thought only how to carry out Supia's wishes, all the more so as circumstances had come so opportunely to his aid. The scandal had reached its cul-minating point. Titin dared not show himself. In the Courts, Mr. Lawyer spoke of him as a common sharper. It seemed as if the unhappy Toinette alone defended him now that he was stripped of all his success. Hardigras himself seemed to have deserted him.

"What did you expect?" said Hippothadee. "The poor fellow lost his head. A swindler whom I know well. He has done me a lot of harm, my brother's willing tool, Odon Odonovitch, said to him: 'You are a prince. You might hope for anything. Meantime you need deny yourself nothing.' Titin, who is not used to society, believed or pretended to believe this fable, but it was Odonovitch who reaped the advantage and got what he wanted for him-

self. . . . All the same they were made to understand each
other, these fine fellows, and Titin never had any schooling—we must do him the justice to say that. All in a
moment he forgot everything. After the 'girls from
Fourca' came dancing stars, and, never fear, he is less to
be pitied than you think. For he will find consolation in
La Fourca, until he makes his appearance again in our
hotels. In short—he bids far to succeed as a crook."

Another thing that "succeeded" and Hippothadee
scarcely expected, was a sharp slap in the face with
which Toinette, who had not interrupted him, punctuated
the end of his last sentence. The conversation had taken
place after lunch, when coffee and liquors were served,
in the Supia's small dining-room, in the presence of Mme.
Supia, simpering and affected, her daughter full of expectation now that her rival had abandoned the prince, and
poor little Toinetta seated huddled in an arm-chair where
she had entrenched herself in her dejection.

It was from this spot that the unexpected and startling
answer had come. M. Supia was in his office. He hurried
in, attracted by the tumult, fearing lest some injury had
befallen his pledge which was daily becoming more valuable
to him.

The Prince held his hand to his cheek and while Thélese
and Caroline were speechless with indignation, Toinette
gave him a piece of her mind. To stop her would have
been no easy matter. For a full ten minutes she embroidered the theme of Titin's honesty, declaring that whatever troubles had befallen him were due to his having been
far too good-natured to a foreign nobleman of doubtful
antecedents from the same country as Vladimar, engaged
by him and the Supia family to bring disgrace to a youth
who was the soul of honor: "But Titin had been through
worse things. He would know how to get out of this
scrape too. As for you, Prince, you are too silly."

The Prince forgot the blow and M. Supia was almost
ready to shout his admiration. . . . So that was the

story she had made up—they had sent for Odon Odonovitch from the depths of Transylvania in order to bring
disgrace on Titin! Entirely taken aback by this instance
of feminine logic, Hippothadee bowed and withdrew.
Supia joined him outside.

"The little thing goes it pretty strong," he said.

"Yes, I thought she had blinded me in one eye."

"I wasn't speaking of that but of this nonsense about
Odonovitch. We should never have thought of it. Oh,
these young girls! They always get the better of us."

"Yes, of course."

"And you couldn't find a word to say."

"That's because my answer was not ready. Wait till I
see you again, M. Supia."

His answer came several days later and it was a pretty
formidable one. . . . It came one golden afternoon, the
herald of approaching spring, at the cool hour when the
throng was returning from the races and the sun already
low in the horizon seemed to be leaving with regret this
Baie des Anges which displayed the glories of Nice. . . .

Facing the road, over which motor cars and carriages
from the race course crowded in a procession, stood "Le
Père la Bique," an inn famous for its cuisine and wines,
and above all for its view. They had brought Antoinette
here on the terrace so that she might "see".

See what? . . . The procession of cars and carriages,
of course. They had to divert her thoughts. Never had
they been so kind to her. And yet Hippothadee had too
quickly forgiven the blow, Thélise was too smiling, Caroline was too sad, and the "tyrant" rubbed his hands too
often not to arouse her suspicions.

She left her glass of port untouched. Hippothadee
was talking unceasingly. Irritated by his flow of words,
Toinetta looked the other way and this is what she saw:
a bungalow amid flowers—a small crimson cottage surrounded by cactus and carob and aloe and mastic trees,
cut off from the road by a thick, high hedge of rushes.

To reach the garden gate it was necessary to clear the
hedge, but behind the gate and the rushes complete seclusion reigned. It was an ideal place for lovers' assigna-
tions. . . . Hippothadee, who seemed to know it and
explained all about it to M. Supia, though he had not
been asked, spoke in such tones as to be overheard by
Antoinette, who shrugged her shoulders, considering the
Prince's comments unseemly.

She was about to turn her eyes from this spot, which
no longer interested her, when a feminine form, wrapped in
a large fringed shawl, appeared in the garden. When she
reached the garden she let the shawl slip off, and a handsome girl of the people clad in her best clothes was revealed. Antoinette saw only her back. She was a tall,
well-proportioned girl and walked briskly with a graceful
stride. She seemed to be somewhat uneasy; but her confusion was not without its charm. Before she went into
the crimson cottage she turned her head—a beautiful dark
head encircled by two black bands, and her dark eyes
gleamed with a somewhat timorous light.

"Nathalie!"

Antoinette could not restrain the slight cry that rose
to her lips as she recognized one of her old playmates
from La Fourca—Nathalie Babazouk, Giaousé's wife. . . .
She now understood why she had been brought there.
And she clung to the hope that these wretched people
were mistaken. Nathalie might have an assignation but
not with Titin, who had always spurned her. That was
well-known in La Fourca and had aroused laughter.
Toinetta was no fool, and grasped at once that she had
been brought there to see Titin in some compromising
situation. But she loved him and prayed that some startling sequel might give Hippothadee the lie.

She turned her back to hide her face from them. . . .
Titin came into view. It was almost dark. He slipped
through the rushes, opened the gate and entered the garden. He was dressed as she was wont to see him in

La Fourca—it was the old Titin. He had the calm step and resolute mien characteristic of him. He crossed the garden but before he reached the cottage, Nathalie's pale face appeared at the door and smilingly greeted him. He bent forward to kiss her. The door closed after them. . . .

A slight moan and Toinetta tottered and fainted. Hippothadee lifted hir in his arms.

"Quick, home," he said.

They drove home. Now she was theirs.

CHAPTER XVII

LOVERS' MEETINGS

WHILE these scenes were taking place at "Le Père la Bique," certain events were happening not far away in an inn whose rustic pergola rose above a path that, skirting the garden in which the crimson cottage stood, intersected at right angles the road from the race course and further along branched into the main road.

From this lodge only the surroundings of the crimson cottage could be seen; nevertheless, from a slightly higher point of the pergola the eye could take in that part of the garden in front of the cottage which could be observed in its entirety from the terraces of "Le Père la Bique."

In this part of the pergola Giaousé and two friends, Norê the smith and Tulip—his real name was Felix Bonifasse—chief clerk to M. Propser Clappa, solicitor in La Fourca, were seated at table with a bottle of white wine before them. Tulip was a great friend of Giaousé's and seemed to have as much admiration for him as Giaousé had for Titin.

He was a curious person and never lost an opportunity to break away from his quill driving. He had a fondness for the "inn" but was clumsy in all physical exercise, thin and long of limb. His skinny neck counterbalanced a huge purple head, hence his nickname of Tulip. In spite of his freaks his employer, M. Clappa, could not make up his mind to get rid of him, for he was an adept at drawing up legal documents, knew a great deal about most people, and, moreover, was discreet. He had begun life as junior clerk to a sheriff's officer in Torre les Tourettes,

201

the town whose ancient walls stood out so picturesquely on the crest of the rocks dominating the Gorges du Loup.

Time was when there was good feeling between the people of Torre les Tourettes and La Fourca. But that friendship, since, had changed to enmity. As it is ancient history and also forms part of our story, it will be as well to say a word about it. In this way we may know something of the manners of these people.

After a game of bowls, which ended in a quarrel, the young men of Torre les Tourettes swore to carry off the May tree which the people of La Fourca were in the habit of planting every year in the square facing St. Helene Church. Forewarned, the young men of La Fourca took up their positions in the cypress and olive trees surrounding the church, and when the assailants came up at night time received them with a shower of stones. Those who persisted in the attempt to tear up the tree were attacked even with knives. One youth, Toton Robin, fell on the battlefield and for a week his life was despaired of.

Smarting under their failure, the young men of Torre les Tourettes returned the following year and succeeded in carrying off the May tree which they planted before their own church. In view of this bold stroke, after evening service on the following Sunday, the pluckiest young men of La Fourca—Toton Robin, Jerome Brocard, Pierre Antoine, and his brother Barthelemy, the two Raybouts, and Titin, then but a boy, headed by their fife and drum band, and supported by well-nigh all the able-bodied population of La Fourca, men, women, and children with Mme Bibi and her two goats bringing up the rear—carried off the May tree at Torre in sight of the people who dared not offer resistance, and marched back in triumph to St. Helene Church, where they sang and danced round their trophy.

That was only the beginning. Three young girls— Thérésia, Félicita, and Madalon—allowed themselves the following year to be lured by three young men of Torre

to leave La Fourca. Their rivals swore to be revenged
for the affront. Five years sped by during which there
was no mean trick which the young men of either side did
not play on the other. Meantime, Titin, increased in
strength and courage, put an end to the feud by a striking
feat.

One féte day in La Fourca twenty-five young men of
Torre les Tourettes appeared at the church door during
the evening service and shouted their insults. Chased by
the infuriated people they took to their heels. But, to
get back to Torre they had to cross a narrow bridge made
up of a few planks thrown across the stream.

They reached the bridge, one after the other, to discover
on the opposite side Titin, who had made a circuit and
was waiting for them, crouching behind an olive tree. Titin
was then fourteen years of age. As each one came up and
set foot upon the plank, he sent him spinning into the
current. One youth, however, named Cauvin, the strongest of the lot, managed to lay hold of him. And in the
scramble they fell into the stream. Here they had other
things to do than to continue the fight. The stream,
swollen by the melting snow, was swift and strong. They
had to set about saving the others, in danger of drowning.

Titin showed as much courage and energy in rescuing
the enemy as he had shown in precipitating them into the
stream. Cauvin and he did wonders. They were helped,
moreover, by some of the La Fourca people who had followed them. Both sides had reason to congratulate themselves; for, on that evening, M. Arthur, the mayor
of Torre, an honest, sensible man, solemnly proclaimed
peace between the two factions—a peace which was celebrated during the following week by sundry banquets.

But human nature is such that we remember humilia-
tions inflicted upon us much longer than the generosity
of those who get the better of us. This generosity, indeed,
is often in itself as humiliating as a defeat; hence many
of those whom Titin had "flung over the bridge," cher-

ished a grudge against him; especially as their girl friends continued to jeer at them for allowing themselves to be put to shame by a youth of fourteen.

These facts are of some consequence because they will enable the reader to understand many things which are about to happen, and particularly the unholy joy with which some of the Torre people heard of Titin's discomfiture.

They lost no opportunity now of making game of "Prince" Titin in the inns in La Fourca. Nothing worse occurred than the exchange of a few blows. Manners had grown somewhat milder with the flight of time. But people in La Fourca, however, were greatly nettled because Titin failed to show himself, putting them in a false position when it came to defend him. . . .

As we have said, Giaousé Babazouk, Tulip, and Toton Robin, all great friends of Titin, were seated at a table in the pergola of the inn not far from "Le Pére la Bique." Presently four young men from Torre, François, and Basil Barraja, Sixte Pastorelle, and an ugly youth known only by the name of Bolacion, came and sat at a table in the court lower down. Bolacion was no favorite on account of his quarrelsome temper and rancorous tongue. As soon as he caught sight of Giaousé and the others he asked after Titin, pretending to be greatly interested in his misfortunes.

"Leave Titin alone," said Toton Robin, the smith. "He's not worrying about your health. You mind your own business."

Bolacion grinned, mumbling a few offensive remarks.

"They're getting at me," growled Robin, rising to his feet. But Giaousé and Tulip held him back.

"Stay where you are. Don't answer them," cried Tulip.

"And whatever you do, don't go for them," added Giaousé, sinking his voice.

"I don't understand you," protested Robin, throwing off their hold. "Don't you see they're kidding us?"

"Yes, you and Titin and all La Fourca into the bargain," shouted Barraja, standing up in his turn.

Both parties were now on their feet, as if they were
ready to exchange blows. Tulip, in a panic, threw himself
between them, thrusting them apart with the full length
of his enormous arms. At the same time he tried to make
them listen to reason.

"Shut up, Tulip," said Giaousé in a harsh voice. "Let
'em come. They want to see Titin. I'll show them Titin."

"Hang it, there's something in that," said Tulip.
"Gentlemen, we invite you to join us. Giaousé will stand
drinks."

"Lord, what am I doing here?" cried Robin, raging
still, "I'm not dotty. I can't make it out."

"You will soon," said Tulip.

"Yes, and pretty quickly," added Giaousé in an undertone. "Just take a look in 'Le Pére la Bique' garden."

They stood on tip-toe and Toton Robin was as amazed
as the newcomers.

"Well, unless I'm mistaken that's Nathalie," said
Bolacion.

"Yes," said Giaousé, whom Tulip watched lest he should
lose his temper. "That's Nathalie, my wife."

She had, in fact, just come and, as we have said, she
entered the crimson house.

"Good Lord, I can't make it out either," said Toton
Robin.

"Have patience," muttered Tulip.

The others sat round them in silence. They exchanged
glances and watched Giaousé pour himself out a drink.
His hand trembled.

"I told you you would see Titin. I keep my word as
we all do in La Fourca. Besides, I said you would see my
wife and I hope you won't forget it."

"There was no need to ask these Torre people to join
us and see that," said Robin with puckered brows, for he
was beginning to understand.

"The more the merrier," grinned Giaousé. "Here's to you all, and if ever your dear wife deceives you, I hope you'll take it as calmly as I do."

"Poor fellow, he used not to be like this," said Pastorelle.

"It's the calm that precedes the storm," said Bolacion.

An awkward silence ensued for fully ten minutes while they waited the course of events. Then Tulip, who was keeping an eye on the garden, said in an undertone:

"Look out, here he is!"

They saw Titin cross the garden and enter the crimson house as though it belonged to him. No one spoke. Giaousé's face was not a pleasant sight to see.

"I say Tulip," he cried in a hoarse voice, "we must now fetch the Commissary of police."

"I'll go," said Tulip, springing up. "I won't be long. He has already been notified. Don't any of you leave Giaousé in case he does anything idiotic."

"Rely on us," returned Bolacion. "It will be better for the thing to be arranged properly. Titin won't be able to get out of it. He's caught this time, the rat."

"I'm disgusted with it all," said Robin. "So long." And he rose to go.

"Stop him," cried Tulip, already at the door. "It's as likely as not he'll warn Titin."

"Damn it all," said Robin clenching his fists, "you clear out and call your Commissary of police as he's expecting you. You don't know me. I never interfere in what doesn't concern me. You are no man, Giaousé."

"No, all my courage is gone," said Giaousé.

"Because of a woman," sneered the smith, shrugging his shoulders. "If I were in your place, with your big fists, I'd have punched his head long ago."

"No, I don't care a rap about Nathalie, but as for Titin. . . ."

"He's quite right," broke in Bolacion. "Its Titin, the beast."

"No one asked for your opinion," said Giaousé.

Tulip took a taxi. Robin went off without looking round. He lighted his pipe and said aloud:

"I see what is happening, of course. But I don't understand Titin. No one understands him now. Still there's no occasion for me to go and drown myself. Besides, the damp brings on rheumatism. All the same it's a nice disappointment for La Fourca to see him spoil such fine work."

Meantime Nathalie, the first to come, had entered the pavilion. She was seeing it for the first time and her heart throbbed loudly. She opened a door and reddened when she saw a bed in the middle of the room, standing between two rugs on a floor gleaming like a mirror. There was no lack of mirrors; they were all around. On a small table lay a china jug containing a large bunch of roses. . . . She had a vision of luxury, and her only regret was that the broken statue, ornamenting the mantelpiece between two large lamps with ground grass globes, had not been replaced in this room so tastefully furnished. It was the statue of a nude woman with the two arms missing!

Continuing her inspection, she opened a door and entered a dressing-room leading out of the bed-room. . . . She returned to the passage and, opening another door, found herself in a dining and drawing-room combined. On the table bearing a figured white cloth, violets and roses lay in artistic and mathematical simplicity, and there were two dainty covers with silver forks and silver-gilt knives. The table might have suggested a little light refreshment for dolls, had not the flasks of wine, the bucket in which champagne was being iced, and a magnificent basket of fruit showed by their presence that the kind of visitors were expected who are not in the habit of sustaining themselves on idle talk.

The whole place was so elegant and pointed to so much delicacy of taste that Nathalie was greatly affected and clapped her hands. But there was no mirror in the room, and she returned to the bed-room where she could see herself from head to foot. She had taken off her shawl. Her woollen dress revealed the graceful lines of her figure. But what she most admired was her nigger silk stockings and patent leather shoes. She could not resist silk stockings, and she had spent her housekeeping savings for these and her little high-heeled shoes. . . . She passed a lip stick over her lips and powdered her face and also her somewhat straight but rather squat nose, which she feared might be shiny. Thus adorned she returned to the dining-room, carefully closing the bed-room door. . . .

She had not been in the room more than twenty minutes and yet it seemed an hour. . . . She was restless, sat down, stood up, sat down again. She tried to restrain herself, to calm her nerves; she held her head in her hands. She had been hoping for that moment, but he kept her waiting so long that she was losing patience. She was thirsty but would not drink. She would wait as long as she could. She drew a letter from her bodice and read for the hundredth time:

"If you still wish to see Hardigras be at 'Le Père la Bique' to-morrow afternoon a little before five o'clock. You will only have to go into the crimson cottage."

It was signed "Hardigras" and written in capital letters. Hardigras seemed never to write in anything but capital letters. She folded the letter and replaced it in her bodice. Suddenly she uttered a stifled cry. It was he. He was crossing the garden.

She ran to the door, and then, before opening it, stopped to take breath. When Titin stood before her no word came to her lips. She lifted her face to him. He kissed her. He kissed her quietly on the cheek and closed the door.

"Is Giaousé here?" he asked.

"No—he is not here," she stammered.

She no longer knew what she was saying nor assuredly

did he to ask such a question. He went into the dining-room.

"It's dark here, why haven't you put on a light?"

He strode over to a table which bore two candlesticks. He lighted one candle, then turned to her:

"Is he coming?"

"Oh my Titin! . . ."

She ran into his arms. Amazed, he roughly thrust her aside.

"Here, none of that, you know."

She had fallen upon a sofa and her head had struck the wall; but she uttered no cry. She remained motionless, staring at him wild-eyed, open-mouthed like an idiot. Indeed, she was perhaps in danger of becoming an idiot. Titin did not even look at her. He noticed the preparations of the little supper—flowers, fruit, champagne. He turned quickly to her:

"It is a regular spread. Will you tell me what it all means?"

With an effort she drew the letter from her bodice and held it out to him. He took it and read with a look of mingled astonishment and rage.

"Who gave you this?" he demanded.

She was still leaning against the wall with stiffened limbs; she had not moved her head.

"I found it yesterday under my door in La Fourca."

He hardly recognized her voice; it was something remote, impersonal. His attention was completely absorbed in the letter he still held in his hand, under the light of the candle.

"Wasn't Giaousé at La Fourca?" he asked, in increasingly harsh tones.

"No, Giaousé hasn't been in La Fourca for a week."

"Where is he?"

"You know as well as I do. He told me he was going to Nice, with Tulip, on your business."

"And you believed I was asking you to meet me here?"

"Yes."

"Bad luck to you!"

She did not stir. He crumpled the letter in a fury, laughing grimly.

"Did you order all these things?" he asked, pointing to the table.

"No."

"Who ordered them?"

She did not answer. But he persisted in shouting: "Who? Who?" as if she knew something about it. At last he fumbled in his pocket-book, drew out a letter, and read it aloud:

"My dear Titin,
Your affairs are improving. I have seen many of those trades-men. The Consul has persuaded them to say what they want. They are willing to hold their hands and wait a few months longer if someone will come forward as security for you. I think I have got a man but he wishes the matter kept secret for reasons which I will explain to you. Be at 'Le Père la Bique' at five o'clock to-morrow. Go straight into the crimson cottage. I shall be there with the man in question. I hope matters will be arranged satisfactorily. I am tired of running about like a dog. Yours, G."

Titin replaced the letter in his pocket-book, putting the letter from Hardigras with it.

"Do you understand now why I am here? . . . Clear out! . . . Giaousé is on his way here. . . . Hang it all, clear out at once."

She collapsed as Toinetta had done a few minutes before. Titin darted towards her. He wanted to get rid of her; but she lay in his arms like a dead thing. Her ice-cold face fell against his cheek; and now he felt sorry for her. She had had no hand in this infamous snare. Indeed, she was to be pitied. Besides, this swoon frightened him.

"Nathalie, my dear Nathalie, forgive me. Unless you pull yourself together we are both done for. . . ." He murmured soft words like a brother. . . . And then he forgot everything—forgot the terrible thing hanging over his head—everything but this lifeless form, everything but this unhappy woman who had always loved him but to whom he had never spoken a word of love.

"Nathalie . . . my dear Nathalie."

Then she opened her eyes—eyes in which distraction dwelt. . . . And a hoarse sob broke in her throat, a long dull cry in which she seemed at last to find relief for her grief. And tears came. She was saved. She heaved a deep breath and, weeping, she bewailed her fate like a child.

He laid her upon the sofa, placed her head upon the pillow, dipped a table napkin into a glass of water, and bathed her temples.

"Thank you, Titin," she said, "I'll get away. I'm sorry."

"No, you must not go until you are yourself again," he said kindly.

"But he is on his way—they are coming here."

"Well, let them come, and all this will have to be cleared up. We must know what it all means."

"You don't know Giaousé. He is meek enough when you are about, but he can be a terror."

"You have nothing to be afraid of, that's all I can say."

"But you—you, Titin. There is danger for you."

"Not a bit of it," returned Titin, shrugging his shoulders.

"It's a bad lookout for you. You don't know him. And to think that I should be telling you that. You will have to bear the weight of the scandal," she said, adding courageously: "Don't forget you wish to marry Toinetta."

Titin started up, turning very pale. He saw the abyss before him.

"You see yourself, you must get away," she went on. "Go now. You can slip out at the back and I'll get out on to the road. If they see me, it can't be helped. Don't worry about me."

"Too late."

The sound of footsteps, indeed, could be heard in the garden.

"Go out through the backdoor—the backdoor," she cried, trying to drag him away.

"No, with a snare like this every precaution must have been taken. I don't intend to be seen running away. Whatever happens, I shall never forget what you said just now. If I were not in love with Toinetta, it would be with you, Nathalie."

"Unfortunately, I'm not worth it. But thanks all the same, Titin."

A door in the passage opened.

"Don't budge," said Titin, recovering his self-possession. "Stay where you are. Why are you wiping your eyes? You have very good reason for crying."

A loud rap came at the door on the other side: "Open in the name of the law!"

A door was opened and closed again. Titin himself opened the door of the room in which Nathalie and he were. The local Commissary of police, M. Galavard, bowed and pointed to his official sash. After him came Babazouk, Tulip, Sixte Pastorelle, and Bolacion. Titin took stock of them all, unmoved.

"Gentlemen, come in," he said. "You will perhaps be good enough to explain what we are doing here!"

The Commissary cast an eye around him, observed the order which prevailed in the room, and turning to Giaousé dissembling himself somewhat furtively behind him, said under his breath:

"In my opinion you were in too much of a hurry," and addressing Nathalie: "Madame, I was asked by your husband, Giaousé, otherwise Babazouk, to verify your presence here."

"Well, have you verified it?" said Titin, in a harsh voice.

"You are M. Titin, I presume?"

"Le Bastardon," added Titin.

"Alias Hardigras," broke in Bolacion, with a malicious laugh.

Titin turned violently to him:

"Who asked you to speak? Why is this man here, monsieur?"

"The husband brought him with the others."

"Come here, Giaousé," burst out Titin. "Are you bent on everyone knowing that your wife has been unfaithful to you? Well, it will have to be some other time, old man, for you have jolly well deserved it. No woman has ever come between us, you old fool—not even your wife. Now, Giaousé, look me in the face. I came here expecting to meet you, I assure you. . . ."

"What was she doing here?" mumbled Giaousé, casting a stealthy look at Nathalie.

"She was crying—crying because she feared the worst from your spitefulness and thought it was you who planned this snare in your own peculiar way. But we'll have the thing out, never fear, here and now, before these gentlemen."

"My presence is no longer required," said the Commissary.

"One moment, monsieur, we're going to have this out before you and these gentlemen. I insist on it. Yes, Giaousé, our friendship is broken since you believed I had played you false with Nathalie and arranged this trip."

"Why is she here?" asked Giaousé roughly, without looking at Titin.

"Well, you know why I, personally, am here. . . . Read this letter, M. Galavard."

The Commissary read the letter signed Giaousé, which Titin handed to him.

"Did you write this letter?" he asked Giaousé.

"Never," he returned, with a look of blank amazement. "Someone has been imitating my handwriting. I didn't write it."

The commissary returned the letter to Titin, who put it into his pocket, shrugging his shoulders.

"That remains to be seen," he said.

"And now, Madame," went on M. Galavard, "will you tell us why you are here? Forgive me if I question you as my task is over, but as M. Titin has invited me to do so, I may possibly be useful to you in unraveling the mystery."

"Madame came here through curiosity," said Titin. "For some time she has been wanting to meet Hardigras. Hardigras must have known that, for he sent her this note." And he placed before Galavard the note addressed to her. "Imagine her surprise," he went on, "when instead of seeing Hardigras she saw me come in. . . ."

"Look here, Titin," said M. Galavard, "Giaousé is right. Anyone in his place would want to know who was making game of him. . . . Did you write this note signed Hardigras?"

"But I am not Hardigras."

"Allow me to press the point: do you positively assert that you did not write this note?"

"I swear it. You forget that I received a letter from Giaousé making an appointment with me here. Why should I send a note signed Hardigras, inviting his wife to come here?"

"You're right, it's not very likely," returned Galavard, returning the note to Titin.

"You hear what the Commissary says, Giaousé. . . . Come, do say something. I am ready to believe you when you say you did not write this letter making an appointment to meet me here, but we must know who did write it. Why did you come here? Who asked you to come?"

"I, too, received a note," said Giaousé, taking from his pocket a very dirty and crumpled piece of paper, which contained a warning of the meeting at "Le Pére la Bique" between Nathalie and Titin. The three of them examined the letter, which, of course, was anonymous.

"Why, this writing is exactly like the writing in the letter from Giaousé. Don't you think, monsieur, that it looks as if the letters to Giaousé and me were written by the same person?"

"That would explain everything," returned the Commissary, only too willing to settle matters. "You have both been the victims of some practical joker."

Titin turned to Giaousé, silent and head bent down like a beast of burden.

"Come, I say, stir yourself. You are not going to stand there like a block of wood."

"What I can't get out of my mind is that she came here with some object. It is possible that someone has been having a game with us, but she acted as if she believed the letter was genuine. She put on her best clothes. There's champagne on the table. If all these preparations are not very suspicious my name's not Giaousé. No, I tell you I can't live with that woman again."

"You're right. I'm going," said Nathalie.

"You hear what she says, monsieur. That gives me a reason for divorce."

Titin stopped Nathalie by a gesture.

"Giaousé, you mustn't do that. You'll go back home with Nathalie, or our friendship is over for good. I have always treated you as a brother and neither Nathalie nor I have ever played you false."

A silence ensued and Titin went on:

"Give and take—do you want to continue friends with me?"

"You know I have always done what you wanted, Titin. It will be the same thing to-day—as usual."

"Shake hands on it, Giaousé."

But Giaousé showed no enthusiasm.

"Hang it all, it's all very well for you," he said. "Come on, Nathalie."

"God bless you. Everything is settled," said the Commissary, taking his leave.

Nathalie began to cry again before she went off with Giaousé, who held her by the wrist.

"Ah, Titin, you should have let me go away alone. . . . You will see . . ."

"I shall be in La Fourca to-morrow. In future you and I, Nathalie, are sworn friends through thick and thin," and turning to the others: "Go back to La Fourca with them. Giaousé is still nursing a grudge against her.

But I know him—it will blow over. Cheer him up, and tell him I am very fond of him, and persuade Nathalie to be nice to him."

"He is very miserable. You would do well to come with us," said Sixte.

"I don't think so. Titin is right. We must wait a bit," said Tulip.

"As for you, I've seen enough of you," said Titin, turning to Bolacion. "Once for all: take it from me, I've no use for blear-eyed people."

"Titin, you have always disliked me without cause," said Bolacion, ignoring the insult. "I have often said to Giaousé: If Titin disliked me less we should get on together. He would have no better friend than me."

"I don't dislike you. To me you are of no more account than a slug," retorted Titin. "Beat it—that's my advice."

"Damn it, I don't know who played that trick on you to-day," growled Bolacion, clenching his fists, "but I look upon him as a friend. . . . Meanwhile our time here has not been entirely wasted."

So saying, he sat down without further ado before the good things at the table. The others, who had gradually left the pergola, followed his example and were soon drinking to the reconcilation between Titin and Giaousé. . . .

Titin had already left. He called at "Le Pére la Bique."

"They are drinking my health over there," he said. "I will pay. You can trust me?"

"Yes, I can trust you with a signature like this."

The proprietor drew out a letter, and Titin knew who had ordered this strange "love feast." But he turned pale as his eyes fell once more upon the signature of— Hardigras!

CHAPTER XVIII

WHEN Antoinette recovered consciousness from her swoon, she found herself in her own room at home. M. and Mme. Supia were lavish in their attentions. When she could speak she asked for Prince Hippothadee. Mme. Supia told her that he was in the next room, greatly pained by what had happened. . . .

"Such a delightful drive and so pleasantly begun! Had the Prince suspected . . ."

"It's all for the best," interrupted M. Supia. "As luck would have it Antoinette was definitely enlightened as to the infamous habits of that youth. Let us hope she has been cured of him once for all."

"I want to see Prince Hippothadee," said Antoinette.

"But, my dear, you will see him to-morrow. It will be as well for you to have a rest to-night."

"No, I want to see him at once, in your presence."

"I'll go and fetch him," said M. Supia. "We must not upset her."

A few minutes later the Prince entered the room. Toinetta looked extremely pale against the pillow, but very pretty. Her eyes shone with a feverish light, and her hand lay listlessly on the coverlet as though she had not the strength to move it. The Prince bent a knee and raised this thing of stone to his lips.

"Will you ever forgive me?"

"No, never," she said in a harsh, clear voice, as cutting as a knife. "Neither you nor anyone who was with you. I asked you to come here to tell you that there can never be anything but enmity and contempt between you and me. Do you understand?"

"But, mademoiselle . . ." stammered the Prince.

"You need not answer. It's no use. I asked to see you not only to tell you this, but to say that I will be your wife."

"Ah . . . Antoinette!"

"I won't allow you to call me Antoinette. Don't say anything. I am willing to be your wife as soon as possible. See to that. Don't lose any time. You may now go."

Hippothadee stood up somewhat embarrassed. Doubtless he had foreseen this solution, and doubtless he had worked for it. But he had not expected such an expeditious result. Nor had he considered the manner in which she had delivered her conclusion to him. The whole position was summed up in the one sentence: She would marry him, but she despised him.

Assuredly there is no such thing as perfect happiness in this world. He would have liked to say something, but the words would not come. The only possible answer in the circumstances to avenge the insult to the Hippothadees from this little nobody in love with a vagabond would be words of farewell. But he could not bring himself to utter those words—it was impossible for many reasons. Thus he was content to say "good-bye" as he turned on his heel with figure erect—the one thing of which he still had reason to be proud. M. Supia saved the situation by escorting him out, saying aloud:

"You were quite right not to take offense. Antoinette is suffering from nerves this evening. Besides, though she may despise you, I think highly of you."

Thélise in the bedroom was more pleased than she could say, by the turn of events. The marriage would bring the Prince and herself together. Suddenly she was startled by the manner in which Toinetta stared at her, and she escaped from the room before Toinetta could utter a word.

Left alone at last, Toinetta let her head fall back upon the pillow. Stifling her sobs, she tried to keep back the tears. . . . Next morning the first thing she did was to return, unopened, a letter from Titin. In the small drawing-room she met Caroline, red-eyed.

"You have been crying because you are not going to marry the Prince. I have been crying because I am going to marry him. But never fear, I will keep him for you. I dislike him as much as you love him. Are you satisfied?"

"Then why are you marrying him?"

"Ask your father. He knows better than I do. I know only one thing—I want to go away and never see you again."

Caroline reflected for some time over her cousin's words and drew from them a momentary consolation, which helped to dry her tears. Before the day was over the whole town learnt that Prince Hippothadee was to marry Mlle. Agagnosc. The broken engagement had been renewed at the express wish of Toinetta herself. The general feeling of amazement soon changed to consternation; for, the town had resumed its interest in Titin. The steps taken by the Transylvanian consul to suppress the scandal brought about by Comte Valdar's financial eccentricities, had convincingly enlightened the parties interested, making clear that Titin was less his partner than his victim. And the rumors about the Son of Carnival's high descent were thereby in a measure confirmed. And though Titin failed to show himself, they ventured once more to mention his name, joining with it that of Hardigras. He had always been the fascinating presentment in which they saw themselves, embodying the high spirits, the love of feasting, the brazen swagger of the Midi—in a word the lightness of heart and whimsical humor without which life would indeed be dull. The vulnerable point in Titin's armor was that he was in love in earnest, poor fellow.

They all knew it. It was not for nothing that Hardigras had stopped Antoinette's wedding. They felt certain that now he would take up, on his own account, the matter where he had left it. And now Antoinette, ignoring Titin,

had given her hand to the Prince. There was amazement
in the town. They failed to understand her.

What would happen when Hardigras learnt a thing
like that? To this question which each one asked himself
M. Bezaudin gave an answer that surprised them all.
He took the opportunity of expressing his opinion one
day when M. Supia and Prince Hippothadee called at
his office to submit a plan for a quick and simple marriage
at an early hour in the morning and asked him to take the
necessary measures of precaution.

"Gentlemen, I shall not take any such steps," he said.
"They would be entirely needless. Nothing further will
happen."

"Have you seen Titin?" asked Supia excitedly.

"Certainly not. He has not set foot in this place since
the incident of Mlle. Agagnosc's temporary disappearance. I don't know what has become of him."

"Then how can you say he won't try the Hardigras
trick again?" interrupted the Prince.

"I think I know him well enough to say for certain that
he won't attempt anything of the kind. You have no idea
of that young man's pride. On the first occasion he took
it into his head to spirit away Mlle. Agagnosc because he
imagined that she would rather appreciate the little incident. And I venture to say he was not mistaken. But
to-day it is very different. To-day Mlle. Agagnosc is not
being led to the altar like a lamb prepared for the sacrifice, but has herself asked for the marriage to take place.
That is how the matter stands now, isn't it? Well, Titin
will not go against her expressed wishes, take it from me.
M. Supia, you will be able to marry your ward in peace.
Good-day!"

"What he said was not too bad," observed the Prince,
when they were outside.

"Possibly," returned M. Supia, "but I remember one
thing—that infernal Titin's threat when he brought back
Antoinette. Do you remember Hardigras's message?"

"I haven't forgotten it. It was all the more annoying

as I was utterly ignored, but I confess that for you and your family it was no joke."

"It was a criminal threat," said Supia, grinding his teeth.

"Tut! tut!" said Hippothadee. "I don't see Titin sending you to kingdom come over this marriage business."

"Nor do I, fortunately. I am convinced that he wanted chiefly to put the wind up. I mean that I treat the message for what it is worth. But there's enough in it to prevent us from sharing the optimism of that silly ass, Bezaudin. That man is the funniest thing in commissaries of police in this country. He puts his confidence only in sharpers whom he is asked to arrest and allows them to go about scot free."

"Suppose we invite MM. Souques and Ordinal," suggested the Prince.

"I think they'll come even if they're not invited, so we shall be spared the expense of bringing them down from Paris. . . ."

Bezaudin was right. Nothing disturbed the serenity of Prince Vladimir Hippothadee and Mlle. Antoinette Agagnosc's marriage. The only peculiar circumstance about it was the dreary fashion in which it was celebrated, and the great gloom of the crowd which, despite the early hour, had put themselves out to be present. They watched the proceedings in a silence more impressive than the most hostile demonstration.

In truth, there was something in this attitude not so much of rage against Hippothadee and the Supias as oppression at the fatality which had brought about this insult to the town. Titin's friends turned sadly away from the wedding party, which might have been a funeral procession, beginning with Antoinette, who seemed, in spite of her wedding dress, more like a widow than a bride —widowed of all her hopes, poor girl! But they no longer pitied her. They pitied only Titin, who was not present.

The morning after this day of ill-omen, when the Bella Nissa stores opened its doors again, it was discov-

ered that most of the articles which had disappeared—
furniture and so forth, as for instance, the famous Louis
XVI bedroom, carpets, knick-knacks, and the many things
pertaining to carnival, had been returned to their former
places as if by magic. In the entrance hall the great
standard was flying once more; but bore now the grim
inscription: *Hardigras is dead.*

This was enough to give rise to the rumor that Titin
had taken his life in despair. The ominous news sent
an icy shudder through the town. Voices were lowered,
as if some great affliction, some irreparable blow, had
struck the people of Nice. Many of them had no heart
to attend to business that day, but shut up their shops
and repaired to the cafés, remaining until a late hour, in
the one hope of seeing Titin, the only conclusive way of
belying the rumor.

Nothing happened during the next few days, and from
Nice to La Fourca, and over the plain to the Gorges du
Loup, desolation reigned. The people of Torre les
Tourettes scarcely ventured out of doors. They were
suspected of rejoicing at the discomfiture of their old
enemies, and violent threats were uttered against them.
The bowlers on the green went on strike, and the Place
d'Arson was deserted, save for the four inseparable
friends, Pistafun, Aiguardente, Tony Bouta, and Tantifla. Their low spirits were obvious, though they did
their utmost to raise them in the inns. It was said that
Gamba Secca and Le Budeu, employed as we know in
Bastardon's Kiosks, were making ready to drape their
newsbags in black. Finally, the sun withdrew from a
land no longer recognizable. During the last week, dark
clouds veiled the blue sky and poured forth torrential
rains. Not all the signs and portents, which proclaimed
and accompanied the death, in a classic age, of Julius
Caesar, were here. But indeed it must be confessed that
in a country little accustomed to the rigors of the gods
they were abnormally plentiful.

CHAPTER XIX

M. SUPIA'S SATISFACTION

THOUGH, as may be imagined, Hippothadee was not free from misgiving as to the success of his marriage, M. Supia on the other hand congratulated himself without reserve on the result of his own finest stroke of business. His ward's fortune passed legally into his hands; in other words, into the coffers of Bella Nissa.

Moreover, the marriage had killed at one blow Hardigras, his pet aversion. Not that M. Supia believed in Titin's suicide. But, by the very fact that Titin had announced Hardigras's death, he had admitted defeat and thrown up the sponge. He had thrown it up so completely that he restored, for nothing, pretty well every advantage derived from his daring pilferings. For nothing! And at a time when M. Supia was ready to give back the little property of which by his astuteness he had formerly relieved Mme. Bibi.

Here was good reason for his satisfaction! He never ceased to thank his stars, especially as this was not the full extent of his gains.

To appreciate the genius of this man it will be well to listen to a little conversation he had with Antoinette's husband a week after the marriage. The Prince had called at the cashier's office to draw the monthly allowance provided for in the contract. But he came away wildly excited after throwing at the cashier's head the two hundred and seventy-five francs offered him in lieu of the bundle of thousand franc notes due to him.

"There's nothing more to come to you. I have my orders," said the cashier politely.

The Prince uttered a few words in a language that the cashier failed to understand. But it was easy to guess their offensive import. At last he shouted in French:

"By God, he shan't have me like this!"

He arrived at the "tyrant's" office in a towering passion. But his sudden appearance in no way caused surprise, it appeared.

"Take a seat, my dear fellow," said Supia. "What's happened to put you in such a state?"

"I've come from the cashier's office," yelped the Prince, restraining himself lest he should fly in his face. "Understand me, Supia, you are a rotten *pezevengh.*"

"*Pezevengh!* I don't know what that means," returned Supia calmly.

"In Transylvania we call a man a *pezevengh* who lives on money from *patchouras.*"

"*Patchouras!*"

"Yes, *patchouras* are women who give money to *pezevengh.*"

"After all you ought to know more about that than I do. You come from that country, my dear Prince. I wish you would sit down. And above all calm yourself."

"Have done with this nonsense. I'm not going to allow myself to be cheated. I am a *palikare.*"

"*Palikare* if you like. I have never said that you were not a *palikare.*"

"A *palikare* is afraid of nothing. And I am going to show you how easily a *palikare* can beat a *pezevengh.*"

"Stuff! We shall end by coming to an understanding," said M. Supia coolly.

The Prince banged his fist upon the desk:

"Why two hundred and seventy-five francs?" he yelled.

"Ah, now we are coming to the point. I prefer that," returned the "tyrant." "Why two hundred and seventy-five francs? Well, my dear Prince, because that's all we owe you."

"Scoundrel!"

"My dear Hippothadee, you call me a scoundrel. I might call you a sharper, and, what is more, have you sent to jail, though you may be a *palikare.* I wish to retain your friendship, though you don't deserve it. You are a regular bad lot, and I preferred once more to advance you money though I have to deduct something from the amount payable to you every month. Of course, nothing much is left after this deduction. But who is to blame for that? In any case, I shall be only too pleased to come to your assistance, you may be sure. It serves no purpose to throttle people, and such has never been my policy. But I won't be confronted by a madman who calls me a *pezevengh.* I don't know what the word means, but it doesn't sound pleasant, and we all have our pride."

The Prince did not interrupt him. He listened, keeping his eyes fixed on him, wondering what the old miser was leading up to; for he had had many opportunities of realizing that the "tyrant" was never so formidable as when he affected this genial tone. At last he asked himself whether Antoinette's ex-guardian had any hold over him. He had spoken of swindling—prison. All that sort of thing was scarcely reassuring, particularly to an aristocrat unaccustomed to trouble himself with the exact system of accounts in which the ordinary prudent lower middle-classes found satisfaction. Suddenly a thought came to him.

"May the great Hippothadee forgive me," he exclaimed. "Can it be that you, M. Supia, are making all this fuss over that little affair of the furniture?"

The "tyrant" grinned without malice.

"Come, come, you have finished behaving like a surly dog, which is something; all the more so as in business matters no one has ever frightened me. That's the one ground on which I am ready to fight, my dear Prince. As a matter of fact it has to do with that little business. Do you know how much that furniture was worth?"

"I never knew and I don't want to know. I don't even know how much I sold it for."

"I could enlighten you. The accounts are here."

"Spare me your figures, if you don't mind."

"And as I have nothing to keep from you I could also tell you how much it cost me to buy it back again."

"You bought back that awful stuff?"

"You can't do without furniture."

"I don't want the flat again. We are very comfortable at the hotel."

"You won't be able to pay your hotel bills out of your monthly allowance. But to return to the furniture, I bought it back for a mere nothing."

"Had you told me otherwise I shouldn't have believed you."

"Hang it all, it was furniture that you had no right to sell and the buyer no right to buy. This business might have gone a great deal further, you know. However, if it were merely a question of this furniture, which is now settled, I should have been less exacting in the amount that must be deducted monthly to enable me to get back my money without feeling it too much. But there's another matter."

"What other matter," gasped the Prince.

"Well, what about the necklace?"

"Necklace—what necklace?" asked the Prince, turning pale.

"Why, you know as well as I do, Mme. Supia's necklace. You must admit that this is much more serious, particularly as Mme. Supia's pearls were very fine ones. I selected them myself, one by one, with a care and, I venture to say, a love, increasing with every birthday and anniversary. With what delight my dear Thélise saw the necklace grow larger and with what pride I saw her wearing it! Those pearls represented a veritable fortune. . . . Mme. Supia's necklace was famous."

"But she still has it," interjected the Prince in a husky voice.

"What an indifferent connoisseur you are! The necklace that Mme. Supia wears now is but an echo of the real one. I don't deny for that matter that the workmanship is first rate. The paste is so excellent an imitation of the real thing that dear Thélise herself has no suspicion of the fraud, inasmuch as the clasp is the actual clasp and adds to the delusion; and I congratulate myself on that fact, for I am very fond of her, and I am in the throes of despair when I see her fretting. You yourself, my dear Prince, who have some liking for her, cannot have wished her to suspect the substitution—and I thank you for it. . . .

"You do things in the grand manner, and I know you didn't haggle with the jeweler over the price charged you for making it when it was a question of his buying the original necklace from you. That was all the more praiseworthy on your part, as he proved to be rather avaricious. I really don't know how you came to be satisfied with those forty-five thousand francs. A necklace like that is worth at the very lowest, two hundred and fifty thousand francs. . . .

"I am well aware that you can say it was a loan and you were free to withdraw the necklace within a fortnight on paying the horrible money-lender fifty-five thousand francs, but you also ran the risk of not having the ready money and of the necklace becoming the property of the scoundrel. You see, my dear Prince, you have too much delicacy not to be cheated by these gentry. Let this be a lesson to you another time! Especially as you acted like a child. To order the jeweler to transfer the genuine clasp to the paste necklace was to give things away! Either you were robbing your fair lady friend, excuse the word, or you were in league with her to cheat her husband, who gave her the necklace.

"I mentioned just now your delicacy, but I ought to

have said 'simplicity.' When I was told about the affair, I assure you that I was grieved for you. You lower your head. You say nothing. You no longer bang the table. You do not even ask me from whom I got this incredible story. But I will tell you, never fear. It will still further enlighten you. I had it from the jeweler himself.

"Mme. Supia's necklace is, I repeat, famous. Our jeweler recognized it. And as he knows the sort of man I am he had no wish to take the responsibility for a shabby transaction of this sort. I told him that it was not for me to interfere in your business, that I had the greatest confidence in you and wished nothing so much as to see you a member of our family, and that if Mme. Supia had ordered a paste necklace through you he had only to execute the order. As he persisted, and indulged in language scarcely flattering to your character, I flatly showed him the door. He got his own back a month later by sending me word that I made a mistake not to listen to him as he was now the owner of the necklace. . . .

"I need not tell you, my dear Prince, how worried I was over the matter. I set great store on this necklace. But that thief, after acquiring it for, as you know, a ridiculous sum, would only give it up on my paying him its full value. The sum total you can work out for yourself, and you will see why I have to deduct so much money at the end of the month. As to the necklace—here it is!"

M. Supia took from his drawer a case containing the real necklace. Suddenly the Prince recovered from his confusion and once more banged the table with his fist.

"Damn you, you are very clever. Why you worked the whole business. It was you who lent me forty-five thousand francs through that jeweler. And now I've got to pay two hundred and fifty thousand francs while you have the necklace!"

"My dear Prince, you are not lacking in a certain imagination," grinned the "tyrant," "but I am not called upon to let you into the secret of my business. I have already said enough about it! . . . Here's another matter settled. And now what are we going to do with the necklace?"

Here the Prince collected himself.

"If you are fair, M. Supia, you will admit that an innocent person is concerned—Mme. Supia. Therefore it would be well to restore the necklace without allowing her to suspect its return any more than she suspected its going. Leave that to me. And in so doing you will be acting like a gentleman."

"My dear Prince, I said that we should end by coming to an understanding. I was going to ask you to do us this little service, especially as I'm no longer afraid of your taking it back to the jeweler since you know, from experience, what this transaction is costing you. However, if you are absolutely bent on repeating the experience . . ."

"No, I understand. I thought I should be a richer man by marrying your ward, and I find myself penniless."

"No man can be penniless if, like you, he has capital in Bella Nissa," returned M. Supia.

"What's the use of capital if it brings me no return, and I am to have to-day's surprise repeated every time I call at your cashier's office?" said Hippothadee lugubriously.

"Stuff! You will have a couple of bad years to get through. . . . It's not worth mentioning. Business is business and this affair is settled for good and all like the other. But we can do more business together, my dear Prince. I am always at your disposal. I admit that you can't run your household on two hundred and seventy-five francs a month. A man like you has need of big sums of money. You'll want a pretty fair amount now and then."

"I want it at once!"

"Not this evening, in any case. We'll discuss the matter again two or three days hence, if you like. At the moment I am in the middle of settling my monthly accounts. Meantime you have two hundred and seventy-five francs. You won't starve. When you have spent that—well, I am not a hard man. I have my security in your interest in my stores. I won't leave you in the lurch."

"Do I need my wife's signature?"

"Not at all. You were married, thanks to me, my dear *palikare* under the system in which all property is held in common. Everything belonging to your wife is yours."

"And everything belonging to me is yours, or soon will be?"

"Protect yourself."

"I will try. So I am to take the necklace?"

"Yes, and you will give it to Thélise at once, you understand."

"But she is at La Fourca with her daughter. I can't leave my young wife alone. She's expecting me."

"No, she is not expecting you. And as to being left alone she will be only too pleased. Everybody knows that the marriage is one in name only."

"Everybody knows that?"

"Well, nothing is being discussed from Nice to Monte Carlo but this little episode. And it's partly your own fault, you must admit. Why did you tell the story to your dear friend the Comtesse d'Azila?"

"Why, that was done to reassure her."

"Well, believe me, she is now reassured and is jeering at you with all those ladies who run our local charities and are waiting to congratulate you when they see you. You had better go off to La Fourca."

While speaking M. Supia closed the case and slipped it into Hippothadee's pocket.

"Am I to bring you back the paste necklace?" asked the Prince helplessly.

"Oh, no. What use would it be to me? It is your property. It is entered on the account. Take it to the

jeweler, if it amuses you, just to see what he will lend
you on it."

M. Supia helped the Prince gently out of the office.
Hippothadee offered no resistance. He reflected that this
was the first time he had a jewel of such value in his possession without being able to turn it to account. Oh,
Supia was a pretty smart fellow! Certainly it would be
better to be his friend than his enemy. He decided not
to go against his wishes in future. He would come to
terms with him to avoid being further cheated. Was not
Antoinette there to pay the score for both of them? She
would get her deserts, it was true. The marriage was
one in name only! Poor Hippothadee rejected by his
wife and laughed at by his mistress! He had nothing
to fall back on but Thélise's affection.

Such were his thoughts as he stepped into the taxi to
drive to La Fourca. His trip, in the circumstances, was
not unwelcome to him. He was unaware, was this noble
palikare that the execrable "tyrant" had warned his wife
by letter that she would have to keep a stricter watch
over her necklace in future than she had done in the
past:

"You have been wearing a paste necklace for the past
three months. I am sending you the genuine one. It
will be placed in your hands by the thief himself. He is
a pretty gentleman, but I ask you not to be too hard on
him since he is now a member of the family."

Supia felt certain that his letter would set them by the
ears, and, as far as both they and Hardigras were concerned, he would cease at last to appear ridiculous. He
was a clever business man, but a poor judge of psychol-
ogy—at least, as will soon be seen, in matters of love.

CHAPTER XX

MORE ABOUT THE NECKLACE

As we have said, the rumor of Titin's death gained ground. No one had seen him. Not a soul had heard from him. Rage, and the spirit of revenge, succeeded dejection in La Fourca. Rage against whom? Revenge for what? For the time being they made a shift to vent their feelings on their adversaries in La Torre les Tourettes, little disposed to bewail Titin's disappearance. Regrettable incidents occurred in the two towns. Now the blame was cast on St. Helene, whose statue was taken without further ado from the church, stripped of its embroidered gold robe, and clothed in a mourning veil as in the days of the great struggle between dwellers in the Gorges du Loup and the Plain de Grasse.

When Hippothadee reached La Fourca Nova during the evening, his taxi was held up by the procession. Torrential rain, as we have said, had fallen. For the time being, the heavenly fountains seemed to be suspended. But the roads were like trenches, and the Grande Rue de la Fourca was a mass of thick, slippery mud, from which vehicular traffic had some difficulty in extricating itself.

And yet young men and girls marched barefooted, through this morass, singing mournful litanies. It recalled the long ago when great catastrophes devastated Provence and the county of Nice, when seas raged wildly, earth shook, winds rocked houses as though they were rushes, while the mountains thundered, and rivers overflowed their banks, carrying disaster and desolation on every hand.

232

Leading the way under a canopy draped in black, resting on a platform devoid of flowers or garlands, and borne on the shoulders of Jerome Brocard, Pierre Antoine, alias Cauva, and the two Ravibands, was the time-honored image of St. Helene in its mourning veil. Mme. Bibi walked behind. Then came Toton Robin, the smith, and his men supporting the mayor, the poor peasant, who likewise was barefooted.

The rector had declined to assist, alleging that to remove St. Helene in such weather, clad like a beggar-woman, with nothing to lose in this world and nothing to gain in the next, was an act of sacrilege. He was told that if she were powerless to help them to trace Titin she was no use in the church, and they would replace her by a new statue, young and all gilt and more beautiful, and the new St. Helene would work miracles.

That such a spirit of medieval superstition should still hold sway in La Fourca was its chief charm. For, in truth, long search would have been needed to find such antiquated ideas in any country spoilt by everyday politics, the traffic of motor-cars, the invasion of foreigners and modern ideas—in a word, by that which it pleases us to call the march of progress.

It was to be the last procession accorded to St. Helene until the day when they would place her outside the walls in a recess above the main gate which led through the plain from the upper and old Fourca to La Fourca Nova. When St. Helene wished to return to the church in the town and resume her place under her gilded canopy, she had but to show that she still possessed some power.

Giaousé, Tulip, Gamba Secca, and Le Budeu were followed by a group of girls singing loudly in voices raised less in supplication than in menace—voices that at times broke into a terrible scream. As the procession passed La Patentaine a general shout went up: "Down with the 'tyrant'!" But by Giaousé's order they continued their march.

Seated in his taxi, Hippothadee felt very uncomfortable. It was fortunate, he thought, that he was unknown in La Fourca, since he had visited it but once before. However, these people might have seen him at the wedding, and he was not anxious to linger among them. At length, the taxi started again and the incident appeared to be over when a group of young men suddenly surrounded it, and called on the driver to shout: "Down with the 'tyrant'!"

The driver, who knew nothing of the circumstances, began to show great irritation against these hotheads.

"Are you going to let me get on, you pack of savages?" he shouted.

They were about to make a rush on him when the Prince, impelled by a sense of danger, lowered the window and yelled: "Down with the 'tyrant'!" Thereupon, they cheered him lustily and the taxi was allowed to proceed.

On arrival at La Patentaine the gate was opened, after a parley, by the scared figure of Madame Cioasa, the concierge. She closed the gate again without a word, and the Prince strode to the villa, whose dark mass could be seen at the end of the garden.

Madame Cioasa scarcely ever spoke, and from the time of a mysterious incident in her life, which occurred in her young days, she had led an entirely solitary existence. It had happened when she was twenty years of age, and she was no worse looking than the average girl. She kept house for her brother and they lived in a small cottage on the outskirts. Her brother began to cut a figure at Grasse before he became chief cashier at Bella Nissa stores. He treated her with scant consideration and never spoke a kindly word to her. She had small love for him.

It was then that she had made the acquaintance of Michel Pincalvin—the facts were fully elicited in the subsequent trial that filled the newspapers for some six months. Michel Pincalvin was then a more than ordinarily sharp youth, and he knew how to talk to young

girls. He was a traveler in perfumery, and was an adept
at telling the tale. Rumor had it that Mlle. Supia had
failed to resist his blandishments. He left the district
shortly afterwards to settle in Arles, where his business
was a failure. He never returned to La Fourca and the
incident was forgotten.

Meanwhile Madame Cioasa had utterly changed. She
was only to be seen on Sundays when she went to mass
at St. Helene church. She spoke to no one. She had no
inclination to dress herself suitably, and her hair was
always in disorder under the kerchief that covered her
head.

At that time she remained indoors for weeks together.
It was said that she was ill. The explanation was plaus-
ible. Mother Bruno, commonly called Boccio, who was
as round as a tub, hunchbacked and looked upon as the
witch of the place, spent some days in her house. She
certainly knew more about her than anyone else. But it
was a part of her business to be close-tongued, and no
one asked her any questions. Boccio undertook every sort
of task, pleasant and unpleasant. She tended the lepers
in Eze, performed the last offices to the dead, acted as
midwife. In a word she always was sent for in moments
of difficulty. She was now a very old woman with nothing
plump about her but her hump.

But to return to Hippothadee hurrying across the
lawn. Night was falling and, in ordinary circumstances,
he would have been surprised to observe the absence of
lights. As things were, he imagined that the villa showed
a dark face on account of the procession and the hostile
cries that went up from it. He was not mistaken. He
had but to knock, and make himself known, to be wel-
comed as a deliverer. Thélise and her daughter Caroline
were shut up in the place without a servant, quaking with
fear. They made a rush on him, after carefully closing
the door.

"Take us back," cried Thélise. "Take us back. We

are terrified. Did you hear them? We've never done anything to them."

"The same here," said the Prince, striking a match. "They refused to allow me to pass until I had shouted: 'Down with the "tyrant"!' "

"Ah, Prince, it's a good thing they didn't knock you about," wailed Thélise.

The Prince was not thinking any more of that affront. His mind was on the necklace, of which he wished to rid himself. He had observed when he entered the room that Thélise was wearing the paste necklace with as much pride as though it were the real one, and he half-glimpsed the tactics which he would have to pursue when Caroline had left them.

"What put it into your head to come and shut yourselves up in this hole? Why are you in La Fourca?"

They both reddened and then Thélise said with a sigh:

"What about you, Prince? Can you tell us to what we owe the pleasure of your visit?"

"I was longing to see you, that's all."

Caroline darted a look at him in which she put her whole soul. But the brigand did not even notice her. Thélise reddened still more and bit her lips.

"We don't believe a word of it," she said.

Hippothadee took her hand.

"I am not at all happy, believe me."

"We are not asking for confidences," said Thélise with dignity.

Caroline could restrain herself no longer. She rose to her feet and, without a word, hurried from the room.

"What's the matter with her?" asked Hippothadee.

"The matter is that since your silly marriage she hasn't left off crying. It was she who wanted to come here. And I needed no pressing to come with her. Ah, your Antoinette. . . . I hate her, Hippothadee."

"Thélise. . . . Thélise. . . . You know I love you. . . ."

Thélise's breath came unevenly.

"Hold your tongue. No lies, if you please. Suppose

the poor little thing heard you! No, don't kiss me, you are a monster. . . . Why did I ever listen to you. I am ashamed of myself, Hippothadee. But, heavens above, how can one resist you. I have not been able to sleep for ever so many nights. Sleeplessness hurts my eyes. I, too, cry when I am alone. Yes, and let me tell you I've never suffered so much in my life before."

"Thélise !"

"All the same you did well to come down. This solitude with only the two of us here and our troubles is more depressing than anything. Still she—she can cry in my arms. But I—I must keep a watch on myself. My sorrow must seem to be hers. I have to lie to her. Why am I not dead? We were within an ace of it."

"I am here, Thélise."

"Good heavens, how scared I was when they shouted: 'Down with the "tyrant" !' "

"Now that I am with you, you need have no fear."

"Take me back at once, Hippothadee."

"I sent the taxi away and was quite right to do so. The roads are not safe to-night. And, besides, I thought you wouldn't refuse me hospitality for one night," he said, kissing her fat, over-manicured hands.

Thélise now nervously clasped his hand. She was greatly embarrassed, shaking her head, turning towards him her bloated face, like that of a Roman emperor.

"Oh, you monster !"

For the moment it was all she could say, but she emphasized it. She gave him a smart rap on the knuckles. He had no need of any explanation, but she went on:

"You will have the spare room. But be careful for Caroline's sake. Her room is upstairs at the end of the passage. Mine is here on the ground floor. You will only have to come downstairs. Poor girl! She has used up six handkerchiefs since this morning."

"Are you sure she suspects nothing?"

"Nothing, or it would be the death of me. How weak I am where you are concerned."

"I have something to tell you. I saw the 'tyrant' before I left."

"Forgive me for interrupting you. Have you brought me the necklace?"

"What—you know!"

"Yes, he wrote and told me. Look, here's his letter. What a wretch!"

"He deserves all he gets," said the Prince coolly, after reading the letter and putting it into his pocket.

"Yes," agreed Thélise, in a tone of indignation, rewarded with a kiss on the ear. "Just that! He accuses you of theft. What answer did you make?"

"Why the truth. What would you have me tell him? I have had a lot to put up with on your account, my poor dear. I thought at one time he suspected you of being in league with me in this business."

"Believe me, I should have been only too pleased. You are too fastidious. You were afraid to tell me that you were in need of money."

"That is so."

"My goodness, how long are you going to be secretive with me? You should have had confidence. Everyone is short of money at times. I see the whole thing. You said to yourself: 'I won't ask Thélise. She mustn't think I am trying to worm money out of her. I'll get a loan on the necklace, give her another like it, but not so fine, and return the original one when I am in funds.' Am I not right, my Hippothadee?"

"Quite right. But try to explain that to the 'tyrant'! Do you know what he did? He redeemed the necklace at my expense. Now he intends to deduct the cost of it from my monthly allowance—in other words, leave me penniless."

"But he gave you back the necklace."

"Well, that was the least he could do! He asked me what I was going to do with it. I told him: 'I shall give it to Mme. Supia.' And here it is. It is yours!"

So saying the Prince drew the necklace from his pocket

and gave it to her with the same simple gesture as though
he were offering her a bunch of violets.

"I won't take it," cried Thélise admiringly, with a catch
in her breath. "Ah, there you have the Prince! He
hasn't a sou and he gives me a necklace worth two hundred
thousand francs. Ah, the poor man!" And she subsided
in his arms, in tears. He valiantly supported her, and
no less valiantly insisted on her accepting the necklace.
She agreed only after he had sworn never to see her
again if she refused to accept it. But at the end of the
scene she all but fell at his feet.

"You are much too good-hearted," she sobbed. "How
do you expect to be anything but poor? You marry a
million, and the day after your wedding you haven't a
sou in your pocket, and yet you contrive to give me a
necklace worth two hundred thousand francs!"

At that moment Caroline returned to the room. She
had drawn on her seventh handkerchief.

"Caroline, do you know what your father has done to
the Prince?" said her mother. "The Prince borrowed
some money on my necklace. He has made him pay the
full value of it. The Prince has just given me the necklace and your father calls him a thief!"

Caroline straightway shared her mother's indignation,
and the "tyrant" was once more held up to execration
by his wife and his daughter. Worn out by the scene,
Thélise declared that she would go to bed early. The
Prince's room was prepared. They all had supper in
the kitchen, so as not to trouble Madame Cioasa, and to
remain undisturbed. Then they retired to their respective
rooms.

The Prince said nothing about Antoinette, though she
was in their thoughts. He made himself most agreeable
to Caroline. And she drew the conclusion that, as her
mother had anticipated, the newly married couple would
not be long together, and her own turn would come. She
fell asleep and dreamed of leaving St. Reparate Church
on the arm of Hippothadee.

CHAPTER XXI

HARDIGRAS COMES TO LIFE AGAIN

At that very hour, M. Supia, delighted with his day's work, entered his flat rubbing his hands after indulging in an extra good dinner in town, a thing that he had not done for many a long day.

On his desk lay his mail. He began to open it with no great interest when suddenly his eyes fell on certain capital letters absent from his table of late. He gave a start. Whence came the letter? From beyond the grave, doubtless, since Hardigras was dead! He deciphered the postmark, his forehead streaming. It came from La Fourca. Greatly unnerved he tore open the envelope. The paper was covered with those ominous capital letters, and the text of the letter, made public later in the Criminal Court, was as follows:

"Monsieur Supia,

You have apparently forgotten the communication that I entrusted Titin to make to you when he brought back Mlle. Agagnosc to your flat. He warned you that whatever the course of events might be, there must be no further question of any marriage between Mlle. Agagnosc and Prince Hippothadee, and that he would hold you and your family responsible with their lives if any undue pressure were brought to bear upon her. To-day, through your maneuvres, Mlle. Agagnosc, to her misfortune and yours, has become Princess of Transylvania. Hardigras has never broken his word."

M. Supia drew himself up on his long legs, trembling all over. He picked up his letters, stuffed them feverishly into his pocket, and rushed out like a person distraught.

He descended to the delivery department.

"Has the van started for La Fourca?" he shouted.

"Not yet. It is still loading up."

"All right. Tell Castel that I'm going with him."

The motor van in question covered the entire district between La Fourca, Grasse, and La Vallée du Loup. It loaded up in the evening with the day's orders. But Castel, the driver, did not start off with his goods until after dinner. The van usually reached La Fourca about eleven o'clock at night, and Castel put it up at La Patentaine, himself sleeping in an out-building, at the rear of the villa. He had a special key with which he opened the main gate of the farm, and no one ever paid any heed to his comings and goings. Even Mme. Cioasa never saw him. He began his deliveries at an early hour and was back again in Nice in the evening before dinner time. Castel knew nothing of what had occurred during the preceding days, nor of what was about to occur that night at La Patentaine.

In the basement M. Supia recovered, in part, his calmness. The cool air from outside, sweeping through the subway with the parcels intended for Castel's van, refreshed him. He took time to think. His alarm had been instinctive. He believed so implicitly that he had done with Hardigras for ever. He withdrew to a corner, and read his letters by the light of a lantern. What new discovery had he made? He did not finish reading them. He ran over to the staff. They had never before seen him in such a state. He hustled them, lent a hand in their work, went out, and mounted the seat beside Castel.

"Off we go, and drive as fast as you can," he cried.

The van swung forward at top speed. An hour later they reached the plain on the edge of which loomed the great crag of La Vieille Fourca. The light of a fire showed on the skyline, the tower, the high gate, and a jumble of small buildings standing close together and rising tier above tier as though about to storm what remained of the castle. The fire was at the base and came from La Fourca Nova.

"Damn it, one might almost think it was La Patentaine," gasped M. Supia.

"No, La Patentaine is farther to the right," said Castel.

"What can have happened?" asked Supia in a voice strained with anxiety.

Castel slowed down for the road was becoming difficult.

"You can never tell. Since this Titin business they have all gone mad. Did you know Nathalie has disappeared?"

"I don't care a hang about her," growled the "tyrant."

"Nor do I," returned Castel. "But I'm only telling you how things are. The other day the La Torre people led by Bolacion came up against Giaousé and his gang. Giaousé had to pretend he was delighted that Nathalie had left him. Bolacion went on to pull his leg about it as usual, and hinted that Nathalie had chosen a good time to go away since Titin had gone too."

"I'm very glad to hear it. . . . Can't you put on more speed?"

"Are you anxious to break your neck? To return to Giaousé and Bolacion. That was enough. They came to blows. The La Fourca people got the worst of it. Yesterday, Bolacion's house in La Torre was burnt down. It may have been an accident. They say it was done out of revenge by the La Fourca people. And to-day it is La Fourca which is on fire. Such a quiet place, too, for so many years! It is all Titin's fault. The unfortunate part is that no one knows what the end of it will be. Meantime he and his Nathalie must be laughing up their sleeves."

"Shut up Castel. Don't ever say such things. Titin is a terrible fellow. He has already done me a lot of harm, and I fear he is going to do me a great deal more, worse luck."

"Yes, guv'nor, I see there's something the matter. You look very upset."

"See how the fire is blazing over there. Do you hear the tocsin? It's ominous. . . ."

It was indeed ominous this nocturnal landscape wrested from its peace and darkness by a flame which rose high on the horizon. Now flashing rocks, old walls, a part of the tower almost completely destroyed, became visible, while in the foreground the dark shadows of clumps of writhing olive trees stood out and the twisted limbs of fig-trees drooped in torment over the crimson-colored road. And above it all sounded the mournful tones of the tocsin in La Fourca, echoed throughout the plain and valley by other and more distant notes, lamenting the desolation of the hour.

M. Supia and Castel had kept silent. The van itself seemed to hesitate to plunge still farther into the fantastic wilderness.

"Did you hear those cries!" suddenly asked Supia. "Are you sure they don't come from La Patentaine?"

"Quite sure, guv'nor. The road makes a bend yonder you know. That's what's deceiving you."

"When I think that my wife and daughter are there!"

"If that's what's worrying you don't be afraid. I know the boys of La Fourca and they never interfere with women."

"No matter, I'm not easy about them. As it happened I asked Prince Hippothadee to go to them. You can say what you like, but he's no coward."

"I couldn't tell you guv'nor. I don't mix with him."

"Have you got your revolver, Castel?"

"Me with a revolver in this place! What should I do with a revolver? For the time being there are differences between these people, and it's a nuisance to everyone, but as I don't meddle in their business I have no cause to worry."

"I always carry my revolver."

"Oh, that's another matter. You have enemies."

"I know quite well that I'm not popular round here.

Therefore I come here as little as I can. And yet I've
done nothing to them. But Titin has worked them up
against me."

In the distance the uproar became louder. They could
hear cries, with an insistent clamor.

"Pull up Castel. Do you hear them?" cried the "tyrant", eyes starting out of his head.

"Yes, there's a devil of a row."

"Listen. It seems as if they're shouting: 'Down
with. . . .' Listen, I say, Castel. Can't you hear them
shouting: 'Down with the "tyrant"'!'?"

"What an idea! And besides we shall find out as soon
as we get down there! I know people say you pay those
chaps in La Torre to annoy them. But I told them that
it's not in your line and you don't fork out your money
like that!"

"If only my wife and daughter weren't there!"

"I'll start the engine again. It was not worth while
to come along at such a pace to stop now. . . ."

"Are you sure they'll let you through."

"As sure as you are sitting there."

"Well, I'm not so sure as you are, for the very reason
that I am sitting here."

"Perhaps you would like me to put you down. In any
case, you know, I can't take you back to Nice. I've
got my work to do to-morrow morning."

"Look here, Castel, you must put me inside the van
and not open it until we get to La Patentaine."

"Perhaps you're right."

The "tyrant" stepped down and allowed himself to be
locked in the van with the goods. Castel drove off once
more; he wanted to make up for lost time. The incident
had no particular effect on him. He was still young and
not easily moved. He had been through the war. On that
particular evening—as was elicited at the trial—he had
an assignation with a girl friend in La Fourca.

When he reached the outskirts he at once realized that
not only was the whole of La Fourca Nova in a tumult,

but that the people of the upper part of the town had come down, too. He had some difficulty in threading his way through. At a turn in the road he saw that Mme. Bibi's cottage was on fire. The old woman was weeping a few paces away, seated on a stone between her two goats nestling against her as though to comfort her. No one knew how the fire had originated. Her little shop with all Titin's fine paintings had blazed up like match-wood.

The La Fourca people round her were in a state of indescribable frenzy. When they recognized the Bella Nissa delivery van they made quick work of it; for, they attributed the calamity to Titin's enemies, chief of whom was the "tyrant." They made a rush, shot Castel to the ground, and pushed the van towards the fire. Castel yelled incoherently like a madman. Suddenly the wings of the van door opened, staved in, and an appalling figure leapt out. It was the "tyrant" making a dash to escape the flames.

He fell into a hundred hands which flung him back into the fire, and his life would not have been worth a moment's purchase had not four stalwarts seized him in time and shielded him from popular fury. They were Aiguardente, Tantifla, Tony Bouta, and Pistafun.

Pistafun not only possessed powerful biceps but a stentorian voice and managed to master the crowd:

"No need to make so much row," he roared. "The "tyrant" belongs to Titin. Titin will know how to deal with him."

Murmurs arose among the crowd, but without waiting for any expression of opinion the four men elbowed their way through the scuffle with their prisoner more dead than alive, and guided his steps to La Patentaine, where they rang the bell and banged at the door. But no one came to open it. Then the "tyrant" remembered that he had his keys.

He opened the garden gate, entered and closed it after him, omitting to thank his benefactors, and passed the lodge at the window of which he perceived the ghostly face of Mme. Cioasa, whom the cries and conflagration outside had kept indoors and who would not have stirred for a kingdom. Then staring wildly round him he reached the villa and went in.

Groping his way he opened a door which happened to be the drawing-room. He took a few steps forward. But suddenly he started back. He had come upon something . . . some obstacle which had yielded and then swung back—some obstacle that "offered no resistance." He wondered if he were going mad. He dared not go forward, he dared not shout for assistance. A few endless seconds ensued. Then it occurred to him that the incidents of the past few minutes had affected his brain. He remembered that he had a cigar-lighter in his pocket. He took it out with a trembling hand. Not until the third attempt was he able to strike a light. At once a hoarse cry broke in his throat, the lighter fell from his hands, and he sank to the floor. . . .

Half an hour later a man fought his way through the crowd still pressing round the smoking wreckage of Mme. Bibi's hovel. He went up to the mayor and dragged him away, spluttering disconnected words in which could be made out: "Horrible! . . . horrible disaster!" It was Hippothadee his face contorted.

Some of them recognized him. They followed him and the mayor to La Patentaine. When they reached the drawing-room, lit by a lamp near which stood Mme. Cioasa like a statue of terror, a terrible cry arose from the group crowding round the door. The mayor himself made a movement as if to escape.

In an arm chair where he looked like a dislocated puppet, arms dangling, head sunk, eyes half-closed, sat the "tyrant". On the divan, in a fainting fit, wrapped in a dressing gown, lay Thélise. In the window recess hanging from a thin rope was the dead body of Caroline bearing a card round her neck with the inscription: "You have brought this on yourself 'tyrant'," signed "Hardigras."

CHAPTER XXII

THE poor girl was clad in a long nightgown which wrapped her about like a shroud.

"Cut her down! Cut her down!" cried twenty voices.

No one ventured to step forward.

"When I discovered the horrible crime, the poor child was already cold," said Hippothadee to the mayor who seemed not to hear him, so greatly the successive misfortunes that had befallen his little town had benumbed his faculties. "But I was conscious that I had a dead body in my arms, and I hurried away to fetch you."

They all stared at him. He was a pitiful sight, half-dressed, without waistcoat, having hurriedly thrown on his trousers and coat, his unbuttoned shirt exposing his long vulture-like neck, sharp, wizened face, disordered hair, cruel nose, trembling lips, and bloodshot eyes. All that had made up the elegance of Prince Hippothadee, his clear-cut profile, his somewhat lean figure—all these things had disappeared giving way to this bird of ill-omen, ravaged and despoiled by the storm.

"In any case we can't leave her like this," groaned the mayor.

"Don't touch anything," said Tulip. "This gentleman is quite right. It is now a matter for the police."

At that moment Thélise, to whom no one was paying any attention, heaved a sigh and opened her eyes. She came to herself, and a terrible sight she was. She gave way to a fit of hysterical sobbing. They had to hold her down for she threatened to kill herself.

"Take her away! Take her away!" they cried.

She was carried to her bedroom in spite of her fierce outbursts and struggles. And then she swooned again. The "tyrant" had risen like a broken mechanical toy which yields to the last impulsion of its spring. With a stupefied look, his head still sunk, he cast a side glance at the people perhaps without seeing them, perhaps in order to see them, and fell upon a seat beside the bed where Thélise was laid.

"Leave us," he said.

Out of doors everyone knew what had happened. The crowd, dismayed, kept silent—a silence which was broken by the arrival, like a meteor, of firemen from Grasse, followed almost immediately by a car containing the Commissary of Police, the Deputy Public Prosecutor, and a clerk. They had assumed from a telephone message from La Fourca that their business was to inquire into a charge of arson. They were about to draw up the first depositions in one of the most extraordinary cases of the day.

La Patentaine was cleared and the crowd dispersed, dejected and oppressed, as though weighed down by a mysterious fate. Not a soul went to bed that night. They all wanted to know the details. The mayor remained at Patentaine with the authorities. The firemen from Grasse finished deluging the ruins of Mme. Bibi's shop. Giaousé managed to take her away with him; her goats would not leave her. Every now and then she lifted the stick on which she leant.

"Where are you, Titin? Is it God's truth there'll be no more dancing at the fête? Come back. I want you."

"Take it from me he'll come back," Giaousé told her. "He's not dead. Meantime, as Nathalie has left me, there's room in my house. We'll look after you. Titin and me—it's the same thing."

"No, no, it's not the same thing," said the old woman, shaking her head.

A number of young men joined the four friends of Mme.

Pieronella's inn, which had reopened its doors. When a man has done his duty he is thirsty, and a crust of bread and cheese is not to be despised. Mme. Pieronella was an elderly woman of jovial and kindly temperament.

Tantifla, Pistafun, Aiguardente, and Tony Bouta had retired to the inn after the excitement of rescuing M. Supia from the fire. They were able to chat together quietly over a glass of white wine. The inn stood in the upper part of La Fourca and nothing was known there of the fatality until groups of people, coming from La Patentaine, told the four men of the discovery of Caroline's body bearing the card round her neck signed "Hardigras."

"It was not Titin who did that," was the unanimous opinion.

"It was done by some cursed devil who has taken this roundabout way of making people believe in the lie," said Tony Bouta. "He ought to be hanged in the same place. He deserves it."

"Yes, yes, he deserves it," they all repeated.

Tantifla and Pistafun alone remained silent. They exchanged glances by stealth, their faces pale with anxiety. Their silence passed unnoticed at the time but was remembered afterwards. Meantime other groups of people came in and argued over words used by the mayor. After the departure of the police officials the mayor observed in gloomy tones: "There's no making anything of it," meaning thereby that the case was an utterly baffling one.

Nevertheless, the result of a preliminary inquiry at which M. Supia and Prince Hippothadee were questioned —Thélise not being in fit state to give evidence—was clear. It was established that Prince Hippothadee had been sent to La Fourca by M. Supia to bring back the ladies to Nice. He had slept on the first floor in a room looking on to the passage at the end of which was Caroline's room. Mme. Supia's room was on the ground floor and led directly to the drawing-room. The three of them had a hurried supper in the kitchen. The ladies wished to retire to bed at an early hour, being worn out by the excitement of the evening. They were to leave La Fourca at daybreak. The Prince borrowed a book to read, from Mme. Supia, and it was found in his room.

M. Supia reached La Patentaine, in his turn, about midnight, escorted by the four friends. On entering the drawing-room he stumbled against his daughter's body and fell in a dead faint. The crime, therefore, must have been committed between nine o'clock and midnight.

The murderer, who seemed well acquainted with La Patentaine and the position of the rooms, must have got in through the kitchen door, which was not locked. He had then made straight for Mlle. Supia's room where the crime was committed; for it was inconceivable that he had carried his victim, even if she were gagged, to the drawing-room and hanged her there without the sound of her struggles awakening the Prince whose door he would have to pass in going down stairs, or Mme. Supia, sleeping in the room next to the drawing-room. Moreover, the disorder in the room pointed to the fact that the tragedy had taken place in that room; and an examination of the body seemed to show that the young girl was strangled and then hanged.

It was ostentatiously to parade his crime that the infamous Hardigras, who had written to M. Supia threatening personal violence and knew that M. Supia, on receiving his letter, would hasten to La Fourca, had hanged his victim in the drawing-room. In that way the hapless father might at once be confronted by his daughter's dead body. That is, indeed, what actually did occur at midnight. How long had the poor child been dead? That was a question which the medical experts would determine on the morrow.

M. Supia at once had fainted. When he recovered consciousness he crawled along in the darkness, attempted to stand up, but fell to the floor again, with no more strength than to moan like an animal at bay. He called out for his wife, in a weak voice. It was these moans that had aroused Mme. Supia. She recognized her husband's voice, got out of bed, terrified, lit a lamp, opened the door, saw at first only her husband on the floor, ran up to him, and suddenly caught sight of the horrible thing.

It was not until then that the Prince, awakened by a terrible cry, followed by the sound of a heavy fall, darted into the drawing-room, lit by a lamp from Mme. Supia's room, the door of which was open. He at first stumbled over M. Supia, stretched on the floor. Over against him Mme. Supia lay huddled, gasping for breath. Between them was the hanging body of their daughter, bearing round her neck the frightful words: "You have brought this on yourself, 'tyrant',", and signed "Hardigras."

The Prince seized Caroline and lifted her in his arms. But life was extinct. M. Supia's evidence left no room for doubt on that point. As to Mme. Cioasa, she had heard nothing. On leaving La Patentaine to fetch the mayor the Prince knocked on her window, telling her to go to the villa at once as a great calamity had befallen them. Lastly, nothing more had been seen of Castel, the chauffeur. Next morning it was ascertained that terrified by what had occurred, and fearing lest the fanatics, who had burnt his van, were about to set fire to La Patentaine, he had slipped away to La Costa, a village hard by, and had stayed the night with Jean Jose Scaliero.

It is easy to picture the commotion roused by the event which, however, was only the beginning of a series of calamities that for some months brought this part of the country, regarded hitherto as a paradise on earth, into turmoil and notoriety.

The excitement in Nice was intense. As at La Fourca, it did not enter the minds of persons knowing and associating with Titin to hold him guilty of such a deed. At Caroline's funeral, attended by the whole town, Antoinette was seen for the first time since her marriage. And this delightful flower of Provence, but lately a beautiful rosebud, seemed like a pitiful stalk. At the cemetery she said aloud: "Titin did not commit this crime." Her heart was heavy, though she deemed it wise to let them all know what she thought.

The judicial investigation conducted by the Nice Public Prosecutor, daily made things look blacker for Titin. His former threats were carefully noted. They all tended to incriminate him. His madness in abducting Toinetta on her wedding day, the manner in which he behaved when he restored her to her family, his remarks at Caramagna's restaurant and elsewhere, declaring that had he been Hardigras it would not have been in effigy that he would have hanged M. Supia, and other wild speeches, were all brought up in evidence against him.

Souques and Ordinal who had come down from Paris when they heard of the new crime, performed a showy piece of work in disclosing that Hardigras's much-talked-of writing in capital letters was exactly similar to that on the sign-boards painted by Titin in La Fourca. Three hand-writing experts proved conclusively that Hardigras's and Titin's writing was the work of one and the same man.

Meantime, M. Bezaudin, the Commissary of Police, blamed for having displayed such unaccountable indulgence towards a youth too ready to play the fool and now become a criminal, was placed on the retired list. Nor could the obstinate silence of Princess Antoinette of Transylvania, summoned to appear at the inquiry, weigh to any extent in Titin's favor. On the other hand, had she been able to speak she would not have failed to emphasize the difference between the Hardigras who had abducted her and the Titin who had brought her home. To every question put to her she made answer that if she had anything to say she would say it at the Criminal Court.

The general public, refusing as yet to abandon Titin, leaned to the opinion that some criminal had merely imitated Titin's handwriting in order to cover up his own tracks. But the three handwriting experts asserted that there was no difference between the handwriting on Hardigras's first manifesto, the early letters received by M. Supia, the last letter found by him among his mail on the eve of the crime, and the letter received at "Le Père la Bique" when the appointment was made with Nathalie. The fact that Titin had taken away at the time Hardigras's letter to Nathalie, making this appointment, was not in his favor. Lastly, her disappearance led people to think that they had linked their fates together, a point which was turned to account to persuade Toinetta to speak. But she, none the less, kept silent. No one knew what to think. If Titin were still alive why did he not come forward and answer the charge?

Mme. Bibi went into mourning. And all his friends mourned for him in their hearts. But the heaviest blow, to those who still pinned their faith to him, was struck by Souques and Ordinal who gloated over their revenge. They were in a transport of delight. The day on which they put the handcuffs on Pistafun was certainly a red-letter day for them. They arrested him by a ruse when his three friends were far away, for had they been together the detectives would never have succeeded in their purpose. But, it must be admitted, it was a master stroke. Souques and Ordinal discovered that it was Pistafun who posted at La Fourca the letter received by M. Supia on the eve of the crime.

Pistafun could not deny posting the letter. The post-mistress's assistant had seen him put the letter in the pillar-box some minutes before the collection. She remembered quite well the envelope with its peculiar handwriting. She said to herself: "Another of Titin's practical jokes!" Now, the envelope bore the mark of a big black thumb— Pistafun at that time was helping to deliver coal. Souques and Ordinal, after obtaining the envelope from M. Supia, sent it with Pistafun's finger-prints to the Criminal Investigation Department and received a conclusive reply.

Pistafun, questioned by the examining magistrate,

answered that Titin had not handed him the letter and
that he did not know Hardigras, though for some time
past, on the initiative of a third party whom he refused
to name, he had done certain jobs for him; he could not
refuse him since he owed him some return for the pleasure
which he had given them all at the last Carnival.

Letters for the post were placed under his door, but he
had no knowledge of how they got there. It was the same
with the last letter. As usual, the letter was enclosed
in a second envelope bearing the design of a scaffold,
Hardigras's seal. This being so, Pistafun knew what he
had to do, and he took a delight in it for, speaking generally, these letters led to amusing practical jokes.

He was asked to produce the outer envelope. He made
answer that he had torn it up, as usual. The examining
magistrate told him that his explanation was intended to
put them off the scent, and that unless he confessed to
receiving the letter from Titin he would pay dearly. He
was responsible for this letter, and they would have to
draw from his silence conclusions unfavorable to the man
who posted it.

Pistafun laughed openly.

"You're not going to believe I did this horrible thing.
Look here, don't say any more or else you'll put me in
a hot rage."

"The letter foretold the murder. That makes you an
accomplice."

"Nothing of the sort. I don't know Hardigras or the
other man either. But Hardigras of the Carnival did not
write that letter. I was deceived like others, and with
all due deference to you, in my opinion you are taken
in also."

Thus he defended himself and defended Titin step by
step. To the warders who took him back to prison, he
said:

"They won't have me."

All the same it followed that Titin was not dead, that

he was charged with murder and was in hiding, and
that Pistafun had posted the letter to M. Supia. At
La Fourca, people were utterly nonplussed. A fever of
uncertainty wrung every heart. The entire district took
sides for or against Titin, and there was a noisy conflict
of opinion. The people of La Torre, led by Bolacion,
bearded the people of La Fourca in their dens. Since the
inquiry lasted some months, ill-feeling during that time
immensely increased.

The foreign element among the workmen mingled in
the fray. Sewerage work was under construction in the
Gorges du Loup and navvies from the four quarters of
Europe were employed in it. The Arabs were not the least
to be feared. Disturbances were multiplied. The ordinary
citizen kept indoors after dark. Not a night passed un-
broken by the sound of firing. Next morning some robbery, effected with marvelous skill, was discovered. The
police, the gendarmery, were worked off their legs. But
no trace of the guilty parties was ever found, and the
whole thing assumed the aspect of an unfathomable mystery. The worst of it was that a feeling was abroad that
these disturbances were the work of some master mind.
Suspicion was rife on every side.

It was then that the worthy mayor, M. Arthur of Torre,
bewailing these calamities, visited La Fourca with his municipal council, the leading citziens, and at least forty
young men among whom were Bolacion, the two Barrajas,
and Sixte Pastorelle.

When the La Fourca men saw this army marching
towards them they sounded the alarm from house to
house and inn to inn, as if the town were threatened with
an attack. But, the enemy had already called a halt at
the Rue Basse facing the statue of St. Helene, which stood,
in its mourning veil, at the entrance to the Town. And
Arthur stepped forward alone.

When they beheld his honest face, stricken by the
calamities of the times, they realized that they need expect

nothing from him but words of wisdom and peace. He
asked to speak to the mayor. Le Petou, the mayor, who
had run up to put himself at the head of his men, observing Arthur's friendly gesture, replied to it by offering
him his hand.

A dead silence fell in the two camps. Arthur, in a voice
whose sympathetic tone found its way to their hearts,
declared that they came as brothers, that the men of
La Torre les Tourettes asked to be received by their
brothers of La Fourca with the same sentiments as those
animating themselves, that is to say without anger or ill-
will—in short, they had confidence in them and left themselves in their hands.

"It is well to clear up this matter," he went on, "and to
put a stop to a state of things that never ought to have
arisen again after the feasts—many years ago, alas!—in
which we celebrated peace between us."

"By all means, if what you say is true you are heartily
welcome," returned Le Petou, "for the evil that is preying
upon us now has been a long-standing sore."

But some of the La Fourca men, recalling Bolacion's
malevolence, pointing to him, cried:

"Leave him out!"

"I brought him here because you have more to forgive
in him than in others."

"Then let him come in."

The two bodies of men watching each other in silence
mounted the winding lanes to the parade. On arrival
Arthur, with a gesture which seemed to embrace the vast
reaches of earth and sky, cried:

"Ah, my friends, what a beautiful country lies before
you. Is there a more delightful spot in the world, more
beflowered, more fragrant, more beloved of the sun king
of the heavens, more graced with the smiles of fair women,
with softer olives, or more golden fruit, or finer or more
sprightly wines for our fêtes? Between our mountains and
the sickle of the blue sky, mirror of loveliness in which

I perceive the picture of our beloved Nice, our land lies
in a hollow like a charmed goblet out of which we should
quaff the joy of life on bended knee. And we put poison
in this divine cup. My friends, does not this fill your
hearts with dismay?"

"Yes, yes," shouted a hundred voices, already touched
by his appeal. He knew what he was about, did Arthur!

"Then let us put a stop to our wrangles. In reality,
while we are quarreling among ourselves the people who
come here from poverty-stricken countries and to whom
we have surrendered, out of good will, a little of our place
in the sun, take advantage of us to do the despicable work
of thieves, ravage our farmyards like foxes and wolves,
disturb our households, harass honest folk, and give us a
bad name. Is this not a disgrace?"

"Yes, yes," they cried.

"It is not merely a matter of shouting 'Yes, yes,' "
returned Arthur, clasping together his plump, soft hands
that might have roused the envy of a Roman prelate, "we
must admit our faults—cry *mea culpa*, strike our breasts
and say: 'We will put a stop to this thing.' We of La
Torre confess our sins. Bolacion admits them. He
wishes to make amends, but none of us, on either side, is
a saint. And no one will be humiliated if you on your
part come to us and say: 'We, too, wish to express our
sorrow.' "

Le Petou drew himself up on his short legs and cried:
"Shake hands on it!" The cry was repeated on all sides,
and when the two mayors fell into each other's arms, loud
cheers went up.

"He can talk as well as our Titin," said Toton Robin.

His words were overheard and spread a feeling of gloom
over the men of La Fourca. Arthur went on:

"My dear friends, I heard some one mention Titin's
name. I should not have spoken of him here because I
know you are greatly troubled on his account, but I should
like to say in my name and in the name of La Torre les

Tourettes: whatever reason there may be for his disappearance and however black things may look against him, we remain at one with you and Toton Robin in saying: 'It was not Titin who did this deed!' "

There were thunders of applause. "Three cheers for Arthur!" they cried.

The men of La Fourca escorted the men of La Torre les Tourettes to their own town. It was a day of rejoicing; and peace, it was believed, would reign once more. But as if to establish the fact that past crimes could not be laid at the door of either party, the mysterious happenings in La Fourca continued in all their horror, uniting in intense and fraternal anger the people of La Fourca, the victims, and the people of La Torre les Tourettes, determined not to allow suspicion to be cast on them.

Some days after the meeting, two persons disappeared: Mme. Paula, otherwise Manchotte, so called because she had lost an arm, and Mme. Cioasa, the "tyrant's" own sister, who had not left La Fourca for thirty years. Both disappeared as if by magic.

Then followed the murder in the Rue de la Toussan. It may be remembered that Mme. Bruno alias Boccia lived in this narrow lane behind St. Helene church. One night at ten o'clock, as she was darning stockings, she heard groans at the top of the lane near the buttresses, reinforcing the ancient building. The ordinary citizen, as we have said, dared not venture out after dark. Doors and shutters were closed and barred, and whatever happened passed unnoticed until the sun rose again and drove away the specters of the night. The neighbors heard the moans which seemed to come from some person in a death struggle, beseeching help. No one thought of venturing out. It was remembered that a week before at La Costa, Cauvin, alias Frussa, allowed himself to be caught by a trick. He opened his shutters, a gang of men made a rush at him, knocked him down, and plundered his house. Terrified by their threats, he had not even dared to call

in the police. And he made answer to every question put
to him by the authorities that the assault was so sudden
that he never quite understood what had happened. He
was unable, therefore, to give any description of his
assailants.

The incident might well have been a lesson to Mme.
Bruno, but the old woman had one failing that proved
her downfall. She was inquisitive, she wanted to see. She
cautiously opened her window. At the same moment, a
shot rang through the room, she was struck in the head.
She collapsed to the ground.

The facts were not established until next day. Shutters were not opened simply because the sound of a gun
was heard. She was found dead near the window. Beneath the window hanging to a bar was a piece of paper
on which was written: "Hardigras." Then it was recalled
that on several occasions she had indiscreetly blurted out
her opinion of Hardigras. Mme. Boccia was the only person to whom Mme. Cioasa, whom she had tended years ago,
ever spoke. The previous Sunday, Mme. Boccia as it happened, went to mass with Mme. Manchotte and stopped
in the church porch to exchange a few words with Mme.
Cioasa, then leaving the church. Instead of indulging
in the usual small talk they discussed Hardigras, and
Mme. Manchotte expressed her opinion, too. Indeed, she
spoke loudly as though challenging those who did not
share her views. This little colloquy, as we have seen,
was to have its sequel.

CHAPTER XXIII

EXAMINING magistrates, judges, counsel, public prosecutors, and other limbs of the law whose office it is to hold even the scales of justice in Nice, are not hard men. The air of Nice is responsible for that. But, in truth, there are occasions in which indulgence would fail if it relapsed into weakness. The case of Titin and Pistafun was one in point. It stood out in so heinous a light and the proofs of guilt were so obviously cumulative that the judges' duty was clearly defined: to present the case in its most lurid colors, set forth the facts to a carefully picked jury so as to prevent any unpleasant surprise, and to insure a death sentence to the first prisoner, and penal servitude, for a goodly number of years, for the second. It was a duty that these gentlemen from the examining magistrate to the public prosecutor, purveyor against his will to the public executioner, did not fail to perform. The indictment was a terrible one. There was nothing in it to provoke laughter. And yet Pistafun laughed.

At length the great day arrived and Pistafun appeared at the Criminal Court between his warders. Titin's place was vacant. Needless to say tickets of admission had been sought for during the preceding month, as though some first night at a theater were in question. Never had the Presiding Judge been the subject of so many touching attentions, invitations, protestations of friendship, and other civilities from those ladies who, however good and virtuous they may be, love the dissection of a scandal.

Hippothadee himself was made much of. He was the man of the moment in circles where to be a somebody you

must be talked about. His great friend, the Comtesse
d'Azila, was proud of him. It was to her that her friends
went for the latest "tips." Through her it was known
that Mme. Supia, still very weak and greatly changed by
the weight of her sorrow, would not be able to give evidence. For that matter, M. Supia himself was emphatically against her presence in Court. But that was not
generally known. It was under the seal of confidence that
the Comtesse d'Azila, from whom her friend Hippothadee
had no secrets, told her circle that the Princess Antoinette
of Transylvania, whatever might be said to the contrary,
had decided to be present. M. Supia and her husband,
the Prince, had vainly striven to persuade her that she,
too, might plead the state of her health, and it would
suffice for her statement to be read in Court.

But she maintained a firm stand. She told them
emphatically:

"No statement of mine is in the examining magistrate's
possession. I said that if I had anything to say I would
say it in Court. Well, I shall say it. . . ." That promised some interesting revelations.

On the day of the trial a great and fashionable crowd
thronged the pretorium, and pressed behind the judges,
the counsel, and the witnesses' seats. The general public
from Nice and the country round were relegated to the
places where there was standing room only. Suddenly
there was an upheaval. Aiguardente, Tony Bouta, and
Tantifla appeared, fighting their way through the crowd.
When Pistafun saw his three friends he seemed ready to
spring from his seat.

"Hang it all, we're a quartette now. We could have a
game of cards!"

The three men, head and shoulders above the crowd,
wore a serious expression. They waved their hands to
Pistafun and shouted advice.

"Don't play the fool. We are with you," said Aiguardente.

"Hang it all, you don't want me to take things too seriously," returned Pistafun.

Just then a commotion was heard outside. Antoinette had arrived. She was very pale in her black dress. She stepped out of a carriage assisted by M. Papajeudi, his wife and three daughters. They, too, were clad in black, as though they were going to a funeral. M. Papajeudi's eyes were red. Neither his wife nor his daughters understood his emotion and he had not thought fit to enlighten them. But as Toinetta had always been on the best of terms with the family and declared that she would only go to the Court with them, they felt highly flattered and shared her sorrow.

At last the Court opened and the trial began. Titin's absence having been duly recorded, the Court proceeded to cross-examine Pistafun, who treated the Presiding Judge's questions with exaggerated politeness. He all but told him that he was delighted to make his acquaintance! A ripple of laughter ensued which the Presiding Judge quickly repressed, threatening to have the Court cleared at the first demonstration. Next he told the accused that the weight of the charge fell on him by the very fact of Titin's absence.

The warning was obviously intended to make Pistafun reflect and to induce him to "give Titin away." But Pistafun was no fool. He grasped the meaning of the maneuver and winked knowingly.

"I'm sorry to interrupt. But if we are to remain good friends you must not set me against Titin. I don't know where he is, I don't know where he comes from, or where he's gone. To my thinking he must have his reasons, and it's not for me in my present position to run after him. But I am easy in my mind. He won't leave me in the lurch. I have nothing more to say."

He left it at that. For the rest he merely repeated his evidence before the examining magistrate. The procession of witnesses began with M. Supia. His statement

was overwhelming. He related the facts as they had been
pieced together at the preliminary investigation. Then
he traced the affair back to its origin, declaring that he
had tried to interest himself in the youth's future to no
purpose, that he had found him a place in his stores but
had been rewarded only with ingratitude, that under the
assumed name of Hardigras he had been up to all sorts
of tricks to ruin him, and had robbed him disgracefully.
Here he turned to the jury, made up, for the most part,
of merchants, and reminded them that these robberies,
unpunished so far, were in themselves an encouragement
to disorder; lastly, that the wretched Titin had imposed
on his ward, had kidnapped her on her wedding day, and
had restored her only after so poisoning her mind that
for some months she refused to hear a word about her
fiancé.

It was then that he had threatened the family in such
a way that the witness and Prince Hippothadee were constrained to postpone the wedding to a later date. And
that when some time after Mlle. Agagnosc, on her own
initiative, asked for the marriage to take place as soon
as possible, he and Prince Hippothadee, still influenced
by Titin's terrible threats, appealed to the police for
advice and protection. Here they found themselves, as
usual, confronted by M. Bezaudin, who had always shown
an unaccountable weakness in dealing with Titin. He
merely laughed at their fears. Titin would not, he said,
go against Mlle. Agagnosc's wishes: 'You have nothing to
be afraid of. He will do nothing. . . .''

"M. Bezaudin bears the weight of a tremendous responsibility. 'Titin will do nothing!' A few days after that,
Hardigras's startling warning was recieved. That same
evening my daughter met her end. Gentlemen, as a father,
I appeal to you to avenge my daughter's death.''

A dead silence ensued. Titin apparently was lost. A
wave of sympathy passed through the court for M. Supia.
Pistafun's counsel thought it well to intervene in order

to minimize the effect of evidence disastrous to his client, as an accomplice to Titin.

"Gentlemen," he said. . . .

But Pistafun came down with one of those blows upon the shoulder that flatten a man and glued the learned counsel to his seat.

"Shut up! Titin has done nothing. But this man's daughter is dead, and he is entitled at least to talk about it."

The Presiding Judge next questioned M. Supia on his sister's mysterious disappearance. M. Supia declared that he had no doubt in his own mind that Mme. Cioasa was another of Titin's victims. Every blow struck at him and his family was part of a scheme of revenge engineered by Titin. He respected no law, human or divine. Accustomed to give free rein to his fancies, he had at first made people laugh, and now he made them cry. He had spread terror everywhere. No one ventured to mention his name, even in La Fourca, without taking the greatest precautions. For daring to express her opinion the poor girl Manchotte had been kidnaped like Mme. Cioasa. And an old woman guilty in Titin's eyes of admitting her friendship with M. Supia and his sister, and of pitying them, was found one morning at her window, shot dead.

"The card bore Hardigras's signature," said the Presiding Judge. "The evidence of handwriting experts shows that the writing on all Hardigras's communications is identical. It is certainly one and the same man who wrote these letters which follow when they do not announce the crime."

When M. Supia left the witness box the usher called Prince Hippothadee. A great commotion arose in Court. The ladies uttered a faint, "Ah! Ah!" of satisfaction. Some of them stood up and there were cries of "Sit down! Sit down!"

The Prince strode forward with great dignity. He wore his monocle, was quietly, but smartly, dressed in a black morning suit, fitting tightly at the waist—he was in mourning for Mlle. Supia—and his hair was lightly waved. His evidence regarding the scene when Titin brought back Mlle. Agagnosc was merely a corroboration of M. Supia's story. As to his engagement and Titin's attitude towards it, he did not think it necessary to refer to the accused's visit on the night when he gave him a piece of his mind with a knife at his throat. That would have been to entrench on the story of his parentage which in the circumstances, Hippothadee preferred to omit.

It may be mentioned that the Transylvania consul, while waiting for instructions, had taken the necessary steps to induce the Court to pass over as lightly as possible, this part of Titin's life, the mention of which might have caused some embarrassment to a friendly power. Other events had arisen which thrust into the background Comte Valdar's meteoric visit. And the evidence in the case was sufficiently preponderant to make it unnecessary to recall a few deplorable attempts to buy furniture and sell jewelry.

Be that as it may, Prince Hippothadee produced the impression, if not of sparing his rival, at least of taking no pains to heap abuse on him. And it was enacted entirely in the grand manner. Lastly, he spoke of the Princess of Transylvania, only to indulge in a tactful eulogy: "As a girl she knew how to enforce her authority on a dangerous madman; as a woman she was the best of wives."

The Prince withdrew from the witness box amid a flattering murmur of approbation. He was succeeded by the handwriting experts whose business it was to establish the identity of Hardigras and Titin from the peculiarity of the writing.

Lastly, Princess Antoinette of Transylvania was called. As they watched her advance so weak and frail, all her energies strained to the breaking point, even the hearts of those most hardened, by daily contact with the great

judicial machine, were softened. It seemed as if she
would not reach the witness box. With an overwhelming
effort she clung to it. At a sign from the Presiding Judge
the usher offered her a seat. She thrust it aside. A cry
burst from hir lips: "He is innocent!" and she sobbed
aloud.

A wave of emotion passed through the Court. The
Presiding Judge himself was moved. After a pause of
a few moments, when she partly had recovered her calmness, he said in a paternal voice:

"Now then, madame. . . . But first swear to tell the
truth and nothing but the truth."

"I swear," she said in a stifled voice. . . . "I swear it
is all my fault. I am the guilty one."

"Come, madame, I will ask you a question or two. You
say Titin is innocent."

"Yes, if he were not innocent I should not have loved
him."

At these words of supreme artlessness a thrill passed
through the Court.

"And yet, madame, it was not he, you married."

"That was my crime. It is I who have killed Titin; for
he is dead or he would be here to answer these charges.
Titin is the best of men. We loved each other. We were
to wait patiently. And then they told me he loved another.
I was disgracefully deceived, and I rushed into this marriage without thinking. Then the thing was done. I
heard nothing more of him. He has taken his own life,
monsieur le President. Titin is dead and the reason that
I too am not dead is because I was determined to come
here and tell you that this Hardigras who has committed
every crime is not Titin. Titin is dead."

Always she harked back to that thought in her despair.
She was beating her head against the barrier behind which
she saw only one thing—Titin's death.

"You will admit that at certain times he disguised himself for Carnival purposes as Hardigras?"

"I don't know," she answered uneasily, aghast at what she had said or at what they were trying to make her say. . . .

"You don't know. You know quite well that Hardigras who kidnapped you, and Titin who brought you back are one and the same person. If they are not one and the same, say so. Remember you have sworn to speak the truth, the whole truth."

She drew herself up, paler and more agitated than before. The Court hung on her words. In a voice that was but a whisper and yet could be heard in the farthest corner, the silence was so tense, she said:

"Yes, since I have sworn to tell the whole truth, I'll tell you that on that day they were the same. They were the same because there could not be two men in the world with the courage to carry off a girl who did not know what she was doing and thought she was deserted by every one, even by him in whom she had put her trust.—There could not be two men in the world to rescue me as Hardigras did and to restore me to my family as Titin did." And she added with clasped hands: "If I have done harm in saying so, may God and Titin forgive me."

"When you returned home your feelings were not the same. There was a change. . . ."

"Yes, there was a change. We had loved each other for a long time, but we had never confessed as much. I was waiting for him to speak. But he was too fastidious. But on that day we fell into each other's arms—that was better than any words. . . . He kissed me as a man kisses his promised wife and he took me back to my family. And now it is said that to be revenged—on whom or what I ask?—he committed this unspeakable crime, when I am the only one at fault. Oh, it is too absurd and you cannot believe it. I appeal to all those who know Titin. No one here believes it, nor even those who accuse him."

As she spoke she recovered her strength, the color came to her cheeks, and a dark gleam lit up her eyes, gazing fixedly at Supia and Hippothadee, who lowered their heads. Some applause broke out at the back of the Court. Then when silence was restored once more, Pistafun's voice was heard:

"Well done, Toinetta. You speak from the heart. But there's nothing to fear. Take it from me, Titin is not dead. If he were here he would perhaps tell us what did occur."

Just then the Presiding Judge, seemingly preoccupied by a communication made to him, turned to the jury:

"Gentlemen, as a matter of fact, Titin is not dead. He was arrested as he was entering the Courts. I have given instructions for him to be brought here."

"Well, there you are! We shall hear the truth," exclaimed Pistafun.

CHAPTER XXIV

MANY scenes are witnessed in a French Criminal Court.
Incidents arise of so unexpected a character that the trial
itself is thrown into confusion and the judges, borne down
by a flood of disclosures, vainly seek to shelter themselves
behind the unstable barrier of procedure. Seldom, however, has there been an instance of the Judge at a Criminal
Court, the Public Prosecutor, the Solicitor-General, the
Counsel for the Defense, and other interested parties, neg-
lecting the usual order of procedure to follow, as dismayed
and powerless onlookers, a duel to the death between two
men whom the course of events had set one against the
other.

The Presiding Judge, whose intention was to suspend
the hearing in order to consult his colleague and take
such measures as might be called for by the unexpected
announcement of Titin's presence, had not uttered a word
when the door of the witnesses' room was noisily flung
open and Titin, dragging behind him MM. Souques and
Ordinal, whom he seemed to have arrested, came rushing
into Court like a man possessed. Doubtless his state of
fury was increased tenfold by the fact that the two detectives had "nabbed" him at the moment when he was entering the Courts on his own initiative. At all events he saw
neither Antoinette, who had fainted in the arms of Mme.
Papajeudi and her daughters, nor Prince Hippothadee,
who had lost all his bravado and wished himself hundreds
of miles away in the fastnesses of Transylvania. His

eyes, his rage, his frenzy, fell on one man whom he seemed to paralyze—and that man was M. Hyacinthe Supia.

Let us at once say that his friends regretted to see him appear before his judges in this half-demented state. They had known him in evil days to display greater self-possession. It was all the more pity that his attitude should support those who, remembering his threats, had represented him as a demon of revenge. There are times when the most prudent are carried away in spite of themselves by the mad gallop in their blood.

"The real murderer is this man!" he yelled.

Had not MM. Souques and Ordinal been present to hold him back he would have thrown himself upon the "tyrant."

"It was he who hanged his daughter after she was already dead. It was he who tied Hardigras's card round her neck."

A general protest of horror and incredulity passed through the Court. Faced by so monstrous an accusation, M. Supia, like an automaton moved by an electric wire, made such convulsive gestures that it looked as if he might scatter into the void. His arms and legs seemed about to fly apart, while the top of the mechanism, before resuming its balance, emitted a grating sound like a broken spring. In any other circumstances his involuntary antics would have caused laughter. Now, however, they appalled.

The Public Prosecutor rose to intervene. But the Presiding Judge motioned to him to keep his seat. From all appearance Titin was half crazy and was in the act of ruining himself. But in truth he was in his right senses and went on:

"You are a criminal—you who do not scruple to send me to the guillotine so that no one should suspect your daughter of hanging herself because she could not bear what was happening under your roof."

"He lies," snarled the "tyrant."

"Do you deny that you hanged your daughter again after discovering that she was dead so as to make it appear as if she had been strangled before she was hanged? Do you deny that you tied round her neck the card that some villain, stealing from me the name of Hardigras, sent you that very night? Gentlemen," went on Titin, turning to the jury, "he not only found among his letters, the letter posted by Pistafun, he found also the card which he hoped would send me to the scaffold."

"He lies, he lies," gasped the "tyrant."

"Where are your proofs?" asked Supia's counsel.

"Proofs! I will give you proofs—the most terrible, the most tragic proofs. As you may suppose if I have delayed coming here to set Pistafun free and to defend myself, it is because I was seeking for those proofs. . . . Pistafun has told you the truth. He knew nothing of the contents of the letter that he had to post by an arrangement often used for this purpose. And I am telling you the truth when I assert that I did not write that letter posted in La Fourca any more than I wrote that card signed Hardigras posted direct in Nice, as the inquiry will prove."

"I deny that," yelped Supia. "No such card was ever in my possession."

"Scoundrel! You were seen fixing the card round your daughter's neck."

"Who saw him?" clamored several voices.

"I will tell you. The things that I will not tell you I will leave you to guess. If that does not satisfy you, you can ask Prince Hippothadee for a few more details. As far as I am concerned I do not ask for them, for there are more sinned against than sinning in this horrible business. . . . Gentlemen, the poor girl in her secret heart loved Prince Hippothadee. She may have believed that she was going to marry him. When he married Mlle. Agagnosc she placed her hopes in a divorce. I can state positively that Mme. Supia won't deny being the first to encourage her in that delusion. . . .

"On the night of the tragedy Caroline was awakened by a sound coming from the ground floor. She went downstairs without troubling to dress. She went down to the drawing-room. Prince Hippothadee was staying the night at La Patentaine. I am in a position to state that he did not spend the night in his own room. And it was because of that fact that the poor girl hanged herself."

"But this is disgraceful," cried Prince Hippothadee, amid the excitement.

"That is the plain speech that I expected from him," returned Titin. "Yes, it is disgraceful and you will have evidence of the disgrace. I swear it or I should be a blackguard. Why cannot I defend myself and pass over in silence these monstrosities? Because my life and honor are at stake—and I must defend myself as best I can. . . . Poor Caroline hanged herself. . . . Meantime, M. Supia arrives. He stumbles against his daughter's dead body. He sinks to the floor with a groan of terror. The door before him opens and it is then Mme. Supia utters a frightful cry of despair which should have awakened the Prince on the first floor had he been on the first floor. Gentlemen, there was no need to call the Prince. He had no need to come downstairs. He had but a few steps to make to hold poor Caroline in his arms and endeavor to restore her to life, while Mme. Supia swooned at the awful sight, and M. Supia thinking only of suppressing a scandal had already taken the infamous card from his pocket. And in this way the frightful farce was stage-managed so that he could demand my head. . . .

"To enable them to take every precaution these gentlemen needed half an hour's grace—half an hour was not too long in which to prepare their scheme and leave nothing to chance. And that is why it was agreed that M. Supia should remain in a faint before Mme. Supia, standing at the door of the drawing-room, uttered her despairing cry. For after that nothing remained for Prince Hippothadee to do but to run for help; that was the obvious thing. We know at what hour M. Supia reached La Patentaine and we know at what hour Prince Hippothadee went for the mayor; in other words, half an hour later. They had to discover, therefore, some means of explaining away this half hour during which the lights at La Patentaine were still out. Well, they found it in the story of Supia's half hour fainting fit and in putting off Mme. Supia's cry of despair for half an hour."

"All this is a ridiculous invention," gasped Hippothadee.

"I challenge this wretched youth to prove what he says," exclaimed the "tyrant".

"Now, this cry that failed to awaken the Prince for good reason, did arouse others who came at once and saw what was taking place during the half hour in question."

"Names, names," clamored several voices.

"Gentlemen," returned Titin seemingly somewhat embarrassed, a fact that did not escape either Supia or the Prince, "you are aware that Castel, M. Supia's chauffeur, slept at La Patentaine."

"It has been proved that he did not sleep there on this particular night," said Supia.

"That's true, but someone was expecting him that night in the servants' quarters."

"That's what you say. Now you must tell us who it was," cried Hippothadee and Supia in unison. "Enough of this humbug. Enough of this nonsense. You promised to give proofs—out with them!"

"Quite right," exclaimed several voices.

"You will understand, Titin," said the Presiding Judge, intervening for the first time, "that everything you have said is so very terrible that it is impossible for you to evade giving proofs any longer."

"Gentlemen, this witness is the mother of a family,"

said Titin after casting a look round the Court, "and I hardly know if I have the right. . . ."

A violent outbreak ensued among Supia and Hippothadee and their friends. And a considerable murmur of disappointment arose from the rest of the assemblage.

"Let not these gentlemen halloo before they are out of the wood," said Titin, whose frenzy had given place to a composure not less tragic. "This person was not the only one to hasten to the spot when Mme. Supia uttered her cry."

"I am waiting," said M. Supia.

"There was also your sister, Mme. Cioasa."

"I could have sworn that!" burst out M. Supia with a hollow laugh. "Mme. Cioasa whom you have caused to disappear so that she should not come here and give you the lie!"

An increasing murmur of hostility towards Titin began to be shown at the back of the Court. The public seemed to be taking umbrage at the promise of evidence that he was in no position to furnish. Titin frequently turned his eyes to the back of the Court. But it was not Toinetta for whom he was looking. At last he seemed to make up his mind:

"Gentlemen," he said, addressing the jury in a voice of despair, "a third person promised to come here and repeat the facts as I have given them to you. That person knew the truth better than anyone, for she was involved in it, and no one could refute her."

"Name! Name!"

"I ask that Mme. Supia should be called."

The effect was overwhelming. Mme. Supia's name was on every lip, and a thrill of excitement stirred the Court. M. Supia straightway resumed his gesticulations. By wildly waving his arms like a semaphone, and by his sharp, frantic tone of voice, he managed to convey that he protested with all his might against his wife's appearance in Court. It would destroy her health, surely, if it did not drive her mad.

"I repeat that it is Mme. Supia herself who asks to be heard," persisted Titin.

Just then an usher strode up behind the Presiding Judge and whispered to him. It was assumed that Mme. Supia had arrived at the Court and, in accordance with Titin's statement, she had asked to be heard. But the Presiding Judge's face betrayed great agitation and it was in a low strained voice that he advised M. Supia to withdraw and asked Prince Hippothadee to be good enough to accompany him to his residence, where his presence was needed. When both had retired, he said:

"Gentlemen of the jury, we shall not hear Mme. Supia's evidence. She has just been discovered—dead."

It was Titin's turn to grow faint as he exclaimed:

"The poor woman has committed suicide!"

.   .   .   .   .   .

Such were the chief events marking the first stage of this amazing trial. Adjourned to the next sessions so that a supplementary inquiry might be held, the case, at the second hearing, developed with startling rapidity. The unhappy Mme. Supia had been discovered with a bullet in her head. The theory of suicide that had been invented, it was said, by Titin—as the only one which would enable him to offer any defense before his judges after the crime—would not hold water. It indicated—in the minds of the authorities—an unspeakable cunning on the part of the prisoner, who had done away with the last witness in a position to comfound him.

Titin no longer defended himself. In the general opinion he alone entered the Supias house hiding himself and taking every possible precaution. His voice was drowned in the hisses of Supia and Hippothadee's friends when he maintained that Mme. Supia had said as he left her: "It is enough for me to have been the cause of my daughter's death. I will give evidence in Court—that will be my punishment."

When the Presiding Judge pronounced sentence of death a loud cry went up in the Court, which aroused him from the terrible lethargy into which he had gradually fallen. Then drawing himself up like a wrestler collecting his strength once more:

"Toinetta, you still believe in my innocence?"

"Yes—to the death."

"Well, we must live, Toinetta, for though I have been condemned to death, I am not yet guillotined."

CHAPTER XXV

PISTAFUN got off with five years' penal servitude.

"Hang it all," he shouted to his friends, "I shall sing to prevent myself from feeling dull. Look after Titin. That's all I have to say to you."

They understood his speech and as the authorities saw some connection between it and Titin's: "I am not yet guillotined," they were able to take their precautions. Titin was subjected to a specially close watch. They were not content with an ordinary cell for him. They confined him, instead, in a small room, on the first floor, which possessed but one small window, well lined with iron bars. The door opened on to a corridor in which a warder mounted guard day and night. On the ground floor looking out on a patrol path was a room occupied by a body of soldiers, the door of which was never closed.

Even had he been a small bird Titin could scarcely have flown away. Four warders selected from the most reliable in the prison kept watch on him in relays of two. These facts were known in the town, and the general opinion was that Titin had but to make his preparations for the end. Meantime he entered an appeal against the sentence.

During the first few days he was somewhat sullen. A sense of hopelessness had come over him. He barely spoke to the warders, refused to play cards with them, and had little inclination for his food.

Thrown back upon himself, confronted by thoughts

which had frequently troubled him but which he had
always thrust aside as unworthy and dishonoring, he was
wounded in his deepest feelings. For, is there anything
finer in life than friendship? After turning over in his
mind for the hundredth time his many misfortunes, he was
forced to a conclusion that pierced him to the heart: his
present misery could only be explained by the treachery
of someone acquainted with his secrets, whom he had of
set purpose refused to suspect, for the crime was too unspeakable. To the question which he had deliberately
refrained from asking himself but which became inevitable
now: "Are you sure of Giaousé?" he was compelled to
reply: "No!"

He wept to think of it. Giaousé brought back to him
his early days, his vagrant boyhood, his happy youth,
their many pleasant trips together, their practical jokes
at Carnival time. Giaousé was all that he could wish him
to be—his dear old friend and slave and also, alas! his
butt. True, he had been somewhat to blame. Was he
certain that he had nothing to reproach himself with in
his relations with Nathalie—Nathalie, who fled from a
place where there was a Titin who had no love for her and
would never have any love for her? Giaousé imagined,
perhaps, that he had stolen her from him. Was it possible to plumb the depths of a jealous man's heart? And
yet he would never have suspected Giaousé of wishing him
to be sentenced to death had not—and this was the horrible part—his underhand influence of late explained
everything.

Possibly Giaousé was not acting of his own volition;
that was indeed probable; but Giaousé was weak. Possibly they had managed to wrest his secrets from him.
Possibly he had allowed himself to drift into things, the
significance of which he had at first failed to comprehend
—things that had ended in blood. To begin with, there
was the meeting at "Le Père la Bique," which had played
into Supia and Hippothadee's hands. Could he assure

himself that Giaousé had not been their accomplice? Titin
had left the place with two letters which, if closely examined, might have led him to the path of truth, but he had
missed them from his pocket. He thought he could positively declare that no one but Giaousé had been near him
that day. With whom was Giaousé acting in concert?
Why and with what object? How he longed to know!
    For instance, there was the disappearance of Mme.
Cioasa whose evidence would have been of great assistance.
He was sure that a day or two before her disappearance
Giaousé had had long talks with her—and she never
spoke to anyone! And, then there was the disappearance
of Mme. Manchotte and the murder of Mme. Boccia.
Giaousé had not been near either of them but the two
women had been seen in conversation with two doubtful
characters with whom Giaousé had made friends and
were, perhaps, his evil geniuses—Tulip and Bolacion.
    Tulip was a curious creature. He did the entire busi-
ness of his employer, the solicitor who had been mixed up,
if gossip in Grasse could be believed, in many shady trans-
actions; a man for every low-down job, full of inventions
and cunning, taking a diabolical delight in the misfortunes
of others. Bolacion was a pretty rough customer, despised in Torre les Tourettes and La Fourca, alike, and
acceptable only to the strange gang who had taken up
their quarters like cave men in the hollows of the Gorges
du Loup, or in primitive huts where navvies and quarry
men speaking the most varied dialects slept after their
rough work. And, when they had a few pence in their
pockets, they abandoned their jobs altogether to indulge
in the lowest form of drunkenness.
    Titin had not wasted his time during the weeks when
he was said to be dead. He had learned a great deal
about their nightly doings, their robberies, the inexpli-
cable misery that had descended on this formerly peaceful
district.
    Then came the last and most terrible blow—Thélise's

death. Who had entered the flat after him? . . . Giaousé
was the only one who knew the way over the roofs. Had
he or some accomplice got in by the balcony? It was
almost a certainty that Giaousé had had a hand in this
last crime, bringing Titin to the scaffold.

The criminal had fired on Thélise from behind with a
revolver found by him in a drawer of Supia's desk. The
papers in the drawer, for some unaccountable reason, were
thrown into disorder. And the revolver was left beside
Thélise to make it seem as if Titin wanted the murder to
be looked upon as a case of suicide. Was Gaousé capable
of arranging a cut and dried scheme of this nature—of
thinking it out in detail? If it were not Giaousé, who did
commit the murder? Bolacion? Who was the leading
spirit in it? Tulip? But who had given them the necessary information unless it were Giaousé? Turn the matter over in his mind as he might, it was always to Giaousé
that his thoughts recurred.

A hoarse moan broke in his throat. Was he to die without solving the hideous problem? No and again no! He
had pledged himself to Toinetta. He was not yet guillotined. Suddenly he asked for wine and cards. They
should see the sort of man he was—the real Hardigras!
It would be Hardigras against Hardigras. The sham
Hardigras would have to look out for himself!

Strengthened by his new resolutions, having nothing
more to fear, and ready once again to dare all to win the
game, he wore a new look which in no way reassured his
warders. Two of them in particular, Paolo Ricci and
Pietro Peruggia—Corsicans—appeared suspicious. After
the third day he managed to induce in them a more cheerful attitude.

Between their games of cards they exchanged a few
words. He learned that the town was interested in nothing but him and that a change of feeling in his favor had
taken place. The ex-Commissary of Police, M. Bezaudin,
whose evidence at the trial was entirely favorable to him,

was trying to bring forward a new fact. He had found handwriting experts whose conclusions were diametrically opposed to those of the official experts.

"You will see that my innocence will be proved when my head is off," said Titin with a laugh.

It was then that he received an unexpected visit from the Public Prosecutor, the Examining Magistrate, and Comte Valdar. Odonovitch seemed greatly distressed.

"Oh, sir, what a blow to Transylvania!" he exclaimed. "And I was so glad to be the bearer of good news—your illustrious father is dead!"

"Is that what you call good news, my dear Comte?" said Titin. "Do you take me for an unnatural son?"

"We wished you to learn from Comte Valdar before you die," said the Public Prosecutor, "that Prince Marie Hippothadee recognized and legitimized you as his son, on his death bed. During the trial you were reproached with assuming a rank to which, it was objected, you were not entitled, and which you made use of to cut a figure as an adventurer. Fortunately the matter is now set straight."

"And your conscience is at rest," said Titin. "It's something for a Public Prosecutor to be able to say to himself that he is going to guillotine an honest man. If you wish to complete your goodness you will call at Durieu's in the Rue de la Poste—he is my stationer—and order some obituary cards bearing a Prince's crown."

"A royal crown," broke in Odonovitch. "His Majesty himself is not in the best of health. According to the latest news he won't live very long."

"He will live as long as I shall, and all the better if he does. What would you have me do with a royal crown if I have no head?"

"You must have faith in Providence," said the worthy Odonovitch. "God and the saints won't permit such a crime to be committed."

"Send me, my dear Odonovitch, a case of that extra dry

1921 champagne, which I so thoroughly enjoyed, and a box of Coronas. They will remind me of the pleasant hours we spent together. That's all I ask you. I am to be a rich man now. That's one comfort, at least."

"Unfortunately, Prince Marie Hippothadee died in exile without a penny, dispossessed of his property. But that doesn't matter for the future belongs to us."

"Thank you for those kind words my dear Comte."

"You can rely on my carrying out your little order."

"Yes I know that we still have the jewelers to fall back on!"

"They are hopeless," returned Odonovitch, and with that they said good-bye. For, the other gentlemen began to show signs of impatience.

Titin, after this visit, displayed a more cheerful humor. His warders regarded him with admiration. It was while left alone for a space with Paolo Ricci that he dilated on the wealth that would have been his had he been going to live. The conversation occurred at six o'clock when Chief Warder Peruggia had betaken himself to the Governor of the prison to make a verbal report of the day's events.

One day Paolo said outright:

"Titin, I am entirely at your disposal. We will help you to get away."

"Do you mean it!"

"The thing is arranged, I tell you."

"By whom?"

"Toinetta. My wife has known her for a long time. She delivers the laundry to the Supias. When the trick's done, I can slip off to Italy. My future is assured. I will tell you all about it to-morrow. Take no risks with Peruggia."

Titin as may be imagined passed an agitated night. At last the moment came when he was alone again with Paolo Ricci. The warder took from his pocket a file, some oil, tow, and bread crumbs. He began to file a bar, explaining in a low voice that it would suffice to weaken two

bars and that Tantifla would undertake to double them up
like liquorice sticks. As the window looked directly out
on to a patrol path inside the prison Titin at first showed
little enthusiasm. It was a plan of escape that seemed
to him rather crude.

"Never mind about that," said Paolo. "We've thought
of everything. Giaousé is running the show."

"Giaousé!" exclaimed Titin taken aback. "Then I'm
done for."

The plan was not fully explained to him until two days
later. He gave a shrug.

"You mustn't make a fool of us, old man," said Paolo.
"We have considered the matter in all its bearings. Our
reason for fixing on this particular scheme is because
there's no choice. It must succeed. With seven of us
on the job it will be devilish bad luck if we don't pull it
off."

"Seven are a good many," said Titin. He felt that he
would have preferred six, leaving out Giaousé, whose part
in it boded him no good.

"Yes, seven of us—Giaousé, Bolacion, Tulip. . . ."

"You have already mentioned three too many."

As you may well think there'll be a few heads smashed.
We shan't be seven when it's all over. The others are
Tantifla, Tony Bouta, and Aiguardente. The thing is
fixed for this particular time of the day. It's dark as
night then, and there's every chance of Peruggia leaving
us alone. If he stays here we shall have to shut his mouth
between us. A nice little gag will do the job without
hurting him. He's my colleague you know."

"Do you think there's any chance?"

"Giaousé promised Toinetta and Mme. Bibi, who came
to Nice the day before yesterday, to have you in a place
of safety by seven o'clock on Sunday. Sunday was
Tulip's idea because a friend of his in the 22nd Chasseurs
will be on sentry duty at La Novi Prison. You know him
perhaps. His name is Sénépon and he is a La Costa man."

"Oh, yes, Sénépon. But I know him very slightly and I don't suppose he'll risk being sent to a penal regiment in Africa just to please me."

"We are not consulting him. He will be marching up and down in front of his sentry box, at the foot of the patrol path. They'll pass him. Tulip will say a word to him and offer him a cigarette; well, he'll manage the thing. For, there are three of them to go for him. They'll hold him and prevent him from kicking up a row. That's where Tulip, Giaousé, and Bolacion come in. Meantime, we'll set to work and you can take it from me, Aiguardente, Tony Bouta, and Tantifla won't waste time over it. These three fellows have the needful to get over the wall. They'll be inside the guard-house before any suspicion is aroused and nab them. You will slip out. Besides, I know some of them believe in your innocence. They'll be content to shut their eyes and ears. I tell you the thing will go off with a bang."

"Which way do I slip out?"

"This way," he said pointing to the window. "Tantifla will double up these bars. The thing is already half done. If anyone knocks at the cell door I shan't open it. I shall be nabbed very likely. But that's part of the program."

"Do you know what I think, Paolo Ricci? The whole scheme is idiotic."

"How changed you are, Titin! In a matter of this sort only the impossible succeeds. You won't be the first to escape from a prison. And they didn't have fellows like our six in the gamble, ready to risk their lives for you."

"After all, time will tell," said Titin, in a tone of philosophy. "But the thing that I can't get out of my head is why Bolacion, with whom I have always been on bad terms, should take a risk like this for me."

"He is now hand and glove with Giaousé."

"We'll talk about this again at seven o'clock on Sunday, my dear Ricci."

His last words fell on deaf ears. For, Ricci was absorbed with the breadcrumbs, the soot, and the rust, getting rid of every trace of his work.

On the following Sunday Sénépon, pacing up and down, saw three dark forms coming towards him, talking and laughing loudly. He recognized Tulip, who shouted a friendly, "Cheerio!"

"Move on, or you'll get me confined to the guard room," said Sénépon.

Without paying any further attention to him they continued their way and Sénépon turned his back on them. He made a few steps when a meteor seemed to crash upon his shoulders. He collapsed to the ground dropping his rifle. A handkerchief was crammed into his mouth to stifle him. A few seconds later Aiguardente, Tantifla, and Tony Bouta, making use of ropes and crampons, climbed over the wall. Meantime Titin and Ricci held themselves in readiness for every contingency. They could distinguish the three forms on the coping of the wall. Titin was very white, and Ricci, was very red. Peruggia would not be back for at least another five minutes.

"That's all right," said Ricci in a husky voice.

At that very moment a shot rang out beyond the patrol path, and straightway they heard the sound of shouts, cries for help, oaths, a rush of men from all sides, and more shots. Aiguardente's voice could be heard yelling:

"Clear out! . . . I am hit. . . ."

Paolo Ricci closed the window, exclaiming:

"It's all up!"

A violent knocking came at the door and Ricci opened it. Peruggia appeared foaming with rage.

"What's up?" Paolo asked.

"Ask Titin," roared Peruggia. "He knows what's up."

"No I don't," said Titin calmly sitting down. "If my opinion had been asked it would have been worked very differently."

The fight in the patrol path was over. The authorities came running in.

"What have they been trying to do?" asked the Governor of the Prison.

"I don't know," returned Titin.

"Besides, if he had stirred a limb I'd have blown his brains out," said Ricci, showing his revolver. . . .

So much for this amazing attempt at escape. Realizing that there was no hope for them, Aiguardente, Tantifla, and Tony Bouta surrendered. Their friends who had overcome the sentry outside were able to make good their escape leaving, however, some traces of blood behind. Sénépon was complimented on his pluck. He had managed, though overwhelmed by the weight of his three adversaries, to reach his rifle and press the hammer. From that moment the game was up.

Next day Titin said to Paolo Ricci.

"If they had wanted to make an attempt at escape impossible and hasten my death they couldn't have done anything worse. You must thank Giaousé on my behalf."

"I certainly will do so," returned Ricci. "It will be a consolation to him. He was stabbed in the arm by a bayonet."

"Is that so?" said Titin.

Titin was right. The incident had the effect of hastening matters.

CHAPTER XXVI

BEWARE! HARDIGRAS!

THE whole town hoped that Titin had made his escape. Had he not practically foretold the event? When it became known that the attempt was a fiasco, and Tantifla, Tony Bouta, and Aiguardente had succeeded only in getting into prison, immense disappointment and regret were shown.

For the past fortnight, M. Bezaudin had undertaken a series of public meetings in the town and villages round about, in an effort to prove Titin's innocence. As the public were only too willing to be convinced, his meetings were everywhere a complete success. He was accompanied on his tour by the two handwriting experts, previously mentioned; and Le Budeu and Gamba Secca, Titin's ex-Auditor and Staff Controller, acted as secretaries.

M. Bezaudin fully realized that the chief part of his reasoning came from the heart, and that it was not with this particular organ that the course of justice could be arrested. Still, in his view, a petition for mercy signed by thousands of citizens might at least save Titin's head. That, after all, was the main point for the moment.

Odon Odonovitch, Comte de Valdar, Lord of Vistritza, Metzoras, Trikala, Triatika, and other places had had visiting cards printed with the object of obtaining admission to the houses of the most influential citizens of Paris before himself submitting the said petition to the President of the Republic. It was then that the untoward business of the attempted escape occurred. M. Bezaudin and Odon

Odonovitch regretted the effort, since it had failed. They had good reason to be cast down. A few days later they learned that Titin's appeal against his sentence had been rejected, that the President had refused to see Comte Valdar, and finally that M. de Paris, the Executioner, had arrived in Nice with his paraphernalia.

From Trayas to Les Roches Rouges, from the confines of L'Esterel to the upper valley of Le Paillon, from bay and headland to plain and mountain, the sinister news spread like a tidal wave. Sea-coast tramways, suburban trains, the Gare du Sud poured forth in an endless stream hosts of sightseers slowly making their way to the Place d'Armes, over the roads leading to Le Novi Prison, where the execution was to take place. Soon the multitude was stopped by a strong force of police, supported by troops brought from Draguignan and Toulon, and companies of Alpine light infantry, seemingly sharing the general grief. Roofs and windows, from which the Place d'Armes and the Rue de la Prison could be seen, quivered with a bewildering and weird throng overflowing and clinging to every point of vantage. . . .

The man and his assistants have disappeared from the door of the prison. He has left to secure his prey, and other men in black pass hurriedly through the gateway with lowered head as though in shame. They too, are after their victim. . . . They want to make sure that he will not escape them. . . .

And Titin—Titin so much in love with life—is Titin to die? . . . Will he no longer gather the olives in May? . . . All his friends are there—friends whose leader he was at the fêtes. What will become of them without him? . . . Weary, the night is fading . . . the night is fading. . . .

* * * * *

But what is this? The terrible forecourt has been deserted for some time. The blood-red sky is merged in a

sheaf of roses and dawn rises calmly triumphant from
the tragic night. One of the most beautiful mornings of
Nice spreads its peace over the land. . . . What does
this period of inaction mean? Why this incomprehensible
delay? No one dares ask the question. An anguish, beyond all bearing, mingled with an impossible hope, wrings
every heart. A silence falls over the city in which the
coming of the angel of death can be heard. And dawn
has come—a lovely dawn—a bright sunlight that no gallows can look in the face. . . . And the gallows is taken
down—is being packed up! Men are at work dismantling
it. The man in red and the men in black are going back
empty handed. Wild scenes break out round the hideous
and futile thing which comes to pieces, disappears and is
swept away. M. de Paris, the Executioner, mounts his
wagon; he takes the road to Paris, does M. de Paris. And
he returns with an empty basket instead of the blood-red
harvest from the Cote d'Azur. Cheerio! M. de Paris.

"Hang it all, we don't want to see you again. . . ."

Titin had played a precious trick on him—a trick which
he was far from expecting. When he appeared in the condemned cell there was but one man there, wearing the
straight waistcoat, but that man was Chief Warder
Peruggia, whose neck bore a card bearing the words:
"Beware—Don't make a mistake. Hardigras." And no
one could fail to see the trick. Titin had written it in
small letters so that there should be no mistake.

The news of this miraculous escape spread like wild
fire. The most circumstantial details were soon current.
And it is easy to imagine the inventions and embellish-
ments with which the first story was embroidered. Titin
had escaped clad in the uniform of a warder, by the complicity of a warder!

CHAPTER XXVII

HARDIGRAS'S ESCAPE

AFTER the unfortunate attempt at escape which proved so
fatal to Aiguardente, Tony Bouta, and Tantifla, Titin
was put into a straight waistcoat. It was an unnecessary
precaution. Deprived of the devoted little band who, had
they been cleverly led, might have been of such great
service, believing also that he was the victim, on this last
occasion, of the duplicity and trickery of him whom he had
always regarded as a brother, Titin confessed, to himself,
his defeat.

Too many people outside and inside the prison were
bent on his destruction to permit him to entertain the
least hope. It was in vain that Paolo Ricci strove to
encourage him. He refused to listen to him. But, he
begged him to set down in writing a few words marked
with the calm dignity of which prisoners of the blood royal
seem to possess the secret in their hour of martyrdom.
Thus his last thoughts and injunctions were to be conveyed to Toinetta by means of her laundress. And he
prepared her to accept his fate without any feeling of
revolt against Providence, sufficiently merciful to allow
them once more to exchange a few words of love.

"I am young and I have no wish to die," Toinetta
made answer to his display of fortitude. "And as I cannot live without you, it is essential for you to live. Have
confidence. We will save you."

Ricci held out the note to him. He was unable to take
it owing to his straight-jacket. But he kissed it. . . .

The day of execution was at hand.

"Don't go to sleep and be ready for anything," Ricci warned him.

"What can I do with this straight-jacket on?" gasped Titin. Ricci did not answer; for, just then Peruggia came into the cell.

Peruggia, after giving final instructions, decided to keep watch over the prisoner that night, with Ricci. He would not leave him, therefore, until the authorities arrived. About three o'clock in the morning a knock came at the door. Ricci, without opening it, asked what was wanted. There was the sound of a voice and Ricci turning to Peruggia, said:

"It's Warder Matteotti. He has a message for you from the Governor of the Prison."

"Ask him in."

Ricci opened the door and at once closed it again. Titin gave a start for he recognized Giaousé clad in a warder's uniform. Peruggia turning round also recognized him. But as Giaousé held a revolver in his hand, pointed at Peruggia's heart, he kept silent.

"Good. Keep quiet. Nobody's going to hurt you."

Ricci also exerted himself. Three minutes later it was Chief Warder Peruggia who was wearing the straight-jacket. He implored them to gag him with a handkerchief, which they did. Titin wished to assume Peruggia's uniform.

"No, they all know the Chief Warder," said Ricci. "It will be easier for you to pass out with my uniform."

"Or with mine," said Giaousé.

"No, you must both of you go out very quietly. You must wait until the clock strikes half-past three to pass the hall porter. That is most important. Do you understand, Giaousé? You know what to do?"

"Well, of course."

"You can see for yourself that you mustn't leave Titin. You will go out together. I'll do my best to look after myself."

They left the cell when the warders were due to be relieved. Five minutes later they were outside the prison. Paolo Ricci, however, was less fortunate. As he was trying to slip out some minutes before the arrival of the authorities, he came up against the Governor of the Prison, who asked him why he was not in the condemned cell with Peruggia. He gave an explanation which seemed suspicious. And, the Governor noticed that he was wearing stripes to which he was not entitled. The fat was in the fire. The magistrates from the Public Prosecutor's office arrived. A very pretty blaze ensued.

To their reprimands and abuse Ricci answered that he had so acted because he was convinced of Titin's innocence, which was true. But, from the reception given to his ingenious defense, he realized that he would have to abandon all thought of a career as a warder.

Meantime, Giaousé and Titin were already far away. They had mounted a motor lorry which was waiting for them behind La Paillon. The van was driven by Bolacion, and seated beside him was Tulip, both disguised as peasants.

As soon as they drove off, Titin and Giaousé divested themselves of their warders' uniforms and put on much worn, wide ribbed velvet clothes, the trousers of which were tucked into long gaiters. These gave them some resemblance to mountain folk—lovers of poaching and even contraband. They were all fully armed.

Telegraph and telephone were kept busy in the mountain district until night time. Motor cars in which the kepis of gendarmes flashed along the roads like meteors, loomed up into sight from the valleys and descended the mountain peaks. But at six o'clock that night Titin and his little band were safe from capture, far beyond St. Martin Vesube, in the depths of a steep crag where Barnabé alias Laguerra, the shepherd, had prepared supper for them.

After supper, when Barnabé had dressed the wound

which an Alpine light infantryman's bayonet had inflicted a few days before in Giaousé's arm, they made their arrangements to part company.

"I am sorry, Giaousé, for having doubted you," said Titin. "You were wounded in trying to save my life, and you would have given your life for me. You are more than a brother to me. I have had bitter thoughts about you. Will you forgive me?"

"I know you have had bitter thoughts about me. But if that is all over now I am satisfied. I have nothing further to say."

"And you, my friends," said Titin, turning to Bolacion and Tulip, "will you forgive me, too?"

"Willingly," said Bolacion and Tulip in unison.

"Where are you going now?" asked Giaousé, after they had ratified their reconciliation, solemnly.

"Have no fear," returned Titin. "Wherever I go I swear that I won't spoil your work. They will never recapture me."

"Good-bye then and may St. Helene be with you," said Giaousé. . . .

Two days later persons trudging up at dawn towards La Fourca gazed with amazement at the high portico commanding the open space in the old town between the Tower and the Town Hall. A dark shape hung outstretched swaying gently in the icy gusts from the mountain. From the distance it was impossible to say exactly what this miserable object could be, but on closer examination it assumed a human shape—a man was hanging there. . . . Nearer still, the hatchet face of the man who was once the "tyrant" could be recognized. He was wearing his last grimace.

CHAPTER XXVIII

PRINCE HIPPOTHADEE DISPLAYS HIS GENEALOGICAL KNOWLEDGE

EVEN though Prince Hippothadee had attended M. Supia's funeral in the morning, he was in high good spirits on that evening. It had been a mournful ceremony. Toinetta had not been present at the cemetery, and in the minds of certain persons there was good reason for her absence—it meant that she could not repeat the gesture which she made at Caroline's grave: "No. Titin did not do this thing." Alas, he had no need this time to sign his name. He knew that the deed would be regarded as the handiwork of the real Hardigras.

His revenge had not been long delayed. The evening following his escape, the "tyrant's" car ran into an obstacle between La Costa and La Fourca, causing it to topple over on its side. The chauffeur in a sorry plight was left on the road while a number of dark forms made a rush on Supia, who had a leg broken and other injuries, and carried him off. At dawn the hatchet face was swinging like a weathercock from the old Tower of La Fourca.

Obviously Titin had tragic reasons for bearing a grudge against M. Supia, and M. Supia shared a considerable part in the responsibility for bringing M. de Paris to the Place d'Armes. Nevertheless, the general opinion was that it was not clever on Titin's part. For, what could he hope for now? . . .

But to return to Hippothadee, who was in sprightly humor that evening. He put the finishing touches to his tie in the dressing-room of the flat in the Promenade des

Anglais, the lease of which had reverted to him. The man servant came in with a letter which some unknown individual had delivered, requesting it to be handed to the Prince at once. Hippothadee opened it, smiled, and said:

"Tell Madame la Princesse that I wish to say a word to her before she goes out."

The man left the room and almost immediately returned:

"Madame la Princesse is waiting to see your Highness in the small drawing-room."

When Toinetta heard the first gruesome report of M. Supia's death she left the Papajeudises with whom she had been staying, to return to the conjugal hearth. For the sake of all concerned her place was there at such a moment. The police might need her and Titin also. Indeed, her place, at the time being, was her home.

In truth, why had she not obeyed her first impulse to go and wait for the man she loved in Barnabé's hut in the mountain? She might have been able to prevent his horrible act of revenge. She would have placed her arms round his neck. He would not have broken that chain. And they would have thought only of their love. Alas! She had been forced to yield to the entreaties of Giaousé and others who told her that she was closely watched, and that the least movement on her part might jeopardize them all.

And now—was not everything jeopardized? Was not everything lost? After escaping the gallows it was as though Titin had executed himself. How utterly senseless! She had not the strength to weep. She sat for hours holding her head in her hands, a grim look on her face.

What could the Prince want of her? She had sent him word that she wished to be left alone. He came in:

"I am sorry to disturb you, Antoinette," he said, "but I have just received a note which gives me food for thought, and I would like to know what you think of it." He handed her the letter. "It is from Souques and Ordi-

nal. They seem to be full of good intentions towards me,
these worthy detectives. But between ourselves I think
they are lacking in psychological insight."

She read:

"Monsieur
We must take the liberty of informing you that your life is in
danger. In our opinion you are marked down as the next victim
to follow M. Hyacinthe Supia, and you cannot take too many
precautions. Do not go out alone, and in particular do not leave
the town. Rely on us in the matter in which we have received
your instructions. We are following up the right clue and shall
have some news for you in this regard before long. The best thing
for you would be to remain indoors this evening. We are, etc."

Toinetta gave him back the letter.

"Well, what can I say? You know better than I do
what you have to do."

"No. I have not disturbed you to receive so vague an
answer. I realize that you are but slightly interested in
the fate of a man whom you do not care for. All the
same my life is at stake. Do you think I am in any danger,
Antoinette?"

"I am too distracted to know anything. I can say no
more. But since you have made me read this letter, I
think my duty is to repeat what those gentlemen say:
Don't go out to-night."

"Thank you, Antoinette. I expected no less from you.
Those words bring us nearer to each other. Well now,
I will tell you something. Personally, I believe these
gentlemen are entirely mistaken. *He* would not dare."

She made no reply. She seemed as if turned to stone.
He sat down facing her, lit a cigarette, and went on in a
delightfully free and easy manner:

"He would not dare, not on my account, but on yours.
He loves you, does this man. There are already sufficient
obstacles to keep you apart. He does not wish to put the
dead body of a husband between him and you. . . . That
is something which you would never forgive him for."

She stared at Hippothadee. A strange light that she had never seen before gleamed in his eyes. He observed the impression which he had made on her and he took a keen and almost cynical pleasure in it.

"No. Titin can do nothing against me," he went on with a smile, venturing to pronounce that name for the first time. "In reality we have no better friend than Titin. He was rather drastic with poor Supia. But when we have finished mourning the poor man, we shall discover that Titin rendered us a priceless service. Supia had become impossible, not only to me who was reduced to borrowing money from the Comtesse d'Azila to pay the rent—our rent my dear Antoinette—but to you whose fortune he had secured entirely for himself. Not only will you be able to get possession of your property. But we are now sole heirs."

Toinetta drew herself up with a tremor, scarcely comprehending him, dazed by what he said. The fiendish glee and peculiar smile that marked his words were loathsome to her.

"The sole heirs," she repeated hollowly.

"Why, of course, thanks to that wonderful Titin, who has taken the precaution. . . ."

"That will do! This does not concern Titin. It concerns us. It concerns me."

"Why of course it concerns you. Please give me your attention and you will understand it all. . . . The man who was your godfather and guardian would have been a relative even if your father had not married poor Thélise's sister, for M. Agagnosc was Supia's cousin. . . ."

"Yes, I know that vaguely, but I perceive that you are at least as well informed as I am. . . ."

"Oh, with us princes, genealogy is about the one thing that we do understand. . . . But to come back to Supia, Agagnosc's cousin. When your father became a partner of M. Delamarre's, the sole director at that time of Bella Nissa, he sent to Grasse for Supia, who was employed in a bank. Then, he made him his chief cashier. Meantime, Agagnosc married Mme. Delamarre's sister—your mother. M. Delamarre died and Supia married M. Delamarre's widow, your aunt, by whom he had one daughter—Caroline. And now, you understand, Caroline is dead. . . . Thélise is dead. . . . Supia is dead. . . . Who is left? Why, you!"

"One moment," said Toinetta, whose teeth were chattering "M. Supia had a sister who comes before me, and fortunately inherits everything."

"You forget, dear Antoinette, that Mme. Cioasa has disappeared," returned the Prince with a smile.

"She has disappeared; but she may not be dead."

"Why do you suppose that she is not dead? All the others are dead. Do you not think she would have given some sign of life when she learnt what had happened in La Fourca since her departure? Come, I assure you, Hardigras can not have spared her any more than the rest. It is obvious that at least some terrible accident has befallen the poor old thing. We must know all about it as soon as possible. I put the matter in Souques and Ordinal's hands, promising them a substantial payment. If we may believe the letter that I asked you to read, they have lost no time."

"You think of everything," said Toinetta in a whisper.

"Everything, Antoinette, where your happiness is concerned."

He bowed low and left her. She remained in her room distraught. . . . "He is the murderer. . . . It was he!" she repeated wildly impelled by a mad feeling of relief.

"He! He!" . . . Those dead bodies all seemed to rise up before her while he was speaking. And the last victim, Supia himself—it was the Prince who had brought about his death. It was he who had committed all these crimes or caused them to be committed. And then she remembered the deadly look that he cast by stealth at Supia the day on which he called on the cashier at Bella Nissa and

returned with two hundred and seventy-five francs. . . .
Murderer! Oh, to be sure he could play the bravado and
laugh at Souques and Ordinal's warnings. He knew well
enough that no one was going to murder him.

A knock came at the door. It was the lady's maid.
She noticed her mistress's agitation. It moved her to
great sympathy for her.

"Leave me. I don't want to see anyone. The Prince
has gone out I suppose. Well, I give you all leave to go
out."

"Madame, some one has just come up the back staircase, some one from La Fourca, from Mme. Bibi, he says.
He would like to see you at once."

"Did he not give you his name?"

"No, madame. But the cook and I recognized him."

"Who is it?" asked Toinetta with a catch in her
breath.

"Titin."

Toinetta uttered a cry.

"Oh! Show him into the lobby—at once—and not a
word to a soul."

"Oh, madame, not for anything in the world. Poor
Titin. If you only knew what a state he is in!"

"Good heavens!"

She went into her boudoir. Titin came in. He leant
against the wall. It seemed as if he were about to drop.
She clasped him in her arms:

"What have they done to you, my Titin?"

He was in rags. He wore a shapeless overcoat, was
without a collar or tie; his shirt was torn and he was
bleeding at the chest. A handkerchief was bound round
his forehead, and beneath was the face of a martyr—as
pale as death . . . with wide-open eyes shining with pain.
. . . He did not return her kisses. He slid into a chair
and she had not the time to hold his head which struck
the wall.

"Something to drink. . . . I'm thirsty . . . hungry."

She rang the bell. The lady's maid came in, looked at Titin, and burst into tears.

Toinetta grew calm.

"Mariette, if you betrayed him, you would be the death of both of us."

"I would die first, madame."

"Then help us. Give him something to eat and drink. Is there any beef tea, champagne, brandy in the place? Get him something."

"Water," gasped Titin.

He began by draining a bottle of Evian water. Later he devoured everything pell-mell as Mariette brought it in—Gruyère cheese, cold meat, fruit, a bottle of wine. At last having satisfied his hunger he smiled and said:

"Now you can bring me some champagne. I feel better."

"What have they done to you?" asked Toinetta, sitting down facing him.

"Nothing, my Toinetta. But for three days and nights they've been hunting me. . . . All over the place. . . . Everywhere. . . . They've stuck to me like leeches. Oh, what a time I've been through—not a moment's breathing space—not even the time for a drink out of a brook! When I thought I had put them off the scent, others sprang up from somewhere or other, and it all began over again. There must be ten of them shadowing me, sworn to do me in. Souques and Ordinal must have had them down from Paris. . . . I don't know their particular mugs. . . .

"They can't be far away. I hadn't an ounce of strength left. I said to myself: See Toinetta for the last time and then. . . . Well, then let things take their course. I won't make another step. What is written is written. So you must be sensible since there is nothing else to be done. . . . Stop kissing my hands like that! . . . They're not hands—they're like nothing at all. . . . Good Lord how comfortable it is here. . . ."

Half an hour had scarcely elapsed though it seemed a

second—an eternity—when three loud knocks came at
the door. Mariette's terrified, breathless voice could be
heard:

"Madame, madame. . . . MM. Souques and Ordinal!"

"You see, my dear," said Toinetta to Titin, "there's
no time to wash your hands." And then to Mariette:
"Did you tell them I was in?"

"I told them you were out. But they said: 'No, your
mistress is not out and we want to speak to her at once.' "

Toinetta opened the door slightly.

"Where are they?"

"I left them in the lobby."

"Show them into the study and tell them I am dressing
but will be with them in ten minutes. Shut the study
door, and don't look so scared."

She turned round. Titin seated with folded arms was
watching her transfixed.

"Well, what are you doing?" she asked, astonished to
see that he had not stirred.

"Nothing. . . . I was looking at you. . . . I have
only another ten minutes to look at you. . . . So you will
understand I am making the most of my opportunity."

"You are right," she said. "Afterwards, time will
show. . . . My love, I know the murderer. Yes, the man
you were looking for—the sham Hardigras. I know him."

Then, she related the scene that had passed between her
and Hippothadee some minutes before his arrival.

"Do you understand now? Do you see how simple the
whole business is. . . . I am the sole heiress. Do you
follow?"

"Yes," he returned, suddenly enlightened. "You are
right. That explains everything. Ah, the villain!"

"Don't you see that nothing is lost."

"As you say, nothing is lost. But we shall want proof."

"I will get it, I promise you. Yes, my Titin, before
very long I shall have him. I shall get him to let out his
secret. I shall pretend to understand him, to share and

to admire his game. He is so conceited. I shall have him, the monster, like the ass that he is. . . . And I'll lead him to say things which others will hear. Don't stir from here. I will tell you what you must do. Let me be for a while. Those two detectives are waiting to see me. They know nothing of the work that I am preparing for them."

She found Souques and Ordinal in the Prince's study, waiting patiently for her, with the look that may be seen on the faces of persons who have undertaken to break disagreeable news.

"What is it, gentlemen? I am sorry to have kept you waiting."

"It is we, madame la Princesse, who must apologize," said Ordinal, bowing. "Believe me, if we could have avoided disturbing you. . . . But we have been entrusted with a very sad duty. You must be brave, madame."

"Good gracious, gentlemen, you frighten me. Speak out. . . . I have had to go through a great deal of late—I expect the worst. . . . What has happened?"

"Something has happened—something serious has happened to his Highness."

"What is it—an accident. Has the Prince been hurt?"

"Madame, we warned his Highness. We sent him word again this evening. We advised him not to go out."

"Yes, I know that. He even gave me to understand that your fears were groundless. Besides, he seemed perfectly easy in his mind. Well?"

"Well, madame, his Highness made a great mistake not to listen to us. He has been murdered."

"Murdered! . . . You say murdered. . . . Why it can't be."

"Why not madame? He was murdered like M. Supia, like Mme. Supia, like. . . ."

"But what you tell me is incredible," burst out Toinetta. "I'm sorry, gentlemen, if I show more astonishment than grief; but if any one ought not to have been murdered, it was he. How was he murdered?"

"You are probably unaware that his Highness was to dine this evening with the Comtesse d'Azilia."

"Very likely, but that is of no sort of interest to me."

"The Prince was in the Comtesse d'Azilia's ground floor flat in the Malausséna quarter when a servant brought him a letter from some person waiting at the garden gate. The Prince read the letter, made his excuses, went out, brought the man into the garden, and had a long talk with him. They disappeared under the trees. It was quite dark. As the Prince did not return, the Comtesse sent the servants to fetch him. Not many minutes elapsed before they were heard shouting. The mysterious visitor was nowhere to be seen, but they had found the Prince hanging from a tree. He bore the card with the one word: 'Hardigras.' "

Toinetta stared at one and then the other. She seemed a prey to great excitement in which there was obviously no trace of despair.

"How long ago was the crime committed?"

"Half an hour, madame."

She seized a hand of each and dragged them after her, though for that matter they offered no resistance. She took them through the flat, flung the door of her room wide open and pointed to Titin, who had not moved.

"He has been here for an hour, and you don't mean to tell me that he murdered the Prince."

Souques and Ordinal seemed in no way surprised by this dramatic gesture.

"We knew that," said Ordinal, quietly.

"How do you mean—you knew that?" asked Toinetta, taken aback.

"We saw Titin enter the flat and we were waiting for him outside. Had we not been waiting for him we should have been prowling round the Comtesse d'Azilia's flat in order to prevent anything unfortunate happening to the Prince, and perhaps he would have been alive now."

"Hippothadee dead!" exclaimed Titin, until then ignorant of what had occurred.

"Hanged like Supia," broke in Toinetta.

Titin threw up his arms in a gesture of despair.

"But who did it. . . . Who? . . . Who?" he cried, for the Prince's death plunged him into a terrible mystery.

"Yes, who did it?" wailed Toinetta bitterly. "Perhaps these gentlemen will tell us—these gentlemen who were waiting below in the street to arrest you."

"No," said Ordinal.

"No?"

"No, we simply wanted to discover what gang it was who have been shadowing Titin for three days and would certainly have taken up the trail again when he left here."

"But was that not your men?" asked Titin.

"We let you slide three days ago."

"How was that?"

"Because we suddenly obtained evidence that you were not guilty."

"What!" said Titin utterly flabbergasted. "Do you really mean that?"

"The day after your escape we never left you," explained Ordinal. "You remember when you came out of Barnabé's hut seeing in the distance two chamois hunters? . . . Well next day at dawn we were on the point of arresting you when news of Supia's murder reached us. You could not have been the murderer since you had never been out of our sight."

"That was a piece of luck," said Titin. "But all the same I've been condemned to death and, I suppose, must get ready to go with you."

"No, we don't want you. We shall discover in the end 'who did it' as you say, but you will have to help us. Do you remember the time when you made a proposal to us to join forces?"

"Ah, so you've come to that," said Titin laughing. "Between ourselves you've been a long time about it."

"Your assistance will be useful," said Ordinal.

"Necessary," added Souques, until then silent. "Ordinal has made us do quite enough idiotic things as it is."

"Thank you," said Ordinal.

"To think that I am laughing instead of crying now," said Toinetta.

"There's nothing to laugh at," said Titin. "What is it you wish me to do, gentlemen?"

"Go back to Barnabé's hut," said Ordinal. "Don't be afraid, we will arrange for you to get there right enough. Once there, you must ask Barnabé to tell Giaousé, Tulip, and Bolacion of your arrival. What's got to be done is to make them talk. Be on your guard."

"But they saved my life."

"Yes, but among the men following your tracks were faces known to them."

"Villainous faces," said Titin.

"Yes, we thought we recognized a few roughs from the Gorges du Loup. They all belong to Bolacion's gang."

"I can't make it out."

"Nor can I," said Ordinal, "but we will make it out, and we shall get light from that quarter. All the principal trouble comes from the Gorges du Loup. The terror that in a few weeks spread over the district originated in that place. They tried to set the people of Torre and La Fourca by the ears so as to bring about still more mischief, but in all this disorder, behind all these nightly attacks, there is some definite plan. In the eyes of certain people it is the work of some international criminal gang, but quite possibly the plan is a very ordinary one."

"Oh, it's a scheme for inheriting certain property," said Toinetta.

"Arising out of certain remarks made in our presence by Prince Hippothadee," confessed Ordinal quietly.

"Did it not occur to you that the Prince himself might be implicated . . .?" asked Toinetta.

"No, madame, for in that case the Prince would have kept silent. He would not have entrusted us with the task of finding the direct heiress to M. Supia's property— Mme. Cioasa who disappeared."

"Then if I understand you aright, these wretched people to whom you allude, are acting in Mme. Cioasa's interests?" said Toinetta.

"Certainly, madame, that is the most logical supposition we can entertain. . . . Yes, they are acting for Mme. Cioasa . . . or for her husband."

"But Mme. Cioasa was not married."

"I don't know if you were acquainted with Mme. Cioasa's history. In her younger days she had had a love affair with a certain Michel Pincalvin—Micheu, as he was called round about here. Micheu had no position, and Supia was against the marriage. Micheu left Grasse and did not return. Well, we now know where Mme. Cioasa is—in a small village in the heart of the Jura mountains. It is to this place that she made off in order to spend her honeymoon with her old lover whom she married exactly a fortnight before Mme. Supia was murdered."

"Well, upon my soul, it's amazing," exclaimed Titin. "But that tells us nothing. At that time M. and Mme. Supia were alive. There was no question of Mme. Cioasa inheriting their property."

"That's why we are entitled to express surprise that a practical old man like Micheu should marry Mme. Cioasa, who had nothing and no expectation of receiving anything."

"I don't agree with you," said Toinetta. "Micheu's calculation was not so far out as all that. At that time M. Supia's daughter was dead. He might tell himself that Mme. Cioasa had a prospect of succeeding to the property one day."

"Mme. Supia was much younger than Mme. Cioasa," observed Ordinal with a grim smile.

"So you believe that Micheu . . . or someone pointed out the facts to Micheu. . . ."

"I think everything is possible in an affair of this sort. Moreover, with Titin's assistance, we shall be able to lay before you certain facts in a few days."

"In any case, I can't yet see where Giaousé and Tulip come in."

"Do you know how we were led to discover Mme. Cioasa's whereabouts?"

"Well, no."

"Through Giaousé and Tulip being in daily correspondence with her."

"You don't say so," exclaimed Titin and Toinetta in unison.

"We are going to make a little investigation in the neighborhood of the newly married couple. Meantime you will have an opportunity of seeing the men in question. Stay in Barnabé's hut until we come to fetch you. We shall be away at most four days. Your chamois hunter won't leave you. And it won't be the police who will trouble you. Within a couple of hours a closed car will come here for you. Two men will be inside. Do exactly as they tell you. You, madame, will remain here. You have duties to fulfill as a result of the disaster that has befallen you. Good-bye for the present, Titin."

M. Ordinal bowed to the Princess and offered Titin his hand:

"Without ill-feeling?"

"Not without ill-feeling, but I'll shake hands all the same. With you, too, my dear M. Souques," said Titin.

"I, too, will shake hands, but not without ill-feeling. . . . Remember Naples," said Souques.

Titin could not help laughing at this reference to that ludicrous, enforced journey.

CHAPTER XXIX

THE SIEGE OF LA FOURCA

A week after these events a terrific beating of drums was
heard throughout the district. It was the work of half a
dozen young men of La Fourca seated in a covered cart
which bore, between two upstanding poles spread out like a
sail, a large white sheet, containing an announcement.

The cart was driven everywhere, stopping at the small-
est turning and open space in the villages. The young
men made music with their drums while the public gathered
in crowds and read:

"To the people of La Fourca and neighborhood—
Greetings!

"Titin le Bastardon, who so often in the past delivered
judgment in matters of dispute to the satisfaction of all
concerned over a friendly glass of wine, claims in his turn
to be judged by the same method. On Sunday next at
two o'clock the said Titin purposes to appear in person,
in the upper square of the old town, in order to vindicate
himself from the many charges of murder, outrage, and
violence, with which his name has been sullied, and that of
Hardigras disgraced. He hereby takes it upon himself
to summon Giaousé, alias Babazouk, Tulip, chief clerk
to the La Fourca solicitor, and Bolacion of Torre les
Tourettes, to appear at the same hour on the same day
to give evidence in their own defense."

The excitement created by this itinerant poster may be
imagined. If Titin, condemned to death, did not hesitate
to appear among them defenseless, it meant that not only
was he certain of the justice of his case but—which was

more important—that he was in a position to prove it. Then it seemed to follow from the actual terms of the poster, that he summoned Giaousé, Tulip, and Bolacion to submit themselves to judgment, not so much to obtain evidence in his own favor as to use this evidence against themselves.   And in this way, Toton Robin's incomprehensible words were confirmed: "Our Titin has been saved by traitors."

To which ordinary common sense made answer:

"But for those traitors he would none the less have been executed."

A new uneasiness took possession of them. Nor was the absence of Babazouk and Bolacion calculated to calm the general anxiety.   As for Tulip, he scarcely ever left his office, absorbed by the work which had resulted from the deaths in the Supia family.   Toton Robin in his smithy rained heavy blows upon his anvil and sent up great sheaves of sparks from the red-hot metal.   Did he know more about the truth than the others to display such scarcely repressed rage?   It was quite possible; for it was in his name and by his orders that arrangements had been made for the ceremony on Sunday.   He had had many consultations with Petou, the worthy mayor of La Fourca, and the Innkeepers of the old town, over the erection and plan of the tables and the bar of honor, which in the old days Titin, as President, used to occupy.

On Tuesday, casks, flasks, and pitchers were hauled to the upper parade in La Fourca, where the "Court" was to be held.   But it was possible that the authorities would not allow the jury time to linger over their wine as was proper in proceedings which would lose their force if they were hurried.   So soon as Titin appeared he might be arrested, and then good-bye to any verdict.   Would it not be as well then, in view of the circumstances, to let judgment be given in his absence?

To this suggestion which came from M. Petou, and was supported by M. Arthur, the mayor of Torre les Tour-

ettes, Toton Robin made answer that he had no idea how
the proceedings would be conducted and his part was
restricted to calling together the jury. Toton Robin, who
had been to the hut in the mountains at Barnabé's request
and had seen Titin with the chamois hunter, knew what
he was about.

Meantime, the entire district was thronged with police,
and the upper and lower Fourca with detectives.   At
Grasse troops were confined to barracks for the following
Sunday, and even the fire brigades of the small towns
round about received orders to hold themselves in readiness, in case of necessity.

Titin had retired to Barnabés hut, according to Souques
and Ordinal's instructions. The chamois hunter was well-
known in the Vesubie district. He was the cleverest shot
in the mountain and had an extensive knowledge of contraband. He was a striking and picturesque figure—the sort
of character that the men attached to Cooks Motor-car
Excursions point out to their tourists. Therefore, he
was invited to lunch at the hotels where the cars pulled up.
During the meal he opened his lips only to eat and drink,
and it was to no purpose that he was invited to relate his
achievements. He was no fool.

Titin and Barnabé were old friends though they had
never indulged in long speeches. Barnabé explained to
him that from where they were they commanded a gun-
range over a radius of more than three miles, and that
no one could come near them unobserved. Neither
Giaousé nor Bolacion—to whom Barnabé had sent word
through the pastry-cook in St. Martin, who received
letters for them, that they were expected by Titin—put in
an appearance. A letter addressed to Tulip by the same
means remained unanswered.

At last after four days Souques and Ordinal appeared
as they had promised. Titin was eagerly and anxiously
on the lookout for them. Had they brought the solution
of the riddle with them?

"We have seen the marriage certificate," said Ordinal. "You will understand what it means. Through this marriage M. and Mme. Pincalvin recognize and legitimize a son born some twenty-five years ago. That son is no other than Giaousé Babazouk, who, therefore, becomes through his mother, the Supia's sole heir. . . .

"We learned a great deal more. This boy was born at Mme. Boccia's. The mother was led to believe that the child died. Mme. Boccia acted under Supia's orders, receiving a sum of money that enabled her to buy the cottage in the Rue de la Tousson and placed her beyond the reach of want. She continued to interest herself in Babazouk. She placed a sealed letter with the La Fourca solicitor in which the facts were set down establishing Babazouk's parentage. This letter was to be delivered to Mme. Cioasa after Mme. Boccia's death, thus assuring Babazouk's future without prejudicing her own position while she lived.

"It was Tulip who received the letter. He was an inquisitive person and an adept at opening letters however carefully sealed. When he learnt the facts, his fiendish mind saw the use to which they could be put. The first thing to do was to involve Giaousé so deeply in the scheme that he could not draw back. It was then that Bolacion and Tulip, close friends, assisted by a gang of men who presently make another appearance in this story, brought about the meeting between Titin and Nathalie at 'Le Père la Bique', and arranged Nathalie's disappearance so as to lead Giaousé Babazouk to believe in an understanding between Titin and her. At the same time they informed Hippothadee who brought Toinetta on the scene, spoiling Titin's chance of marrying her. They shunted Giaousé on to Toinetta out of a spirit of revenge. It was an easy matter. Giaousé's liking for Toinetta had not escaped Nathalie's notice and she had warned Titin of it on several occasions.

"That, of course, would be a masterly stroke, a crowning triumph for Tulip's scheme. Both fortunes in one hand! Babazouk, the sole heir of the Supias and Agagnoscs. . . . The immediate necessity was to discover Micheu. They soon traced him. Micheu was almost an honest man. He knew that in the circumstances he was doing a good stroke of business for himself. But he had no suspicion of the many crimes that lay behind his marriage. Mme. Cioasa was a worthy, but unhappy woman. She had never ceased to think of Micheu. She readily returned to him. They were anxious, of course, for the marriage and the subsequent recognition of their son to be kept secret in order that no suspicion should be aroused. Hence their retirement to that lost corner of the world in the Jura mountains.

"Meantime, they hinted to Mme. Cioasa that her son was still alive. They prepared her for the joyful news. But they had to act quickly. The letter containing the necessary proofs would not be handed over to her until Mme. Boccia's death. That explained the murder in the Rue de la Tousson and the disappearance of Mme. Manchotte whom Mme. Boccia had taken into her confidence. . . . They undoubtedly sent Mme. Manchotte to join Nathalie. . . . Where? . . . Poor women! . . .

"Well," ended Ordinal excitedly collecting together his bundle of papers, "what have you to say?"

"The whole thing is too awful," returned Titin. "But I should like to know exactly what part Giaousé played in all these horrors. That's the question I'm going to ask him."

"But are you mad?" exclaimed Ordinal. "You must not think of doing that. We have in this report full proof of your innocence. You should come back with us to Nice. As to Giaousé, we will undertake to bring him to you escorted by two gendarmes, and in safe company. . . ."

"But I've been condemned to death, my dear Ordinal," said Titin. "It is for you two to go back to Nice and let me know when I can turn up there without danger to myself."

They left him with a gesture of dissent. Titin said to Barnabé:

"Certainly there are things which should be cleared up. But I can't forget that Giaousé risked his life to save mine."

It was then that Titin with the help of Toton Robin announced with a flourish of drums the "judgment over a glass of wine". One of the darkest days in the history of La Fourca, one of those days which are long remembered, and the story of which is handed down from generation to generation, was about to dawn. On Saturday the inns remained open for the best part of the night. No one knew what was going to happen. Toton Robin was not to be seen. The mayor and the rector were ill at ease.

The mayor had made his money in the olive trade, and besides possessing two or three houses between La Fourca Nova and La Costa, he had a good substantial house in the old town. It was here that Mme. Petou invited her friends to sample her famous jams and liqueurs. It was here, too, that the mayors seated facing each other were waiting impatiently for Toton Robin, who had not come.

"There's going to be more trouble," said Arthur.

"I fear so," agreed Mme. Petou.

Arthur, the mayor of Torre les Tourettes, had reached La Fourca on the stroke of midnight and was remaining with Petou, who told him as much as he himself had heard from Toton Robin.

"By Jove, if this is the case we may fear the worst," exclaimed Arthur. "They'll do their best to prevent Titin from turning up."

Just then a loud knock came at the street door. Mme. Petou went and slid back the shutter of the wicket.

"Toton Robin!" she cried.

They made a rush on him. She closed the door. His face was distorted.

"No news of Titin! He ought to have been in hiding at the doctor's last night. I suggested to the doctor: 'Let's get to Barnabé's.' We drove off in a motor-car for St. Martins Vesubie. Barnabé did not come down the mountain to meet us. We went up to him. . . . We found him up there in his hut . . . alone . . . murdered."

M. and Mme. Petou and M. Arthur uttered a cry:

"What about Titin?"

"That's just it. Where is he? What's happened to him? They took him by surprise, obviously. Titin wanted to see Giaousé and Bolacion, and sent for them. They came. But they didn't come alone, you may be sure. And as they've got him, they've got us as long as they hold him prisoner. I drove back to St. Martin's. The doctor and I telephoned the news to Grasse and Nice, and here we are. I said to myself: perhaps you may have heard something. . . . Listen. . . . Someone's calling you, Petou. It's Mme. Closs's voice."

They heard, too, the sound of the cart being drawn by the mule. They ran to the door. The market gardener had pulled up outside and was holding her lantern above a body lying stretched upon her baskets and vegetables.

"Ah, my friends, I lifted her up as best I could. She was almost dead. . ₂ . I found her a little way past La Costa in the middle of the road."

"But who is it?"

"Oh, you don't recognize her all at once. It's Nathalie, poor thing."

Toton Robin had already lifted her out of the cart.

"She is covered with blood. Put her to my bed and send for the doctor," said Petou.

Meantime Arthur felt her heart.

"She's still alive. Good Lord, how they have knocked her about."

Petou slid a glass of brandy between the poor girl's lips.

"If she could only speak," said Robin. "We shouldn't need to look very far to find Titin."

As though she were waiting for the mention of that name she suddenly recovered consciousness and opened her eyes.

"Titin!" she said in a weak voice. "You want to know where Titin is. ، . . Ah, that's you Toton Robin. . . . Petou. . . . Have I come in time? They're going to murder him."

"Where is he?"

"At Touet du Loup."

"In the quarries?"

"Yes."

"Off we go!" said Toton Robin.

"How can you think of doing such a thing! You must all go there—there'll be none too many of you. But don't lose time. When Mme. Manchotte told me they had brought Titin there, and what they were going to do with him, I thought to myself I must save him. Mme. Manchotte helped me. I learnt all about it from her, and I will tell you everything. . . ."

An hour later the people of La Fourca poured out of the town once more through every lane and footpath. But it was no question now of witnessing Titin's execution. They were determined to save him, to wrest him from the rabble in the Gorges du Loup. In silence, long files of men wound their way like black serpents over the roads. They disappeared from view and came into sight again on the ridge of the mountain, and at length effected a junction at the entrance to the passes where they were joined by Arthur's men. For, the people of Torre les Tourettes declined to leave the honor and danger of an expedition which would make history, to La Fourca, alone.

The men of La Fourca marching further ahead, reached the narrow pass to the quarries from which the eye could take in Touet du Loup. Meantime the men of Torre les Tourettes led by the wily Arthur, struggled up numerous

rocks and down numerous precipices to attain the enemy's
rear beyond Touet du Loup and close in upon him the
circle of death.

When the men below led by Toton Robin, assisted by
Petou's prudent counsels saw that Arthur had completed
his encircling movement, they made ready to attack. The
assault must needs be overwhelming to succeed. They
brought up a large number of ladders and ropes. Their
main object was first to rescue Titin. A resin torch lit
by Mme. Manchotte, as had been agreed between Nathalie
and her, was to indicate the exact spot to which he had
been taken. A last council of war at which Nathalie, carried on a stretcher, was present, enabled them to arrange
the details of their plan of campaign. Truth to tell the
attack was bound to succeed for the enemy camp was in
a merry mood. Titin's capture had been the signal for a
wild outburst of drinking.

It was four o'clock in the morning when this side of the
mountain became transformed into a volcano. Multi-
colored fire, mine explosions, the sound of guns, yells,
despairing appeals, harrowing cries, an indescribable
frenzy—all these things seemed to combine to create the
illusion of hell let loose wherein everyone of these unhappy
madmen would meet his death and his damnation.

In the background of a sort of tunnel, which crossed
the mountain, could be seen two men with bare breasts
dripping with the blood of the enemy, advancing, retiring,
smashing, crushing with uplifted, or whirling club like
two splendid and terrible heroes from the pages of Homer.
It proved to be Toton Robin at one end of the tunnel and
Titin at the other. A voice from below shouted words of
encouragement: "Go for them! Go for them!" It was
Nathalie's voice.

The battle was over in less than an hour. The seriously
wounded surrendered and "there were not many of them,"
to quote the traditional account of the battle. It was no
more than the truth, for the rabble in the Gorges du Loup

received that night a right royal "thrashing", quite sufficient to keep them quiet for many a long day. And peace descended once more on the district.

The victors returned in triumph. They brought with them a few prisoners intended to create a sensation in the "judgment over the wine". Bolacion had received a blow from Titin's club cutting open his head, and he was losing his demoniacal brain. All the same he was brought along in a cart to be "judged", side by side with Giaousé, who was also severely wounded. Tulip alone was missing. He had been far too cautious to set foot in the incriminating haunts of Touet du Loup.

As the cart containing the prisoners passed La Costa, Jean José Scaliero's wife opened her door and handed over Tulip. She feared lest the people of La Fourca might learn one day that she had given refuge to him, and set fire to her house. She, probably, was not far wrong. Tulip could not stand on his legs and his limp form was pushed at the back of the cart. Titin was nowhere to be seen. He had disappeared under a tarpaulin while Nathalie unburdened herself to him. She told him the story of her martyrdom, bringing tears to his eyes. It was on his account that she had so greatly suffered.

While the procession marched towards the place of "judgment", the rumor of the battle reached the government authorities, who at once gave orders for the police and others forces to hasten to Touet du Loup and put an end to the slaughter. But, of course, the forces arrived after the battle was over. And, on returning to La Fourca, they found the old town in a position of defense, about to deliver its "judgment", and opposed to any outside interference. La Fourca was surrounded as though it were to be carried by assault. The story of the siege, which lasted twelve hours only, was no more grotesque than the siege of Fort Chabrol in the heart of Paris in 1899, when one man for three weeks kept at bay the entire forces of the capital.

Orders were despatched from Nice and even from Paris, insisting on an immediate intervention; but the besieged announced that since Souques and Ordinal had been careless enough to enter the place they would hold them as hostages and not scruple to make short work of them if any attempt were made to break through.

While this farce was being played outside, the tragedy was continuing in the upper town. And with great dispatch! Toton Robin had been nominated Presiding Judge. In a few words he put them in possession of the facts. The bodies of Bolacion and Tulip were even now hanging at the main gate, and it was Giaousé's turn to be tried.

Giaousé threw himself upon his knees. He begged for mercy. He appealed to Titin to help him. Titin rose to his feet, pale and trembling.

"I ask pardon for him," he said. "He allowed himself to be led away. I cannot forget that we loved each other like brothers. And if you have any regard for me, remember that he saved my life."

But a pitiless voice behind him was heard. It was the voice of a dying woman who had retained sufficient strength to be present at his punishment.

"He is the most guilty of them all because the others were not your friends," she gasped. "This man pretended to be a brother to you and deceived you more than a man has the right to deceive his worst enemy. The reason he saved your life, Titin, was that he wanted you to live so that people might continue to believe that you committed these murders. And he got you out of prison merely to enable Hardigras to continue his crimes. Do you still ask mercy for him, Titin?"

At this deadly explanation a tremendous clamor arose. Giaousé was carried to the scaffold without further ado. As to Titin, after uttering a dull moan, he turned to Souques and Ordinal:

"Now all is over. There is nothing more to be done.
I am at your service."

But the people protested:

"We alone are to blame. It is we who should give ourselves up. We have acted with strict justice like good and
impartial judges. Do with us whatever you like."

And so ended the siege of La Fourca. Souques and
Ordinal, unaided, made the entire town prisoners. There
were barely sufficient troops and police to take charge of
the people, increased by the crowd demanding to be tried
with Titin.

The end is a matter of history. The trial was trans-
ferred to a Court in the South West, the Court at Nice
being set aside on the grounds of prejudice. The prisoners were all found guilty and bound over. Titin was
triumphantly acquitted.

The marriage of Titin and Toinetta was celebrated with
rural pomp, Aiguardente, Tantifla, Tony Bouta, and the
worthy Pistafun, discharged from prison some weeks before, continued to celebrate the festivity for a year on
end without intermission. At the first banquet the bride
insisted on M. Bezaudin being placed on her right. Odonovitch was on her left and addressed her as, "Your
Majesty."

"Queen of La Fourca," she corrected. "I want no
better title."

Before the ball Titin and Toinetta went to St. Helene
Church. For ten days in succession Mme. Bibi opened
the dance with M. Papajeudi, who was the first to call a
halt. . . .

The curious, who may wish to obtain some knowledge
of the amount of food and drink of all kinds consumed
in those ten days, may be referred to a learned work
which the first magistrate of Torre les Tourettes has been
engaged in compiling in his spare time. The worthy mayor
of the Round Table, the noble and well-beloved Arthur,
has taken it upon himself to collect together all the facts

bearing upon the Chronicles of Hardigras. And like all chronicles truly worthy of the name, these which do not take their rise in the imagination of romancers, they will serve one day to complete the great and glorious history of France.

THE END